THE SHADOW WEAVE

SPELL WEAVER: BOOK 2

ANNETTE MARIE

dark owl
fantasy

The Shadow Weave
Book Two of the Spell Weaver Trilogy

Dark Owl Fantasy Inc.
PO Box 88106, Rabbit Hill Post Office
Edmonton, AB, Canada T6R 0M5
www.darkowlfantasy.com

Cover Copyright © 2018 by Annette Ahner
Cover and Book Interior by Midnight Whimsy Designs
www.midnightwhimsydesigns.com

Editing by Elizabeth Darkley
arrowheadediting.wordpress.com

ISBN 978-1-988153-18-6

BOOKS BY ANNETTE MARIE

STEEL & STONE UNIVERSE

Steel & Stone Series
Chase the Dark
Bind the Soul
Yield the Night
Feed the Flames
Reap the Shadows
Unleash the Storm
Steel & Stone

Spell Weaver Trilogy
The Night Realm
The Shadow Weave
The Blood Curse

OTHER WORKS

Red Winter Trilogy
Red Winter
Dark Tempest
Immortal Fire

THE SHADOW WEAVE

ONE

CLIO'S SPINE prickled under the weight of watchful stares.

She shot a glower over her shoulder. The five daemons lingering around the oversized table avoided her gaze.

Facing the stovetop again, she slapped the spatula down on the pan and flipped a pancake in one smooth motion. The ring of flames circling the gas burner jumped as she overturned the second and third cakes. The glowing oven window offered a blurred view of the thick bacon strips baking to a perfect crisp.

She should have known better than to cook bacon. The smell had permeated the sprawling manor, and it had taken all of five minutes for the first daemon to wander into the kitchen as though by coincidence.

Grumbling, she scooped the pancakes onto the plate beside her and spooned more batter into the pan. When the third daemon had appeared—*not* summoned by the smell of cooking meat, or so his nonchalant attitude had suggested—she'd doubled the pancake recipe.

Now she was wondering if she and Lyre would have to fight the other daemons for their shares. Not that Lyre couldn't defeat them all with a choice weaving or two, but he was trying to keep his identity as a notorious Chrysalis spell weaver a secret.

She cracked the oven door open to check on the bacon. A blast of hot air, heavy with the mouthwatering aroma, wafted over her and she nodded as she closed the door again. Almost ready.

Her neck prickled again.

She whirled around. The daemons at the table, staring hungrily at the oven, immediately resumed their attempts to look occupied. She glared at them, waiting to see if any would *ask* if they could share in her cooking, but she wasn't surprised when they said nothing. Daemons didn't like asking for things.

Four males, one female. She had no idea what their castes were, why they were here, or how dangerous they might be. But daemons also didn't like those sorts of questions, especially in a place like this.

As she reached for the carton of eggs and a large bowl, she glanced around the spacious room. It was so different from the dinky kitchen in her townhouse that it was almost like a dream. Shiny granite countertops, a huge center island, stainless steel appliances, recessed lights under the glossy cabinets. She'd never been to a Consulate before, but she hadn't expected this.

Demons that visited Earth knew about Consulates—sanctuaries where trained Consuls offered daemons free room, board, and protection. The daemons at the table behind her could have hailed from the Overworld or the Underworld, and short of caste-identifying features, it was impossible to tell where a daemon came from. She was trusting that same ambiguity to protect her identity as a nymph.

Still, she probably should have kept out of sight. She and Lyre had already stayed here too long. Since their escape from Asphodel two days ago, they'd mostly slept—especially Lyre, whose magic reserves had been completely depleted. She would have slept almost as much except their room had only one bed. No matter how many blankets she piled into a barrier between them, he somehow always shifted closer and closer until she was hanging off the edge of the bed.

This evening, she'd woken up with his spicy cherry scent filling her nose, his hard body pressed against her side, his warm breath whispering against her neck—sending hot swirls of heat deep into her center and making her twitchy. Even fast asleep he was sinfully alluring. And when she'd forcefully untangled herself, he'd opened his eyes, shadow-dusted amber that could take her prisoner with only a glance.

Incubus. Lord of seduction. Master of lust. *Sex fiend.*

And she'd already had a brief introduction to the taste of his mouth, the feel of his body, the way he could—

She shook her head violently, almost dislodging her loose ponytail. Growling to herself, she whisked the eggs with more force than necessary. She'd left him in the room to wake up and shower while she scrounged up something to eat. The Consuls provided a few meals a day but also allowed guests to help themselves to anything in the kitchen.

As though summoned by her thoughts, the sex fiend himself breezed into the room. Hair damp and tousled, the kind of face that made women's hearts skip, broad shoulders that tapered to a toned torso. His tattered clothes should have ruined the look, but they added an extra edge—dangerous and exotic.

The others in the kitchen noticed his arrival, but they dismissed him just as quickly. Unlike most daemons, incubi were easy to recognize even in glamour. No other caste possessed that stunning combination of golds—white-gold hair, warm golden skin, vibrant irises like a dark patina over rich yellow gold.

Yes, they recognized him as an incubus—and they didn't bother to hide their curling lips and wrinkling noses. Lyre either didn't notice or didn't care as he swept over to her, his expression brightening for the first time in two days.

"Clio," he purred, voice too low for even keen-eared strangers to hear, "your powers of seduction would put any succubus to shame."

She blinked at him, the bowl of whisked eggs in her hands and a hot pan sizzling in front of her. His mood was so different from earlier that she couldn't quite grasp it.

"Huh?" she managed. How articulate.

"This is entirely unfair. I have no power to resist such tactics." He waited a beat. "Are you planning to do something with those eggs?"

She blinked again, trying to unscramble her brain. Scramble. Right, the eggs. She dumped the mixture into the hot pan. "What *are* you going on about, Lyre?"

"Bacon," he sighed dreamily. "Pancakes. Scrambled eggs. You slay me, my love."

On the words "my love," her heart screeched to a stop so fast it might have left skid marks on her ribs. It kicked back into gear at three times its previous speed and she concentrated so hard on the spatula that she almost went cross-eyed. "You—you can't be that excited about my cooking. You don't even know if it's any good."

"I can tell already. It'll be *delicious*."

She shivered. The way he said that word should be illegal. As she hurriedly stirred the eggs with a spatula, he stood so close he was almost touching her, his body angled toward her as though she held his entire attention. But his gaze, sliding coolly from one watching daemon to another, was distinctly unfriendly.

She scraped the eggs off the pan, then rescued the bacon from the oven—triggering a stir among the waiting daemons. With her bottom lip caught between her teeth, she pulled a plate from the cupboard, loaded it with food, and held it out to Lyre. She'd cooked an elaborate late-night breakfast to cheer him up, but now second thoughts were crowding her brain. Too late to change her plan now.

His smile only fueled her blush as he fished a fork out of a nearby drawer, loaded it with eggs, and scooped them into his mouth. She held her breath. The entire room went silent.

His eyes rolled back in ecstasy. "So *good*," he moaned.

Bang.

She jerked around. The female daemon had dropped her heavy book on the floor. As everyone looked over at her, pink tinged the woman's cheeks. She snatched up her book and beat a hasty retreat out of the room.

Clio swallowed hard, envious of the woman's ability to flee. Lyre's moan had been so sensual it had been downright scandalous, and if Clio didn't put space between them, she was going to start swooning like a complete fool.

The male daemons didn't look scandalized, though. They looked irritated. The largest, a bulky guy with a bald head and a thick beard, pushed away from the table. Clio went still as the daemon came up to the island, his glower fixed on Lyre.

"You gonna share some of that, incubus?"

Lyre smiled and bit the end off a strip of bacon. "Ask the cook."

The daemon faced her and she had to stiffen her spine to keep from shrinking away. She'd fully intended to share the excessive amount of food, but she didn't like his attitude—or the way he'd sneered "incubus" when he'd spoken to Lyre.

"Well?" the daemon growled when she didn't say anything.

She turned to the counter, grabbed another plate, and piled it so high that eggs threatened to tumble off the edge. She pulled out a fork and stuck it into the top like a flagpole. The daemon reached eagerly for the overloaded plate.

Raising her chin, she carried it right past him and walked to the doorway.

"Whoever wants some can have it," she announced. "But if you eat, then you can clean up too."

The aggressive daemon and the other three stared at her.

She tilted her head at Lyre. "Come on."

Casting a brief smirk at the other guy, Lyre sauntered across the kitchen to join her, and she led the way to their tiny room on the lower level.

Setting her plate on the desk, she dropped into the wooden chair. "They're so rude. Would it kill them to *ask* for some? Why do they have to play power games?"

Lyre pushed the door closed with one foot and waved his fork in an indecipherable gesture. "They probably intended to be polite until I showed up."

She frowned. "What do you mean?"

"Male daemons always feel like they have something to prove when there's an incubus in the room." He shrugged and shoveled half a pancake into his mouth.

She picked up her fork, dismayed by the mountain of food, then lowered her cutlery with a groan. "Oh no."

"Huh?" Lyre grunted through a mouthful.

"I forgot syrup." She looked up at him, embarrassed. "I gave you a plate without syrup too. I'm sorry."

"Clio, it's fantastic as is. It doesn't need syrup."

"But …" Her brows scrunched together. His plate was already half empty. When had he eaten that much? The food was vanishing at an alarming rate. Maybe it was a good thing she'd overloaded her plate.

As she watched him scarf it down, a strange feeling twisted through her middle. The last time she'd been this nervous about someone liking her cooking, she'd been treating her half-brother, Bastian, to a meal. No matter what she cooked for him, however simple or extravagant, he'd eat a few bites, compliment her efforts, then put his cutlery down. But Lyre didn't even have syrup for his pancakes and he was devouring everything like it was the best meal he'd ever tasted.

The feeling in her middle twisted tighter and she quickly focused on her food before he commented on her gawking. Once she'd eaten her fill, he finished off her plate too.

Finally done, he sat on the bed with a satisfied sigh. "I could get used to eating like that."

As another blush threatened, she stacked the plates and utensils on the desk. "Did you not eat well in Asphodel?"

"Hmm, I guess I did." He squinched his eyes in thought. "The cook makes whatever I want and there are dozens of places to eat, but …" He shrugged. "It's not the same, somehow."

Yep, she was blushing again. "You had your own cook?"

"S'pose so. Cook, maid, maintenance staff. We don't really …" He trailed off, frowning. "I didn't do any of that stuff."

She said nothing, recognizing his change of tense from present to past. He wasn't a pampered master weaver anymore. There were no more cooks or maids in his future.

The same thought seemed to occur to him. The light in his eyes faded into dull exhaustion. His spurt of good spirits, brought on by the shower and food, withered and he slumped back on the blankets.

She winced. During the brief periods he'd been awake since arriving here, his mood had been dark, grim … defeated. She'd tried to discuss what to do next but hadn't gotten further than him agreeing that they needed to get his clock spell back from her traitorous bodyguard Eryx.

"Lyre," she said softly, facing the bed. "I know you're tired, but we need to plan our next move. We can't stay here any longer."

He opened his eyes but his stare was lifeless, and she wondered how he'd grown despondent so fast. Unless his energetic confidence in the kitchen had been a show for the other daemons?

"I don't know what to do next." He rubbed his face. "We should head into Brinford, I guess. It'll be easier to hide there."

"We can't hide forever. We need to get your clock spell back."

"How?" He slouched into the pillows. "That asshole Eryx could have taken it anywhere."

"He took it to the Overworld." She hardened her voice. "Now quit moping and help me figure out a plan."

"How do you know he took it to the Overworld?"

"Because he's Prince Bastian's bodyguard. He's taken the clock to Irida to give to Bastian, I'm sure of it."

"You mean the prince who submitted Irida's proposal to Chrysalis?" He finally sat up and focused, but his expression was bleakly incredulous. "You're saying a *ruling family* in the *Overworld* has my KLOC? How am I supposed to get it back from *them*?"

She pursed her lips. "Well, I was planning to just ask Bastian."

He blinked.

"Eryx betrayed me and … and left me to die." The words caught in her throat and she had to force them out. "But Bastian would be horrified if he knew what happened. If I can explain how dangerous the clock is, I can convince him to destroy it."

"Eryx overheard me explaining how the KLOC's power spreads," Lyre said skeptically. "To him and to your prince, it sounds like a weapon that can wipe out a daemon army's magic. You think he'd destroy something that powerful?"

"If we explain how catastrophic it could be, he will," she said, burying her doubts. "Everything else aside, *the* most important thing to Bastian is the safety of our people. His highest priority is protecting Irida."

Clio and Kassia had often disagreed about Bastian, but no matter what, Clio could trust him to put Irida first. He always had, and always would, protect his people. Not even Kassia would have disagreed with her on that. The challenging part would be convincing Bastian that the spell was too dangerous to use against their enemies. It devoured magic, and the more it consumed, the further the magic expanded in a chain reaction that could spread and spread until it devoured everything.

"Well, I guess we'll find out if you're right about that." Lyre's shoulders slumped. "So we need to go to the Overworld, then. Great."

"It won't be that bad," she assured him. "If I can survive Asphodel, then you'll have no problem in Irida."

He nodded, weariness clinging to him like a miasma. He was still in shock. His entire life had been torn away, and he was adrift in a different world with no resources and no plan—and lethal hunters that would soon close in.

He'd lost everything: his esteemed position as a master weaver, his home, his family, his belongings. He had only the clothes on his back, a bow and quiver of arrows, a few chains of lodestones, and whatever he carried beneath his glamour. In a single Underworld cycle, he'd gone from a nearly unassailable Chrysalis weaver to a hunted outcast.

And it was her fault.

If not for her, he wouldn't have fought his psychotic brother Dulcet. If not for her, no one would know his secret magic-eating clock spell existed. If not for her, his family wouldn't have turned on him and he would still be in Asphodel—not happy, but safe.

Now he was on his own on Earth, with nowhere to go and no one to help him—except her. But what could she do?

"Lyre." She hesitated. "Are you okay? You haven't been …"

Ghosts of emotion gathered in his eyes—fear, pain, bitterness, dread, defeat. Toeing off his shoes, he pulled his legs onto the bed, half turning away from her.

"What next?" he asked tonelessly. "Back to the ley line?"

She opened her mouth, then closed it. Tightness spread through her chest. "I wish it was that simple, but unfortunately …"

"What?"

She forced herself to take a deep breath. "I've never traveled to Irida myself. I don't know the ley lines so I ... I can't take us."

He twisted around to stare at her like he couldn't believe his ears. "You've never traveled to Irida? *Never?* How do you not know how to travel to your own territory?"

"I didn't learn how to travel the lines until after I'd left!" Choking back her defensiveness, she pressed her hands to her thighs. "My situation was ... unusual. I learned ley line travel after coming to Earth, but I haven't been to Irida since I left. I was counting on Kassia to show me the way home, but she's ..."

Pain cut into her chest at the reminder of her friend's death, and she squeezed her eyes shut before the tears could start again.

"You learned ley line travel *here*?" he asked incredulously. "How long ago was that?"

"Two years."

"Why haven't you been back?"

"I was ... it was a special request from Bastian."

She couldn't say more than that. Only a dozen people, all of them in Irida, knew her real identity. Lyre knew nothing about her ties to the Nereid royal family, the true nature of the mission that had brought her to his homeland in the Underworld, or her rare ability to mimic any magic she saw. She couldn't reveal such a dangerous secret to *anyone*.

"How the hell do you propose we get to the Overworld, then?" he demanded. "This might come as a surprise, but I don't know any of your world's ley lines either."

"We'll need to find a guide."

"A guide," he repeated flatly.

"An Overworlder who can take us through the ley lines to Irida — or at least get us *close* to Irida. I'm sure we can find someone who will take us."

"For a price, maybe. I don't know about you, but as a newly destitute fugitive, I'm fresh out of cash."

"Do you have a better idea?"

Something dark and unfriendly passed through his eyes, then he rolled onto his side with his back to her. "No."

She reached toward him, then withdrew her hand. She couldn't imagine what he was feeling, but considering his precarious situation was her fault, she was probably the last person he would accept comfort from.

"Why don't you sleep for a couple more hours?" she suggested as she rose to her feet. "We can leave at midnight."

He said nothing, so she let him be and headed for the door.

He was too smart to believe that a daemon who'd only learned to travel ley lines two years ago, and hadn't been in the Overworld since then, was a royal envoy. Maybe he'd suspected before, but now he knew for certain she was someone else entirely—and she couldn't tell him who.

She quietly closed the door, her shoulders drooping. Whether she revealed the truth or not, she wasn't sure it would be enough to erase the suspicion in his eyes.

TWO

Stopping halfway down the corridor, Clio hurriedly wiped her eyes before turning toward the unfamiliar voice.

The female daemon from the kitchen waited a few paces away, a heavy textbook under her arm. Her dark hair was pulled into a bun and thick-rimmed glasses perched on her small nose.

Clio scrubbed her face, embarrassed she'd been caught in tears. While Lyre was sleeping, she'd wandered the manor, lost in anxious thoughts. Overwhelmed by worry and loneliness and wishing Kassia was still with her, she'd given in to a few tears. Had it only been a few days since Eryx had murdered her best friend? It felt like half a lifetime ago.

"Yes?" Clio replied.

The woman smiled, but the expression was empty of genuine warmth. "I hope I'm not intruding, but I was wondering about your companion, the incubus?"

Wariness flared through Clio. "What about him?"

"Is he"—she cleared her throat delicately—"available?"

"Available?" Clio repeated blankly.

The woman adjusted her glasses. "I heard you two arrived together, so I thought I'd ask."

"Wait, you—you want to …" Clio's cheeks heated and something sharp twisted in her gut. "Why are you asking me?"

"I was merely being polite. Some women react poorly to competition."

"Well, he's not … I mean, we're not …"

The woman rolled her eyes, her earlier politeness nowhere in sight. "I was just inquiring if you were done with him. A 'yes' or 'no' is all I need."

Done with him? Like he was a toy she would get bored with? "I'm not *done* with him, so you can move right along."

The vehemence of her words surprised her. Where had *that* come from?

The woman smirked. "But how long until he's done with *you*?"

"Mind your own business."

The daemon pushed her glasses up her nose again, then laughed softly.

"You're in for a world of pain, girl," she called over her shoulder as she walked away. "You should have known better."

She disappeared around a corner and Clio folded her arms.

"Known better than to what?" she muttered to herself.

As she headed in the opposite direction, she supposed she shouldn't be surprised. Incubi attracted attention. Women desired them and men wanted to "prove something" as soon as they showed up. For a caste with limited defensive magic, that much attention must be nerve-racking.

But she had bigger things to worry about, like what she and Lyre would do once they got to Brinford. Though many cities had daemon populations of only a few dozen, Brinford was a major hub. Embassies, businesses, shops, gatherings of all sorts. For that reason, Bastian had selected the city as her home-in-exile, and it was the same reason Lyre had chosen it as a hiding place.

Returning to her townhouse was her first instinct, but the depth of Eryx's betrayal was a complete unknown. If he realized she was alive and back in Brinford, he might return to finish her off before she could reveal to Bastian what he'd done. She and Lyre would have to find temporary accommodations far from her old home while they located a guide to take them to the Overworld.

In Irida, she'd had no need to learn ley line travel, and when Bastian had sent her away, she'd been brought through the ley line to Earth while in a protective state of unconsciousness. She didn't know a single Overworld ley line, and if you didn't know where a ley line was, you couldn't travel to it.

Irregular thudding sounds broke into her thoughts. Alarmed, Clio crept to the doorway the noise emanated from and peeked inside.

The huge room wasn't what she'd expected. On the nearest wall hung a multitude of weapons. Exercise mats covered the floors and the farther end was full of training equipment—foam dummies, climbing ropes, targets, weights.

In the center, a girl was kicking a punching bag like she was trying to split it open. She slammed her shin into the bag over and over, then unleashed a flurry of lightning-fast punches up and down the bag where a man's head and stomach would have been.

Clio hung in the doorway, mouth falling open. The girl couldn't have been older than twelve or thirteen, with a leggy build and auburn hair cropped close to her head in a boyish style. Sweat shone on her face and neck as she whirled around and jammed her foot into the bag, sending it swinging on its chain.

The girl backed up a few steps, breathing hard, then jerked to face the doorway where Clio stood, surprise flashing in her green eyes. Curious as to what the girl was, Clio blinked her asper into focus.

A faint shimmer surrounded the girl—an aura so weak there was no way it would support magic casting. But the blue glow of a weaving embedded deep in the girl's body surprised Clio more. The weblike construct was staggeringly complex and woven through her head and chest, almost like—

"What are you looking at?" the girl demanded aggressively.

Clio blinked her asper away so she wouldn't keep staring. "Are you human?" she blurted in confusion.

"Haemon," the girl snapped. "I'm a haemon."

Haemon? Clio frowned, trying to dredge up her flimsy knowledge of half-daemons. They weren't all that common; most daemons had no interest in procreating with humans. Haemons were physically human but possessed limited magic inherited from their daemon parent. All Consuls were haemons, she'd heard.

"I'm a junior apprentice," the girl added defensively, misinterpreting Clio's frown. "I'm Piper. The Head Consul is my father."

"I'm Clio," she replied, smiling quickly to diffuse the tension. Piper had introduced herself as though Clio should recognize her name, but she was completely out to sea. "Is the Head Consul in charge of this Consulate, then?"

Piper pushed her damp bangs off her forehead. "The Head Consul oversees *all* Consulates. Haven't you ever been to a Consulate before?"

"No, this is my first."

Piper dropped onto the mats and started a set of stretches. "You're the one who came in unconscious two days ago, right? With the incubus?"

When Clio nodded, the girl opened her mouth, then closed it, a pained expression on her face. She muttered something.

"Pardon me?"

"I said, 'Stupid rule.'"

"What rule?"

Piper extended her legs into a perfect split and leaned forward into the stretch. "The one where I'm not supposed to ask you questions. Like who hurt you, or why the incubus was in such bad shape too. He collapsed as soon as he got here. My uncle—he was the Consul on duty when you two came in—thinks the incubus must have carried you for a while." She straightened and added, "Those weren't questions."

Leaning against the doorframe, Clio bit her lip. "I lost consciousness before we went through the ley line, so I'm not sure how far he had to carry me."

"The ley line? That's a three-hour walk." Piper glanced up from her next stretch with an incredulous expression. "He carried you the whole way? He must be tougher than he looks."

"He is."

"So what hap—" The girl bit off the question.

"What's it like being an apprentice Consul?" Clio asked, steering the conversation away from her dramatic arrival at the Consulate.

Piper shrugged. "I only started official training a few months ago. Before that, I wasn't allowed downstairs without my father or my uncle with me, so it's nice to have more freedom."

"Downstairs? You mean the basement where the guest rooms are?"

"No, I mean anywhere except the family level upstairs." She smiled mischievously, green eyes sparkling. "Not that I didn't sneak down here all the time anyway. Just don't tell my father."

"You're awfully good at that"—Clio waved at the punching bag— "for having only started a few months ago."

"I've been training in martial arts since I was five." She lifted her chin proudly. "I already have a second-degree black belt, and I'm taking the test for the third-degree later this year."

"Wow." Clio stared bemusedly at the wall of weapons. Kassia had shown Clio how to throw a punch and hold a dagger, but her strength lay in magical defense.

Piper gave Clio an appraising once-over. "Those clothes look terrible on you."

Clio didn't need to be told. The oversized white t-shirt hung off her frame like a sail and she'd had to pull the drawstring on the cotton sweatpants so tight they'd bunched up around her waist. "This is what they gave me."

Piper pushed to her feet and canted her head. "You're so *small*. What, five feet?"

"Five foot one," she muttered.

"I'm five foot three," Piper responded smugly. And she could expect another growth spurt or two in her future.

"Congratulations."

Piper laughed. Bounding toward the door—still full of energy after her workout—she waved at Clio to follow her out. "Come on. I'm sure I have something that will fit you."

"You—you don't have to do that," Clio protested half-heartedly. She didn't want to take the girl's clothes, but she was desperate to get out of her current outfit.

"It's fine." Piper frowned as she led Clio toward the foyer. "You're not a succubus, are you?"

"No."

"Okay, I didn't think so. You don't really have the look." Clio choked slightly and Piper grimaced. "I didn't mean it like that. You're really pretty. It's just you're not, you know, supernaturally beautiful."

Clio sighed. Considering how gorgeous Lyre was compared to the average male, she understood Piper's point.

"Plus," Piper continued, "it would be weird to see an incubus and a succubus together." She paused at the bottom of the grand staircase in the foyer. "Daemons aren't technically allowed upstairs, but we'll be quick."

She darted up the steps and Clio followed on her heels. On the upper floor, worn furniture and thick rugs filled a cozy living room, and a small kitchen peeked out of a wide doorway. So this level was like a penthouse suite, then.

Piper led her down a hall and into a small bedroom. A blanket was tangled over the bed and discarded clothes, books, and a few weapons carpeted the floor. Clio picked her way into the room as Piper crunched straight across the mess to the closet, its doors hanging open and clothes spilling out like an overturned bucket.

"What were you saying before?" Clio asked. "About incubi and succubi?"

Piper burrowed into the closet, riffling through the hangers. "They're the same caste—males and females, right? But they don't get along. They even have different names. What other caste has two names like that?"

None that Clio could think of. Piper backed out of the closet and held up two different shirts. "Which one?"

Clio picked the looser-fitting black tank top with a white paint-splatter graphic over the chest.

"My textbooks basically say if both an incubus and a succubus end up at a Consulate at the same time, expect trouble." Piper pulled out a pair of gray jeans with a horizontal tear across the front of one thigh. "I was going to throw these out, but you can get a bit more wear out of them."

Clio accepted the pants and turned her back to change. She dropped the sweatpants to the floor and shimmied into the jeans. The legs fit just fine—minus the thigh-baring tear—but she had a lot more in the hips department than the young teen did. She quickly swapped shirts, pleased that the new one wasn't too tight.

When she turned around, Piper was holding out a thin leather jacket. "This was a present from my uncle but it doesn't fit me right. Give it a try."

"Your *uncle* bought you a leather jacket?" Clio muttered dubiously as she accepted it and examined the silver buttons and aggressive cut to the collar. For a spunky eighteen-year-old, sure. But for a twelve-year-old?

Piper snickered. "Yeah, he's kind of dense sometimes. I think my father was relieved when it didn't fit. Go on, try it." As soon as Clio pulled it on, Piper whooped. "It's perfect! All you need is eyeliner and you'll look like a rocker chick."

"A what?"

"Never mind. But it's a good look on you." Piper headed for the door. "We'd better get downstairs before someone catches you here."

Clio followed the girl back to the living room and staircase. The open style offered a clear view of the foyer below—where three daemons had just walked in through the front door. Men in inconspicuous black clothes, with bland faces and neutral expressions.

Ice cascaded through Clio's veins. She grabbed Piper's arm and hauled the girl back around the corner.

"What's wrong?" Piper hissed.

Clio clamped her hand over the girl's mouth and held her breath as the daemons paused in the foyer, their gazes sliding around the space. The centermost daemon. Tall, thin build, ashy-silver hair pulled into a low ponytail at the back of his neck.

She knew him. He was the daemon from the Hades embassy, the one who'd guided her, Kassia, and Eryx from the ley line to Chrysalis's doorstep in Asphodel.

A reaper.

She and Lyre had waited too long. Hades had found them, and asleep in the basement, Lyre was trapped.

THREE

LYRE OPENED his eyes with an irritated grunt as the tapping on the door sounded again. Who the hell was knocking? Not Clio. She could disarm his lock spell herself. He sat up, rubbing his face as the light knock sounded a third time. He could sense a female presence.

Tugging his rumpled shirt straight, he padded across the tiny room and pressed his hand against the door. In his other hand, he prepped a lethal cast, golden light sparking over his fingers. After disarming the ward on the door, he pulled it open.

A woman with dark-rimmed glasses stood in the hall. He recognized her from the kitchen—the one who'd dropped her book. He was tempted to slam the door shut again.

"Um." She smiled shyly. "Hi."

"A stunning apparition outside my door?" The words came automatically, sultry and crooning, as long-practiced habit kicked in. He kept his ready-to-unleash cast hidden behind his back. "Am I still dreaming?"

Her eyes, lighting with eagerness, slid down his torso and lingered suggestively, then rose back to his face. Bold enough to come to his door, but too shy to ask him outright for what she wanted.

He glanced down the hall but saw no sign of Clio. Mentally pulling himself together, he focused on the willing victim in front of him. He might as well take advantage of the opportunity and see what came of it.

As he harmlessly dispersed his spell, he let a few wisps of aphrodesia uncoil around him. "I'd invite you in from that cold, lonely hallway, but an incubus can't invite just *any* daemon into his room, no matter how beautiful she may be."

Catching his drift, she raised an eyebrow. "I'm an Underworlder like you."

Damn. Not what he'd been hoping for. But she was already moving forward so he stepped aside to let her in. She glanced at the bow and quiver leaning in the corner then focused on him, her gaze hazy from his aphrodesia. She licked her lips as he swung the door shut and gave her a slow smile.

"What brings a fine woman such as yourself to the Consulate? Business?" He lowered his voice into a purr. "Or pleasure?"

She shivered at the word. "Business," she answered, her voice fluttering. "But at the moment … I would say pleasure."

Her presence in his mind grew as she slipped under his influence. Pushing off the door, he circled behind her and put his mouth by her ear.

"Business can be fun too." He backed up a step as she tried to press into him and continued his circle around her. "Do you like to play games, beautiful?"

"What kind of games?" Her face was slack, her guard down as anticipation dominated her emotions. She reached for him and he caught her wrists, caressing her skin as he gauged the focus—or lack thereof—in her eyes. He unraveled more aphrodesia around them.

"The naughty kind," he breathed as he lifted her arms and wound them around his neck. "How many times have you stayed at this Consulate?"

She frowned at the unexpected question. "Three times."

"Three." He turned his head and brushed his lips against her wrist—once, twice, three times. She inhaled, her heart racing so fast he could hear it. "How many times have you been to Brinford?"

"Dozens," she answered eagerly.

"That number is too high for this game," he pouted. "How many years have you been coming to Brinford, then?"

"Three."

"Three." He slid his fingers down her throat, then plucked apart the top three buttons of her fitted blouse, baring most of her cleavage. Her chest heaved and she stretched up for his mouth. Hands on her waist, he stopped her with a chuckle. "What's the rush, sweetheart?"

"No rush," she said quickly.

"Mm." He massaged her waist. "The Consulate is boring. What other interesting places do you know of in Brinford?"

"What sort of places?"

"Fun places," he crooned. "Dangerous places."

"Dangerous?"

He slipped his fingers under her blouse and ran them across the small of her back. "A little danger is exhilarating, don't you think?"

Shivering, she pushed him backward with unexpected strength. His legs hit the bed and he dropped to sit on it. She was on him in an instant, straddling his lap, and he caught her by the hair before she could get her lips to his. Kissing her would be counterproductive to getting the answers he wanted.

"Do *you* like a little danger?" he asked.

She nodded, clutching the front of his shirt.

"Tell me ..." He smiled teasingly. "What if I wanted to play a dangerous game with ... hmm ... with an Overworlder? Where would I find Overworlders in Brinford?"

"You can play games with me."

"I will," he purred. "But incubi thrive on variety, you know."

"The best place to find Overworlders is the Ra embassy, but you wouldn't have any fun *there*." Giggling, she arched back, letting him support her head, her breasts almost bursting from her partially undone shirt. "I bet you'd like the dance clubs on Altaire Avenue."

"I've been there before. I want something more ... adventurous."

"There's an Overworlder hostel on the north end." She trailed a finger down his throat, the tip of her tongue caressing her upper lip as she watched him. "A few restaurants downtown, a gentlemen's club ...

but if you really want adventure, I've heard rumors of an underground conclave."

"Underground? That sounds intriguing." Encouragingly, he caressed her back under her shirt. Keep it light. Keep it playful. Nothing to make her suspicious. Nothing to leave her wondering too much about the questions he was asking.

"I don't think it's *your* kind of fun." Arching an eyebrow, she slid her hands into his hair. "Unless you're daring enough to play games with thieves and smugglers?"

He pulled her hard against him and added another dose of aphrodesia.

"I won't know unless I check it out, will I?" he crooned, keeping a hold on her hair. "Where would I find this conclave?"

She rattled off an address. "At least that's where I heard it is." She lowered her eyelids in an provocative stare and wound her arms around his neck. "I've heard a lot about incubi too."

"Whatever they say about us"—he brought her mouth closer to his—"I can do even better."

The door flew open.

Clio burst into the room, her ponytail swinging wildly as she caught herself on the doorframe. Her gaze landed on him—and the woman straddling him with her arms around his neck—and her mouth fell open. Her face went beet red in the time it took her to gasp, choke, and start sputtering.

He blinked, distracted by her new outfit. Tight jeans, a black top that hugged her curves, and a fitted leather jacket. *Leather?* On the sweet, innocent nymph?

Oh yes, he liked the leather.

Clio coughed, caught her breath, and pointed at the woman on his lap. "*You!*"

The daemon gave Clio that catty smile women reserved exclusively for other women. "I told you he'd be done with you soon."

Clio bared her teeth, and to his shock, her eyes darkened from summer-sky blue to the color of stormy seas. Holy shit. She was *shading?* Over this? The only time he'd seen her fall into full daemon aggression was when her bodyguard friend had been murdered.

He stood up so quickly the woman fell off his lap and landed on her ass.

"Clio," he began warily. "I was just—"

Her focus snapped to him—and her irises darkened even more. He swallowed the rest of his sentence. She glowered at him, her face red and her eyes shifting closer to ebony, then she lurched back a step and shook her head. Blue returned to her eyes, but the vibrant color was ice cold.

"We need to leave," she said, her normally soft voice as sharp as a machete. "Right now."

He gawked at her, then lunged for the corner and grabbed his bow and quiver. He shoved his feet into his shoes, pushed past the woman who'd just climbed to her feet, and rushed to Clio's side as she dissolved his spells on the door, erasing the evidence of their presence.

"Hey, wait—" the woman began angrily.

He slammed the door in her face as he followed Clio down the hall. "What happened?"

"Three reapers just arrived," she replied tersely. "We have maybe five minutes to get out of here while they're distracted."

"Distracted by what?" he asked as they dashed across the basement common room to the back stairs.

"The Consul girl is stalling them with about ten different forms to fill out. She'll delay them with paperwork as long as she can." She frowned worriedly. "If they hurt her ..."

"They won't." As he raced up the stairs, he tried to remember if he'd seen a female Consul but none came to mind. "Short of complete anarchy, not even a reaper would mess up a Consul inside a Consulate, especially not this one."

They came out on the main level near the kitchen and escaped out the back door. As they sprinted across the lawn and into the trees that surrounded the manor, Lyre cast a cloaking spell over himself, and Clio followed his lead. It was almost midnight and the woods were pitch black, the moonlight scarcely breaching the leafy canopy. They pushed through the undergrowth, trying to move fast without creating too much noise.

"Now what?" Clio whispered. "Do we walk to the city cross-country? What if they find our trail?"

He frowned. "I guess we'll have to …"

They came out of the trees into a clearing where a small building stood alone—a garage with a narrow dirt road leading to it. He hadn't thought the Consulate had a vehicle, but they'd just been keeping it out of sight of the main building. How convenient for him and Clio.

"So," he drawled, arching an eyebrow. "Morally speaking, do you have any objections to stealing?"

IN AN EMPTY LOT in the city's rotting heart, Lyre and Clio abandoned the car and set out on foot. Though slower, it was the least conspicuous way to travel.

He trailed after Clio, letting her determine their route through the alleyways. His skin prickled, nerves winding tight. His bow and quiver were too noticeable to carry around, so he'd taken a moment away from Clio to wrap them in his glamour with his other weapons. But now he was empty-handed and he didn't like it.

They skirted the worst of the garbage, passing graffiti-marked brick walls, boarded-up windows, and the rusting skeletons of cars from a bygone age. Once, these sprawling human cities had been very different. He could only imagine what Brinford had been like at full population, but that had been well before his time. For the last six decades, the city had housed barely a third of its potential capacity.

And that, he supposed, was partly the fault of daemons.

For as long as anyone remembered, daemons had used ley lines to visit Earth. This world bound the two daemon realms together, but centuries ago, venturing here had required great care. Humans were numerous and fearful—a dangerous combination. Back then, daemons had come and gone in secret, their presence known only to the Consuls who ran clandestine sanctuaries.

Sixty years ago, that had changed. War had broken out among the humans and swiftly consumed the planet. With humanity wielding weapons of mass destruction and threatening to eradicate all life, daemons of both realms had come together for the first time. Samael, warlord of Hades, and his Underworld subordinates had been joined by the most powerful families of the Overworld: the Ras, the Valkyrs, and the jinns.

Combining information, resources, and forces, they'd concocted a plan to save the bridge between the daemon realms. In a masterfully timed coup, the daemons simultaneously assassinated all the top-ranking human leaders involved in the war, then tracked down and eradicated the worst of the humans' weapons of mass destruction.

With that, the war had ended—but the chaos had just begun. Daemons were no longer a myth. Their anonymity among humans had been forever lost.

Humans, with their population crippled and their cities in ruins, fled the urban centers and formed small towns and villages in the countryside. Only the brave, the desperate, and the rich had stuck around in the cities where daemons no longer bothered to hide. Maybe Brinford would someday recover its former glory, but for now, it was a hellhole with a few respectable neighborhoods. Lyre had never liked it much; it was dirty, it stank, and it was full of nervous humans.

He supposed he'd better get used to it. Brinford, or somewhere like it, was the best home he could expect for the rest of his life.

Before those thoughts could suck away the last of his waning energy, he glanced at Clio. She stalked several long paces ahead of him, her untidy ponytail swinging with each step.

"I wasn't messing around with that woman," he informed her without preamble.

She stumbled. Catching herself, she fixed him with the meanest glare he could ever have imagined from a five-foot-nothing nymph.

"Whatever." She faced forward again. "You can do what you want."

"So you don't care?" he prompted.

"Not one bit."

Uh-huh. "Then I guess you don't care about the information I coaxed out of her."

She looked over her shoulder again, confusion flitting across her face. "Wait, what?"

"You said you didn't know where to find an Overworld guide, so ..." He shrugged. "I figured I might as well start somewhere."

"You were getting *information*?"

"Why else would I let her in our room? Besides, she's not my type. I prefer blonds."

As pink stained her cheeks, Clio finally stopped and faced him. "Did you learn anything?"

"There's an Overworlder black market by the city center mall. Not ideal, but probably our best bet for finding a guide. Unlike more straight-laced daemons, smugglers should be willing to bargain with us." He raised an eyebrow. "Do you forgive me for getting cozy with that lady?"

"I don't care what you did with her." She bit her lip. "But I guess that information is useful. It'll save us a step."

He quashed his smile as she continued, her renewed silence more thoughtful than hostile. The alley they were following met a narrow street lined with dark shop windows and they paused in the shadows. Lyre scrutinized every doorway and cranny for signs of life. Tension crept through his muscles, and the hunted prickle running down his spine—a trick of his mind, he hoped—wouldn't let up.

"Where are we?" he asked, wishing he could sit down but unwilling to admit how tired he was. Losing his magic had taken a toll on his body.

A hint of mischief sparked in her eyes. "Don't you recognize it?"

Frowning, he scanned a row of small, sad little shops, then turned to the other row where inviting yellow light still lit a single window. A familiar window.

"Wait. Isn't that the spellcraft shop where—"

"Where we first met," she finished. "We can't do anything without money, and this shopkeeper deals in human and daemon currency."

He scrubbed a hand through his hair, trying to wake up his brain. He should have realized a place like this would be their first stop. Why was it so hard to focus on the obstacles in front of them? Why was it so hard to care?

"Now that Hades knows we're in the city, we'll need a safe place to camp out," he said. "Finding temporary accommodations comes first, then we can worry about locating a guide."

"That's what I was thinking as well."

At least one of them had been thinking. He sighed as he reached for his pocket where he'd stashed his pouch of diamonds. "I hate to part with lodestones, but even one will buy us—"

"No." She touched his wrist, stopping him. "You need your lodestones. Wait here."

"Huh? Clio, what—"

"Just wait." She walked back down the alleyway and vanished into the darkness. After a moment, the soft jingle of chains broke the silence. Chains? She wasn't carrying chains, was she?

She returned within a minute, holding a long gold necklace lined with dozens of sapphires, rubies, and emeralds. She held it out to him. "Will this be enough?"

"Uh." He took the chain and slid his fingers over the finely tooled links and sparkling gems. "Yeah, this is more than enough." He gave her another long look. Since she hadn't been wearing any jewelry before, especially not a chain worth a small fortune, she must have been carrying it under her glamour. "Are you sure you're okay with selling this? All these lodestones—"

"It's fine." She smiled faintly. "The necklace is just a decoration."

He shook his head. Nymphs were known for their rich territory loaded with precious stones and metals, but to wear perfectly good lodestones as jewelry was kind of absurd.

"Shall we, then?" He took a step into the street, but she didn't move.

"You go ahead," she murmured. "I'll wait here."

"It's not safe. We should stick together."

"Bargaining isn't my strong suit, as I'm sure you've figured out already. It's better if you handle it." A smile—the first he'd seen in a while—tugged at her lips. "Plus, remember how you broke into that cabinet and smashed the quicksilver, then walked out the door?"

"Yes?"

She folded her arms. "Well, the shopkeeper turned up twenty seconds after you left. So guess who got blamed for *your* thievery?"

"Oh."

"Yeah. So, I'll wait here."

"I guess that's for the best." He thought back on their first encounter. "I know I said it then, but ..."

He stepped closer, and she gasped when he slid his arm around her waist and pulled her close the way he had during that first meeting. And just like that first time, he brought his mouth to her ear, lips brushing across her soft skin. Her sweet scent, tantalizing and familiar, filled his nose.

"Thanks," he whispered.

She shivered. He'd intended to release her immediately, but his arms tightened instead. Wrapped around her small frame, his cheek pressed against her hair and his eyes squeezed shut, he held her to him. For one brief moment, he allowed himself to acknowledge his pathetic relief that he wasn't alone in this.

And how petrified he was of the moment when he'd have to face this new future on his own.

Forcing his arms to loosen, he released her and stepped back. She wobbled, cheeks bright with a fresh blush. Unable to help himself, he brushed his thumb across her rosy cheek.

"Stay safe, Clio. I won't be long."

Leaving her in the shadows, he hastened across the street to pawn her jewelry and buy them a little of the safety they would desperately need very soon.

FOUR

"I DON'T KNOW if this is a good idea," Clio muttered. "Why would we want a room anywhere near a … a party street?"

"Altaire Avenue," Lyre told her as they cut through another dark alley, homing in on the loud thud of conflicting dance beats. "Haven't you been here before?"

"Of course not," she huffed. "Why would I?"

He didn't comment as he surveyed the surrounding buildings before venturing out. They'd been out in the streets for a couple hours and he was jumping at every shadow. After he'd traded Clio's necklace for a mix of human money and the platinum coins that formed most daemon currency, they'd trekked across downtown. They needed to find shelter soon.

They rounded a corner and Altaire Avenue stretched ahead of them — rows of buildings flooded with lights and glaring neon signs. Despite the late hour, a couple hundred people wandered the pavement, young and old, some in casual dress, others in flashy club wear. The music pounded in an unpleasant cacophony as each club's sound system vied for dominance.

Humans were strange creatures. Terrified of the dark, paranoid about daemons attacking them, but give them bright lights and cheap beer and they were as brave as lions. It might have seemed odd that so many were out reveling when the average resident was barely scraping by, but the tougher the times, the more people craved a release from the stress.

A group of laughing women in skintight dresses that barely covered their asses sauntered by, leaving a trail of alcohol-scented air in their wake. Clio cringed back into the shadows of the alley.

"It's easier to hide in a crowd," Lyre explained. "And this is the busiest street in the downtown area."

"But how will we sleep with all this noise?"

"The clubs are quiet during the day, and that's when we'll be sleeping."

"Oh, right. How do we find a room to rent?" A wrinkle formed between her brows. "I've never done anything like this before."

He looked at the bustling humans, laughing as though they had no cares in the world, and uncertainty settled in his stomach—right beside the anxiety and dread. "Me neither."

A soft touch on his hand. Warm fingers curled around his, and Clio smiled at him encouragingly. "We'll figure it out together. Let's go."

She started forward, tugging him after her. He lengthened his stride to keep pace and watched her out of the corner of his eye.

By almost any standard, he was an expert when it came to women. He knew how to read their faces, bodies, and scents. He could predict their thoughts, emotions, and reactions to what he said and did. And he could manipulate those thoughts, emotions, and reactions as needed, with or without magic. It was his business, his *nature*, as an incubus to understand exactly how to deal with females.

So why didn't he understand the way Clio's smile had tightened his chest as though she'd grasped his heart and plucked it through his ribs?

"*Hi.*" A face appeared in front of him, bright red lips smiling.

He reflexively jerked to a halt. As soon as he stopped moving, five women surrounded him and Clio. Shit.

"Wow," someone breathed. "You are *gorgeous.*"

"Babe, you want to come dancing with us?"

"Forget the clubs. I want to take him home."

"I saw him first."

"No, *I* did."

They pressed closer, jostling for his attention, and he silently swore. What was wrong with him? Walking into a crowd of inebriated women with his face uncovered? Drunk, uninhibited, and human—three factors that made women so susceptible to his aphrodesia that he didn't even have to unleash it to attract them.

As they crowded him, pushing Clio away, he tightened his grip on her hand. A woman draped herself over his side, arms wrapping around him as she slurred something about taking his clothes off. As though that had given them permission, two other women grabbed him.

"Ladies," he crooned, projecting his voice with a touch of power. "Give me a little space, hmm?"

His voice—and the seduction magic in it—blanked their faces. They obediently stepped back, bumping into the small crowd that had formed around him. He pulled Clio to his side and pushed through the group. The nearest women hastened to follow and he flicked his fingers behind him, casting an invisible tripwire. The girl in the lead caught on it and fell. The others tripped over her.

Dragging Clio with him, he ducked into the shadowy entrance to a bar where three guys were smoking cigarettes. He focused on the one close to his size.

"Hey," he said. "I want to buy your sweater."

"Huh?" the man grunted

"Your sweater—your hoodie. How much?"

"I'm not selling my—"

Releasing Clio, Lyre stepped closer, smiled, and unleashed a hard punch of aphrodesia. His victim's eyes glazed over and his mouth fell open.

"Your sweater," Lyre purred. "I want it."

"You … yeah, sure, man." With dazed motions, he pulled the dark green hoodie off and held it out, staring at Lyre. "Hey, uh, you want a beer?"

"No thanks," Lyre said, taking the sweater.

He pulled a couple bills from his pocket and tossed them at the guy. As he strode away, he yanked the sweater over his head—relieved it didn't stink too badly of human or smoke—and tugged the hood up, adjusting it to cover his hair and shadow his face.

Clio grabbed his arm, slowing his fast pace as they reentered the crowded street. "Lyre, did you just use your aphrodesia *on a man?*"

"Attraction is attraction," he said grimly. "Gender doesn't matter."

"But—I mean—you—" She jerked to a halt and her fingers bit into his arm. Alarmed, he spun toward her as her face went from rosy-cheeked to bleached white in two seconds.

"That man just vanished," she gasped. "I think it was a reaper. He was watching us, and I looked at him, and he disappeared."

Snarling, he grabbed her arm and launched into motion again. "Definitely a reaper. When you spotted him, he teleported. What an amateur. Someone is going to beat his ass for that."

"How did they find us so fast?" Panic raised her voice an octave.

"They must have been waiting to see if I'd turn up. Bloody hell."

He ducked through a doorway and into a dark bar. Breezing past the tables, he pulled Clio through the kitchen door as though he knew where he was going. A greasy line cook glanced up from a deep fryer. "Hey, what—"

Lyre walked right by and straight out the back door. In the alley beyond, he swore again. "This is my fault. I suspected they might be watching this area, but I figured we could blend in. But then, like a complete idiot, I forgot to hide my face."

And the boisterous crowd of women had acted like a flashing sign, drawing the hunters right to him.

Scanning the shadows, he led Clio down the alley to a narrow gap between buildings where they could peek into the busy street. He leaned back against the wall and raked his fingers through his hair, then tugged his hood low again.

"Lyre," Clio whispered, "shouldn't we be getting away?"

"They might be following us." He squeezed his temples. "Probably waiting to catch us in a less public place. If we move too far from the busy street, they'll attack."

"Hmm."

Her thoughtful murmur surprised him. She peered down the alley, then looked up at the dark roofs of the buildings. She moved closer to the busy street and gave it a slow, thorough study.

"I don't see any reaper auras. I think we lost him."

"Any ... what?"

She dusted her hands together like she'd just taken care of business. "You aren't the only one with useful skills," she said tartly. "I can see all magic—even cloaking spells. I can spot daemons easily, and reapers' red magic is especially conspicuous."

He stared at her. Astral perception, the unique gift of nymphs. "You can see auras?"

"Magical auras, yes. Yours is gold." She smiled. "It's very pretty."

"Pretty?"

"Yes." She tilted her head toward the street. "There are six daemons out there—two blue, two pink, one purple, and one bronze. No red. Even if a reaper used magic to hide, I would see him."

"Huh. But what if he's staying out of your line of sight?"

"My asper doesn't work through walls, but if he tries to follow us, I'll probably see him."

He took a deep breath. Her asper wasn't foolproof, but it gave them an advantage. "Okay, I guess we can—"

"Wait." She leaned toward the street again, her voice hushed. "He's back. Walking south and—ha! He's searching for us."

Stepping close behind her, Lyre spotted the daemon—all too obvious now that he knew where to look. The man, dressed in casual black clothes, was strolling along the sidewalk, hands in his pockets and his head swiveling constantly.

"He lost us," Lyre murmured. A cold, calculating stillness slid over him. "But he'll bring others to search this area until they find our trail ... unless we stop him from reporting to anyone."

She stiffened. "You ... you mean ..."

"This is life or death, Clio. Our enemies won't show us mercy."

He waited to see how she would react—and what she would decide. She didn't like violence. To her, death was shocking, appalling, a tragedy. He suspected her hands and her conscience were clean of blood. She had never killed before.

Unlike him.

Her eyes darted between his, her focus shifting back and forth as she thought hard and fast. He braced himself, already planning where he would leave her while he did what needed to be done.

She pushed her shoulders back. "All right. What's the plan?"

Damn. She kept surprising him. With a tight smile, he cast his most powerful cloaking spell over himself. Before she could cast her own, he touched the base of her throat, her pulse fluttering against his fingertips, and cast the same spell on her.

"Mine is stronger," he said, answering her questioning look.

She nodded without argument. "I'll follow your lead."

He checked the reaper's position, then slipped into the street. Trailing at a distance, he and Clio shadowed the reaper for several blocks. Eventually, the daemon gave up on relocating his quarry and turned down a side street.

Lyre and Clio followed him away from Altaire Avenue. The streets grew darker and quieter until the throb of music was too distant to hear. The daemon slowed, then stopped in a small, empty parking lot behind a row of shops.

Lyre paused. Beside them, a door hung off its hinges, revealing a dark hallway that led into an abandoned office building. Drawing Clio with him, he headed inside and upstairs into an empty office where a broken window overlooked the parking lot. The reaper stood in the same spot, shifting his weight from foot to foot.

"He activated a signal spell," Clio whispered. "I can see it."

"Summoning his team. We don't have much time." He backed toward the door. "Wait here a sec."

"Lyre—"

He ducked out of the room and around the corner, out of sight. Closing his eyes, he dropped his glamour. The weight of his weapons materialized on his back. He pulled his bow and quiver off, then shifted into glamour again and hastened back into the room with Clio. As he knelt and pulled out an arrow, she glanced at him but didn't comment. He was hiding his true form from her, but she'd done the same. There were things an Underworlder just didn't do in front of an Overworlder.

Nocking the arrow, he raised the bow and took aim. An easy shot, an unsuspecting target. With Clio crouched beside him, tense and silent, he drew the string back to his cheek.

She grabbed his wrist, stopping him just before he could release it.

An instant later, footsteps crunched on loose gravel. The reaper agent turned around as three men walked into view, wrapped in shadows. Two silhouettes revealed average-sized men in simple clothes, but the third's outline was distorted by the bulky shapes of weapons—multiple swords, including a hilt jutting above his shoulder.

An icy prickle ran down Lyre's spine.

"Two reapers," Clio whispered. "The third is … human? I can't see an aura on him."

No, the third one wasn't human. The arctic chill in Lyre's gut told him that much.

"You summoned us?" a reaper asked, a note of sharp command in his voice. His words, though quiet, echoed off the buildings.

"I saw them," the agent replied, shifting nervously. "They were heading down Altaire Avenue, then they disappeared."

"Disappeared?" the reaper demanded. "How?"

"I—I'm not sure. It was crowded."

The heavily armed daemon faced the agent, who cringed back. "They saw you. You lost them because they saw you."

That voice. Deep and sepulchral in a way that reached into his bones. Lyre knew that voice. He knew why the mere silhouette of that daemon sent trepidation twisting through him.

He was so, so dead.

Beside him, Clio had stopped breathing. She gasped in a lungful of air, the sound full of terror.

"Black aura," she whispered faintly. "Not a missing aura. A black aura."

The agent stumbled back a step. "The nymph's astral perception makes it impossible to—"

The motion was so fast. The other daemon grabbed the agent by the throat. A crunch, a gurgle, then the agent hit the ground, twitching and wheezing in the throes of death.

"Ash," the lead reaper growled.

"I don't have the patience for incompetence and excuses. Call off the rest of your idiot spies before they slow me down even more."

"I'm not—"

"Then I'll keep killing them as I see them."

"You aren't in charge here, draconian. Samael assigned the contract to you, but *we* are overseeing—"

"I don't give a fuck what you do. Stay out of my way and this will be over a lot faster."

A long moment of silence.

"You're confident you can kill a master weaver on your own?"

"I can kill anyone."

The reaper snorted. "Arrogance will be your downfall."

"Human or daemon, powerful or weak, everyone bleeds. Everyone dies." He turned away. "Especially when you shove a sword through them."

As he walked out of the lot, shimmers rippled over his body. Black wings rose from his back, flaring wide, and he sprang into the air. With two beats of those sinister, dragon-like wings, he vanished, swallowed by the night.

Lyre clutched his chest as a bolt of terror seized his lungs. Beside him, Clio had curled in on herself, her frantic breath hissing through her clenched teeth. The panic waned almost as soon as it had manifested, but he recognized it. He'd felt a similar surge of paralyzing fear just before his last encounter with Ash. The fear was triggered by the draconian—a magic similar to Lyre's aphrodesia, except it fed on terror instead of lust.

The two reapers stood for a moment more, then without a word, they disappeared in flashes of red light, teleporting away.

Clio sucked in air. "That—that daemon was …"

Lyre nodded, his fingers digging into his sternum. Though the exacerbated panic was fading, a block of icy dread had lodged inside his ribcage, and he doubted it would abate anytime soon.

"But Ash won't … he wouldn't kill us … would he?"

"He's one of Samael's best assassins," Lyre answered dully. "And he has orders to follow. Whether he wants to or not, he's going to kill us."

Growing up in Chrysalis, Lyre had learned how to toe the line of defiance. He'd learned where he could resist and where he had to obey. And sometimes he'd obeyed orders that killed pieces of his soul because that's what it had taken to survive.

Ash knew where the line was too. To survive, he would follow his orders. He was coming for Lyre and Clio, and the only mercy he could give them was a fast death.

Clio's mouth trembled. "He helped me escape the bastille."

Lyre looked at her sharply. "He did?"

She nodded, her eyes huge and shining with tears. "You and I would never have made it out of Asphodel without him. Will he really …"

"He will." Lyre's voice cracked, and he caught her hand and squeezed it gently. "What happened before—what he did—doesn't matter anymore. He can't defy direct orders any more than I could when I was at Chrysalis."

Her fingers clenched around his. "What do we do?"

"We get to the Overworld before he can catch us. If he finds us first …"

"Will you be able to stop him?"

"Will I be able to *kill* him," Lyre corrected. He looked at his bow. "Maybe. If I see him before he sees me."

She too glanced at his bow, and her throat moved as she swallowed. "Lyre, you know how I said no daemon can hide from me because I can see their magic?"

"Yeah."

"His aura, his magic … it's black."

His stomach sank. "You won't be able to see him coming, will you?"

"Not in the dark."

He closed his eyes. One of Samael's deadliest assassins was hunting them, and he belonged to the only caste that could defeat Clio's astral perception.

She wrapped her other hand around his, her skin cold and clammy. He held on tightly, his jaw tense as he tried not to imagine Ash's hand around her neck, crushing her fragile throat the way he'd crushed that reaper's.

Their only chance was to stay ahead of Ash. If they could find a guide quickly enough, he could get Clio to the Overworld where she would be safe. If he could get her home, she would survive.

His survival, on the other hand …

He couldn't stay in her realm indefinitely. Eventually, he would have to return to Earth. His death warrant had been signed, his executioner was already waiting, and it was only a matter of time before he was another tally on the assassin's kill list.

FIVE

HE WISHED there was a way to make his brain stop. Just stop.

Lying on a sofa that smelled of stale smoke and old beer, he stared at the water-spotted ceiling. The breeze outside whistled through cracks in the ill-fitting balcony door and ruffled the moldy drapes he'd pulled across the glass to block out the daylight. Soft scurrying sounds confirmed the reek of rodents was as recent as he'd feared. He'd never considered himself squeamish, but this place made his skin crawl.

A dart of movement near the ceiling. A cockroach as long as his palm scurried down the wall and disappeared behind a crooked power socket.

This room had been the best they could find before sunrise. With the money he'd gotten for Clio's jewelry, they could have afforded something much better. They just hadn't been able to *find* something better after trekking several miles away from Altaire Avenue.

The unit held a sofa and a double bed, separated by a room divider and a dinky kitchen he intended to never enter. The cupboards held more cockroaches than cookware.

On the other side of the divider, Clio was already sleeping—what he should have been doing as well. Casting defensive wards throughout the room and trip spells all around the building and halls had exhausted him. He was still recovering his magic.

Every daemon had a well of magic within them, the maximum quantity of power their body could hold. For daemons who couldn't naturally wield a metric crap-ton of magic, lodestones acted like mini magical batteries they could drain and recharge as needed. That's how Lyre and his brothers could spend countless hours weaving magic without exhausting themselves.

Clio had rescued Lyre's diamond lodestones, but he'd drained them all at once. Even that much power hadn't done much to offset the toll his KLOC spell had taken on him when it had blasted through all his magic in one shot.

He shifted on the sofa, unable to escape the springs jabbing him through the scant padding of the cushions. He would've loved to pass out and sleep away the unrelenting anxiety, but he'd already been lying here for over an hour. Short of knocking himself out with a blow to the head, he probably wouldn't sleep at all.

Instead, he kept dwelling on his newfound "freedom." Despite craving it his entire life, he'd never attempted to escape because he'd known the reality would be painfully harsh. To survive, he would have to run, hide, and sneak around in the darkest and dirtiest places—like this one. He would have to isolate himself, but he'd also have to support himself. Selling spellwork would draw too much attention, and he had no other marketable skills.

Well, except for one. But he wasn't eager to fall back on the old incubus stereotype. Not that he wouldn't make a damn good prostitute, but still. He wasn't that desperate … yet. He'd have to survive long enough to run out of money first.

His thoughts kept turning in circles, and he finally gave up. Heaving himself off the sofa, he walked to the paneled divider and peered around the edge. Murky shadows draped the bed. Clio was curled in a tight ball under the blankets and her blond hair, splayed in a tangle over the single pillow, was the only visible part of her body.

For a long moment, he stood still and silent, watching her. Debating. Pride pitted against weakness. Dignity against desperation.

Screw pride.

He stepped across the invisible line between his space and hers. He hesitated at the edge of the bed, then gave in.

When the mattress dipped under his weight, she stirred. He slipped under the blankets and found her warmth. As he slid in next to her, she stiffened. Ignoring the unspoken protest, he curled around her, his chest pressed against her back.

"What are you doing?" she demanded in a whisper, as though afraid to wake a sleeping neighbor. Lucky for them, the only eavesdroppers were rats.

"I …" He closed his eyes. "I can't sleep."

"So you woke me up?"

"Were you sleeping?" he asked. She didn't sound groggy.

A moment of silence. "No. I can't sleep either. But this is—I mean … you said I could have the bed."

He let out a slow, silent breath. She didn't like him in bed with her. At the Consulate, they'd had to share, but she'd piled the blankets into a barricade between them. He couldn't blame her. Her experiences with his caste hadn't been positive.

"Just a few minutes," he whispered. "I just need … give me a few minutes."

The blankets rustled as she turned her head. She said nothing, but her silence was answer enough. He took a moment to appreciate the unfamiliar sting of rejection. Women had turned him away before—rarely—but this … this felt different. Sighing, he pushed himself up.

Her hand closed around his arm, stopping his retreat.

"You can stay," she murmured. "If you want."

He almost asked if she was sure, but he didn't want her to reconsider. Settling down again, he tucked himself against her back and gently slid his arm around her. She lay stiffly, but after a minute, she relaxed into the lumpy mattress.

Closing his eyes again, he concentrated on the scent of her hair to block out the unfamiliar odors of the room. Slowly, the tension in his muscles eased.

"This place is really gross," she eventually commented.

"Yeah."

"There's a centipede in the bathtub."

"There are cockroaches in the walls."

She shuddered and he reflexively pulled her closer. Her fingers curled around his wrist.

"It's only for a few days," she said reassuringly.

His eyes cracked open but he could see only the back of her head. Despite everything, she was comforting him? He turned his hand and took her wrist instead, rubbing his thumb across the soft underside.

"A few days," he agreed. For her, at least.

"What next? Are we going to the Overworld smugglers market tonight?"

He hesitated. "We could, but I don't know how dangerous it will be. And if any of our pursuers catch up with us, I'm not fit for a fight. Part of the reason I wanted a room near Altaire Avenue was so I could charge my lodestones."

"Oh." She thought for a moment. "Um, how do you charge your stones ... exactly?"

He smirked since she couldn't see it. The question was justified.

Charging lodestones with magical energy required an unexpected ingredient: non-magical humans. A daemon's energy was tied to their own magic, so it couldn't be stolen by another daemon. But daemons could siphon human energy—their auras, so to speak—into lodestones to fuel magic.

The tricky part was siphoning the energy. It required the human to be in a heightened emotional state where their energy radiated off them. Different daemons had different strategies for inciting emotion, but it was easy to guess how an incubus "excited" his human targets.

"I prefer dance clubs," he explained. "I can charge all my stones just by wandering across the dance floor a few times."

It was insanely easy. Take one crowd of humans, add booze, scanty outfits, and loud music, then presto—a virtual cloud of sexual energy waiting for him to draw into lodestones. Lyre almost felt bad for daemons who specialized in other emotions. A fear-inducing daemon like Ash couldn't just waltz into the local terror pub to get a power fix.

Clio shifted on the mattress as she mulled it over, and he had to force his thoughts onto a different track. Thinking about arousal in any fashion while she was pressed against him wasn't a smart idea.

"We can't go back to Altaire Avenue," she said. "They might be waiting for us."

"Yeah, someone will be watching. Since they saw us there already, I'm sure they've figured out that I want to top up my lodestones."

"Where can you go, then? There aren't that many dance clubs in the city."

He mentally ran through his various options. He'd considered them all already, but he kept hoping he would come up with a different conclusion.

"They'll be watching any club I've ever gone to with my brothers." He pressed his lips together. "But there's another one I know of with a reputation for … an extreme lack of inhibition."

"And you've never been there?"

"No." He huffed out a breath. "It's a succubus club."

A long pause. "Oh."

He knew she was waiting for him to explain further but he didn't want to elaborate on how messed up his caste was.

His caste was unique in that males and females were each other's worst enemies. Because of the nature of their magic, they were forever pitted against one another. In the same way an innocent mind and body possessed a natural immunity, incubi—with their constantly lascivious minds and heightened sexuality—had zero ability to resist the aphrodesia of their female counterparts, and vice versa.

So, obviously, him walking into a succubus lair was like a lamb walking into a wolf's den. But continuing to traipse around Brinford with barely any magic and a draconian assassin on his tail was worse.

"If the succubi in the club notice I'm there, they'll attack me," he finally said. "But if we're quick, I think we could get in and out without any trouble. You could spot any succubi before they got close, right?"

She nodded, her head bobbing against the limp pillow. "So we go to the succubus club first, then on to the smugglers market?"

"That's what I'm thinking."

She chuckled. "It's a date, then."

"That might have been sarcastic, but I guarantee any date with me will be romantic."

"Oh, right, of course."

He snorted at her dry tone. They both fell silent, and she nestled into the blankets. He rubbed his thumb back and forth over her wrist, listening to her breathing soften and trying not to read into her "date" comment. She knew incubi didn't date, right? No incubus was capable of long-term commitment. They couldn't even manage short-term commitment most of the time.

Exhaling, he closed his eyes. It was always the same. He wanted what he hadn't yet had, but once he got it, he would lose interest. That's how it went with incubi. The ultimate playboys, not by choice but by nature. They couldn't resist the next new flavor.

But right now, she was all he could focus on, and as he buried his face in her hair, he let her scent, her warmth, and her fingers twined in his lull him to sleep.

SIX

PEEKING AROUND Lyre's shoulder, Clio reminded herself to take a deep breath. She could do this. It was just a dance club, for crying out loud.

Tell that to her churning stomach.

Without the line out front and the pulsating dance beat leaking through the walls, she never would have guessed what the abandoned warehouse was. The street was filthy and otherwise abandoned, and she'd thought it was a weird location for a club. But as she stood in line, watching the other club goers, she began to understand how this place was different.

For starters, its patrons were the next level up from Altaire Avenue in terms of extreme outfits. Fishnet stockings and miniskirts were the standard. Hair in all colors, dark makeup—on men *and* women—lots and lots of bare skin. There were no average-looking people in t-shirts and jeans.

But there were a few very *un*average-looking daemons.

To her asper, their auras were obvious, and most daemons could sense their own kind. But, somehow, the humans recognized the daemons too. Each daemon was surrounded by half a dozen admirers, usually of the opposite sex, who couldn't get enough of the daemon's attention. It wasn't something she was used to seeing.

As the line shuffled closer to the door, she nervously adjusted her hair. It fell down her back in loose waves. Before approaching the building, she and Lyre had made a few quick wardrobe adjustments. Her jacket and his sweater were tucked in a hidden nook in the alley, and she'd knotted the hem of her shirt so a hand's width of her midriff was bare. Lyre had ripped the sleeves off his shirt—already damaged anyway, so no big loss. A simple illusion spell had darkened his hair to brown, which wasn't quite as striking as his natural pale blond, but he was already attracting attention.

The bouncers, two daemons roughly the size of grizzly bears, waved her and Lyre forward. They followed a scantily clad couple down a long, empty hall. In a small room at the end, a smiling woman held a black velvet box. The first couple each took something from inside it before continuing.

"First time here?" the woman asked as Clio and Lyre walked up. "The Styx is for indulgence of all kinds. Leave your inhibitions at the door by donning a complimentary masquerade mask. Here, you can be whoever you want to be."

"Is it mandatory?" Lyre asked.

The woman stared at him before recovering her composure. "No, and it would be a shame to cover a face like yours." She cleared her throat. "Black masks are for humans, while silver masks are for our *other* guests."

The woman held out the box and Clio took a black mask—not wanting to announce herself as a daemon—then she and Lyre walked into the main club. Red and blue lights flashed and zoomed all over, but they did little to illuminate the darkness. A long bar ran along one side, surrounded by a few tiny tables with stools, and in the center was a dance floor where hundreds of bodies writhed in time to the driving beat.

That part she'd expected, but she hadn't anticipated the platforms with silver poles where women in their underwear gyrated against the metal. And she hadn't expected the stage at the back where dancers in scandalous costumes were sinuously twisting either alone or up against each other, their hips moving ceaselessly.

Squinting, Clio scanned the room again, this time using her asper. Minimal spellwork around the perimeter—all in the golden magic she'd come to associate with incubi—and a smattering of colorful daemon auras throughout the space. No sign of succubi, though.

The daemon clubbers in shining silver masks were the center of attention wherever they went. Humans followed them in worshipful awe, and Clio understood why the club was so notorious. This sort of human/daemon mingling wasn't exactly taboo, but daemons generally hid their true natures around humans. The Styx was a haven for humans to indulge in daemon fantasies and fetishes, and it was an open hunting ground for daemons who thrived on human attention.

Like a certain incubus.

Beside her, Lyre was fixated on the dance floor. Taking his arm, she pulled him off to one side so they weren't blocking foot traffic. Tense and unblinking, he took it all in with dilated pupils and parted lips.

"Are you ready?" When he didn't respond, she squeezed his arm and raised her voice over the music. "Lyre, are you ready?"

"Huh?" He finally looked at her but his gaze wasn't quite in focus.

"Are you okay?"

"Yeah." His attention twitched away from her as though inexorably drawn to the dance floor. "This place is … off the charts."

She didn't know what charts he was talking about or whether being off them was a good thing. "Can you charge your lodestones?"

"Oh, yeah. In here? No problem."

His gaze flashed around the room again, but when he turned back to her, his sudden somber concentration took her by surprise.

"Are *you* ready?" he asked. "Once I get out there, I won't be able to sense a succubus approaching. If you see anything suspicious at all, you need to get us out—even if you have to drag me away."

"Drag you?" she repeated with a frown.

A feverish light sparked in his eyes. "This place is a literal sauna of lust, and everyone here is basking in it. I'll try to stick to the edge of the dance floor, but …" He smiled crookedly. "I'll be *very* distracted."

"Oh." That sounded ominous. "Okay."

His smile faded and he brushed his fingers across her hand. "I'm counting on you, Clio."

Her breath caught. "I'll watch your back, I promise."

His smile bloomed again, stealing the last of the air from her lungs, then he was moving. She let him get ten steps ahead of her before pulling her silly black mask on and following him to the dance floor. Once there, she got a front row seat to just what an incubus on the prowl could do.

His natural grace multiplied as he swayed to the music, and each smooth movement embodied seduction. Even at a distance, Clio couldn't control her racing pulse.

The female dancers didn't miss his approach either. Within moments, he had one girl in front of him and one behind, both rubbing their bodies against his in the guise of dancing. In another few seconds, dancers swarmed him, but he somehow slid through the group, briefly falling into sync with one woman after another, his hands sliding over her hips or his eyes capturing hers until she couldn't look away from him.

It was good Clio had more important things to focus on, because watching those girls hang all over him was causing her some unwelcome twists of jealousy. She kept her attention moving, her asper in focus. The bright, colorful auras of the daemons in the club were like glowing signs, easy to spot and track, but she kept scanning anyway. The dance floor, the bar, the tables, the doors, back to the dance floor, over and over.

Lyre moved along the edge of the crowd, slipping from one group of women to the next with practiced grace. She wondered why he kept moving. Why not stay in one spot and siphon energy from the women who came to him? Gold mist swirled around him: his aphrodesia, visible only to her. He wasn't using much, probably because he didn't need it. Everyone was riled up like the entire club was already infected with seduction magic.

Her eyes narrowed, and she again scanned the room. Was there a faint golden tinge to the air?

"Hey, baby." Hot breath that reeked of alcohol washed over her ear. "You look lonely."

A guy leaned over her, his buddies behind him. This, she did not need. Silently, she pointed to a random spot behind the men. Obediently, they all looked toward the other end of the room, and while they were turned, she cast a cloaking spell on herself—the same powerful one Lyre had demonstrated for her last night.

She walked away as the guys turned back, their bewilderment increasing when they discovered her gone. Cloaking spells weren't true invisibility spells, but in a dark building full of drunk, unobservant humans … close enough.

On the dance floor, a willowy girl with long raven hair was undulating against Lyre as though she were boneless. His hands were on her waist, his hips moving in time with hers. Clio bit her lip, her cheeks heating. She wanted to look away, but the way he moved was mesmerizing and somehow thrilling.

A forbidden thought crept into her head: the wish that *she* was pressed against him, that his hands were on *her* hips and his body was moving against *her* like that. Not that she knew how to dance, or grind, or whatever that girl was doing.

The frenzied beat of the song changed, and the crowd swelled outward. Caught in the expanding horde of dancers, Lyre disappeared from her view.

She hurried to the spot where he'd vanished. Catching a glimpse of his shimmering gold aura, she pushed onto the packed dance floor. How many people were they going to jam in here? The club had grown more crowded since their arrival.

As she squeezed between writhing dancers, her cloaking spell lost its effectiveness and men tried to catch her eye. People bumped her, elbows and gyrating hips and swinging arms everywhere, and the frenzied movements pushed her around like violent ocean waves. Where was Lyre? She was shorter than almost everyone and all she could see were unfamiliar heads and shoulders.

His aura was nowhere in sight. Neither was the edge of the dance floor. All she could see was the crush of people, and the gap around her closed like a vise. Three dancers wedged her between them before shifting away. Someone's sleeve caught on her mask and pulled it off her head, tearing out a few strands of hair with it.

She would never find Lyre in this insanity. She needed to get out.

She spun in a circle. Where was the edge of the dance floor? Where was the exit? She whirled around again, gasping in the hot air that smelled of human sweat.

Someone bumped her and she almost fell. Terror rocketed through her at a sudden vision of being trampled under the packed dancers. She lunged toward a gap between two women, desperate to escape.

Hands caught her around the waist and pulled her back into a hot male body. The scent of spicy cherry filled her nose.

"Gotcha," Lyre crooned in her ear as he lifted her off her feet, bringing her eyes level with his. She could see over the dancers' heads and fresh air washed over her.

The crowd closed in even tighter. At least a dozen women pressed into him, shouting garbled words over the music to reclaim his attention. Clio wrapped her arms around his neck, afraid she might get knocked from his grasp.

"Dance with me!" a girl shrieked, red splotches all over her pale cheeks. She pushed into him, inadvertently mashing her breasts against Clio.

Lyre staggered forward, and when grasping hands fumbled against Clio's legs, she realized people were grabbing him from behind. The women—and a few men too—pushed closer, crushing Lyre and Clio.

Now she understood why he'd kept moving when he was working through the crowd. The mood of these women was rapidly shifting from excitement to desperate aggression—like a mob turning violent. Keeping his encounters short had allowed Lyre to stay in control of his interactions … and that control was gone.

No sooner did she realize they were in big trouble than someone grabbed her hair and tore her out of Lyre's arms.

She slammed down on the floor. Lyre dove after her, shouldering two dancers away before they stepped on her. He scooped her up and launched forward. A woman grabbed his shirt to drag him backward. With a loud tearing sound, the seam of his shirt ripped and he pulled out of her grip.

Not bothering with subtlety, he rammed through the crowd with his daemon strength. As they burst into the less crowded bar area, Clio cast the same cloaking spell on him before any women could chase him down.

He headed for an abandoned corner, and in the relative safety of the shadows, he set her on her feet. Wobbling a few steps, she leaned against a pillar to catch her breath as adrenaline faded from her system.

"Holy shit," he said on an explosive exhale. "That was *intense*. Are you okay?"

"I'm fine." She squinted at him, taking in his rumpled hair and ripped shirt. "Are you?"

He grinned, his eyes overly bright. "I'm good."

"Your pupils are the size of dinner plates."

"Oh? Huh, well, I might ..." He raised his hands in an innocent shrug. "I might be just a liiiiiittle drunk."

"Drunk?" She blinked. When had he had a chance to drink anything? "Wait, you mean ... drunk off the energy in here?"

"Mhmm." He leaned closer, still grinning, but it was more goofy than sexy. "Not the first time it's happened, but *this*—this is something else. I *like* this club."

"And the women here like you—a bit too much," she replied, shaking her head. How long would his high from the lustful energy last? She wasn't used to seeing him so ... relaxed. "Did you charge your lodestones?"

He blinked. "Did I ... what?"

Her amusement vanished. "Charge your lodestones. You know, the whole purpose of this trip."

He stared at her.

"I don't believe it." Her hands balled into fists. "Do *not* tell me you got so distracted by those women rubbing all over you that you *forgot* to—"

His befuddled expression cracked into a grin and he threw his head back in a boisterous laugh. Her face blanked. Okay, the drunken silliness was no longer overriding his hotness factor.

In fact, it was adding to his appeal—not the inebriation, but the way it softened him. Even when he teased her, there was always a subtle edge to him—a certain caution as though he were considering the repercussions of every word he spoke. But that edge was gone.

"Of course I charged them." He chuckled. "All taken care of. We can leave any time now."

She sucked in a deep breath and let it out through clenched teeth. "Then why did you—"

"Because," he drawled, stepping closer. His fingers brushed a lock of hair off her forehead. "You're sexier than usual when you're pissed off."

She froze, her back pressed against the pillar. "I'm … not …"

"Oh, you are." His voice shifted to a purr and he braced his hand on the pillar beside her head. "Like when you got all jealous over that female daemon in the Consulate and shaded for a second. *Mmm.*"

Blood rushed to her cheeks. "I—I wasn't jealous."

"No? Are you jealous now?"

"No."

"It didn't bother you," he crooned, his heat all around her, his amber eyes darkening to bronze, "that they were touching me? That I was dancing with them?"

"Absolutely not."

"Hmm. That's too bad."

She swallowed hard, unable to look away from him. "W-why is that?"

Braced against the pillar with one hand, he lightly ran his thumb along her jaw. "Because you were the one I wanted to dance with."

Her lungs deflated and refused to expand again.

"You," he purred, his dark gaze drifting over her face, "are the one I want touching me."

He caught her wrist and pressed her palm against his hot skin, exposed by the torn seam of his shirt.

"Are you sure"—he guided her hand over the muscular planes of his stomach—"you aren't a *little* jealous?"

Her pulse raced frantically in her ears and it was hard to breathe. Slow heat rolled through her center, and without intending to, she focused on his mouth.

Those lips curved into a seductive smile. Her heart thudded as he leaned down, but he didn't close the distance. His mouth hovered just above hers, barely any space between them.

"So, Clio? Which is it?"

"Which is … what?"

"I just told you I want you." His lips brushed across hers like the touch of butterfly wings before he drew back again. "Don't you have anything to say?"

She couldn't help it. As he drew away, she leaned forward, chasing his retreating lips. "Like what?"

"You can't think of *anything*?" He leaned in again, almost kissing her, before pulling back.

She lurched after him, stretching onto her tiptoes, but his mouth was still out of reach. "I—I don't know what …"

His warm hands closed around her hips, then slid up to her exposed midriff, caressing her bare skin. She shuddered at his touch, still stretching toward his tauntingly close mouth.

"Lyre," she gasped.

"Yes?" He raised his eyebrows as though he had no idea what she could possibly want.

"You—" Her brain refused to produce a single coherent word for her to speak.

"So you'd rather pretend you don't want me?" His hands slid around her waist then down over her backside. He pulled her hips hard into his and his mouth dropped closer again, lips brushing against hers as he spoke. "Because I don't want to pretend anymore."

She gasped, one hand still pressed to his bare stomach and the other clutching his arm. He rocked his hips back and forth, matching the booming tempo as he held her against him, guiding her movements. She panted as the erotic rhythm teased her with sensations and longings she was desperate to explore.

His dark, scorching eyes held hers as he moved their bodies together, and it was sweet torture—hot and exciting and teasing. He slid his lips across hers in a feathery touch before pulling back again. Unable to take it anymore, she grabbed him by the hair to yank his head down.

He suddenly stopped moving.

His brow furrowed. He stepped back, pulling away from her hands, and looked her over with a frown pulling at his lips.

"Is that my cloaking weave?"

Her whole body flashed from hot to cold.

His confusion grew as he studied the spell she'd cast on herself then checked the one she'd cast on him. "This is *my* spell. How did you learn it so quickly?"

Frantic denials spun through her head. "I watched you last night with my asper, and I remembered how …"

"This spell is too advanced for your weaving skill."

"I—I know a lot of advanced—"

His expression hardened. "I gave you a lesson in weaving. I *know* what level you're at. How did you learn *and* cast my weave after only seeing it once?"

After their impromptu lesson back in Asphodel, he'd gotten a rough idea about her weaving *knowledge*. But for her, knowledge and skill didn't correlate. She could duplicate any spell she saw, no matter how advanced.

How stupid was she? His cloaking spell was so much better than hers and she'd used it without considering the possibility that he might recognize it.

"Clio," he growled. "I want an answer."

"I … I don't …"

"How did you cast my spell?"

She stepped back but he followed, his pupils constricting with focus.

"Clio."

Her back hit the pillar. He towered over her, and all she could do was stare at him, her mouth open but her voice absent. What did she say? How could she explain without revealing she was a mimic—and therefore a Nereid?

He glared down at her, waiting for an answer.

"Clio," he growled again—and this time there was a hint of power in his voice.

She grabbed the front of his shirt, her fist braced against his chest, preventing him from shifting any closer. Her other hand lifted, fingers curled.

"I blasted you once," she said, her voice low and marred by a faint quiver. "Don't make me do it again."

His face went blank, then he stepped back. His shirt pulled from her grip, and she straightened, her pulse skittering from the adrenaline rush.

Before he could say anything, she marched away from him, walking the length of the bar before glancing back. He hadn't moved, a mere shadow in the dark corner. Breathing harshly through her nose, she went into the women's restroom and braced herself against the sink.

Had Lyre been about to force an answer out of her with aphrodesia?

She wasn't sure. Power had touched his voice, easy to recognize after her recent incubus experiences, but sometimes he unintentionally leaked seduction magic.

She wanted to trust him, but maybe that was naïve. Maybe she was a fool. Mimicking his advanced weaves right in front of him certainly suggested she was an idiot. If she planned to keep her abilities a secret, she needed to be more careful.

Her blue eyes, vivid against her skin, stared back at her in the mirror. If she wasn't willing to trust him with her most dangerous secrets, how could she trust his equally dangerous power?

SEVEN

WHAT THE HELL was wrong with him?

Lyre rested his forehead against the pillar and pressed his clenched fist into the unyielding concrete. He pressed harder until pain cut through the buzzing in his head and the hungry euphoria waned.

He could still feel them—hundreds of swirling presences, the dancers lost in lust and excitement. Their energy was like a drug and it called to him. For an incubus, this place was the worst combination of everything they loved and everything that made them weak. Aroused, uninhibited women everywhere. So much lust energy. It was overwhelming. It was glorious.

His hunger raged under the surface, ravenous and unsatiated. Temptation flaunted itself everywhere he turned. Stimulation, scents and sounds and willing bodies. He ached from it—ached *for* it.

He dug his fist into the concrete. He'd almost used aphrodesia on Clio. Even if he'd wanted an answer and not her body, it didn't make much difference. If he was willing to compromise her will for that, then he was willing to compromise it for anything he wanted badly enough.

But damn, it was so difficult around her. He'd been fighting the urge to let his magic loose since he'd pulled her against him on the dance floor. Since he'd carried her out of the crowd. Since he'd touched her face, touched her body, pulled her to him, moved against her the way he wanted to move inside her.

In short, since he'd started seducing her.

Hadn't he decided he wouldn't risk sleeping with her? Somehow she kept erasing that decision right out of his head. In a club full of eager women, he wanted her. Only her. The moment he'd touched her on the dance floor, the other women had virtually disappeared, and all his hunger and need had locked onto her.

Just her. The girl he'd decided he couldn't have.

An Overworlder. A nymph. A virgin. Three reasons to keep his distance that should have been more than enough. Three reasons that were doing shit all to stop him from trying anyway.

He breathed deeply to clear his head. He should find her and apologize for being an ass. She shouldn't be alone, not when there were so many hunters from Asphodel after them.

But first, he needed to get a grip on himself. Even alone, he burned for her. He couldn't stop thinking about her mouth, her body, her warmth, her scent, her taste. He was going insane with it. A prickling sensation ran up his arms, his skin over-sensitized and painful. Instead of receding, the desire lighting him on fire kept building.

He pulled his fist off the pillar and opened his fingers. Confused, he watched his hand tremble. He couldn't think. The searing lust had become pure torment, and he panted for air as the tremor in his limbs increased.

A flutter of fear pierced him before the flames within him consumed it too. Caught in a maelstrom of raging need, he turned around.

And looked into the yellow eyes of the woman behind him.

CLIO SPLASHED water on her face and grimaced at her reflection. Grabbing some paper towel, she patted her face dry. She couldn't hide in the bathroom forever. She needed to go back out there and face him.

Passing a group of tipsy girls, she returned to the main club where the flashing lights and hammering beat assaulted her all over again. She would get Lyre and they would make their getaway now that he'd charged his lodestones.

And, she decided as she headed toward the dark corner where she'd left him, once they were out of here, she would tell him she was a mimic. Considering what they'd gone through together already, he deserved to know. But would he understand the implications of her rare ability? Would he realize only members of the royal nymph bloodline possessed the mimic gift?

She chewed her lip as she scanned the dark corner. Where was he? This was the same spot, wasn't it? She was certain of it.

Cold slipped through her veins. Had he left without her? He wouldn't do that, would he?

Blinking rapidly, she focused her asper. A golden cloud of aphrodesia hung in the air, as thick as Madrigal's had been when he'd tried to control her mind. The wispy trail of magical fog ran along the perimeter wall and disappeared through a curtained doorway — guarded by two beefy bouncers.

She looked from the mysterious doorway back to the aphrodesia mist. Why would Lyre unleash his seduction magic like that? Unless …

Unless that wasn't *his* aphrodesia.

The chill in her blood turned to ice. She had left him alone. She'd promised to watch his back, then she'd left him alone in a succubus club. The lust-energy high had impaired his judgment. She'd seen it herself. Why had she left him alone?

Controlling her urgency, she headed for the curtained doorway. The bouncers watched the clubbers, their gazes shifting from person to person but never turning her way. Her powerful cloaking spell was still working. Keeping to the shadows, she crept closer, and when both men focused on a catfight near the bar, she ducked between them and through the curtain. On the other side, the corridor opened into a posh sitting area — a private place for VIP guests?

Muffled laughter reached her ears. The last of the faint aphrodesia clung to a closed door with a fine web of gold light crisscrossing the handle—a lock spell. Hurrying to the door, she pressed her ear to the wood and heard female voices on the other side.

Carefully, she broke the spell and turned the handle. The latch clicked quietly and she cracked the door open to peek inside.

The small room was open in the center while plush built-in sofas lined the walls on three sides. Soft blue light glowed from behind the bench seats, giving the whole space an eerie twilight cast. Small tables for drinks were pushed into a corner as though the room wasn't in use right now.

In the middle, three women stood—the most beautiful women Clio had ever seen. Waves of silken blond hair, tanned skin, huge golden eyes lined with thick lashes, sculpted cheekbones and full lips. Flawless, exotic beauty. They were impossibly stunning—walking fantasies instead of flesh-and-blood women.

And standing in their center was Lyre.

The illusion spell that had changed his hair color was gone, his pale locks tinted by the blue lights. A succubus stood in front of him, two fingers under his chin as she gazed unblinkingly into his eyes. He stared back at her with pitch-black irises, his expression eerily blank.

The other two succubi circled him like he was a prized stallion.

"He really is quite fine," one commented as she squeezed his bicep. He didn't react, his stare still locked on the succubus in front of him. "Ten out of ten, even for an incubus."

Lyre's voice was otherworldly in its musical tones, but the succubus's was too beautiful for words. An entire symphony would have been hard-pressed to produce a more pleasing sound.

"We should dock him a point for stupidity," the shortest of the three said. "Do you think he knows this place is run by succubi?"

"Either way, I'm pleased." She stroked his arm again and smirked when he shuddered. "Rosa, has he submitted yet?"

The succubus holding eye contact with him smiled. "He's fighting my control. He does *not* want to obey." She ran her tongue over her upper lip. "I do enjoy a fighter."

Clio swallowed down her stomach. Lyre had said the succubi in the club would attack him, but she hadn't expected *this*.

She should have, though. She'd seen how swiftly and viciously a female's aphrodesia could overwhelm an incubus—because she had done exactly that to Madrigal and, by extension, Lyre when she'd mimicked their auras. Just as Madrigal had lost his will to Clio, Lyre had lost his to these succubi. *Three* of them. He hadn't stood a chance.

With two fingers still under his chin, Rosa slid her other hand down his chest. Another shudder ran through his body, almost as though the light touch was hurting him.

"What shall we do with him first?" she purred. "Zinnia, what do you think?"

The short succubi flipped her waist-length hair over her shoulders. Much like the clubbers on the dance floor, she wore a tight miniskirt and a shimmering top with a plunging neckline. Clio pressed her face against the crack in the door and tried desperately to think of a plan— a way she could take on three daemons without Lyre getting caught in the crossfire.

"Why don't we see exactly what we have before we decide?" Zinnia suggested. "Have him release his glamour."

"Ooh," the third succubi exclaimed. "Excellent idea. Let's see him."

Rosa laughed and tightened her grip on Lyre's chin. "Release your glamour, darling."

He bared his teeth at her.

Zinnia chimed a laugh. Despite the hair-raising beauty of the sound, a clear note of cruel amusement rang in it. "*Still* fighting, oh my."

Rosa's fingers dug into Lyre's jaw and when she spoke again, even Clio heard the power in her voice.

"*Release your glamour.*"

The tension tightening his muscles relaxed and his black eyes dulled with sudden passivity. Shimmers of light washed over him like heat waves, and when they faded, the glamour that disguised him as human was gone.

Clio couldn't breathe.

A god descended from the heavens couldn't have been as perfect. A fallen angel couldn't have been as magnificent. His body remained essentially the same, but everything about him that was already mouthwateringly gorgeous had been magnified to a whole new level.

His hair, silken and tousled, had paled closer to white. A thin braid, longer than the rest of his hair, hung down one side of his face to just below his jaw, the end adorned with a sparkling ruby. His skin, tanned honey, was radiant, almost luminescent, as though the golden light of his aura was leaking from within him. His ears came to sharp points, and the left one was pierced with two tiny gold hoops and a diamond stud.

Mysterious garb she'd glimpsed once before had replaced his torn shirt and black pants. The midnight blue garments were fitted to his body, the seams accented with silver thread and black edging. The exotic cut was simple but flattering, and the sleeveless shirt exposed the finely tooled leather armguard on his left forearm and the short sheaths holding knives strapped to his other arm. A strung bow and bristling quiver hung off his shoulders, and more gear was belted over his body. He looked ready to walk onto a battlefield.

The succubi were silent, as stunned as Clio. Had his brilliant allure stolen their breath too? Were their hearts locked in their chests, too stunned to beat, as though only his touch could awaken them? Or had his battle-ready appearance silenced them?

"Wow," Zinnia murmured. She plucked at his shirt. "This is high quality."

Rosa didn't move, still holding eye contact. "Jessamine, what's his family mark?"

The third succubus peered at Lyre's right cheekbone. Beneath his eye, a delicate design was tattooed in black ink.

"I don't recognize it," Jessamine said.

Zinnia joined her to squint at the marking, then slipped her fingers under the neckline of his shirt. She pulled out two chains laden with sparkling gems—and the small silver key that armed the clock spell.

"No way!" Jessamine gasped. "Are those all lodestones?"

"Whoa." Zinnia lifted them over his head. "These are worth a fortune. This guy is *loaded*."

Rosa smirked as she rubbed her thumb along Lyre's jaw. "I'm impressed. I wonder how else he might be well endowed."

Clio's hands clenched as the two succubi pulled off his bow and quiver, unstrapped his larger weapons, then checked him for more valuables. They carelessly ran their hands over his body, uncovering several more lodestones from his pockets, and he did nothing, held firmly under Rosa's power. Giggling, Zinnia unbuckled his belt and wiggled her hand into his pants. Clio looked away, unable to watch.

Helpless fury burned through her. She wanted to burst in there and blast the succubi to pieces, but she had to wait for her best opportunity to act. If she used an attack to hit all three daemons at once, she would hurt Lyre too. If she only attacked one succubus, the other two might harm Lyre while he was helpless.

After stripping Lyre of his valuables and piling them on a sofa, Jessamine and Zinnia returned to Rosa's side.

"Well then," Zinnia purred. "We need to wear down his resistance before we can have any real fun with him. Do you think I can make him scream like the last one?"

"No, it was the one before that who screamed," Rosa corrected. "The last one *cried*, remember?"

"Oh yes. And he kept begging." Zinnia pulled Lyre's arms behind his back and light flashed as she bound his wrists together with a spell. "I want to hear this one beg."

Jessamine sighed. "Can we *not* torment him? It isn't necessary to control him."

Zinnia shot the succubi an incredulous look. "Are you serious?"

"I don't like …" She shifted uncomfortably. "I don't like using aphrodesia to break them. It's so … undignified."

"And you think he would treat *you* with dignity if he had caught you in his aphrodesia instead?" Rosa snapped. "You're so naïve, Jessamine."

"Fine, do what you want." Scowling, Jessamine retreated to a sofa and sat, her arms folded.

"You're just going to watch instead?" Zinnia taunted. "Then I'll give you a show."

She turned to Lyre, grabbed him by the hair, and pulled his mouth down to hers.

Clio flinched, unable to do anything as the succubus kissed him, her face plastered against his. With his arms bound, he could do nothing but stand there, not that Clio could expect him to resist when he was so deeply caught in—

Zinnia shrieked and reeled backward, her hand flying to her mouth.

"He bit me!" She slapped him hard in the face and he stumbled away from her—opening a gap between him and the two succubi.

Clio flung the door open and charged into the room. Her swift blast knocked them over, and her second spell shoved Lyre clear of the fight. Pivoting back to the succubi, she began a binding spell.

A flash of movement in Jessamine's corner. A golden surge slammed Clio off her feet. She hit the floor and rolled, holding on to her in-progress cast. Lurching onto her knees, she flung the spell at Rosa and Zinnia, catching them both in the binding.

Jessamine raised her hands to cast another spell. Clio cast a reflective barrier—the one she'd learned from Lyre's brother Viol—and the attack bounced off. Jessamine yelped as the power rebounded and crackled over her. Clio curled her fingers, another binding spell almost ready to throw.

A magical blow hit her in the back. She landed on her face, her arms bound to her sides.

A shoe—one with a stiletto heel—came down on her back and threatened to punch through her ribcage. The person standing over her *tsked* softly.

"Incubus," the newcomer purred, her voice like harmonized bells and brimming with power. "Do not move."

Panting shallowly, Clio glimpsed the blond hair of the woman pinning her down. A *fourth* succubus.

"Jessamine, free Rosa and Zinnia."

"Yes, ma'am," Jessamine mumbled, hurrying to her friends.

Clio gritted her teeth. She'd been *so close*. Thirty seconds more and she would have been ready to fight the unexpected arrival.

Jessamine broke the binding spell, and Zinnia and Rosa launched to their feet. Rosa hurried to the corner where Clio had shoved Lyre. The foot disappeared from Clio's back, then she was hauled up and thrown onto the sofa. Her back hit the leather and she sat awkwardly with her arms still bound.

The fourth succubus put her hands on her hips. Unlike the others, she wasn't wearing skimpy club clothes. Her pencil skirt, fitted red blouse, and matching four-inch pumps were reminiscent of a businesswoman. She had pulled her hair into a high ponytail, and dark makeup gave her a sultry look. Her lips were the same cherry red, vivid and inviting.

She scanned Clio from head to toe, then glanced at Lyre, who knelt with his wrists still bound. Rosa was in front of him again, resuming eye contact so he couldn't throw off the mind-controlling aphrodesia.

"Who," the new succubus said, "might you be, my dear?"

"She came in with the incubus," Zinnia answered.

"Oh? A companion of his?"

Clio surreptitiously wiggled her arms, testing the binding. "Yes. And those three kidnapped and assaulted him."

"He invaded our club," Zinnia snapped.

"Did we miss a 'no incubi' sign on the door?" Clio retorted. "He hasn't done anything to harm you or this club. We were about to leave."

"Hasn't harmed us?" Zinnia pulled her lips back to reveal her bloodstained teeth. "He *bit* me."

"You forced yourself on him."

"He *wanted* me to—"

"If he wanted you, he wouldn't have bitten you."

"Impertinent chit," Zinnia snapped. "Lilith, what should we do with her?"

The businesswoman tapped a glossy red fingernail against her full lower lip, then shrugged. "Have the bouncers throw her out."

Clio jerked upright. "I'm not leaving without my friend!"

"Your *friend*?" Lilith's eyebrows rose. "An incubus is no woman's friend. Have you slept with him yet?"

Her cheeks heated. "N-no. We're—we're not—"

"She's a *virgin*," Jessamine gasped in what might have been shock or delight. "You are, aren't you?"

"I—I'm not—"

"Oh, honey," Lilith sighed. She glanced at Lyre then back to Clio. "You have no idea the game he's playing, do you?"

Clio stiffened at Lilith's condescending pity.

The succubus lowered herself onto the sofa beside Clio. "Let me explain something to you, girl. You have a superficial ability to resist an incubus's power and that makes you feel safe around him, doesn't it?" She leaned closer to Clio, her caramel eyes intense. "But the truth is an incubus is *more* dangerous to a virgin than any other woman."

Clio set her jaw, determined to disregard everything the succubus said.

"If he unleashes the full scope of his aphrodesia on you, you'll overdose on his power," Lilith told her grimly. "He'll warp your mind, tear apart your senses, and ruin you for sex forever afterward."

Madrigal's insidiously beautiful voice whispered in her memory. *I'm going to destroy you with pleasure.*

Clio shook her head. "He—he would never do that to me."

"Even if he has the best intentions—which I sincerely doubt—he could still accidentally damage you. Incubi naturally release their aphrodesia when aroused, and they don't normally have to worry about controlling it since an experienced partner isn't at risk."

"He wants to toy with you," Jessamine added unexpectedly. "They enjoy the chase. Most women give in to them immediately, so incubi will target inexperienced girls instead."

"He hasn't bedded you yet because he's still having fun," Zinnia added. "Look, girl. Take it from us, would you? We know what incubi are like."

Clio pressed her lips together.

Lilith rose to her feet. "There's no reasoning with a virgin in love, is there?"

Clio scowled. She wasn't *in love* with Lyre. She hadn't even known him that long.

"Well," Lilith murmured, "I suppose in this case we will—"

A high-pitched moan rose over Lilith's words.

In the corner, Rosa had her mouth glued to Lyre's. He held her jaw with one hand as he kissed her—but hadn't his wrists been bound? The sound coming from the succubus rose even higher, no longer sounding like pleasure.

He drew back, pulling on her lower lip—held between his teeth. Blood ran down her chin. She yanked away from him with a pained cry, splattering the floor with red droplets.

"Rosa!" Zinnia cried.

All three succubi lunged at him and electric power sizzled the air. Clio didn't need her asper to know they had unleashed their aphrodesia on him, and the uncomfortable warmth she'd felt since entering the room flashed hot in her veins. Breathless, she couldn't react as Jessamine grabbed Rosa and pulled her away. Zinnia took her place, her blazing eyes locking on Lyre's black irises as she crooned a constant stream of commands. *"Hold still. Stop using magic. Don't speak."*

"Rosa, what happened?" Jessamine asked, holding her companion tightly.

"I—I was listening to you talking." Rosa sniffled as she held her mouth, trying to staunch the blood. "I didn't notice he'd started to hum. His voice is …" She shuddered from head to toe. "We shouldn't have made him drop glamour."

"No, you shouldn't have," Lilith reprimanded, her tone sharp. "You shouldn't play with toys you can't control. Concentrated aphrodesia makes some daemons violent instead of passive. You know this."

"But that's not usually an issue with incubi," Jessamine protested in a small voice as she glanced nervously at Lyre. He knelt with Zinnia in front of him, once again submissive, his magnetic daemon form luminous and irresistible. "He's … different."

"You should have been prepared to stay in control regardless." Lilith strode to Lyre and grabbed his chin, pulling his face up. "And he isn't any different from—"

She broke off, her gaze fixed on the dark tattoo on his cheekbone. For a long moment, she stared at the marking. Then she snatched her hand back as though his skin had burned her.

"Lilith?" Rosa asked worriedly.

The succubus inhaled, her breath trembling and shoulders shifting, then she pivoted. "Everyone out."

"W-what?"

"You three should never have touched this incubus." Lilith's eyes darkened with fear. "Out. Now."

"But we can't just leave him here like this. He'll—"

"Some time alone will settle him down. Just hope he decides to leave without indulging in revenge." Lilith snapped her fingers. "Move."

Wide-eyed, Jessamine and Rosa hurried to the door.

Lilith waved at Clio. "Hurry up, girl."

She folded her arms. "I'm not leaving without him."

"Once he's free of Zinnia's control, he'll go for the first female he sees. I'm going to lock him in until he calms down. You can wait outside the door."

Clio shook her head, not trusting the succubus.

"Are you not *listening*?" Zinnia said without looking away from Lyre. "She's saying your incubus friend will attack you the moment we're gone."

"I can handle him," she replied stiffly. Whether Lyre would attack her remained to be seen, but if he came after her, she knew what to do. In Chrysalis, when she'd used aphrodesia on him and Madrigal, all it had taken was a few minutes under a sleep spell to return him to his senses.

"You can't." Jessamine hovered in the doorway, her voice soft with concern. "You won't be able to stop him. He'll—"

"If she wants to stay, fine," Lilith snapped. She flicked Clio's arm, dissolving the binding spell. "Let's go, ladies. I have much to explain to you about your reckless lack of due diligence."

Rosa, still holding her bleeding mouth, disappeared from the threshold but Jessamine hesitated, her perfect forehead wrinkled.

"But Lilith, that girl has no idea what—"

"Go, Jessamine."

Jessamine's throat bobbed as she gulped back another protest, then she vanished as well. Zinnia gave Lyre a final command to hold still, then hastened out with a pitying look at Clio.

Lilith stepped up to the door. "Last chance, girl. You don't want to be in this room." When Clio didn't move, the succubus snorted softly. "Virgins. Fools, every one of you."

She swung the door shut. Golden magic webbed across it, forming a strong lock spell.

Clio pressed against the sofa as Lyre lifted his head. His black eyes, burning with mindless lust and rage, locked on her—and there was nothing submissive left in his stare.

EIGHT

"LYRE?" Clio whispered.

He watched her with terrifying intensity and no sign of recognition. Only heat and fury.

When a daemon was pushed too far, their instincts could become so overwhelming that it drowned out their higher consciousness—including the part that recognized allies and loved ones. And the way he was watching her, she knew beneath the violence the succubi had spurred in him, Lyre didn't know her right now.

But she'd resisted an incubus on the offensive before, and following the advice he had given her, she looked away from his dangerously compelling eyes and focused on his chin instead—except it was almost impossible to hold her attention there. His daemon form was utterly spectacular, so subtle in its inhumanity compared to most daemons, yet so much more than she could have imagined. He was fascinating, enticing, glorious, irresistible. His presence alone was fogging her thoughts.

A cold wave ran through her, fear countering the warmth of his power, and she wondered if she'd miscalculated. She'd resisted aphrodesia before—but not from an incubus out of glamour.

Lyre smiled a predator's smile, vicious and cold and hungry ... and so damn sexy.

Panic shot through her and she lunged to her feet, a binding spell crackling over her fingers. Her hand snapped up, ready to throw the spell.

"*Stop.*"

That voice. Impossibly beautiful, the sound layered with enchanting harmonics that vibrated with soft power. With a single word, he erased all thoughts of self-defense from her head and left her floating in a blissful haze.

Obediently, she stopped.

He approached with slow, prowling steps and their eyes met. Conscious thought vanished from her mind, lost in the bottomless darkness of his eyes. Her spell fizzled to nothing.

Then his hands were on her, and any chance she might have had of resisting him was gone.

He pulled her off her feet. Her back hit the wall and he pressed into her, his body hot and hard. He caught her hair and yanked her head back, then his mouth was crushing hers.

He kissed her savagely, his tongue in her mouth, each stroke sending molten heat diving through her. She couldn't move—her hair in his fist, his body pinning her in place, his other hand gripping her backside. She could scarcely breathe as his mouth relentlessly covered hers and she clutched his shoulders, her fingers digging in.

Her blood had turned to fire. She was combusting inside. Her head was spinning but she needed more. She had to have more of him or she would die.

His hand slid down her leg and he pulled her knee over his hip, then he pushed into her even harder, his hips grinding against hers. He lifted his mouth and latched onto her neck. Sucking, biting kisses, more possessive than sensual, sent pleasure and darts of pain shooting down her spine like bolts of electricity. Every nerve in her body screamed with need. She was helpless to his desire—an insatiable fire consuming her from within, his mouth consuming her from without. She could do nothing but hold him, nothing but submit, nothing but drown in his touch.

He pulled on her hair, forcing her head to the side as his teeth grazed her neck, creating another shot of delicious, fleeting pain. He hummed, his otherworldly voice wreaking more havoc on her mind and body. The sensations and the need and the fire grew stronger, hotter, more overwhelming until she couldn't breathe at all. Pleasure raced through her like a cocktail of drugs, but with every touch of his hands and mouth, the craving for release burned hotter, dug deeper, twisted tighter, building and building and building. She couldn't stand it. She couldn't bear it. The worst hunger, the most parched thirst, didn't even compare. It was excruciating. It was torture.

She had to have more, and the need was so powerful, so devastating that tears spilled down her cheeks.

His hands stopped moving. His mouth lifted from her skin.

Vaguely, she realized she was openly weeping. She hung in his arms as the searing heat and torturous cravings drilled even deeper. A sob shook her body, but the desperate need for him pushed everything else from her mind.

Except he had stopped, and without his touch, the hot euphoria he had stirred in her diminished—and pain grew in its place. Her overstimulated nerves ached and burned, and a terrible hollowness filled her—an unbearable emptiness he had to fill. She would go insane if he didn't.

He stepped back from the wall, holding her with a gentleness that had been missing from his touch before now. With careful movements, he turned her back to his chest and sank down, pulling her with him until they were sitting on the floor. She shuddered in his grip, gasping and shaking with pain and need. Arms wrapped around her and fistfuls of her shirt in his clenched hands, he pressed his face against her shoulder.

"I'm sorry, Clio," he whispered. "I'm so sorry. I'm so sorry."

Over and over, he repeated the words as she trembled in his arms. The heat faded, leaving her aching with a strange, cold emptiness, and when her thoughts eventually cleared, she wept again as she understood what had happened—what he had done to her.

He held her, whispering apologies against her shoulder. She wondered dully if she should leave. There was nothing stopping her.

She could break the spell on the door easily, and if she left now, he wouldn't follow her. He would let her go.

If she were smart, she would leave.

Instead, she let him hold her and listened to his whispering voice, musical and hypnotizing even with its power suppressed. Pain weighed down each word, and she searched out his tight fist. She stroked the back of his hand until his grip on her shirt loosened. After a minute, he trailed into silence, but he didn't lift his head from her shoulder.

A long time passed before she felt steady again. Hesitantly, she gave Lyre's hand a gentle tug. He released her and she clambered to her feet, wobbling on stiff legs. Aches twinged in her muscles as though she were recovering from a bad fever.

Lyre stood as well, but when she turned to him, he wouldn't meet her eyes, his face pale and a smear of Rosa's blood on his chin.

She dropped her gaze too. "Let's get out of here."

He nodded and crossed to the couch where his gear was piled. As he strapped his weapons into place, she turned her back on him. The magnetic pull he exerted had her shaking again. Only when he'd shifted back into glamour did the feeling of being drawn to him lessen.

She broke the lock spell, pushed the door open, and waited for Lyre to go ahead of her. He didn't look at her as he passed, heading for the hall that would take them back into the main club. Clio started after him when she caught a glimpse of movement.

In a curtained doorway at the room's opposite end, holding the fabric aside, Lilith watched her with an unreadable expression.

Clio stared back. She didn't know what she felt, only that ice pulsed through her at the sight of the succubus. She turned her back to the woman and hurried to catch up with Lyre.

Lilith had been wrong about Lyre, but she'd also been right. And Clio didn't know how much of the ice in her veins was a residual chill from the fading heat of his aphrodesia … and how much was terror of the power he could wield against her.

THE SPACE between her and Lyre had grown far greater than the physical distance that separated them.

She wrapped her arms around her knees as the cold breeze tugged at her hair. They sat on a rooftop, the dark sky overhead spattered with dim stars and the street below even darker. The only light came from a four-story shopping mall with a few glowing security lights.

According to the daemon Lyre had questioned at the Consulate, this was where they would find an illicit Overworld conclave—a place where daemons gathered to trade in illegal or taboo goods and services. The problem was she and Lyre didn't know exactly where the smugglers market was happening. So far, they'd seen four daemons go into the closed mall and not come out. Now she and Lyre were waiting for another daemon to show up so they could follow him to the mystery location.

The wind gusted and she suppressed a shiver. Lyre glanced at her. They hadn't talked much since leaving the succubus club. He'd brought up what had happened, but she'd cut him off, assuring him it hadn't been his fault and she wanted to put it behind them.

He hadn't been in control of himself, and it was astounding that he'd come back to his senses at all. She didn't blame him, but understanding and logic couldn't erase how she felt. And she felt fear.

The distance between them hadn't changed, but she could feel the chasm yawning wider.

Daemons tended to stick with their own kind, and Earth was the only place where daemons of different realms interacted with any regularity. She and Lyre were beings of opposite worlds. Was it so surprising that irreconcilable differences existed between them?

Irreconcilable differences. Was that how she wanted to describe his ruthless ability to make her a slave to his desires?

"Clio?"

Her head jerked up. He watched her, his brow furrowed and shadows lurking in his eyes.

"What?" she asked, looking away.

"Are you all right?"

"I'm fine." Why was he suddenly asking? She was fine. She was just sitting here. Just …

She belatedly noticed she was trembling, and it wasn't from the cold.

"I'm fine," she repeated more firmly.

"It's okay if you're not." His voice was soft, the words almost inaudible. He lifted his hand, palm up and fingers splayed. She looked blankly at his hand, then she saw the faint quiver in his fingers. *He* was trembling?

"That much aphrodesia is a shock to the system," he mumbled as he tucked his hands under his arms. "It can leave you feeling weak for … a while …"

He trailed off, his stare fixed on nothing, and her heart constricted. She'd been so wrapped up in her own trauma that she had given no thought to how he was coping with the assault *he* had experienced at the succubi's hands.

"Are *you* okay?" she asked gently.

He nodded.

She hesitated, then murmured, "It's okay if you're not."

He smiled faintly at his words echoed back at him. "That's … never happened to me before."

"Which part?"

"That much aphrodesia. Those succubi went way overboard."

"You did bite two of them," she pointed out.

"Not that I regret it"—a growl crept into his voice—"but that was their own damn fault."

"They seemed surprised that you fought back like that."

"Probably because the incubi they've caught before weren't prepared for it."

"You were prepared?"

He shifted uncomfortably. "No, not like … I just meant that the first time is the worst because you've never experienced it before."

She studied his profile, but before she could ask anything else, he straightened sharply and focused on the street. "Someone is coming. Look."

A lone figure wearing a dark, casual coat moved swiftly up the street toward the mall, his head turning as though checking for witnesses. This many interlopers in a shopping center that had been closed for hours was too much of a coincidence.

"He's a daemon," she whispered, her asper confirming it. "Let's go."

Lyre led the way back to ground level and they sped down the street. Ahead, the daemon slipped into the building. Lyre slowed, a shimmer of golden light rippling over him as he cast a cloaking spell. He canted a sideways look at her.

"Do you need …?"

She grimaced at the wary edge in his voice, then sighed and pressed a hand to her chest. As she cast the same cloaking spell on herself, he watched with uncomfortable concentration.

"Identical," he muttered, shaking his head.

To her relief, he said nothing else. Since he hadn't guessed she was a mimic, he must not have been familiar with the rare ability.

They slipped through the doors and into a wide, empty concourse lined on either side with dark storefronts behind metal cages. Harsh security lights cast the scuffs and cracks in the worn linoleum floor into sharp relief.

"I can see his aura up ahead," she murmured.

They hastened after their target, following as closely as they dared. The daemon, his coat wrapped around him, hurried into a spacious center plaza and stopped beside a rectangular opening in the floor where a staircase descended from the ground level. He glanced around, then trotted down the steps.

When he didn't reappear, Clio approached the railing and peeked over the edge, Lyre behind her. Partway down, a plywood barrier was nailed to the walls, blocking any passage to the lower level—but the daemon was gone. She focused her asper, scanning the stairs and wood.

"It isn't spelled," she told him.

"Let's take a look." He led the way down and stopped two stairs up from the barricade, hands on his hips as he surveyed it. His pale hair shone in the security lights, reminding her of the iridescent shimmer of his true form beneath his glamour. And that reminded her of his pointed ears and tattooed cheek—a family mark, the succubi had called it. Her memory plucked up more visceral visions: his teeth dragging across Rosa's bloody lower lip, his predatory smile, his ravenous black eyes fixed on her.

Fear trickled through her, but her brain wasn't done tormenting her yet, because behind the fear came a wave of hot desire. She glanced at Lyre to make sure he wasn't using aphrodesia. He was focused on the wooden barricade, his aura calm.

Her breath hissed through her clenched teeth. Regardless of how insanely attractive he was, she would never allow him to kiss her again, let alone anything else. All it would take was one slip of his control, and she would no longer have the ability to say "no," to say "wait," to say "stop." His power was too dangerous, too devastating, and she couldn't trust it. She couldn't trust him.

Shoving those thoughts out of her mind, she focused on the plaza. There were no signs of life, not a sound or a whisper of movement, but a faint chill crept over her, raising gooseflesh on the back of her neck.

"Aha!"

Clio jumped and almost fell over backward. Lyre stood beside the plywood wall where a panel shaped like a door hung open on hinges.

Grinning, he gestured grandly at the entrance. "Now we're in business."

How could his grin still make her heart flutter like an overexcited butterfly? She joined him at the doorway and peered into the darkness on the other side. "Where does it go?"

"A metro station, I think. The city has an underground train system, but it hasn't been used in decades."

She checked it over with her asper—no sign of magic—then looked at him expectantly.

His eyebrows rose. "I remember you saying you aren't afraid of the dark."

"I'm not."

"So you're waiting for me to go first because …?"

"Because you're the big, strong male. It's only proper that you take point."

He rolled his eyes and stepped in front of her. "I can't decide if you're being sexist or just plain chicken."

She followed him down, moving slowly to allow her eyes to adjust to the dark. The damp reek of mold overtook the stuffy mall smell, and the sound of dripping water echoed off concrete walls. The stairs descended two full stories, and at the bottom, the light leaking from the upper level scarcely penetrated the darkness. A long platform ran alongside a pit where rusting train tracks stretched. Nonsensical graffiti layered the slimy walls and a carpet of grime and garbage covered the cracked floor tiles.

The platform was empty. So were the tracks. There was no sign of the daemon they'd followed or a gathering of Overworld smugglers.

"Hmm," Lyre mused. "Which way, do you think?"

Which way? There was nowhere to go except back up the stairs. Unless he meant …

She looked toward one end of the station, then the other. Though the platform ended in a blank wall, the tracks continued, vanishing into pitch-black tunnels.

"Um." She swallowed, her mouth dry. "Maybe we should wait for someone else to show us the way."

"We don't have time to hang around." He tapped his chin, by all appearances unfazed by the prospect of venturing into an inky tunnel. "The breeze is flowing out of the south one, so let's go that way."

"You're picking a direction at random?" she asked, her voice going higher. "And planning to walk in there with no idea where you're going?"

"It's a straight line, Clio. It's not like we can get lost." He smirked. "Are you sure you aren't scared of the dark?"

"Yes." The way her voice quavered wasn't exactly convincing. "Very sure. I just don't like … *underground* darkness very much."

"Hmm. Well." He hesitated, eyeing her as though she might bite him, then lifted his hand in invitation. "I'll stay with you. If that … helps."

She went still. When she didn't respond, his eyes shuttered, but before he could lower his arm, she grabbed his hand and squeezed it tightly.

He relaxed, his expression softening again. With a brief smile, he drew her to the platform's edge and hopped down. She jumped after him, her feet crunching on what was either very fine gravel or an extra thick layer of dust. Stepping into the center of the tracks, he started toward the south tunnel.

She walked beside him, all too aware of his warm fingers around hers. It was the first time they'd touched since the succubus club, and she couldn't figure out why her heart was drumming against her ribs. Either she was afraid of the dark tunnel, afraid of his touch, or afraid of what his touch was doing to her.

As they ventured deeper into the suffocating darkness, she was glad for the warm, solid connection between them. Without thinking, she turned her hand to twine their fingers together more comfortably.

Eventually, the pitch black defeated their night vision, and he cast a tiny light to guide them. The tunnel stretched on forever, empty and untouched except for the old graffiti scrawled across every wall.

"See?" Lyre remarked. "The underground thing isn't that bad."

She arched an eyebrow. "Of course it doesn't bother *you*. You're a night-realm ghoul who barely ever sees a sun."

"Excuse me? A *ghoul*?"

"Nymphs, on the other hand," she continued primly, "prefer to see the sun and sky. I'd take a cliff over a cave any day."

He wrinkled his nose. "Heights are the worst."

"You're scared of heights?"

"Not *scared*. It's just that, where the possibility of plummeting to my death is concerned, I maintain a healthy wariness."

"I don't mind heights at all."

"Good for you."

"Tell you what." She grinned teasingly and raised their entwined fingers. "If we have to go somewhere high up, I'll hold *your* hand."

To her surprise, he didn't return her smile. Instead, he glanced at their hands, then lifted his gaze to hers. "Deal."

She stared into his somber amber eyes, dimmed by shadows of emotion she couldn't identify, and forgot how to breathe. Then she tripped on a rail track tie.

She pitched forward. He caught her and she grabbed his sweater for balance.

It should have been a simple matter for her to straighten and resume walking, but she didn't. And he could have casually released her, but he didn't. Instead, she leaned against him, her cheek resting against his chest. His arms wrapped around her, engulfing her in his warmth and spicy cherry scent.

In the silent darkness, broken only by his flickering light, they stood like that, unmoving and unspeaking. His hand slid into her hair, his touch so gentle and careful that tears pricked her eyes. She hesitated, then lightly stroked his back.

"Why are you so different, Lyre?" The question escaped her before she could stop it. "You're nothing like your brothers."

"I don't know." He combed his fingers through the long loose waves of her hair to their ends. "They were always the talented ones. The favorites. They never had to fear someone else's power."

She exhaled slowly, controlling the surge of emotion rising in her. He was silent for so long she didn't think he would say anything more.

"You're the first person," he whispered, "to ever put their life on the line to protect mine."

Her arms tightened around him. In that dangerous, treacherous world, he'd been on his own from the start? No wonder he always had that sharp edge hiding beneath his easygoing exterior. It was the honed vigilance of a daemon whose survival had never been a guarantee.

He tensed. "Do you hear that?"

"What?" She went still, listening. A soft murmur was scarcely audible over the drip of water. "Douse your light."

He flicked his fingers and his hovering spell blinked out. Darkness plunged over them, and stepping away from him, she squinted her asper into focus.

There. Faint, almost invisible but unmistakable, was the glow of magic far down the tunnel.

"Lyre," she breathed, "I think we've found it."

And now the real work—and the real danger—would begin.

NINE

THEY DIDN'T get far before a new obstacle brought them up short.

Clio stood beside Lyre, arms folded as she examined the ward that spanned the width of the tunnel. Runes and symbols formed complex geometric shapes, all glowing with an unfamiliar pale lavender light. Near the base of the spell, a red shade tinged the magic.

"There's a blood magic element to this," Lyre said before she could speak. "But it isn't an offensive ward. It won't stop anyone from walking through, but—"

"But if you don't meet the criteria of the ward, it'll sound an alarm," she finished for him.

He knelt to study the ward's base. "This weaver's work isn't half bad. He has some clever arrangements."

She crouched at his side. "By my best guess, this ward is keyed to specific daemon castes. If you don't belong to a caste set in the spell, the alarm function will trigger."

"How much do you want to bet that 'incubus' isn't among the acceptable castes?"

"I think that's a safe bet."

On the other side of the ward, the train tracks curved around a bend, and somewhere beyond that, light and sound trickled down the tunnel. Voices rumbled in a steady jumble of conversation. They'd definitely found the right place.

She glanced curiously at Lyre. "How would you get through this ward?"

"Me? Well." He shrugged. "I've already found a dozen weak points that would be easy to break."

"Ah," she said, just a little smug. "But it's woven to—"

"To trigger an alarm if it's broken," he said just as smugly. "Which is why I would first isolate and shut down that portion of the weave, which is, all things considered, poorly hidden."

She puffed out a breath and he flashed her a grin. Her stomach flipped.

"Well, I can do one better," she told him. "I can disable it without breaking it."

"Oh?" Interest sparked in his eyes. "Where? How?"

She'd expected him to be annoyed or defensive about her asper giving her an advantage over his years of experience and training, but his genuine curiosity made sense. If he didn't love to learn, he wouldn't have accomplished so much at a relatively young age.

She showed him that part of the weave, then stuck her hand into the ward and cut off the flow of power through one of its main arteries. The threads went dark, and Lyre walked through it to the other side. She crossed as well, then pulled her hand out. The ward lit up again, unaware that an Underworlder had bypassed its defenses.

"So," he murmured as he pulled his hood over his head. "I can either use an illusion spell, which an observant daemon might notice, or I can try to blend in and let you do the talking."

"I'll do the talking, I guess." Nervousness fluttered in her stomach. "Just keep your head down."

Following the bend in the tracks, they rounded the wide corner into another metro station, and it couldn't have been more different from the last one.

Interconnecting arches formed elegant domes above the platform, and soft light shone through the stained-glass mosaics—except it was the middle of the night. Squinting, she spotted the illusion spell that mimicked sunlight streaming through the stained glass.

The colorful light sparkled across the long platform, which flowed in a gentle curve that was interrupted by an arched exit where a wide staircase led to the upper level. The nearer half of the platform was filled with clusters of fat, round cushions in colorful patterns, placed on woven rugs, some surrounded by fabric screens for privacy. Daemons sat on the cushions or milled around, chatting casually with the owners of each little sitting area.

The platform's other half, on the far side of the exit, was a colorful line of booths. It looked like a flea market had been dropped into the station, except the wares were nothing a human would ever expect to see. All in all, there were probably a hundred daemons present, with about a quarter clustered around a booth at the far end of the market.

"This closer side," Lyre murmured, "is probably for networking and negotiating. The other side is for commerce."

"I don't even know where to start." How would she find someone to take them to Irida? Talking to the wrong daemon could get them in trouble. "Let's check out the market. If anyone is selling Iridian goods, I can talk to them first."

"Good idea."

Lyre trailed after her as she climbed onto the platform and strode into the clustered cushions with all the confidence she could muster. A few daemons glanced curiously at her and Lyre, but everyone was in glamour, casually dressed as humans, and enough people had their faces hidden that Lyre didn't stand out.

She tried to keep her pace and body language casual as they meandered through the gatherings. Some of these daemons did not look like people she wanted to mess with. She passed a trio sitting around a bowl of smoke with a sweet, tangy smell, their narrow faces hard and humorless. Snippets of conversation flowed all around her, some in languages she recognized and some she didn't.

She breathed easier once they'd moved into the open space between the two halves of the platform. Ahead, the first booth of the market was laden with clothing in a variety of styles. She paused in front of it, scanning the items while the seller watched her closely. Lyre lurked behind her, turned at an angle to keep his face hidden.

Seeing nothing from Irida, she moved to the next booth, this one scattered with weapons and mismatched leather gear. A few items bore splatters of dried blood. She walked right past that stall.

The next booth was all foods from the Overworld—buns, cakes, preserves, dried roots and vegetables, even some candies. Her mouth immediately watered at the sight. She hadn't eaten *real* food in two years, and even the preserves looked delicious. Nothing was particular to Irida but she was familiar with almost everything.

The stand was popular. Six daemons stood around it, haggling with the seller or waiting their turn. She wasn't the only one pining for a taste of home.

Lyre leaned over her shoulder, checking out the table with interest. Squeezing in beside a tall woman, Clio waved to get the seller's attention and pointed at two meat buns. He held up three fingers and she dug platinum coins from her pocket and passed them over. He handed her the buns wrapped in brown paper. Backing out of the crowd, she gave one to Lyre and unwrapped hers as she moved down the line.

She bit into the bun and almost moaned. It was cold and a bit stale, but the flavor sent a thousand memories rolling through her. The pastry was flaky and sweet, the meat and vegetables coated in a savory cream sauce. As she took another bite, the noise of the market faded away and she wandered forward at a slow stroll, passing a handful of stalls while she savored the treat.

As she popped the last bite in her mouth, she realized she'd stopped entirely and Lyre was standing beside her. Holding his half-eaten bun, he looked at her with raised eyebrows from the shadows of his hood.

"What?" she muttered, crumpling the empty wrapper.

"Nothing." He touched his thumb to the corner of her mouth. "You have crumbs on your face."

His thumb slid lightly across her lower lip and her heart fluttered. Pulling back, she self-consciously wiped her mouth, but she didn't notice any crumbs. He took another bite of his bun, watching her with an odd intensity.

Looking around, she discovered they had drawn close to the crowd gathered around the end booth. Just off from the fringes of the group, a small table caught her eye: a garden of bright leaves in a dozen shapes and sizes covered its surface. A few larger potted plants sat on the floor beside the booth.

Clio made a beeline to the booth and excitedly scanned the plants. One had thick waxy leaves with blue veins, one had thin blue leaves, and one had pink flowers the size of her outspread hand. All three grew in the mountains of her homeland.

As she examined the plants, a slight chill ran over her. Of the ones she recognized, most were plants her mother had taught her to avoid, the leaves or seeds used for poisons, narcotics, or hallucinogens.

The seller behind the counter was younger than she would have expected—early twenties, maybe—with dark brown hair pulled into a short tail, the fuzzy scruff of a few missed shaves, and square, black-rimmed glasses in front of brown eyes flecked with purple. Squinting, she brought his aura into focus—silvery-gray with an odd, sparkly outer layer. She had no idea what caste it signified.

"Is that ghalia thorn?" she asked, pointing to the plant with blue-veined leaves that could be brewed into a tea to make a mild stimulant, or eaten whole for a buzz that would keep a daemon wide awake even if they were exhausted.

He nodded.

"Is it wild-harvested or do you cultivate the plants yourself?"

"This one is from my greenhouse," he said, and she had to lean closer to hear his low, husky voice. "But the cutting came from a wild specimen."

"It's in wonderful condition," she complimented. "Outside the mountain forests, they're finicky to grow at the best of times."

He glanced over her as though sizing her up, but she had no idea what he was thinking. He wasn't particularly forthcoming, and if she asked too many questions, she might put him off conversation entirely.

She perused the plants again, then pointed. "Could I see that one?"

"This?" He picked up a ceramic pot with a spindly vine coiling up a supporting stick, unremarkable except for the blue sheen of its tiny green leaves.

She took the pot and examined the little vine. Healthy, and with a few weeks of extra care, it would probably flower. Behind her, Lyre shifted away from the noisy crowd, tucking closer to Clio but keeping his back to the plant merchant.

"How much?" she inquired.

"Do you even know what it is?" he asked flatly.

"Sea-shine vine. The latex can be used to treat minor cuts and burns, and it makes a lovely decorative plant as well."

His eyebrows crept up in either surprise or skepticism, and she had to work to keep her smile in place, befuddled by his attitude. Didn't he want to sell his plants? She'd thought he might warm up to her if she bought something. And would it kill him to speak up? The boisterous gathering only a few paces away was growing noisier.

"How much?" she asked again, keeping her tone pleasant. Just her luck that she'd find a possible guide only for him to be completely unsociable. "I'd like to buy it."

He looked from the pot to her face. "Two plat."

She offered two coins. He took the money and she bit her lip, wondering how to broach the topic of his familiarity with Overworld territories—and most importantly, Irida. Straight up asking wasn't smart. Daemons were suspicious by nature.

If Lyre had been doing the talking, he would have known exactly what to say. He was the smooth talker, not her. She was lucky if she could make it three sentences without stammering or blushing.

An animal shriek cut through the rumble of voices. The small crowd around the nearby booth jerked backward, bumping into Clio and Lyre, and a gap opened, revealing the popular table. It was triple the length of the other booths and stacked with cages of all sizes. Small creatures flitted or cowered behind wire bars, some colorful and feathered, some with shimmering wings, some with fur or scales. All creatures native to the Overworld.

The largest cage sat on the floor in front of the table, and it had drawn the interest of the gathered daemons. Inside it was a wolf-like creature with blue and black patterned fur, bright yellow feathers sprouting in a fringe across its shoulders, and lean legs that morphed into birdlike toes and talons. Someone rapped their knuckles on the top of the cage and the creature ducked, mouth opening in another wail—a sound aching with fear and distress.

"What's wrong?" Lyre's warm breath brushed her ear, making her shiver.

She realized how tense she was and forced herself to relax. The trade of native Overworld creatures was restricted or forbidden in many territories, so it made a twisted sort of sense that poachers would bring their catches to Earth to sell. But seeing it herself made her chest tighten.

"That's a lycaon—a baby one," she told him. "They live in the mountains near Irida."

"Do you want to talk to that seller instead?"

"I don't want to deal with a poacher," she muttered. "I think this plant merchant has been near Irida, but he doesn't want to talk to me."

Lyre leaned closer, ostensibly checking out her new vine, and his gleaming amber eyes caught the light from under his hood. "Flirt with him."

"Huh?"

"Flirt with him," Lyre repeated, his teeth flashing as he grinned.

She gawked, then shook her head. "No, I can't—"

"*Trust* me, Clio," he purred, nudging her around to face the plant booth again.

"But—"

He gave her a gentle shove in the back and she stumbled forward a step, clutching her vine. The plant seller glanced up, his eyes flat behind his glasses. *Flirt* with him? The guy could barely stand to look at her.

Trust him, Lyre had said. After a moment's thought, she leaned forward and braced one hand on the tabletop, putting her breasts at eye level with the daemon. His gaze flicked down to her bosom then back up to her face, and she felt like a complete idiot. If their mission hadn't been so serious, she might have thought Lyre was tricking her into making a fool of herself.

"I …" She smiled, mentally flailing. "I'm really impressed by your plant collection."

Behind her, Lyre coughed. The sound was full of swallowed laughter. She gritted her teeth, almost ready to abandon ship before she humiliated herself.

"Many of these plants are difficult to grow and maintain," she continued determinedly. She nodded at a bushy plant with spiky, serrated leaves. "Vandela is notoriously fussy. You're clearly a skilled botanist."

The daemon seemed confused, but he focused on her with a hint of interest. "Thanks."

"I'd love to know more about your collection," she suggested. What else should she say? If she'd been flirting with *Lyre*, it would have been easy, but …

Hmm. Flirting with Lyre was ridiculously easy, wasn't it?

She reassessed the daemon in front of her. With warm bronze skin to contrast his dark hair and eyes, he was handsome in an exotic way, though his scruffy chin wasn't helping. Nowhere near Lyre's league. She lowered her face and peeked up through her eyelashes, trying to pretend this daemon was Lyre.

Lyre's sensual mouth was always distracting her. She let her gaze fall to the daemon's thin lips, then looked back up and smiled again. She held out her hand. "I'm Clio. It's wonderful to meet you."

The daemon hesitated, then took her hand. "Sabir."

"Hi, Sabir," she said, trying to sound breathy as if Lyre had touched her. "How long have you been studying plants and herbs?"

"Uh." His brow furrowed and he seemed at a loss for words. He was still holding her hand, though their brief shake was over. "My entire life. I apprenticed under my father."

"That's amazing. You must be very experienced."

"Yeah …"

"I learned from my mother." Reclaiming her hand, she touched the thin blue leaves of an Iridian plant. "I was making kanavus tea for her from the moment I could lift a kettle."

"I prefer a tincture over infusion for kanavus."

"A tincture is more potent," she agreed, "but we drank the tea as a mild relaxant, so we didn't want it that strong."

"Interesting." He sat up straighter. "I've only prepared it as a sedative. How do you create the infusion?"

"Three leaves if fresh, one crushed leaf if dried. I like to add a drop of honey to sweeten it. It's lovely as a hot drink before bed after a stressful day."

He nodded thoughtfully as though filing the information away. She stared intently into his eyes, hoping she didn't look like a complete moron. "Kanavus only grows in the northeastern mountains. Have you been there? It's very beautiful."

"You mean Kyo Kawa Valley?"

"Kyo Kawa is a closed territory, so I wouldn't expect you to have been there." She gave an empty-headed giggle. "That would be far too dangerous."

"It's not dangerous if you know what you're doing."

"You've been inside ryujin territory?" This time, she didn't have to fake her amazement.

Sabir pushed his glasses up his nose. "Many times."

"Wow. That's ..." She made her voice breathy again. "You're so brave."

Lyre coughed again. She ignored him, keeping her focus on Sabir. His full attention was on her, his brown eyes brighter. She still didn't know what he thought of her, but he was being friendlier, at least. Flirting. Who would have thought?

"What about the other mountain regions?" she asked. "Irida and the northern reaches of Ra territory?"

"I've visited Irida a few times, but the nymphs don't buy much, and I'd rather collect my own plants than purchase from them. Griffin cities can be profitable, but only if you know where to sell. Their taxes aren't friendly to small merchants."

Her eyebrows shot up. For a seemingly bland, unassuming guy, he was playing with fire. Entering Kyo Kawa, a closed territory renowned for murdering trespassers, and selling goods illegally within Ra borders? He *was* brave—or stupid. Maybe both.

"I was wondering ..." She trailed off coyly.

He tilted his head, waiting for her to continue.

"I need to make a quick visit to Irida, but I've never traveled there before." She did the peeking-through-her-eyelashes thing again. "Is there any chance you'd be interested in a brief engagement as my guide?"

He blinked. "Uh ..."

"I'd compensate you, of course."

His dark eyes met hers and an inexplicable chill ran down her spine. He smiled for the first time, a brief curving of his lips before he pursed them in thought.

"I've never traveled into Irida by ley line, and going cross-country ... the terrain can be grueling." When she wilted in disappointment, he hurried on. "But I'm heading to the mountains for my next trip. I'll be passing close to Irida's southwestern border, so I could drop you off there?"

Excitement flashed through her but she acted mildly pleased instead. "Really? You would do that for me?"

He smiled again, a warm expression that made her reevaluate him. "Yes, though there's still the matter of compensation."

"Right," she agreed. "Name your price."

He stated a number and she countered at half that. They haggled for a minute before agreeing to a price that would severely deplete her and Lyre's stock of coins.

"When can we leave?" she asked. "The sooner, the better."

He leaned back warily. "I have a lot of stock to sell first."

"I'm on a tight schedule, to be honest. I need to—" She cut herself off, not wanting to reveal how desperate she was. "If we can't go in the next few days, I'll have to cancel. I'd hate to miss out."

"The next few *days*?" He rubbed his forehead. "Uh. I guess ... two nights from now? That's the earliest I can leave."

"That would be *wonderful*." She caught his hand and squeezed it. "Thank you so much, Sabir. Should I meet you here, then?"

"Yes, that would be simplest."

"Lovely!" She withdrew her pouch and counted out plats. "Twenty-five percent now, twenty-five percent when we leave, and the rest when we reach Irida."

Sabir accepted the money and slipped it out of sight under his table. "Make sure to bring—"

With a crash and a loud screech, the crowd around the table of poached creatures surged backward. Daemons fell over each other to get out of the way as yellow feathers flashed.

The young lycaon sprang out of its collapsed cage, screaming furiously with its huge ears flattened to its wolfish head. It launched onto a daemon's back, its eagle talons tearing through the man's shirt in a spray of blood.

Clio flinched as the retreating crowd backed into her and Lyre. Sabir's table rocked violently and he grabbed his plants before they fell. The lycaon howled and leaped into the crowd, talons slashing, and the daemons shoved backward, knocking Clio into the table. Another daemon crashed into Lyre and they both fell in a tangle of limbs.

The shrieking creature bounded across the platform and leaped off. With its seller chasing after it, it bolted down a tunnel. Half the present daemons could have stopped the lycaon, but no one had even tried— probably fearing the merchant would charge them for damaging his merchandise.

As the sounds of the chase faded, conversation resumed. A couple daemons picked up the bleeding guy, examined his injuries, and offered to heal him—for a price, of course. Clio straightened a few of Sabir's plants, glad to see none had fallen.

"*Underworlder!*"

The accusing shout rang over all the other voices. Clio whipped around.

Two daemons—the ones who'd knocked Lyre over—held him by the arms. His hood had fallen off, his pale hair and amber eyes on display for all to see. Everyone nearby went quiet.

One of Lyre's captors grabbed him by the hair and shoved his head forward.

"An *incubus*," the daemon sneered. "How did you get in here, mongrel?"

Clio stood frozen, unable to react. What did she do? Against fifty daemons—a hundred if those on the platform's other half joined in— not even a master weaver stood a ghost of a chance. Lyre didn't move either, his expression strangely blank. Something passed over him—an invisible shift she couldn't quite quantify.

Then the most lascivious smile she'd ever seen spread across his face. He canted his head, his hair still in the Overworlder's grip.

"That kind of treatment costs extra, darling," he drawled in a deep, sultry purr. "Just so you know."

The daemon blinked, then yanked his hand away. Lyre straightened, but his body language had completely changed. There was a loose fluidity to his limbs—a soft, enticing openness.

"I'm afraid I'm booked for the night, love," he crooned to the daemon on his other side. "But if you're interested, I could arrange something to your liking, hmm?"

Both daemons released him, disgust crossing their faces. Lyre rolled his shoulders, then stretched his arms over his head, his shirt lifting to display a glimpse of his toned abdomen. He relaxed again, completely unconcerned by the danger he was in.

"What the hell are you doing here, incubus?" someone demanded, their voice loud beneath the blanket of silence.

"Working," he answered, his salacious smile reappearing.

He slid sideways, his gait swaying in a way that was both erotically suggestive and aggressively masculine. He slipped his arm around Clio's waist, pulling her against his side. She clutched her potted vine as though it were a shield against the stares that snapped her way.

"Bought and paid for already, I'm afraid," he cooed at the two daemons who'd grabbed him. "But just for tonight."

"Why did you bring that incubus slut down here, girl?" a daemon barked at her.

She stared gormlessly, heat rising in her cheeks. Again, Lyre jumped in to rescue her.

"Can't a lady enjoy a night of shopping with pleasurable company?" His voice lowered and deepened. "Clearly, you boys don't know how to play the game."

The male daemons recoiled as though Lyre had admitted to something utterly grotesque. The female daemons, however, watched him with varying degrees of interest and embarrassment.

Clio had surpassed embarrassment. She was somewhere between "absolute mortification" and "just kill me now."

Lyre ran a finger down her hot cheek. "Let's take our fun somewhere else, sweetheart. I don't mind an audience, but I know you prefer … mmm … we'll talk about your preferences later, shall we?"

"Get your whore out of here," a daemon spat at Clio. "We don't want that filth in our business."

Lyre smiled, slid his arm up her back, and draped it over her shoulders. "Your loss." His gaze flicked across his audience, lingering on the women, and he ran his tongue slowly across his upper lip. "You don't even know what you're missing."

With a husky laugh, he tugged Clio into motion. She stumbled a step, then pulled herself together. Glancing at Sabir, who was watching her with an appalled expression, she mouthed an apology and held up two fingers, hoping he understood she would return in two nights.

He hesitated, then nodded.

Relieved, she let Lyre pull her toward the stairs. Every daemon in the station watched them leave with hostility clogging the air. A ward spanned the staircase halfway up but Lyre didn't pause, and she followed him through it. Magic sparked over her skin, but if the "alarm" had triggered, she couldn't tell and didn't bother studying the spell to figure it out.

She didn't breathe properly until they reached a small lobby with double glass doors. Lyre pushed one open and they stepped onto a dark street across from a tall, old-style theater that had seen better days. The entrance to the station sat beneath a tall structure with an excessive number of windows. A cold wind had picked up while they'd been underground, and it whipped across them, smelling of rain.

Lyre took three steps out of the doorway, then dropped his arm from Clio and vigorously rubbed his face. Head tilting skyward, he let out a long, violent exhale. She stared at him, still speechless. She hadn't managed a single word since his transformation from spell weaver to lewd prostitute.

"That," he grumbled, sounding normal again, meaning sexy as hell but not lecherous, "was a close call. I thought I was a dead man."

She opened her mouth, but only a croak came out. Swallowing, she tried again. "How did you do that?"

"Do what?"

"Start acting like …"

He raised his eyebrows. "Was I convincing?"

"Uh." Her cheeks heated again. "You seemed convincing to me."

"Good." He smiled crookedly. "I would hate to have sacrificed all that dignity for nothing."

"Have you ever … um …"

"What?"

"Never mind."

"Have I ever what?"

"Nothing. Never mind."

He leaned closer, his smile growing more wicked than playful. "Have I ever traded my body for money? Is that what you wanted to ask?"

"N-no," she stammered, backing up a step.

He followed, not allowing her to put space between them. "It's a fair question. Sex is our primary skill set. Most incubi choose to monetize it. Why not?"

She continued to inch backward. His tone held an edge she didn't understand, but the heat in his eyes was easy to recognize.

"It's not *your* primary skill set," she protested weakly.

"Actually," he purred, his eyes darkening to bronze, "it is."

She gawked at him, unable to form a coherent thought. Was he suggesting he was better at sex than he was at spell weaving? Because she didn't think that was possible.

And why was she thinking about sex at all? Why was she thinking about what it would be like to let him show her those skills? To let him demonstrate them on her? To give in to the longings he had woken in her and discover the pleasure he was promising?

Wasn't she afraid of him? Hadn't she decided she would never so much as kiss him again?

She stumbled back another step and blinked her asper into focus, but his aura was quiet. No aphrodesia. Not even a hint. He had it tightly under control.

His dark eyes moved across her face, then he stepped back. The hot demand in his gaze cooled. "Two nights."

She blinked, confused. Had he realized she was checking him for signs of seduction magic? Could he read her that easily? "Two nights of what?"

"Two nights of … waiting? Until the supremely uncharismatic plant guy can lead us to the Overworld?"

"Oh … right."

"What did you think I meant?"

"N-nothing. I didn't …" Damn it, she was blushing again.

"You were thinking *something*. Come on, tell me."

No way in hell was she admitting that her mind had jumped to two nights of *him*—in the most inappropriate sense. What was wrong with her? It had only been a few hours since he'd coerced her with his magic, and all she could think about was kissing him again?

With her lower lip caught between her teeth, she peeked at him out of the corner of her eye—and saw his half-hidden smirk.

That incubus! He knew *exactly* what conclusion she'd jumped to. He'd led her right to it!

Teeth gritted, she stomped past him, heading down the street. The wind carried his quiet chuckle to her ears, and her stomach did a fluttery little dance at the sound.

Focus. She needed to focus. They had to survive two more days in the city, then they would escape to the Overworld. She almost looked back at Lyre, his footsteps only a few feet behind her, but she resisted. Once back in Irida, she would be safe, but for an Underworlder like him, the Overworld was a temporary refuge that harbored many dangers.

Chewing on her lip, she put those questions out of her mind. For now, she would focus on getting through the next forty-eight hours alive. After that, she would worry about how to keep Lyre alive in the Overworld … and beyond.

TEN

FOLLOWING CLIO down the dark streets, Lyre waited for his heart rate to slow. After three blocks, he would've figured he'd calm the hell down, but no. Adrenaline still coursed through his veins. Nothing like having a hundred dangerous Overworlders turn on you all at once to give the old heart a workout.

Amusement sparked amid his lingering anxiety and he swallowed another snicker at Clio's reaction to his prostitute impersonation. He'd been worried her beet-red face would give them away, but he supposed anyone would be embarrassed by such a public reveal of their "indiscretions." He was tempted to tease her about it more, but she was already in a huff.

Teasing her was just too much fun. He was glad that hadn't changed. After what those succubi had done, he'd feared Clio would never smile for him again.

Later, he would acknowledge the dark pit of bitter rage and humiliation that burned deep inside him. Later, he would privately expunge the violence clinging to the edges of his mind, the sick desire to twist those succubi into broken corpses. Later, he would quell the simmering hunger that had been sucking at his mind and soul since entering the club.

As soon as they got back to their room, he was going to take the longest, coldest shower of his life.

Clio stalked down the middle of the street ahead of him, her arms wrapped around herself and hands tucked into the sleeves of her jacket as the wind howled between skyscrapers. The first few spatters of rain shone on the black leather. That little plant she'd bought was tucked in the crook of her arm and bobbed with each step.

Lengthening his stride, he fell into step beside her. She glanced at him, her full lips pressed into an annoyed pout. He filled his expression with exaggerated innocence, and those lips twitched as she fought back a smile.

"I was wondering," he said, keeping his voice low so the wind wouldn't carry it, "what's with the plant?"

She glanced at the potted vine. "What about it?"

"Why did you buy it?"

"I thought buying something might soften up Sabir." She frowned at the plant, then at him. "How did you know flirting with him would get better results?"

"How did you *not* know?" he asked with a laugh. "He was watching you long before you noticed him."

Her frown deepened, doubt written all over her face. "Why was he so aloof at the start, then?"

"Because he has zero natural charm and no idea how to talk to women."

"Hm." She walked in thoughtful silence. "Did it bother you?"

"Huh?"

"Me flirting with another guy." Her blue eyes widened in question. "In the club, you asked if I was jealous over you dancing with other girls. Were you jealous of me flirting with Sabir?"

He kept his expression neutral, but a hundred thoughts buzzed in his head, and he warned himself not to read into her question too much. "Nope."

Was that a flicker of disappointment? She dropped her gaze before he could be sure. "Oh."

He swung in front of her, forcing her to a stop. "If I'd thought even for a moment he might be competition, I would have been jealous." Smiling down at her, he brushed his finger across her soft lips. "But I'm not worried about a guy like him stealing you away from me."

Her eyes widened.

With an extra enthusiastic gust of wind, the clouds opened up. Icy rain swept over them and he grimaced. Lovely. He pulled Clio into the sheltered alcove of a boarded-up doorway. The rain fell in sheets, carried on the sporadic wind.

As she huddled beside him, the vine trembling with her shivers, he was secretly grateful the weather had interrupted him. Where exactly had he been planning to go after the part about not letting anyone steal her away from him? He closed his eyes. Only a few hours had passed since he'd assaulted her in a blind, lust-fueled rage. Why couldn't he keep his damn mouth shut?

If he kept spouting stupid shit like that, she might think he was pretending to be in love with her or something. And that would only shatter her trust in him—whatever trust might remain—because *no one* would believe an incubus might be in love. Not even a naïve nymph.

Incubi couldn't fall in love. Only in lust.

"Lyre? Are you okay?"

His eyes flew open to find her gazing up at him in concern. Shit. What expression had been on his face?

"I'm fine," he said quickly. When she frowned, unconvinced, he cast around for a change of topic. "You never explained about the plant."

"Yes, I did. I bought it to butter up Sabir."

"No, I mean, why *that* plant? Surely he had something more useful for sale."

"Well … yes, I suppose he did."

"So why buy that one?"

She looked down at the plant. "I just thought …"

He canted his head, her hesitant tone surprising him. "Thought what?"

"Nothing." Her shoulders curled inward. "I picked it randomly."

"No, you didn't."

"I figured it would be cheap. Would you just drop it?"

He almost did as she asked—but then he saw the pink tinge to her cheeks. She was blushing?

"Why won't you tell me? Your reason can't be *that* bad."

She shook her head. "It was … just a silly …" She trailed off into an unintelligible mutter, the wrinkle in her forehead deepening.

"A silly what?" he coaxed. "I won't make fun of you."

"Yes, you will," she mumbled.

"I won't, I promise."

He waited as the rain poured, filling the streets with dark puddles and washing away the persistent reek of the city. She stared at the ground, clutching the plant as she chewed on her lower lip.

"I picked this plant because …" She tried to start again, stopped, then spoke in a bare whisper. "I thought you might like it."

He wasn't sure what he'd been expecting, but it hadn't been that.

"Me?" His voice cracked on the word.

She hunched over the plant, her cheeks glowing. "I thought … I don't know what things will be like for you after … but you'll probably be living in cities like this, and they're ugly with no grass or trees, so I thought … it's medicinal and you can treat scrapes and cuts with it, and it's a really hardy plant, so you won't have to worry about it dying, and it's small, so you can take it with you and … and I thought, you might have to move around a lot while you figure things out, and it would be comforting to have something familiar to bring with you … something to bring a little life to your … new …"

The rain continued to fall, the gurgling patter filling the silence between them. He stared at her, speechless, unable to form words. Unable to respond. He had no idea what to say.

No idea what to feel.

She peeked at him, then hunched a little more. "I know it's stupid. You'll have way too many important things to worry about and carrying a plant around will be a needless burden. It was a silly—"

"You picked it for me?" He hadn't meant to interrupt her. The question had slipped from him, confusion and disbelief thick in his voice.

She looked at him properly, her brow furrowed. "Yes?"

He focused on the small vine as though seeing it for the first time. Its stem coiled elegantly around the supporting stick and pointed green leaves shimmered blue in the faint light. Small, plain, but with a quiet beauty.

He couldn't quite take a real breath. Why did his chest hurt? What was this heavy weight rolling through him? She had picked out a plant to give him. It wasn't a big deal. Just a plant—a living memento, a bit of life and warmth to take with him wherever he went. A gift that was special and meaningful to her and she hoped he would treasure.

Except she had convinced herself he wouldn't want it, and she watched him with vulnerable eyes and a crease in her forehead, expecting rejection.

It took everything he had to hold still, to keep his hands at his sides, to resist the urge to reach for her. Because he didn't know what he would do if he touched her. Because he wanted to touch her more than he'd ever wanted to do anything in his life.

He wanted to touch her, but not for his pleasure or hers. He wanted to touch her because something hot and painful had tightened in his chest and it hurt to breathe. He wanted to kiss her slowly, to taste her and know her and forge a connection between them so he could understand this strange pain. He wanted to hold her and never let go.

He wanted her so badly, but in a way he'd never felt before. And he was afraid.

Without his conscious instruction, his hand rose toward her as though drawn by an invisible force—drawn as inexorably as if she could wield aphrodesia and he was caught under her spell.

His fingers brushed across her soft cheek, her skin warm from her blush and splattered with raindrops. His touch trailed lightly across the side of her face and his hand curled around the back of her neck. He ran his thumb along her jaw to the corner of her mouth.

He was going to kiss her. Even though he knew he shouldn't. Even though it was stupid and dangerous for both of them. He couldn't stop himself.

Before he could lean in, before he could capture her lips with his, a cold thrill ran down his spine and splintered into shards of ice. He stiffened, his instincts screaming at him.

They weren't alone.

With his hand still cradling Clio's neck, he strained his senses. The dark street stretched away on either side of them, obscured by the downpour, the irregular streetlights reflecting off the water and further obscuring his vision.

"Lyre?" Clio whispered, alarm sharpening her voice.

Focused on finding the threat, he didn't answer. Fear skittered through him, growing stronger, edging into panic. He scanned the street again, searching for a sign of danger.

Then he saw it. Not hidden, but in plain view. Watching. Waiting.

At the end of the street, just within his reduced visibility, a dark figure stood. Feet set wide, the silhouette of weapons bulking his form, arms folded. Rain cascaded around the shadowed watcher, but he didn't flinch. Waiting.

Waiting to be noticed.

Lyre's heart hammered against his ribs. That silhouette was unmistakable, as was the arctic fear chilling his body.

Ash.

Ash had found them.

When Lyre's attention fixed on him, the draconian assassin moved. He reached over his shoulder and drew a long, curved sword. Faint light gleamed across the blade as the daemon brought it to his side in a ready position. And waited.

Lyre's fear cracked, crumbling away as his survival instincts took over.

Why was Ash waiting? Why reveal himself? Why sacrifice the element of surprise? If he'd attacked instead, he could have killed Lyre and Clio in a single strike without any risk to himself.

Why, Ash? He wanted to shout the words across the distance between them. He knew it wasn't an invitation to talk or a truce—the drawn sword made that clear. Revealing himself wasn't a meaningless gesture, nor was it misguided chivalry driving him to outwardly challenge Lyre instead of ambushing him.

There was no such thing as a fair fight for those who had learned to do battle in Hades's training grounds. So what, then?

"Lyre?" Clio whispered again and started to turn.

Ash's sword shifted, light flashing on the blade.

Lyre tightened his hand on Clio, holding her in place as cold understanding cut through him.

"Why do you need to find her?"

"Everything here is foul. This town. The daemons in it. Us. We're black with the filth of this place. But she isn't. And I can't let them ruin her. I don't want to see her end up like us."

In his mind's eye, Lyre could see the dark rooftop where they had exchanged those words just days ago. He remembered every word, every moment, and he knew Ash did too.

He and Ash harbored souls blackened by Asphodel's darkness. But Clio didn't.

Tightening his hold on Clio, Lyre steeled himself for the coming betrayal. He had no choice. He wouldn't waste the chance Ash was giving him. Casting his weak emotions aside, he let instinct rule him. Sharp, calculating aggression swept through him.

He dropped his glamour.

As shimmers rippled over his body, Clio gasped. He caught her face with both hands, palms pressed to her cheeks. *Touch.*

He locked his eyes on hers. *Eye contact.*

"Clio," he purred, using the hypnotic tones of his full incubus form. *Voice.*

And then he unleashed the full scope of his seduction magic.

She arched, mouth gaping open, pupils dilating. Touch, eyes, voice—the three conduits that heightened the power of his aphrodesia to their maximum level. His magic swept away her conscious will, leaving her helpless to his command.

"*Run*," he ordered, power thrumming through his voice, his eyes, his touch. "Run straight to the metro station. Don't stop. Don't come back."

She stared at him blankly, quaking beneath his magic.

He released her and stepped back. "*Go!*"

The flowerpot fell from her hands and shattered on the pavement. She launched into a breakneck run back down the street. She didn't pause, didn't look back, and in moments, she vanished around a corner, fleeing toward the metro station and the relative safety of the smugglers market.

Lyre exhaled slowly. He had told Clio that Ash would show no mercy, but this … this was his mercy. He had given Lyre a chance to save Clio.

Lyre glanced once at the vine, flattened by the rain, its broken pot scattered across the pavement and the downpour already washing the dirt away. He didn't allow himself to feel, to hurt, to regret. He didn't wonder if Clio would ever forgive him.

In all likelihood, he'd be dead before his aphrodesia wore off enough for her to realize what he'd done—and why.

ELEVEN

STEPPING OUT of the alcove, Lyre activated the defensive spells embedded in the chain around his neck: one for magical defense, one for physical. At the same time, he untucked a three-fingered archery glove from his belt and pulled it on.

As the rain poured down in sheets, he turned to face the dark street where Ash waited—except the street was empty.

Oh hell.

He grabbed his bow off his shoulder and pulled three arrows from his quiver. As he set the first one, frigid panic hit him like an ocean wave. The terror clawed at his mind, freezing his body as though chains of ice had formed around his limbs.

If this had been his first experience with a draconian's manufactured panic, he would have died right then.

He wrenched free of the paralysis and spun, bringing his bow up. From out of the rain and darkness, huge curved wings spread wide as Ash plummeted out of the sky.

Lyre loosed his arrow with a dozen feet between them. Ash twisted and the arrow shot past his throat with an inch to spare. He slammed down beside Lyre, the monstrous blade in his hand already swinging. Lyre sprang out of reach and snapped his second arrow into place.

Faced with a point-blank shot from an archer, every opponent Lyre had ever encountered had backpedaled as fast as they could.

Instead, Ash lunged closer. He grabbed the bow, the arrowhead grinding against his armored glove, and shoved it upward, forcing Lyre's guard wide open. Ash swung that damn sword again, the blade shining in the rain.

Lyre activated the weaving on the arrowhead. The spell exploded as Ash's sword slammed into Lyre's chest.

They both flew backward. Lyre crashed down on the pavement, lungs locking from the impact. His shields had protected him from the weapon's sharp edge and deflected some of the force, but it couldn't deflect the entire blow—and Ash had hit him hard.

Not waiting for his lungs to recover, Lyre lunged up, his arrow still nocked and ready to shoot. Ash had kept on his feet, his damp clothes smoking from the explosion. He shifted his stance, his steely stare the color of dark thunderclouds. Cold, emotionless.

Fear pounded in Lyre as the draconian's false terror infected him, and Lyre understood why draconians, like incubi, stayed in glamour even in their own world.

Black dragon wings rose off Ash's back, balanced by a long whiplike tail that ended in a black tuft. Obsidian scales edged his cheekbones, and six horns, three on either side of his head, curved back from behind his ears, giving his face a malevolent cast.

The same black scales ran down the tops of his arms, and armguards protected the bare undersides. Weapons were strapped across his body, but he moved with easy grace, unrestricted by the weight. A black wrap covered the lower half of his face, and the only thing familiar about his appearance was the red tie braided into his dark hair on one side.

Ash's hand clenched and his sword—a long, curved weapon designed solely to kill—twitched. Power rippled down the blade and black fire lapped at the steel like it had been dipped in oil.

Lyre yanked the bowstring back and shot his second arrow. Ash sprang aside, wings tucked close to avoid the bolt, then darted in.

Lyre snapped his third arrow up and loosed it.

With a flick of his sword, the draconian cut the arrow out of the air. His blade whipped up and Lyre lurched back. The flat of the blade hit his bow, ripping it out of his hands. It spun through the air and clattered on the pavement ten feet away.

Ash rammed his shoulder into Lyre and his sword came right after. It hit Lyre's torso and raked sideways across his shield, dark flames surging over it.

This time, Lyre felt his flesh part beneath the lethal edge.

The sword swung free and Lyre staggered, disbelief fogging his thoughts. Blood soaked into his shirt. His shield had failed? Ash had cut through it? *How?*

Ash snapped the sword toward him once more.

Wrapping his hands in tight shields to double their protection, Lyre caught the blade and grunted as the force shoved him back. Wings flaring, Ash drove into Lyre, forcing the blade down.

The fire coating the sword scorched Lyre's shields, eating through them. Jaw clenched, Lyre sent magic spiraling into the draconian's blade. Faster than he ever had, he wove a simple spell that would survive the consuming flames. Then he shoved the blade up and let go.

Golden light burst over the steel. A blast of electricity surged down the blade and into Ash. The draconian's legs buckled and Lyre raced for his bow.

Crackling power that had nothing to do with Lyre's spell infused the air. Black magic exploded out of Ash—a detonation of power and force that tore apart the paralysis weave. The concussion slammed into Lyre's back and threw him down. He landed two feet away from his bow.

He grabbed the bow with one hand and an arrow with his other as he rolled onto his back. He was armed again, but the pieces were in the wrong hands—his bow in his right hand instead of his left.

Ash charged him, magic surging over his body. He didn't shield or evade, certain Lyre didn't have time to switch hands and get a shot off.

On his back, Lyre snapped the arrow onto the bow and shot point-blank at the draconian.

Ash jerked sideways. The shield-piercing arrow missed his chest and hit just above his bracer, lodging in his forearm.

Wings pulling in and tail snapping, Ash sprang backward a few steps. He grabbed the arrow sticking out of his arm, broke it, and tossed the point away. As the draconian yanked the other half out, Lyre switched his bow to the correct hand and grabbed the chain around his neck. Finally, he had the time and space he needed to turn this fight in his favor. He broke off a gem, activated the weaving, and threw it into the space between him and Ash.

Light flashed from the stone in a complex spiderweb of lines and runes. They glowed as blades of magic burst out from the weave—an attack that would rip through Ash's shields and impale him.

Ash raised his hand and cast, but it was too late to stop the weaving.

Flames spiraled out from the draconian in a violent maelstrom and collided with Lyre's weaving. Golden light met ebony fire in a howling detonation of power, evaporating the rain into billows of hissing steam. With a final burst, the explosion died.

Lyre's spell was gone, devoured by the draconian's fire.

Snapping his wings down, Ash launched across the space between them. Lyre grabbed a handful of arrows and shot one at Ash's face. The bolt sliced his cheek on its way past.

He slammed into Lyre. They tangled as Ash tried to hammer his fire-coated sword through Lyre's shields. Lyre used a flash of magic and another arrow to break away, but Ash came after him, pressing hard, driving his sword in again and again, waves of black magic searing Lyre.

With each strike, his shield deteriorated. Which each hit, a new tear appeared in his barrier and the blade found his flesh. Ash aimed for the same spots, slicing into existing wounds.

Lyre ignored the pain, the blood, the chill in his body. An arrow caught Ash in the shoulder. Another nicked his thigh. One went through his right hand, but Ash simply swapped his sword into his other hand, as ambidextrous with his weapon as Lyre was.

They clashed again and the draconian flung a spell at his face. Lyre jerked away and Ash's sword caught him in the back with the sound of splintering wood. His spare bow fell to the ground in pieces.

Landing hard on his shoulder, Lyre threw his hand up and cast a blinding flare. Ash flinched, shielding his face. Rolling to his feet, Lyre sped backward, keeping his eyes on the enemy as he pulled two arrows from his quiver. He couldn't miss this time.

Ash dropped his hand, still squinting, then sprang into motion.

Lyre slapped the two arrows side by side on the string and activated one's spell. With a single pull of the bow, he fired them both.

The spell unleashed in a burst of wire-like bands that shot ahead of the bolt. They spun around Ash, bringing him up short, and the two arrows came in right behind the magic.

Ash could only defend against one and he cut the spelled arrow out of the air before it struck his chest. The second one hit his thigh and lodged deep in the muscle. With a burst of fire, the draconian tore the binding weave apart. He yanked the arrow out of his leg and stepped toward Lyre.

His leg buckled.

He dropped to his knees and his sword hit the ground, the hilt in his grasp but its weight too heavy to lift. He pitched forward and caught himself on one arm to keep from collapsing entirely. His wings arched off his back, shuddering violently.

Lyre swallowed back his sick regret. A poisoned arrow wasn't how he wanted to win this fight, but he had no other choice. Steeling himself, he withdrew one more arrow, activated its shield-piercing weave, and nocked it. He drew the string back to his cheek, aiming for Ash's bowed head.

The poison worked quickly, but Lyre would give him a clean death. It was the only thing he could do to repay Ash's mercy toward Clio. He let his fingers relax, and the bowstring snapped away with a soft twang.

Jerking up, Ash slapped the arrow out of the air.

Blood sprayed from his torn hand, the red droplets lost instantly in the rain. His sword scraped on the ground as he lurched to his feet with painful effort. Unable to believe his eyes, Lyre snatched another arrow.

Ash dragged his sword up with both hands, then slammed the point into the asphalt. Blades of ebony fire exploded out of the sword in an expanding spiral with Ash at its center. Lyre took one look at the lethal cast and bolted in the opposite direction, buying himself a few precious seconds to cast his strongest shield and reinforce it with as much power as he could.

The blast hit him in the back, ripping through his bubble shield, and hurled him forward. His defensive weaves, already weakened, tore under the onslaught and when he rolled to a stop, every nerve screaming, there was almost nothing left of either weaving.

Those defensive shields were the only things that had kept him alive this long. Without them, Ash would kill him with one strike of his sword.

Sucking in air, Lyre staggered to his feet and squinted through the rain and dust. Around him, the street was cracked—giant gouges torn into the asphalt by Ash's attack—and chunks of concrete crumbled off the nearby buildings.

Lyre's skill as a master weaver had always given him an edge over other daemons, and his power hadn't mattered nearly as much as his skill. But for the first time, he understood just how wide the chasm of power between an incubus and a draconian really was. Incubi were at the bottom of the totem pole, and draconians stood alone at the top as the most powerful Underworld caste of all.

Through the rainy haze, a silhouette rose—Ash staggering to his feet. He lifted his sword and slowly turned toward Lyre. Impossible. The poison on that arrow was debilitating in seconds and lethal in minutes. Ash shouldn't be able to stand. He shouldn't be able to *move*.

He was too strong. He could rip apart Lyre's best weavings with brute magical force, carelessly throwing around quantities of power that Lyre couldn't wield and could scarcely grasp. Lyre could weave powerful spells, but he couldn't unleash them instantly in the heat of battle. Even with fully charged lodestones going into this fight, he was already tiring, his reserves half depleted and draining fast.

But if he didn't meet Ash's power with equal force, he wouldn't survive the draconian's next attack.

Open space. He needed open space.

Slinging his bow over his shoulder and pressing his hand to his bleeding side, Lyre sprinted down the street, praying the poison and Ash's injuries would slow him down enough.

Ahead, the buildings ended abruptly. The road continued across a dark river, its surface dancing under the pouring rain.

Lyre ran onto the bridge and stopped in the center. Whirling around, he put his chain between his teeth, a gem resting on his tongue for the physical contact he needed to activate it. Then he reached over his shoulder, fingers brushing across his arrows, the nocks embedded with tiny weaves that told him which arrow held what spell.

He pulled out an arrow, its black fletching standing out harshly against his drenched skin. Wetting his fingers in the blood leaking from one of his many wounds, he wiped it on the arrowhead, then nocked the arrow and lifted his bow, ready to draw.

But he didn't activate the weaving. Not yet.

Eyes narrowed, he watched the street, waiting for Ash to appear — waiting for the moment he would unleash his second greatest weapon. The KLOC was his most powerful creation, but he'd never intended to use it as a weapon. This arrow held his second most powerful invention: the same spell he'd used to kill Dulcet.

And now he would use it to kill Ash.

The draconian couldn't evade this one. He couldn't counter it with his power. He couldn't consume it with his black fire. The blood arrow was too devastating. It was unstoppable once unleashed.

Teeth gritted, Lyre waited. Ash would come. Unless the poison had done its work, he would come. And Lyre would end this once and for all — before he bled out from his wounds.

Seconds ticked by.

Fear slithered along his nerves, intensifying into shuddering terror. As panic constricted his throat, he realized his oversight.

He whipped his gaze toward the sky.

Out of the rain, black wings flashed. Ash dropped out of the darkness, diving toward the bridge deck with black power rippling off him. Lyre swung his bow up but it was already too late. Ash was too close. If Lyre fired the blood arrow, it would kill them both.

He activated the gem between his teeth. His best dome barrier snapped around him — and Ash plunged into the golden light. The draconian's power ripped through the weave before it could solidify, and he slammed into Lyre with bone-breaking force.

His bowstring snapped and the blood arrow flew out of his grasp. He hit the bridge's railing so hard the metal bowed with the shriek of tearing bolts. Ash drove into him with the momentum of his dive and pinned him against the rail.

Lyre hung in his grip, dazed and in too much pain to move. His ribs were broken. Bones in his shoulder and left arm were broken. His bow was gone, knocked from his grip.

Ash lifted his sword with one hand, the blade shining in the rain, the point aimed at Lyre's chest. Lyre met those eyes, darkened to the same ebony as his fire, and could read nothing in them. Just blank emotionlessness.

Just a mercenary following orders. Just an assassin making the kill.

But Lyre wasn't ready to die.

With no defenses and no time to cast, he used the only weapon he had left. In the instant Ash's sword began to move, Lyre unleashed his aphrodesia—the full, awful power of his seduction magic.

The sword faltered, Ash's hand stuttering with the point inches from Lyre's torso.

Lyre grabbed Ash's face. Agony tore through his body but he ignored it, focused on pumping aphrodesia into the draconian. Pushing Ash's face wrap down, he pressed his hands against the draconian's skin, unfamiliar scales under his fingers. His voice wrapped around his victim in hypnotizing harmonics. Words flowed from him in a constant stream, but he had no idea what he was saying. He only knew he had to keep speaking or risk losing control.

Ash stared at him, his eyes wide and blank. His sword wavered. He wasn't naturally attracted to the male body, and most men thought that made them immune to incubi's power.

No one was immune.

Lyre's magic flooded Ash, overwhelming his mind and will. The draconian's sword wavered again, then fell from his hand and hit the concrete with a metallic bang.

His will belonged to Lyre now.

Ash was helpless, his superior strength useless. His presence pulsed in Lyre's mind. The draconian was his to control, to command … to kill.

He stared into Ash's blank eyes. Saw the flicker deep in their depths. Felt the shudder in his mind—Ash resisting. Ash fighting for control. Ash struggling desperately to regain his will, just as Lyre had struggled against the succubi.

Weave the death spell. That's all he had to do.

If he'd hated the thought of winning with a poisoned arrow, the idea of killing Ash like *this* was a hundred times more revolting. They'd spent their lives struggling under someone else's power, and now Ash would die under Lyre's power.

Weave the death spell.

Why had it come to this? Why did they have to kill each other? Why couldn't they have found a way to keep this from happening?

Weave the death spell!

A tremor ran through him. With a shuddering breath, he pulled Ash's head closer, shifting against the bent railing.

Metal creaked. With a clanging snap, the railing broke.

He fell backward, dragging Ash with him. They pitched off the edge, plummeted fifty feet, and plunged into the icy river.

TWELVE

RUN.

Clio stood on the shadowed stairs, staring blankly at the familiar row of booths as merchants made their final transactions and began packing up their merchandise. No one glanced her way, too busy with their own things.

Run straight to the metro station.

Her lungs burned and she couldn't catch her breath. A painful tremor shuddered through her leg muscles. She braced a hand on the dusty wall.

Don't stop.

She looked from the merchants and their booths, to the sitting areas set up on the platform's other side, to the interconnected domes in the ceiling filled with stained glass and the illusion of soft sunlight.

Don't come back.

Why was she here? Where was Lyre? Hadn't she been outside with him, heading to their rented room? Why had she run back here without him? She rubbed her face, wet with rain, and started to turn away from the platform.

Don't come back.

Her muscles seized, refusing to obey, and she stumbled into the wall.

Don't come back.

That hypnotic command spun around and around in her head. The weight of the words pulled her toward the metro station and she gripped the handrail, fighting the need to continue down the stairs.

Run to the metro station.

What was wrong with her?

Don't stop.

Why was she here alone?

Don't come back.

Don't go back where?

She pinched the bridge of her nose. She remembered walking down the street with Lyre when it had started to rain. She remembered standing in the alcove with him and admitting that she'd bought the sea-shine vine as a gift for him.

He'd seen something in the street that had made his face pale and his eyes go black. And then—

His glamour falling away, the released power spilling over her body in a wash of tingles.

His black eyes locking on hers, his hands on her face, his aphrodesia pouring over her in a tidal wave of heat and need.

His mesmerizing voice wrapping around her, power vibrating through each command: Run. Run to the metro station. Don't stop. Don't come back. Go!

She'd run away. She'd left him alone to face whatever he had seen in the street that had sent fear crawling across his face. And she knew which hunter he feared most.

Shoving away from the wall, she charged back up the stairs, slammed through the doors at the top, and careened into the pouring rain.

Lyre, that idiot. That stupid, self-sacrificing incubus. Why had he sent her away? She could have helped. Ash's magic might be difficult to see, but she was a mimic. She could have—

But Lyre didn't know she was a mimic. She hadn't told him.

She ran back the way she'd come, feet pounding on the pavement, heedless of the wind and rain. Whipping around a corner, she spotted the alcove where she and Lyre had sheltered from the downpour.

The sea-shine vine lay flat in a puddle, its pot broken. Nearby, ten-foot-wide gouges marred the pavement. Building walls crumbled and windows that had been intact a few minutes ago were shattered. An arrowhead, the shaft snapped in two, glinted in the middle of the street.

Standing motionless and holding her breath despite her screaming lungs, she listened. With her asper in focus, she scanned the street for a glimpse of golden magic. Where was Lyre? Where had he gone?

He couldn't be dead. He couldn't be gone, murdered and dragged off by his killer.

A boom of unleashed magic erupted over the sound of the rain. The sheets of falling water shuddered and a shock wave of power rushed over her like an electrified breeze. She could taste dark, savage magic.

She launched into motion, racing toward the magic's source.

FRIGID WATER and pitch darkness closed over him. Lyre sank like a rock before kicking his feet. Fighting the pain in his bruised and broken body, he clawed his way to the surface and gasped in a frantic breath.

The current was sluggish and he was able to half float, half swim for the shore. His feet found the bottom and he crawled onto the gravel bank, his left arm useless. Halfway out of the water, his good arm buckled and he collapsed, his vision going white from the agony of his ribs hitting the ground. With icy water still tugging at his legs, he panted for air and tried desperately not to pass out.

Gravel crunched under heavy, uneven footsteps drawing closer. Lyre turned his head.

Ash stopped three long paces away. His face wrap hung around his neck, dripping water, and his mouth was pressed into a thin, furious line. His face was pale and blood streaked his limbs from arrow wounds. His wings were furled tight against his back and his long tail snapped from side to side.

He grasped the hilt strapped to his thigh and drew a katana-style short sword. "Get up."

Lyre blinked. It was the first time either of them had spoken since Ash had revealed himself. "What?"

"Get up." He pointed at Lyre with his sword. "Don't make me kill you while you're lying in the fucking mud."

A wheezing breath slid from Lyre. He didn't want to die on the ground. Gathering his strength, he got his good arm under him and pushed, but his trembling limbs weren't cooperating.

"Get up!"

Lyre snarled in answer as he struggled to make his limbs obey. Agony ripped through his chest and he feared he might puncture a lung. Not that it mattered. Ash was going to put an even bigger hole through him in the next sixty seconds.

Ash grabbed the strap of his quiver and hauled him off the ground. Lyre had barely caught his balance before Ash skittered backward, wary of getting too close, but Lyre knew better than to use aphrodesia again. Without the element of surprise, Ash would kill Lyre before he could take control. He had nothing left. He was done.

Bracing his feet on the uneven gravel, arms hanging at his sides, he lifted his heavy head.

Ash's jaw flexed. "It was a good fight."

Lyre smiled faintly as his vision shifted in and out of focus. Losing sucked. Dying would suck even more. "It was."

Ash brought his sword up. A shimmer of black flames ran down it as he prepared it to pierce shields and flesh with equal ease. Lyre kept his eyes on Ash's, unwilling to look away in this final moment.

The draconian's weight shifted as he prepared to lunge in for the killing strike.

A ripple of cold, unfamiliar power sizzled in the air. Ash's gaze snapped to a point directly behind Lyre and his dark eyes widened.

Something hit Lyre in the back, a punch to the ribs that sent agony flaring through his body. He stumbled from the blow—and felt the razor edges of a blade sliding out of his flesh.

He staggered forward, the blade in his back tearing free, then dropped to his knees. Ash stood before him, sword in hand, the steel shining in the rain. Lyre stared at the draconian, his thoughts too slow.

He'd been stabbed in the back. Someone had stabbed him in the damn back.

What a stupid way to die.

With no strength left, not even enough to spit a curse at whatever coward had snuck up behind him, he crumpled to the ground and his vision went dark.

CLIO SPRINTED onto the bridge. Halfway across, the twisted, broken metal railing told the tale of a battle and she raced toward it, scanning for any sign of Lyre or his magic.

Her foot caught on something and she crashed to the concrete, skinning her hands and knees. Gasping, she twisted around to see her feet tangled in Lyre's bow, the broken string hanging from one end. Her stomach turned to stone and she lurched up again.

Light caught on something half submerged in a puddle—a long, wickedly curved sword. Another weapon, but where were the warriors? She was alone on the bridge.

"Get up!"

The barked words rang out, carried on the wind, distant but audible over the rain. Clio threw herself at the railing and scanned the dark water and shorelines.

Shimmering gold, Lyre's aura, a hundred feet away on the riverbank. She thought he was alone, then she saw the glimmer of light sliding down a steel blade. Unnatural terror slammed through her.

Ash was little more than a dark silhouette against the shore, the sword in his hand reflecting light as he backed up a few steps. Directly across from him, Lyre stood with no weapons. His arms hung limply at his sides and he made no move to defend himself.

Clio clutched the railing, her heart in her throat. Too far. She was too far to do anything.

Ash said something, the quiet words inaudible over the rain. He raised his sword, preparing to strike. Lyre didn't move.

No. No, this wasn't happening. This couldn't happen.

"Don't do it, Ash," she choked. "*Don't!*"

The last word came out in a shriek and was immediately whipped away by the wind.

Ash froze, but not because of her cry.

Time slowed as red light flashed directly behind Lyre. He jerked forward, stumbled, then fell to his knees. Behind him, a man—a reaper—held a long dagger.

A dagger he had used to stab Lyre.

Lyre collapsed onto his side, motionless.

Clio didn't move. Didn't breathe. Didn't even exist as every fiber of her being screamed in denial.

"What the hell are you doing?" Ash snarled, the wind carrying his voice across the water.

The reaper tucked his dagger back into a hidden sheath. "It's not like you to play with your food for so long."

Ash lowered his sword. "It was my contract. My kill."

Buzzing filled Clio's head, the same words repeating a thousand times per second. *He's not dead he's not dead he's not dead.* Lyre couldn't be dead. It wasn't possible.

Grief constricted her heart, crushing it until her body threatened to implode from the torment. First Kassia, now Lyre. She couldn't lose him too. She couldn't bear it. The anguish howled through her, growing louder and more violent until she heard nothing else.

Then it stopped.

And she no longer felt grief or anguish or torment.

She felt rage.

She hadn't decided to drop her glamour, but when she released the railing and turned, it was already gone. Strength flooded her body as rain washed over her bare skin, her simple chest wrap and shorts offering no protection. She leaned down and wrapped both hands around the hilt of the sword abandoned beside the broken rail.

As she heaved the sword up and turned back to the figures on the riverbank below, her aura was already changing. The flood of alien power fueled her fury as red light hazed her vision. Baring her teeth, she stepped forward.

The world disappeared. Black nothingness sucked the air from her lungs and crushed her eardrums with all-consuming silence.

The world popped back in with a blaze of sound and sensation: the cold rain pounding down on her head, the splash of the river, the sharp gravel under her bare feet, the cold hilt of the sword in her hands. And in front of her, the broad back of the reaper whose aura she had mimicked.

She thrust the sword with all her weight behind it.

The blade plunged into his body up to the hilt, sliding through flesh with no resistance. The force shoved the reaper forward onto his knees and he gaped at the sword protruding from his chest. Leaving the weapon embedded in his body, she stepped into his field of vision.

"How does it feel?" she hissed.

His eyes bulged. Blood bubbled from his mouth and he toppled over with the sword impaled in his back.

A few feet away, Lyre was curled on his side, unmoving, his skin ghostly pale and his hair white against the dark gravel. Rage pounded through her, consuming her grief. She raised her gaze to Ash.

Shock and disbelief brushed across his features. Disbelief at what he'd seen. Disbelief that she had teleported like a reaper.

Fear scraped at her, but her deadly focus was enough to keep it at bay. If not for that, the sight of him out of glamour would have had her cowering. With his wings and tail, horns and black scales, and eerie, menacing designs that coiled wherever scales met skin, he was a nightmare come to life. A dark wraith escaped from the realm of night.

"You're next," she whispered, her voice unfamiliar to her ears—ice dipped in sweet poison.

His eyes widened.

She snapped her hand out and her first cast shot toward him. He shielded, his reflexes faster than she'd expected, and her cast exploded against the barrier—but her second cast, formed in her other hand, was already flashing for him. The whip of power slammed into his ankles, below the edge of his shield.

He fell.

She flung a third cast, but he rolled, wings snapping outward. He lurched to his feet and whipped a band of black fire at her. She cast a master-weaver shield just long enough to deflect the attack, then hurled the spell in her other hand.

He shielded again but her attack tore through it, throwing him back. He barely kept on his feet. She advanced, casting so fast he had no time to unleash his more powerful magic against her.

If he'd been fresh, it would have been a different fight. She could see his injuries. She could see his weakness.

It made her want to kill him even more.

He cast a different shield—a type she'd never encountered before—but she could see the shape of it, see its flaws. With a flick of magic, she shattered the barrier and whipped a spinning disk of power at his injured leg. Her spell struck the arrow wound in a splatter of blood and his leg buckled.

He caught himself, somehow staying upright. Stepping over Lyre, she advanced on the draconian, hurling another spell and forcing him to defend instead of attack. He staggered back, heavily favoring one leg, and she lifted her hands, two lethal casts spinning across her fingers.

Something touched her leg.

She leaped back and looked down, deadly spells ready to fly.

On the ground at her feet, Lyre's hand was stretched toward her. Amber eyes, hazed and out of focus, squinted up at her and blood trickled from his mouth as his lips formed a soundless word: *Clio.*

He was alive. He was still alive.

Her casts dispersed in an instant and she dropped to her knees, both hands going to his chest as she spun a thread of healing magic into him. Alive. Still alive. Broken bones, blood loss, a collapsed lung.

She could save him. There was enough time. Just enough.

She grabbed the chain hanging around his neck and pinched a familiar gemstone. A dome-shaped shield burst into existence around her and Lyre, enclosing them safely within it.

With uneven footsteps, Ash approached the barrier, its light casting eerie shadows over his face. Wings tucked tight to his back, he studied her for a long moment, his expression indiscernible. Cold. Empty. Then he turned, limped to the fallen reaper, and wrenched his sword out of the daemon's body.

Weapon in hand, wings tightly furled, he walked away with lurching steps. A dozen yards down the riverbank, his form blurred. With the rain, the darkness, and his cloaking spell, he'd vanished between one step and the next.

Clio clutched Lyre's shoulder and focused on his healing. Everything else could wait.

THIRTEEN

PERCHED on the edge of the bed, Clio held Lyre's hand. Every few moments, she stroked her fingers across his palm, his knuckles, his wrist, memorizing the subtle shapes and forms. His skin was warm to the touch—finally warm after hours of feeling clammy and chilled.

Behind her, he slept beneath every blanket she'd scrounged up in the tiny suite. She'd even thrown a few heavy bath towels across him for extra warmth.

Four broken ribs. A shattered shoulder and collarbone. A deep slice in his side. Half a dozen other cuts and slices over his body. Those were the injuries she presumed Ash had given him.

The final wound was a hole running through his back into his left lung, just missing his heart: the lethal blow the reaper had dealt.

She stared blankly at the wall, painful tension spreading through her body. Memories flashed through her mind. Ash's sword. The shining blade. The reaper's unprotected back. Her hands, as though belonging to a stranger, ramming that deadly length of steel into the reaper's torso.

She'd never killed anyone before. As a race, daemons were violent creatures, but nymphs were a comparatively passive caste. They rarely devolved into the brutal violence of self-preservation that others were so prone to.

She'd never lost control like that before. She'd never felt that kind of bloodlust. Now, calm and composed once again, she kept returning to that moment where she'd teleported behind the reaper and stabbed him in the back just as he'd done to Lyre. And she couldn't summon any remorse. Even with the shaded rage long behind her, she didn't regret killing that daemon. Did that make her a terrible person?

She glanced behind her. Lyre slept the deep, silent sleep of the recently healed. It would be hours more before he stirred. She gently rubbed his hand, making sure his skin was still warm.

She couldn't regret murdering the reaper who'd almost killed Lyre, but when it came to the other daemon who'd tried to take the incubus's life, she was quietly relieved Ash had walked away.

She glanced at Lyre's face again, at the dark tattoo marking his cheekbone. He hadn't recovered enough to regain his glamour—which was why she had her back to him. She'd watched him at first, but she'd kept falling under the spell of his otherworldly radiance. She wanted to trace the design on his cheekbone, the delicate points of his ears, the fine braid that hung down the side of his face, adorned with a ruby at the end. Even while unconscious, his power over her was frightening.

On the riverbank, he'd seen her out of glamour for the first time, but she wasn't sure he would remember. He'd been halfway comatose.

Releasing his hand, she rose to her feet and stretched. Exhaustion dragged at her limbs and aching hunger had settled deep in her belly, but there was no food in the apartment. Before Lyre woke, she'd have to venture outside to restock.

She'd never healed wounds as severe as Lyre's before and the magic's toll had left her weak and woozy. Healing magic required both training and natural talent, and daemons without an affinity for it were limited in what they could learn. Clio had inherited a gift for healing from her mother, but that didn't make it any less exhausting.

Rolling her stiff shoulders, she turned to the suite's main door and squinted her asper into focus. Tangled green lines and complex runes spanned the doors, the walls, and even the floor and ceiling: multiple wards layered one atop the other.

Not just any wards. Lyre's wards. The same powerful, lethal spells he had used to protect his house in Asphodel.

Beneath her weaving, the faint golden shimmer of his original wards on the room glowed. They were good wards, but with Lyre helpless and her magic nearly depleted, she hadn't trusted them to be enough.

She carefully examined the weavings, ensuring they were perfect and functional. After a quick circle around the tiny unit, she returned to the bed and looked down at him. So close. She'd come so close to losing him.

She saw it again: the blade in the reaper's hand. Then she saw another blade in a different hand, shining with red blood.

Kassia's blood.

Images flashed in her mind. Kassia falling. Lyre falling. Kassia's blood. Lyre's blood. Kassia's eyes wide with shock, her hands clutching her chest. Lyre's eyes, hazed with pain and fading consciousness, his hand stretched toward her across the muddy gravel.

A shudder ran through her. With jerky movements, she crawled onto the bed and tucked herself against Lyre's side. Trusting the deep healing sleep to keep him unaware, she took his hand tight in hers, pressed her face into the blankets, and let the tears fall.

Tears of grief, of fear, of loss, of regret.

She'd saved Lyre. Why couldn't she have saved Kassia too?

RAIN SPLATTERED Clio's face and she hunched her shoulders against the stiff breeze. Her new hat, a black courier-style cap with a short brim, did little to keep her head dry, but she'd hidden her hair under it. That was its most important job.

A heavyset man bumped her and she cringed, clutching her paper bags of purchases. The weekly market was closing as the sun dipped behind the tall skyscrapers that surrounded the downtown square. When it had been Clio and Kassia, they'd usually shop in the afternoons when humans dominated the market. But now, with the shadows stretching across the square and the light fading fast, daemons appeared in numbers she wouldn't have expected.

Glowing auras filled her vision, and she didn't dare let her asper out of focus even for a moment. A headache throbbed in her skull from the strain, but there were too many daemons—including a smattering of red auras—for her to take the chance.

Being out in the open at all was a huge risk, but she and Lyre— especially Lyre—needed food. She hadn't had a single bite to eat since that bun in the smugglers market. Their meeting with Sabir was still scheduled for that night, and she'd picked up supplies for their journey—or as many as she could find in a human market. Now she just needed something for them to eat.

Adjusting her heavy shopping bags, she approached a table with a few foil-wrapped packets still available. The aroma of pork and garlic made her mouth water. A shopper moved away from the table and the seller turned to Clio, one eye twitching nervously.

"I'm packing up," he grunted. "What do you want?"

She held back her grimace. What was with the unfriendly merchants lately? Pointing to the four remaining meal packets, she said, "I'll take them all."

"Eighty dollars."

"*Eighty!* That's—"

Golden light blazed in her peripheral vision. She recoiled from the table, prepared to run for her life. But it wasn't an incubus with a golden aura she'd glimpsed.

Four tall men walked past the booths. Their hair ranged from wheat-yellow to ashy cream, and their eyes were varying shades of green. Not Underworld incubi, but Overworld griffins. Almost as bad, seeing as the Ra family ruled the griffin caste and she considered them all her enemies. But unlike incubi, any griffins in this market weren't likely to be looking for her. They were just passing by.

She turned back to the table, ignoring their pale yellow auras so similar to incubi's golden magic.

"Fine, eighty dollars," she agreed since it didn't matter what she paid, even if the seller was ripping her off. "Pack them up, please."

As the seller dropped the foil bundles into a paper bag, she fished out the money. They exchanged items and she tucked the new bag against her side, grateful for the warmth of the food. Turning, she hurried back across the market, dodging shoppers as she headed for a side street to make her escape.

Why did it seem like every daemon in the square was watching her?

It had to be her imagination. Three red auras were moving around at the other end of the square, but her path out of the market was clear. She hastened her steps and glanced over her shoulder. Her gaze passed across two indigo auras and a bright violet one.

Her steps faltered, but she forced herself to keep walking.

She'd seen those three auras while at the other booth. Now they were only twenty paces away: two men with beefy builds and one short, scrawny one, all with dark, nondescript clothes. Was it a coincidence, or had they followed her across the square?

Gulping down her fear, she made a sharp turn and headed along a new row of booths with fresh produce that was mostly picked over. As she dashed past the tables, she peeked behind her.

The three daemons had turned down the same aisle.

Shit. They *were* following her. Why? They weren't reapers, draconians, or incubi, but she didn't know what castes their colors represented.

Buying herself a moment to think, she stopped at a booth with a few scrawny carrots and potatoes displayed in worn baskets. Her stalkers conveniently paused to examine the vegetables at a different table, maintaining the same twenty paces between them. They didn't want to get close yet. They were probably waiting for her to leave the public square and walk into a nice abandoned alleyway.

She picked up a potato and pretended to examine it as she fought down her panic. What should she do? She had to get back to Lyre without her new stalkers jumping her, *and* she needed to make sure they didn't track her to their room.

Damn it all. She didn't know how to prevent either outcome.

With rumbling voices, two of the griffins she'd spotted earlier ambled down the same aisle of booths. She focused on the potato in her hand, feigning obliviousness, but the daemon pair walked past her without so much as a glance in her direction. The wind gusted, whipping rain into her face.

A black umbrella appeared over her head, blocking the rain. She straightened in surprise and turned to the umbrella's owner.

The potato fell from her hand and hit the table with a thud.

Amber eyes looked down at her, cool and expressionless. The daemon's golden aura glowed brightly in her asper, and complex weavings wrapped his body from head to toe, layered around his neck and wrists where he carried heavily spelled chains and bracelets. A deep hood hid his pale hair, and dark clothes disguised the strong, limber body underneath.

"Reed?" she whispered, panic and confusion warring for dominance.

Lyre's brother tilted his umbrella, keeping it over their heads and blocking them from her stalkers' view. His free hand rose, and a gemstone between his fingers sparked. Invisible magic, discernible only to her, leaped from the stone to the human merchant on the other side of the table. A glowing weave wrapped around him and the man's eyes went completely blank.

Clio's mouth hung open. That spell had simultaneously immobilized the man and knocked him unconscious. He hadn't moved, but he was no longer aware of anything around him.

"You shouldn't be here." Reed's voice was soft, the words thrumming with that deep, irresistible timbre only incubi possessed.

"Why are *you* here?" she whispered back, her voice shrill with urgency. "How did you find me?"

"The same way *they* found you." He tilted his head toward her three daemon stalkers. "You're alone. Where is Lyre?"

"He's … nearby."

"Alive?"

"Yes." Her eyes narrowed and she asked again, "Why are you here?"

Reed's expression hardened. "To tell Lyre he's a fool. He's been here too long. You have to leave the city."

"That's our plan," she snapped, unimpressed by his tone. "We just need to—"

"You have to leave *now*." His gaze flicked across the square. "Samael's best killer returned empty-handed and injured. Samael has put out a bounty for an incubus and a nymph, with descriptions of you both. You're to be captured alive and presented in Asphodel for a generous reward."

An icy shiver ran through her.

"Every bounty hunter affiliated with Hades is either here or on their way. It won't take long for news of the bounty to reach other mercenaries."

"We're leaving tonight," she whispered, gripping her shopping more tightly to suppress her shivering.

"Good." Reed pressed closer, jostling her shopping bags as he brought his mouth to her ear. His breath warmed her skin as he whispered, "I'll distract the bounty hunters while you escape."

"But—but why are you—"

"I can't stay here any longer." He stepped back. "Get Lyre out of the city."

"But—"

"Go."

She stared at him helplessly, then ducked under the table. Popping out on the same side as the immobilized seller, she stayed in a crouch, hidden behind the rows of bulky booths, and raced toward the nearest dark alley.

As she dove into it, she glanced back. Reed stood with his umbrella resting on his shoulder, watching her. When their eyes met, he casually raised his hand in front of his chest. Light flashed from between his fingers.

In a silent whoosh, a golden cloud burst from the gem he held. The fog billowed outward, blanketing the entire square in seconds. Alarmed cries rose and colorful lights flashed as daemons tried to counter the unnatural mist with their magic.

Sucking in a breath, Clio turned and ran, leaving the square behind.

If Reed had found her so easily, that meant others could too. And with every mercenary from the Hades territory hunting them, their chances of evading capture had dropped to a terrifying new low.

Getting out of the city had never been more critical, and she desperately hoped their Overworld guide would be waiting for them in a few hours as promised.

CLIO DISARMED the wards on the door and slipped into the room, then reengaged them. Still catching her breath, she half-heartedly wiped her wet boots on the mat and crossed to the screen that separated the bed from the rest of the cramped unit.

Lyre lay under the patchy blankets. His skin had regained its usual warm tan, and he was back in glamour. He was staring at the ceiling, and when she stuck her head into view, his amber eyes dropped to hers.

"You're awake," she said with a sigh of relief as she hurried to the bed, fumbling with her shopping bags.

"Hmm," he agreed, his gaze again lifting to the ceiling, a small wrinkle between his eyebrows.

She frowned worriedly at him, then glanced up to see what he was so focused on. The ceiling was blank and boring, marked with water spots and weird brown splatters. A faint shimmer of green magic hinted at the wards she'd embedded throughout the apartment, barely visible without her asper in focus.

Lyre squinted at the ceiling, his gaze shifting from one spot to another. There was nothing there but the wards.

Her stomach sank to the floor.

He finally looked at her, a strange blankness in his eyes. "My wards," he murmured.

Swallowing hard, she nodded. When she'd cast his wards over their unit, she'd figured he would notice them before she could remove them. She just hadn't expected he'd notice within minutes of waking up.

"How?" His question was calm, but something in its simplicity demanded an answer.

She sat on the edge of the bed and piled her shopping bags beside him. Breathe in. Breathe out. "All nymphs can use astral perception, but some of us ... a very few nymphs possess an additional ability. It's called mimicking."

His expression went even more blank than before. He said nothing.

"I can mimic any magic I see with my asper. When I was at your house in Asphodel, I had to examine the wards to disable them. Since they're the best wards I've ever seen—the best you've ever created, I'm guessing—I used them to protect us here."

She pressed her hands together and waited for him to respond. The silence stretched between them, crackling with things unsaid.

"A mimic," he echoed flatly.

"Yes," she whispered, staring at her lap. "I'm sorry. I'm sorry I didn't tell you before."

The painful quiet was broken only by the rain drumming on the roof. Then, out of nowhere, his laughter rang out.

Head jerking up, she gaped at him. He laughed for half a minute before gulping back his amusement and pushing up into a sitting position, one hand pressed to his side where his ribs had been broken.

"A *mimic*," he gasped, catching his breath. "Oh man. I can't believe it."

Merriment danced in his eyes and she clenched her hands, wanting to check if he was feverish but afraid of insulting him. "What's so funny?"

"It explains *everything*. Your tour. Your obsession with those damn prototypes." He barked another laugh. "How much did you see? All our best wards. All our—damn." He leaned against the wall at the head of the bed, grinning at her. "You were never going to *buy* something, were you? Damn that scheming prince."

"Um." She blinked at him. "You're not ... angry?"

"Angry? Hell no." He squinted at the ceiling. "Okay, I'm annoyed that you've been pilfering *my* weavings, but ripping off Chrysalis—I would love to be a fly on the wall if my father ever finds out what you were up to."

She blinked a few more times, struggling to reconcile his reaction with her fears about how he would respond.

He tensed. "You said you can mimic anything. Does that include the KLOC?"

"No," she answered quickly. "That's the only spell I've ever seen that I can't copy. With the moving parts, I couldn't even figure out how to activate it."

He relaxed again, his amused grin returning. She stared at him. All this time worrying about his reaction, and he thought it was *funny*?

His eyebrows rose. "What's that scowl for?"

She hastily cleared her expression. "Nothing."

"That was a mean scowl." He leaned forward and his bright eyes captured her. "Are you angry with me?"

"The only thing I'm upset about is you almost dying on me."

"Oh, right." He glanced around the room. "Didn't I get stabbed in the back? How am I alive?"

"I healed you."

"But how did we get back here? You couldn't have carried me."

"We walked."

"We did?"

She nodded. "It took a shock of magic to wake you up. I also got your bow and as many of your arrows as I could find. You don't remember any of that?"

As he scrunched his face, struggling to remember, she glanced at his bow and quiver leaning in the corner. While collecting his arrows, most damaged with their spells spent, she'd found one on the bridge that hadn't been used. Later, she would ask him about the terrifying blood-magic weave embedded in that black-fletched bolt.

The irony was painful. After all her life-risking efforts to search Chrysalis for a weapon powerful enough to terrify Irida's enemies, he'd been carrying one all along.

"I can't remember anything after getting stabbed." Lyre frowned. "What happened to Ash?"

"He was injured, though not as badly as you. I threw a few spells at him and he took off."

"I shot him with a poison-tipped arrow. Not sure why it didn't kill him, but it must have had *some* sort of effect." His attention fixed on her shopping bags. "Is that food I smell?"

Amused, she opened the food bag and lifted out a tinfoil packet. Warmth seeped into her skin and she passed it to him before pulling out a second one for herself. She stared at it for a moment.

"Actually," she said abruptly, "I am angry with you."

He paused halfway through ripping open the wrapper, his expression wary.

"You made me run away from Ash."

His gaze dropped from hers and he pressed his lips together. "I didn't have time to explain or argue about it."

"You forced me to leave with aphrodesia."

"I didn't have a choice. I don't expect you to forgive me, but I only did it to—"

"You almost *died*." Her hands clenched, crushing her dinner. "Why didn't you let me help? We could have fought him together!"

His eyes darted up, surprise flickering across his face. "Against Ash? He would've killed us both. You had a chance to—"

"To run away and leave you to die?" She glared at him. "That is not an acceptable outcome. Not for *anything*. We're in this together, Lyre."

"Together?" he repeated, his voice oddly quiet.

"We escaped Asphodel together, and we're going to the Overworld together to get your clock back. So do not *ever* send me away like that again. If I want to leave, then *I'll* decide. You don't get to decide for me."

He nodded, his attention returning to his food, but he didn't resume opening the foil. She pursed her lips, then reached out and smacked him upside the head.

"Hey!"

"That was for using aphrodesia on me. *Again*."

He rubbed his ear, casting her a flinty look. "I was saving your life."

"You were being a self-sacrificing idiot. I'm not useless, you know." When he smirked, she gave him her meanest glower. "Whatever you're thinking about saying, I suggest you reconsider."

He snickered and ripped his dinner open to reveal a thick bun loaded with shredded pork and strips of roasted vegetables. In the time it took her to eat her bun, he ate the other three.

He crumpled the foil wrappings into a ball and tossed it in the direction of the kitchen. "What else did you buy?"

"Supplies for the Overworld." She pulled the nearest bag toward her. "A change of clothes, water bottles, a blanket, dried food—"

As she moved the first bag, the second one tipped over, and the clank and clatter of metallic objects accompanied the expected sound of crinkling paper. Clio went still, staring at it in confusion. Cautiously, she reached for the paper bag, pinched the bottom corner, and upended it. A pair of khaki pants and a gray shirt fell out, along with a black cloth bag with a drawstring—a bag she hadn't purchased.

Before she could warn him, Lyre picked it up. The contents clinked energetically as he untied the drawstring, pulled it open, and poured a mixture of uncut gems, steel marbles, and arrowheads into his palm.

"What the hell?" he growled.

"I didn't buy that," she stammered.

"I know. These are my spells. This is everything … *everything* I left behind. All the spells I had stashed in my house, my workroom, and a few other locations."

"Reed," she whispered.

His sharp stare snapped up. "What?"

"I didn't have a chance to tell you yet. Reed found me at the market. He came to warn you that Samael put a bounty on us." She looked at the bag in disbelief. "I had no idea he'd slipped that in with my shopping."

Lyre's terse suspicion morphed into surprise. "Reed came to warn me? Did he say anything else?"

"Just that he couldn't stay here any longer."

He nodded slowly. "He must have snuck out, but his absence won't go unnoticed for long. I doubt he'll be able to get away a second time."

"What's your relationship like with Reed?" she asked, hesitating over the question. "He seems different from your other brothers."

Lyre poured the bag's contents into his lap and sorted through it. "Reed and I worked together a lot since our talents are complementary. He isn't competitive like the others, so he never had a problem with me."

Reed seemed to care a lot more than just "not having a problem" with Lyre. She nibbled on her lower lip. "Is he like you? Is he trapped by Chrysalis too?"

"He ..." Lyre's hand paused above a ruby shard. "Reed just likes to weave. He doesn't care what, or why, or for who. Chrysalis is exactly where he wants to be—the one place where he'll never run out of weaving projects."

"He doesn't care if he's making evil spells?"

"How the spell is used doesn't matter to him. He's all about the weaving—the process of it." He selected three steel marbles and lined them up on his palm. "Coming all the way here to warn me ... it's more than I would have expected from him."

"Do you think it's a trick?"

"Doubt it. Reed is the least deceptive daemon I know." He arched an eyebrow. "He makes you look like an outright con man."

"Me? A con man?"

"Con woman," he corrected as he shoveled the spells back into the bag. "Either way, his warning about the bounty means—" A yawn overtook him. "The bounty means we need to—" Another jaw-popping yawn.

She pulled the bag from his hands and stood. "We're safe here for now. You should sleep for a few more hours."

He nodded, his eyelids already drooping, and slumped back onto the limp pillow. She cleared off the mattress and tucked their new belongings in the corner. By the time she returned to the bed, he was asleep again, his body shutting down to conserve strength as he recovered from the toll his battle and healing had taken on him.

She hesitated, then brushed a lock of hair off his forehead. He'd used his aphrodesia to make her flee from Ash, proving once again he could control her mind whenever he wanted to. Yet he hadn't done it to hurt her, to take advantage of her, or to betray her.

He'd done it to save her life. And he'd done it expecting she would never forgive him.

Her fingers slid down his cheek and brushed across his lips—the lips that had kissed her with fierce lust and soft passion. The latter made her heart race, but the former sent a thrill of fear running down her spine.

His soft, sweet charm was one side of him. The brutally aggressive lust was the other side. Gentle and fierce. Charmer and seducer. He was both, and she kept forgetting that.

She brushed her fingers across his lips one more time, memorizing the zing of fear, the terror of his aphrodesia sweeping through her mind and erasing her will. She had to hold on to that fear or she would have no shields left to barricade her heart.

Charmer, seducer … and, if she wasn't careful, heartbreaker.

FOURTEEN

LYRE HELD his arms out to the sides and waited for Clio's judgment. Her summer-sky eyes ran over him from head to toe before returning to his face.

She wrinkled her nose. "It looks terrible. Black doesn't suit you at all."

"It's a disguise. It's not supposed to be flattering."

"But …" She pursed her lips. "Well, you don't look like an incubus anymore."

"That's the important part." He glanced at his reflection in the glass balcony door. The illusion that had darkened his hair to raven black and his eyes to the color of tree bark wasn't doing him any favors, but even a terrible color scheme didn't take away from his looks that much. "Maybe I should create the illusion of an ugly nose or something."

"You're fine. The bounty hunters are looking for a blond guy." She grabbed a sweater off the bed and tossed it at him. "Let's go before we miss Sabir."

As he pulled it over his head and drew the hood up, she twisted her hair into a bun and jammed her new hat on top of it. They checked the room one more time, then headed down the stairs. He couldn't say he would miss the place. The cockroaches would probably miss them, though.

The rain had finally let up, but the street shone with puddles and the air was heavy with the threat of more precipitation. The moment they set foot outside, Lyre's senses jumped into high gear.

Ash had given him advance warning once, but the draconian wouldn't extend that mercy a second time. Not after the way their last fight had gone. Women weren't forgiving of incubi who used aphrodesia on them, but men got damn vicious over it. Having their mind wiped by male sex magic tended to shake them to their very core—and leave them feeling especially vengeful.

And now, according to Reed, he and Clio could expect more mercenary company to show up.

Walking briskly at Clio's side, he took a moment to marvel at the idea of Reed coming to Brinford to pass on a warning—and to deliver his lost spellwork. That black bag of magic was the source of the complex illusion disguising him. Creating a simple illusion for hair color was easy, but creating one that other daemons couldn't detect was much harder.

His brother's visit had come in the nick of time; a few hours later and Clio would have missed him entirely. Lyre appreciated Reed delivering his lost spells, but that wasn't what had drawn his brother into the city. Nor had he come to deliver a warning—at least not a warning about bounty hunters.

Reed wasn't the type to go out of his way for anything less than the most dire of circumstances. A bounty was bad, but Lyre was a master weaver. He had more than enough spells to deal with the average mercenary—Ash being an exception, but the draconian wasn't "average" in any sense of the word.

Reed had come to deliver a different warning, one he hadn't shared with Clio. Lyre could guess what it was, though. So far, his hunters had come from Hades—reapers, draconians, and now mercenaries. But there was someone else who would be even more brutally determined to see Lyre killed as quickly as possible.

Lyceus. His father.

Reed wouldn't bother to warn Lyre about mercenaries. He wouldn't bother to warn Lyre if Andante, Ariose, or Madrigal were coming to Earth to hunt him down.

But if their father had joined the hunt … that was something Reed would see as dire enough to require a warning. It also explained why Reed had anticipated that his first attempt to contact Lyre would also be his last. If Lyceus guessed what Reed had been up to, he'd ensure his wandering son stayed home for a good long while.

Lyre shivered at the thought of his father hunting him, and he was damn grateful he'd soon be out of this city—and out of this realm.

He and Clio traversed the dark downtown streets in silence, watching for any signs of danger. They lingered near the closed shopping mall for half an hour before venturing inside and sneaking through the hidden door to the abandoned metro station. The walk down the tracks was the most frightening part of their journey—a long, empty stretch of darkness where an ambush would be only too easy.

They quickly bypassed the ward at the next station and slipped in among the bustle of the market. Lyre's gaze traveled from daemon to daemon and his skin prickled.

When they stopped to wait for a group to move out of their way, Clio leaned closer to him.

"Is it just me," she whispered, "or is it a lot busier than last time?"

"Seems like it," he answered grimly.

Their path cleared and she walked ahead of him, her shoulders rigid. Shivers crawled up and down his spine as he followed her to the merchant booths. Again, a large crowd had gathered around the poacher's booth, and Lyre wondered if that wolfish creature with feathers—the lycaon—had been recaptured.

Sabir the plant seller was perched on a stool behind his booth of leafy things, but the table was far emptier than two nights ago and all the large plants were gone. His gaze found Clio well before she approached his table.

Lyre almost felt bad for the guy—he didn't have a charismatic bone in his body—but he mostly felt annoyed that they had to rely on the daemon to get to the Overworld. Despite his assurances to Clio that he wasn't jealous, the Overworlder gave him a bad feeling.

"Sabir," Clio gushed, resuming her terrible attempts at flirting. Lyre quashed his automatic smile. "I'm so glad you're here. I was worried ..."

The daemon glanced at Lyre, who raised his eyebrows in a silent challenge. Sabir flicked his attention to Clio, his expression darkening ominously. "I didn't expect you to bring the incubus back."

Damn. His disguise wasn't good enough.

"He, uh, well ..." She leaned forward, getting nice and close to Sabir. Hmm. Maybe her seduction skills weren't as amateurish as he'd thought. "He's actually my ... business partner. Last time—that was just an act so he didn't get ripped apart."

Sabir's mouth flattened. "What sort of business?"

"Um ..."

Lyre smiled condescendingly at the daemon. "Is that really a question you want *anyone* around here to ask?"

Sabir's scowl deepened. "You aren't part of my agreement with Clio."

Having expected this, Lyre pulled a pouch from his pocket and dropped it on the table. "Double the people, then double the payment. Only fair, right?"

Oozing displeasure, Sabir opened the pouch and peeked inside. His expression didn't change, but he tied the bag shut and slipped it out of sight. A practiced merchant—no reaction to the money and he removed it from the table immediately. He knew what he was doing, and like most businessmen, he wasn't about to turn down money just because he wasn't excited about taking an incubus along.

"When do we leave?" Clio asked brightly.

Sabir shifted on his stool, probably still adjusting to his disappointment that he wouldn't get Clio all to himself for the journey. "It's unusually busy tonight. I'll pack up after things settle down."

Lyre's instincts sharpened. So it wasn't just his inexperience with the market that had made it seem more crowded. If this was unusual enough for Sabir to notice, then ...

He took a step back and carefully scanned every daemon in his line of sight. Clio seemed to have the same idea, because she turned the other way as she casually swiped her hand across her eyes—a signal he'd come to recognize as her using her astral perception.

Daemons went about their business, none paying any attention to Lyre or Clio, but he didn't trust it. Too many wore hoods, hats, sunglasses, and other more conspicuous methods of covering their faces. He shifted closer to Clio but he couldn't see anyone looking their way. Busy booths, small groups in discussion, two men haggling over a glowing glass orb—

His gaze stalled on a dark nook near the stairs—the only spot on the entire bustling platform empty of daemons.

Except it wasn't empty.

He'd almost missed it. He'd almost assumed it was just a shadowy corner. But a haggling daemon lifted his orb in a vehement gesture and its light sparkled across the wall, piercing those deep shadows. The shape of a man was cast into sharp relief before disappearing again.

Lyre sucked in a breath so fast he almost choked. The hidden man wore a long trench coat with the deep hood pulled over his head—and a black wrap covering the lower half of his face. *Already?*

He almost jumped out of his skin when Clio grabbed his arm. He tilted his head, not daring to take his eyes off the shadowed corner.

"Lyre," she hissed in alarm. "I think we're about to have trouble."

"I know," he whispered back.

A pause. "What are you looking at?"

He tensed even more. "Apparently not what you're looking at."

Her hand tightened on his arm. "Half a dozen griffins are converging on that poacher's booth. It looks like it's going to get ugly."

"Griffins?" Sabir barked before Lyre could respond. He grabbed a thick canvas bag and started shoving his merchandise into it. "We're leaving now."

"Are griffins bad?" Lyre asked, still watching the corner. Let the damn draconian know Lyre had seen him.

"Griffins aren't allowed in here." Sabir lowered his voice and shoveled plants into his bag with no care whatsoever. "They control or influence half the trade in the Overworld. It's *their* laws and tariffs we're all here to avoid."

Clio pressed closer to Lyre. "There's another eight of them mixed into the crowd. They all have their faces or heads covered, but they look the same. They might be soldiers."

"Why didn't the ward trigger?" Sabir spat a foreign curse. "There's an old cathedral ten blocks north of here. Meet me there. I don't want to be seen leaving with anyone."

He threw his rucksack over his shoulder, grabbed his last ceramic pot off the table, and got exactly three steps before all hell broke loose.

Lyre didn't see what happened, but magic exploded from the vicinity of the poacher's table. Screams and furious shouts erupted, something hit the floor with a bang, and steel blades rang as they were pulled from sheaths all across the platform.

Lyre scooped Clio against his side and sprang over Sabir's emptied table. Landing on the other side, he pulled it over to form a barricade. Magic burst all around as the griffin raiders attacked the poacher—and the poacher's customers attacked the griffins. The violence spread like wildfire, and daemons dropped glamour as they went into full battle mode. Sabir had vanished in the pandemonium, hopefully making a successful escape.

Clio flinched at another whistling burst of power. "We have to get out of here!"

Lyre agreed, but—

With a flash of yellow light, six daemons went flying—and half of them crashed down on him and Clio. Lyre hit the floor with a grunt, some idiot sprawled half on top of him. The daemon snarled as he pushed up, tearing at Lyre's shirt.

His illusion gem tumbled out of his pocket, and the daemon's eyes widened as Lyre's appearance changed. With his own snarl, Lyre punched the daemon in the gut, shoved him off, and grabbed the guy who'd flattened Clio. He flung the man aside and hauled her up.

Light blazed and the volume reached ear-splitting levels as magic went off on all sides. The griffins on the other end of the platform had launched attacks, and battle consumed the whole station.

Instead of rejoining the fray, the daemons Lyre had thrown seemed to decide he was a griffin too. They charged him. He slammed paralysis spells into them and they crumpled to the floor.

Coming from directly behind them was Ash.

His short katana blade gleamed as he leaped over the fallen daemons and rammed into Lyre. As he went over backward and hit the floor a second time, Lyre grabbed Ash's forearm before he got impaled.

With a twist of his wrist, Ash freed his sword arm and the blade flashed down.

A rogue ball of purple flame flew out of a nearby fight and smacked Ash in the back of the head. He jerked forward and Lyre shoved him off. Rolling away, he jumped to his feet—and a hunk of wood, thrown by an explosion, hit him in the back. He crumpled to his knees and swore.

Ash lunged up and pivoted toward Lyre, when a random daemon snatched the draconian's coat and yanked him off balance.

Lyre sprang away, leaving Ash with the poor fool who'd grabbed him, and looked around frantically for Clio. Out of the chaos, she jumped to his side, and he blinked at the magic swirling over her hands. She flung two spells into the nearest daemons. One went down in a binding spell, and the other went flying from an invisible impact.

He blinked again. He could do simultaneous casts too, but two completely *different* spells?

She was already casting again, green light flickering across her fingers. A black-eyed daemon, frothing with bloodlust, shot toward Lyre. He grabbed the guy by the shirt front and threw him with an extra dose of magical force. Ash sprang out of the way as the body sailed past him.

The draconian whipped back toward Lyre, his trench coat discarded to reveal the myriad of weapons strapped over his dark clothes.

"Underworlders!" a daemon howled, his voice rising above the cacophony.

"Seriously?" Lyre snarled as a dozen nearby daemons turned from whatever fights they were having to focus on Ash and Lyre, standing in plain view.

Clio popped up between them and threw her two spells into the nearest daemons' faces.

Lyre swore again and wrenched her away from Ash. The draconian lunged for Lyre but had to duck as a blast went over his head. Then the other daemons were on them.

Close-quarters fighting wasn't Lyre's strong suit, but he had one advantage. Grabbing the chain around his neck, he activated his defensive shields—new ones, replaced by Reed's spell delivery. The closest daemon, wielding a short dagger, tried to ram his blade into Lyre's chest. It hit his invisible shield and skidded off to the side.

Lyre coated both hands in one of his favorite little weaves—a shield that also enhanced force—and slammed his fist into the daemon's jaw. The guy flew six feet backward and collapsed. One down, eleven to go—except the original dozen was rapidly growing into twenty as more bloodthirsty daemons headed their way.

That was the problem with daemon instincts. Once a fight got going, those who were aggressive by nature didn't simmer down when the initial conflict was over. They craved bloodshed.

Lyre took a few blasts of magic straight on as he dealt more punches to anyone who got close enough. Three beefy Overworlders closed in on him, and he dodged a blow that would have hurt even with a shield. Hands raised defensively, he darted backward—and thumped into someone else.

He looked over his shoulder and found himself back-to-back with Ash, Overworlders surrounding them on three sides.

Ash glanced at him, a sword in each hand, then lunged forward to meet the oncoming daemons. Blood sprayed and a daemon went down screaming—no mercy from the draconian.

Jaw clenched, Lyre sprang at his assailants. Clio stayed in the background, magic flashing as she cast multiple spells with ambidextrous perfection, whipping them one after another at the attacking Overworlders.

Lyre pummeled his way through a couple more daemons but found himself encircled. He slammed his fist into one daemon while dissolving the shield on his other hand so he could cast. His binding spell slammed into the second daemon.

Someone grabbed him by the back of the neck. Fear shot through him. His defensive shields protected him from blows and flesh wounds, but it had to be flexible so he could move—which meant his attacker could break his neck. He started a rapid cast.

Clio flew out of her corner and charged straight at the huge daemon holding Lyre. She sprang off the ground and let her fist fly—her hand wrapped in a perfect copy of the force-enhancing weave he'd been using.

Her fist connected with a crack. The daemon's hold vanished and Lyre was flung away. He landed on his feet and staggered, grabbing for the nearest support—Ash's arm. Ash staggered too, missing his next strike, his blade glistening with blood. Jumping back a step, Lyre whipped around in time to see Clio jam another punch into her victim's throat. The daemon keeled over backward.

Lyre blinked. Two steps away, Ash had also turned, and he stared at Clio with a slightly bewildered crease between his eyebrows.

Clio whirled toward them, her eyes wild. "Watch out!"

Lyre and Ash spun around at the same time. Two griffins, their blond braids streaming like banners, sprang at them with casts forming in their hands. Ash slashed with his swords, forcing them back, and Lyre cast a bubble shield—covering himself *and* the draconian. The griffins' attacks exploded harmlessly against the barrier.

Ash leaped forward, and Lyre dissolved the shield before the draconian hit it. He tore into the lead griffin, and Lyre jumped in behind him. As Ash whipped toward the second daemon, the griffin threw up a shield. Lyre flung a dart that shattered the shield, and Ash's sword plunged into the griffin's chest.

The daemon fell, and Lyre glanced warily at Ash. The draconian's eyes were unreadable, his face mostly covered.

Clio raced over and put her back to them. Ash promptly turned away and Lyre put his back to theirs as they formed a defensive triangle to face the brand-new horde of angry griffins moving into position around them.

The griffins clearly didn't appreciate the slaughter of their comrades, and these guys—unlike the idiots he, Ash, and Clio had mowed through—weren't your average daemons. The griffins moved like soldiers. A few punches with added magic wouldn't stop them.

Ash raised his sword, pointing it straight ahead, and the air crackled with the gathering weight of his power. Eyes widening, Lyre looked over his shoulder.

Ash met his look, calm and cold, and flicked his gaze toward the ceiling.

Lyre glanced at the interconnected domes formed of steel framing and thick stained glass. Oh shit. He snatched the chain around his neck and grasped for the right gemstone. The air hissed and sparks danced as electricity built.

Ash swung his sword up to point at the ceiling.

Power exploded out of it, racing up the steel and bursting into spirals of howling black fire. The whirling blasts crashed into the stained glass, ripping it apart, and a thousand pounds of steel and heavy glass shards plunged toward the platform.

Lyre activated his shield. The golden dome snapped over the three of them an instant before the lethal deluge hit. Screams erupted as glass and metal impaled daemons. The griffin soldiers frantically shielded, and every daemon went down, shielded, or jumped for cover.

As soon as the debris had stopped falling, Lyre dissolved his barrier and whirled to face Ash. The draconian was already moving—but not to run his sword through Lyre. Instead, he sprang over the nearest daemons and sprinted for the stairs.

Realizing Ash had the right idea—their reprieve would be over in seconds—Lyre grabbed Clio's hand and bolted after the draconian. As they reached the stairs, a blast of magic hit the wall, spraying concrete chips across their path. He didn't look back to see how many griffins were back on their feet.

He and Clio charged up the stairs. As they came to ground level, Lyre saw the closed doors. If Ash had gone through them, they would have been swinging—but they remained untouched. To his left, the lobby bent in on itself and another staircase ascended into the building that sat atop the metro station.

Lyre chucked a raw blast of power at the doors. It blew them open and shattered the windows. Dragging Clio with him, he whipped around the corner and raced up the stairs. Behind them, footsteps thundered into the lobby then crunched across the broken glass as their pursuers ran outside.

Not sure how long his deception would last, Lyre pushed faster. Clio's breath rasped as she struggled to keep pace with his longer stride. The stairs kept rising and he started to panic. He'd expected to go up one or two levels, but the damn stairs weren't ending.

Finally, they leveled out into an open plaza. Connected to the space was a pedway bridge that spanned the street, linking the office building on the other side. A heavy gate, bolted shut, blocked the pedway and there was nowhere else to go.

Lyre slid to a stop. In front of the floor-to-ceiling windows, Ash was sheathing his swords. He stiffened at Lyre and Clio's arrival.

Angry shouts echoed up the stairwell.

Ash's gaze flicked to the stairs, then he faced the window and blasted the glass with his magic.

Damn it. Lyre had run himself and Clio to a dead end only Ash could escape, and the griffins were closing in from behind.

As Ash's body shimmered like he'd been engulfed in a heat wave, Lyre squeezed Clio's hand and launched forward. As the distortion around Ash faded, his dragon wings unfurled and a long tail snapped out behind him. Terror hit Lyre like a punch to the gut but he didn't slow, charging across the space.

Ash glanced back, his eyes dark and horns sweeping alongside his head. Then he launched out the window.

"Lyre!" Clio cried, her steps slowing.

Lyre grabbed her under his arm, lifted her right off her feet, and sprinted for the opening as Ash vanished out of it. Lyre hit the edge and jumped, casting a push spell behind him to propel himself forward.

For an instant, they soared over nothingness. Then they slammed into Ash in midair.

Lyre clamped his arm around the draconian's waist and held on for dear life. Ash roared furiously as the sudden weight sent him spinning in the air. The pavement—farther below than Lyre had expected— whirled dizzyingly as Ash pumped his wings. He grabbed Lyre's arm to pry it off, but his talons scraped harmlessly against Lyre's shield.

They careened through the air in a wide arc, barely missing the corner of a building. As they plunged into a narrow alley and a wall rushed to meet him, Ash desperately beat his wings, but he couldn't stop their momentum.

And that's about when Lyre realized Ash couldn't control his flight with two people hanging off his waist.

The three of them crashed face first into the wall. They bounced off and fell in a tangle of limbs and wings. A shimmer ran over Ash and his wings vanished just before they all slammed into an open dumpster.

Lyre pushed Clio on top of him as they hit, cushioning her impact with his body. Pain ricocheted through every inch of him. It freaking hurt. Weren't dumpsters supposed to make perfect fall-breaks?

He had only a moment to painfully stew about how misled he'd been before his senses registered something far more pressing than his pain: the stench.

He lurched up and unceremoniously threw Clio out of the dumpster ahead of him, then grabbed the slimy edge and hauled himself over. *Ugh.* Disgusting. Like dead animals and food so rotted it had turned to bubbling puddles.

Dropping to the pavement, he rushed a few steps away from the toxic cloud around the dumpster, then remembered they weren't alone. Tensing, he whipped back around.

Ash swung over the edge of the dumpster and landed heavily, one hand clamped over his nose and mouth. With a sense of smell far more sensitive than Lyre's, the reek had to be outright torturous for the draconian.

Ash's eyes, black with fury, locked on Lyre.

Lyre opened his mouth, but even if he'd known what to say, he didn't get a chance to speak. Ash bore down on him with violence brimming in every movement. Lyre backpedaled, but not fast enough. Ash didn't even bother to draw a weapon, just pulled his arm back.

His fist slammed into Lyre's face. His head snapped back, pain exploding through his cheek.

"Shit-eating son of a whore!" Ash yelled. "What the fuck is wrong with you?"

He drew his arm back again. Still reeling from the first hit, Lyre snarled and threw himself into Ash. He landed exactly one glancing blow before Ash tackled him. They hit the ground and rolled across the asphalt as they pummeled each other. Or rather, as Ash beat on Lyre while Lyre got in maybe three good hits on the draconian.

A dart of movement from Clio, then a flash of green light. An electric shock slammed through him. His limbs convulsed and Ash's weight flattened him as the draconian collapsed from the same spell.

Ash recovered first and shoved off Lyre. Blood ran from the corner of his mouth as he turned on Clio. Lyre scrambled to rise, but before he was even sitting up properly, a shout rang out from a nearby street—the griffins.

Ash's head snapped toward the sound, then his glare flashed across Clio and stopped on Lyre. He bared his teeth as though debating whether ripping Lyre's arms off was worth fighting the griffins.

Apparently deciding against it, he snarled another curse, whirled on his heel, and strode down the alley in the opposite direction of the griffins' voices. Ten steps away, a dark ripple passed over him, and his form faded into the shadows.

Lyre gingerly prodded his cheek. His eye was already swelling and splitting pain had lodged in his skull.

Clio looked down at him. "You're crazy, did you know that?"

"Yeah."

"And stupid."

"Can't argue there either. But at least we're still alive, right?"

She shook her head and, without another word, started down the alley into the deeper darkness. Pushing to his feet, Lyre followed a step behind her, warily searching the shadows for any sign of Ash. The sooner they left for the Overworld, the better. He didn't want to find out what would happen next time Ash caught up with him. Lyre just kept piling on the reasons for Ash to hurry up and kill him.

He rubbed his throbbing cheek again. Damn draconian hit hard.

FIFTEEN

FOR TWO YEARS, Clio had been adrift in an unfamiliar world. Exiled among humans with no ties to the people there, with no purpose, she'd never felt a bond with Earth or with her townhouse in the city. For two years, she'd longed for that subtle but encompassing warmth a real home had brought her.

But now she could feel it. She could smell it in the air. She could feel it in the earth beneath her feet. She could taste it in the soft thrum of power that saturated this world.

Her world.

The moment she stepped out of the ley line, clutching Sabir's hand, her senses went into overdrive, drinking in everything both familiar and alien. Sand shifted under her feet as she stumbled forward. Sunlight blinded her and a hot breeze carried the scents of sun-scorched rock, dried leaves, and a hint of water. She squinted, her heart throbbing painfully in the back of her throat.

Wind-carved rock formed a deep bowl in the earth, its contoured walls flowing like waves frozen into stone, and natural pillars bent in precarious arches that crisscrossed the bowl. The rock was burnt orange veined with pale blue crystal that sparkled under the two sister suns.

Sand filled the basin, the same burnt orange as the rocky walls with a sprinkling of blue crystal that shimmered as the breeze teased it. In a shadowed corner, two narrow waterfalls spilled from a lip of rock and poured into a small pool. Low bushes flourished around the waterhole and vines with large, waxy leaves climbed the stone walls. The Overworld's subtle, ancient life filled the air.

She tried to take a step forward and felt a tug on her hand. Sabir was still holding her. He smiled, his eyes behind his black-rimmed glasses warmer than she'd seen before. "What do you think?"

"It's beautiful," she answered automatically, her gaze sweeping over the basin again. "Where are we?"

"Near Ra's northeastern border. We'll head north from here, then east toward Irida. The journey will take about three days."

"I'm looking forward to it," she gushed vapidly, gently tugging her hand out of his. "You should get Lyre before he thinks we've forgotten him."

Sabir's pleasant expression soured, and it was abundantly clear that forgetting about Lyre would have made his day. With a nod, the daemon returned to the ley line. The rippling band of blue and green light spanned a short gap in the rocky wall, barely ten feet across. He stepped into the line and vanished, his passage causing the steady flow of power to stutter.

Beams of light beat down on the barren sand in the basin's center and heat made it dance and shimmer like water. She stepped out of the shade and the temperature shot up as though she'd walked into an oven. She inhaled the dry air and tipped her face toward the two suns. After the chill and rain on Earth, the heat felt delicious on her skin.

What would Lyre think of her world?

After their violent parting of ways with Ash, she and Lyre had located Sabir easily enough. He'd been waiting exactly where he'd said he'd be, his rucksack of plants replaced with a traveling pack. With griffins and bounty hunters on the prowl, Sabir had wasted no time whisking them to the ley line south of Brinford. And after days of struggle and stress, here she was, back in the Overworld.

Behind her, the power of the ley line jittered. She turned as Sabir and Lyre appeared, clutching arms so they weren't pulled apart during the shift from one realm to the next.

Lyre took a few stumbling steps, his eyes widening as they flashed across the basin. He'd changed out of his dumpster-splattered clothes into a gray button-up shirt and sturdy khaki pants, and the backpack with their supplies hung from his shoulders. The bruising on his face was gone; she'd healed it on the journey to the ley line.

Lyre finished his study of the basin and turned to her. Even in the shade, his amber eyes glinted brightly, the warm color complemented by the orange stone behind him. Quiet wonder softened his features.

Elation bubbled in her and she wanted to run to him, to throw her arms around him and celebrate their successful arrival. But with Sabir watching her, she could only smile and pretend it wasn't a big deal to be home again.

"We should get moving," Sabir said, adjusting the pack on his shoulders. "The first leg of the journey won't be fun, but once we reach the mountains, the heat won't be as much of an issue."

"How far to the mountains?" she asked as he trudged through the sand to a cluster of boulders near the waterfall.

Sabir dug around in the rocks. "Depends how fast you two can go, but it'll take the better part of the day, I expect. I can move faster alone, but the heat takes a toll if you aren't used to it."

He heaved a rock aside and fumbled with something out of sight. When he straightened, he held several bundles of white fabric and three large waterskins.

"Fill these up," he said, tossing them to Lyre. "And have a drink now. We'll have to ration those skins for the rest of the day."

While Lyre held the first skin under the waterfall, Sabir shook out a swath of white fabric and approached her. "Hold your arms out."

She obeyed, and he draped the cloth over her head to form a deep hood, wrapped the rest around her body like a cross between a cloak and a dress, then knotted the corners behind her shoulder.

"Where did you get these?" she asked as he stepped back to examine his work. "Do you always keep supplies here?"

"They aren't specifically mine." He flipped a second white garment over his head and wrapped it swiftly around his body to cover his exposed skin, then pulled off his glasses, folded them, and tucked them under his robes. "My people have used this oasis for hundreds of years, and we always keep shared supplies here."

"Wow," she murmured. She wanted to ask who his people were, but questioning a daemon about his caste was not only rude but often taken as an act of aggression.

Lyre joined them with the waterskins and Sabir wrapped him in the third white robe, then showed them how to tie their waterskins under the fabric.

"Don't lose them," he warned. "That's your life source in the desert."

He stepped back to appraise them, and his scruffy beard, long hair in a loose ponytail, and exotic complexion didn't look so out of place with the fabric shading his face.

"One last thing," he said to Lyre. "I recommend you stay in glamour. It mutes your magical signature, which could attract unwanted attention."

Clio frowned. She'd dropped glamour in the Underworld, but maybe her aura had been too buried beneath the dense magic of Asphodel's inhabitants for anyone to sense it. She was already itching to return to her true form—this was her first time using glamour in her home world—but she'd decided to keep her caste hidden from Sabir for now. Assuming he hadn't guessed already, keeping her asper a secret gave her a slight advantage.

"Let's go, then," Sabir said. "Stay close, and if you feel lightheaded, speak up immediately. Heatstroke can hit fast and hard."

Clio and Lyre exchanged uneasy looks, then followed Sabir around a bend in the basin's wall. On the other side, a rocky path had been carved into the bowl, steep and narrow but nothing an agile-footed daemon couldn't handle.

When she reached the top of the basin, the sputtering breeze transformed into a gusting wind. It hit her like a battering ram and almost blew her over. She grabbed her hood as the wind whipped hot grains of sand at her face.

The ground sloped away from the rock basin, and stretching for miles in every direction was nothing but rolling orange dunes shimmering in the baking heat. Wisps and eddies of sand fluttered at the dune peaks, and the suns blazed down from a cloudless sky.

Sabir took her arm, pulled her around, and pointed. On the northern horizon, almost invisible through the rippling heat waves, were the faint silhouettes of mountains. She rose on her tiptoes, straining to see the easternmost summits, hoping vainly she might recognize her homeland. But it was too far.

On her other side, Lyre let out a low whistle. "I knew to expect it, but damn. There it is."

She didn't have to ask what he meant. Hovering above the distant mountains was a massive planet. Clouds swirled across its alien surface, white in the bright suns. As they traveled toward it, the planet would appear to rise higher into the blue expanse of sky, but it didn't actually move; its position was fixed, the Overworld and the other planet locked together in orbit.

Sabir led them around the basin and they started toward the distant mountains. Five minutes in, she was sweating from the heat. Ten minutes in, she was ready to gulp down her water despite Sabir's warning to ration it. Thirty minutes in, her legs were aching from the constant need to correct her balance on the sand.

After an hour, she knew this would be one of the most physically demanding days of her life.

The vista rippled with heat more intense than anything she'd experienced, and the air was so painfully dry it sucked the moisture out of her body with each breath. She was baking under the layers of fabric Sabir had wrapped her in, but she didn't remove them. He had covered them up for a reason.

The dunes rose and fell, forcing them to climb and descend, climb and descend. The sand, though, was what made the journey truly miserable. It slipped and shifted beneath her feet, forcing her to work harder for every step. Sabir gave them handkerchiefs to wrap over their lower faces so they didn't breathe in too much dust, but that didn't keep the tireless wind from whipping sand into her eyes.

The mountains never seemed to draw any closer. Their pale shapes on the horizon taunted her—close but out of reach. As the hours of toil dragged on, Sabir encouraged her with updates on how far they'd come and how far they had left to go, but she didn't trust his estimates. She and Lyre were slowing him down.

Clutching Lyre's arm, Clio forced her aching, exhausted body up the slope of another dune. Sabir, fifty yards ahead, was approaching its peak. Some dunes were as large as foothills, but this one was the largest they'd climbed so far.

At the top, Sabir waved her and Lyre onward. "There's a good view up here," he called. "We can take a short break."

A break? Though considerate of his less fit and climate-adjusted traveling companions, Sabir hadn't allowed them to stop for more than a minute or two all afternoon, claiming it would tire them out faster to constantly stop and start.

Gritting her teeth, Clio forced herself to continue upward. Her leg muscles burned, but she climbed with Lyre at her side until they reached the dune's top. Panting, she grabbed Sabir's extended hand and he pulled her up onto the narrow top of the dune with him. Lyre hobbled up beside her, breathing just as hard.

"Take a look," Sabir said, pointing east.

Clio turned, putting her back to the sun, and gasped.

From this height, the giant waves of sand stretched for endless miles, but near the horizon, a different shape broke the monotony. In the same burnt orange shades as the sand, towers rose. The spires clustered within a surrounding wall, and she could make out touches of green plant life around it.

"That's Aldrendahar," Sabir told them. "The northeasternmost griffin city. There's a natural spring in the center of the town, so walking into its walls is like walking into a tropical oasis."

Aldrendahar. Clio knew the name. It was the closest Ra city to the borders of Irida, and she could finally place their location on the map in her head.

"Irida is northeast of there, then," she said, gesturing. "Why are we traveling straight north?"

"It's less direct, but it'll get us out of the desert faster." Sabir caught her arm before a powerful gust of wind could blow her off the dune. "And if we went that way, we'd have to stop in Aldrendahar for water."

Visiting a griffin city was something she'd rather avoid. "If we head north from here into the mountains, that would put us west of Irida — but that's Kyo Kawa Valley."

He nodded, unfazed by her alarmed tone. "We'll stick to the edges of their territory. It's perfectly safe."

"Whose territory?" Lyre asked.

"The ryujin," Clio answered nervously.

"Never heard of them."

"A reptilian water caste," Sabir told the incubus. "They're hostile to pretty much everyone, but Kyo Kawa Valley is a massive network of interconnected rivers and valleys, and it's easy to avoid the ryujin if you know your way around."

"Trespassing in Kyo Kawa is not a good idea." Clio shifted her weight uneasily. "The ryujin are vicious to outsiders."

"I know how to avoid them," Sabir assured her with perfect confidence.

"Sabir?" A hesitant note touched Lyre's voice. "This might be a stupid question, but … is it supposed to look like that?"

"Huh?" Sabir turned to peer in the direction Lyre was pointing.

Following suit, Clio squinted across the endless desert where dark clouds had settled over the horizon. Clouds? On the horizon?

"Ah, shit." Sabir puffed out a breath. "That would be a sandstorm."

Lyre tugged on his hood. "Sounds bad."

"Yes. Especially since it's headed this way."

Clio scanned the brown billows of dust. "It looks far away. It might die off before it reaches us."

"Distances are deceptive in the desert," Sabir said grimly, taking Clio's and Lyre's arms. "And it's moving fast. Let's go."

He jumped, pulling Clio and Lyre off the dune's peak. They half slid, half ran down two hundred yards of steep sand to the valley between the dunes.

"There's shelter nearby—we might reach it in time. Don't slow down!"

He broke into a quick jog and Clio raced after him, but running in the sand was even more difficult than walking in it. Sabir's light-footed grace made it look easy, but she and Lyre lumbered awkwardly, wasting twice as much energy. Her throat was parched and painful, but Sabir called at them to hurry, turning to trot backward as he waved them onward.

"We don't want to be out in the open for this. Hurry up!"

She ran on. Lyre followed behind her, and his harsh breathing was slowly drowned out by the increasing roar of distant wind. Sabir had said the storm was moving fast, but how could it be here *already*?

"Come on!" Sabir yelled.

She pushed her aching legs harder but she didn't seem to be running any faster. The groan of the approaching storm grew louder, accompanied by a sharp whistling noise. Wind blew over the dunes, whipping sand off the tops.

Sabir spun around. He ran back to her and Lyre, grabbed her around the middle, and threw her over his shoulder. She squeaked in alarm and clutched at him for balance as he sprinted toward the unseen shelter. He flew over the sand, barely touching it, and Lyre fell behind.

"Sabir, slow down!" she cried. "Lyre can't keep up."

"He'll catch up," Sabir grunted, breathless for the first time. "We're almost there."

Her heart constricted as the gap between them and Lyre stretched wider. Lyre was running hard but he couldn't match Sabir's speed. An orange haze thickened the air and the whistling scream of the oncoming storm grew louder.

"Lyre!" she yelled. "Sabir, slow down!"

Sabir ignored her and raced around a bend in the dune valley. Lyre disappeared from her line of sight.

"Sabir, stop!" She shoved against his shoulder. "Put me down!"

"We're almost there. I'll go back for Lyre."

She bit her lip, panicking but unsure what to do. Running back for Lyre seemed foolish. What use would that be? Sabir would get Lyre as soon as she was safe.

He ran through another valley of dunes, then slowed to a stop, breathing hard. Just ahead, a wedge of weathered blue crystal jutted from the earth, with orange sand piled on one side of it. Sabir hauled her to the leeward side and pushed her down.

The sunlight dimmed. The howling wind grew deafening.

Sabir whirled around and took two running steps back the way they'd come, then pulled up short.

With a sound like a deep bellow and an ear-splitting shriek combined, a wall of sand blasted down the dune and engulfed their crystal shelter. The light disappeared, and as dust screamed past them in a choking cloud, the entire world turned to a black nightmare of wind and sand.

SIXTEEN

SABIR had to physically hold her down as the sandstorm engulfed them. She almost blasted him off so she could run back to find Lyre, but the sand was a solid, screaming wall and she couldn't see beyond a few feet. She'd never find him.

"This is your fault!" she yelled at Sabir, struggling against his constricting arms. "You shouldn't have left him behind!"

"I couldn't carry you both," he snapped, more upset than she'd expected. He pulled her deeper into the crystal shelter as dust eddied around them. "Stop talking before you get sand in your mouth."

She hunched her shoulders, holding back her furious, panicked criticisms. Even with the cloth tied over her face, her mouth felt gritty and her throat hurt. The sand boiled past their shelter in a mixture of dust, sharp orange particles, and larger bits of rock. What would that abrasive barrage do to Lyre, caught in the open with no shelter to break the wind and block the sand?

Would it shred his skin? Would it blind him? Would he suffocate, choking on sand?

Tremors ran through her and her eyes watered, though whether from fright or the grit in them, she wasn't sure. For what felt like hours, the sandstorm raged without relief. Finally, the whistling scream of flying sand died, leaving only the whooshing wind and clouds of roiling dust.

Releasing her, Sabir sidled cautiously to the edge of their shelter. "You can wait here while I look for—"

"No," she snapped. "I'm coming with you to find Lyre."

His eyes narrowed, then he shrugged. "You'll just needlessly exhaust yourself. Stay close. Visibility is poor."

Before venturing out, they both took a long drink from their waterskins, then Sabir led her back into the dune valley. The loose sand, heaped and piled in strange new ripples, sucked at her feet. Sabir moved quickly, forcing her to jog every few steps to keep up. A thick haze hung in the air, dimming the sunlight, and the wind wasn't as painfully hot as before.

"He should be around here, based on how fast he was moving." Sabir stopped to scan the sandy gorge. "If he fell and got buried, we might have trouble finding him."

Fell. Buried. Those words triggered a fresh wave of panic. She lurched forward, blinking her asper into focus. His aura. Where was his aura? Had he fallen? Was he buried? Had he suffocated? She couldn't see the faintest glimmer of golden light in the endless sea of orange.

"Lyre?" she shouted, turning in a circle. "Lyre, where are y—"

She faced the way they'd come and a shimmer leaked through a heap of sand. With a frantic gasp, she sprinted to the spot and thrust her hands out. Her fingers slammed into something hard only a few inches under the sand and pain shot through her joints.

"Ow!" she gasped, stumbling back a step.

Sabir appeared beside her. "What the hell?"

He brushed the sand aside to reveal a smooth surface that glowed gold. Runes and interconnecting lines formed an intricate, powerful barrier. She swept her arms across it to expose the top of a dome.

Sitting inside it, his chin propped on one hand and eyes closed, was Lyre.

"Lyre!" she cried.

His eyes popped open. At the sight of her and Sabir leaning over the top of his barrier, he sat up and reached for the glowing gemstone in front of him. He touched the gem, golden light flashed, and the barrier dissolved. All the sand piled against its sides collapsed into the gap where he sat.

"Shit," he yelped as he was swamped. "Damn it."

With a bemused expression, Sabir held out his hand. Lyre grabbed it, and Sabir pulled him out. Lyre brushed himself off, sand flying everywhere, and pulled his backpack off to shake it clean.

"Glad you made it," Sabir said, a note of caution in his voice. "That's one hell of a barrier. I've never seen anything like that."

"Good thing I had it," Lyre commented evasively, cool as could be considering he'd just weathered a brutal sandstorm alone and exposed in an Overworld desert. "Glad you two showed up. I couldn't tell if the storm had ended."

"Looked like you were taking a nap in there."

Lyre shrugged. "It was boring. Nothing else to do."

Sabir shook his head. "You're tougher than you look, incubus."

"Thanks … I think."

Clio said nothing, her hands clenched into fists and her expression as blank as she could make it. Her heart pounded from residual fear, and relief rolled through her, so strong it made her knees weak. She'd been so afraid he was dead.

Sabir scanned her face as though checking to see if she would burst into tears or throw herself into Lyre's arms. "Let's get moving then. Navigating in the dust will be tricky, but I have a good sense of direction."

He started out again, glancing back frequently to make sure she and Lyre were following. She didn't move, letting Sabir draw ahead, and Lyre waited beside her.

"I'm fine," he whispered, guessing exactly what she needed to hear. "Absolutely fine."

She nodded, on the verge of tears, and pressed her lips together so he wouldn't see them tremble.

"Are you okay?" he asked.

"I'm fine."

"Good." He put his hand on the small of her back to guide her forward—and hot tingles rushed up her spine.

She jumped in surprise. He smiled conspiratorially and winked at her. She stared for a moment, then laughed softly and hurried to catch up with Sabir, Lyre following right behind her.

A little jolt of aphrodesia to calm her nerves and reassure her he was fine. Later, she would tell him off for using his seduction magic on her *again*, but for now, she would hold on to that feeling of warmth and pleasure for as long as she could.

Miles of desert lay behind them, and they still had a long way to go.

CLIO LOST COUNT of the hours, and with the haze left by the sandstorm, she couldn't see the mountain range to judge their progress. Eventually, rough orange crags and jutting formations of blue crystal overtook the endless sand dunes, and the occasional clump of grass, cluster of shrubs, or lonely tree appeared. By the time the suns hung low on the horizon, struggling to burn through the dusty haze, the desert dunes were far behind them and the rocky foothills had taken over.

Despite the reduced visibility, Sabir led them unerringly. He never tired, his stride unfaltering while Clio's and Lyre's strength flagged more with each hour.

"We'll make camp in the next ravine," he told them as they climbed a rocky hill dotted with dry grass and a few bushes with bluish leaves. "I'd intended to get farther into the mountains before nightfall, but the storm slowed us down. We'll make up the time tomorrow."

Clio cringed at the thought of another day of travel like this one. She'd run out of water a few miles ago and was now sharing the last of Sabir's waterskin with Lyre. Her legs throbbed mercilessly, and she wholeheartedly agreed with Sabir's no-stopping policy—if she stopped, she'd never start again.

They crested the hill, and just beyond it, the hillside fell steeply into a ravine. Short trees grew in scattered clusters of four or five, and winding through the center was a narrow creek, its surface reflecting the planet's glowing light, now brighter than the last streaks of sunlight in the west.

She dredged up the last of her energy as they half slid, half trotted down the slope. She wanted to throw herself into the water and wash off the dust and sweat of their journey, but when she got to the bottom, she discovered it wasn't a creek so much as a shallow stream only a few inches deep, trickling merrily over smooth pebbles and bits of crystal. Far too shallow to bathe in.

Sabir hustled her and Lyre to a thicket of trees. Clio sank down in a patch of soft sand, too tired to drink the fresh water only a few feet away.

"We'll camp here." Sabir pulled off his pack and propped it against a tree. "This spot is sheltered enough for a fire. Once the suns go down, it'll get cold."

"How cold is cold?" Lyre asked as he shed his backpack and crouched beside the stream. He dunked his empty waterskin into the shallow flow.

"Cold enough that you'll want a fire and a blanket."

"Fun," Lyre muttered.

"There isn't much firewood here," the daemon continued, gesturing at the nearest spindly tree, its upper branches decorated with six-inch thorns. "I'll collect some from nearby, then make something to eat."

"Do you need any help?" Clio offered, even though the thought of standing again made her want to curl into a ball and cry.

"No." He pulled off his white robe and shook out the sand. "The next wooded area is a bit of a hike. I can get there and back faster on my own."

"Thanks, Sabir," she murmured tiredly.

"Just rest for now. Drink. Wash up. I'll be back in an hour." With a glance at the sky—gauging the time by the partially eclipsed planet above—Sabir hopped over the stream, no sign of weariness in his movements, and swiftly climbed the opposite side of the gully. He vanished over the crest.

"I didn't think much of him at first," Lyre said as he capped his waterskin and filled hers, "but that guy is hardcore."

"Yeah, he's a lot tougher than I would have guessed." She arched an eyebrow at Lyre. "Does that mean you'll be jealous now if I flirt with him?"

He huffed and handed her the filled waterskin. "Maybe a little. If nothing else, he's making me look pathetically out of shape."

"If you're out of shape, then what does that make me?" She stifled a groan as she sat up and untied her white garment, dislodging a cascade of sand. She folded the fabric, then moved to their pack and retrieved her spare shirt. "I'm going to go rinse off."

Finding a spot downstream with some privacy, she used the cloth she had tied around her face to scrub off, then changed into her clean top. Washing her hair wouldn't work without a bucket, so the best she could do was shake the dust out. As clean as she could get and feeling reasonably refreshed, she gave her old shirt a quick wash and returned to their camp.

Lyre was crouched beside the water, his handkerchief dripping wet. His shirt was untucked, the first few buttons undone, and his hair was damp. He must have washed off too. As she approached, he pressed the cloth to the side of his head just at his hairline, then lowered it to look at the fabric as though expecting to see something.

"What's wrong?" she asked as she flipped her washed shirt over a tree branch to dry.

He prodded the side of his head again. "Do I have a scratch here?"

She knelt beside him and found a scrape near his temple. It had already scabbed over but she took his cloth and carefully cleaned it anyway.

"It's not bad," she told him. "What happened?"

"Just a rock from the sandstorm. It took me a minute to get my shield up," he added at her confused look.

She lowered the cloth. A sick feeling twisted deep in her gut, the same nausea she'd felt as she desperately worked to heal him on the riverbank in Brinford after the reaper had stabbed him.

"If you hadn't had such a powerful shield," she murmured, twisting the cloth into a knot, "what would have happened to you?"

"I don't know." He pulled the cloth from her hands before she mangled it. "But I did have a shield that could hold against the storm, and I made it through just fine. I might even have done better than you and Sabir."

She smiled wanly, but that sick feeling of what might have happened still churned inside her.

"Clio." He touched her cheek. "Don't make that face."

Her pulse quickened at the warmth of his hand against her skin. "What face?"

He rubbed his thumb across her jaw. "The heartbroken one."

"I just …" She exhaled unsteadily. "I can't do this without you."

"Yes, you can."

"I don't want to."

"You don't have to. I'm right here."

She gripped his wrist, holding his hand against the side of her face. "Good. Stay right here."

"Yes, ma'am."

"Ugh." She wrinkled her nose. "Please don't call me 'ma'am.'"

"Yes, Clio."

A flush rose through her. The way he said her name—the way his deep voice caressed each sound. Suddenly, her heart was pounding loudly in her ears. His eyes held hers and she was drowning in warm amber.

She'd promised herself there could be nothing between them because the power imbalance between an incubus and a woman was too catastrophic to allow trust. But she couldn't remember the fear.

She leaned toward him. Shadows flitted across his eyes and he shifted out of her reach. She froze, the sting of rejection cutting through her. He slid his hand away from her and stood. Confused and hurt, she dropped her gaze, biting her lower lip.

"Clio," he groaned. "I *really* can't handle that heartbroken look."

Even more confused, she peeked at him.

He retreated a few steps and sank back down, leaning against a narrow tree trunk and propping his elbow on his knee. "Do you really think I don't want to kiss you?"

Her cheeks flushed. "I … I didn't …"

"I'm exhausted, Clio. My self-control is shot. I can't kiss you right now." His eyes darkened. "But I can assure you I want to. You have no idea how much I want you."

His voice deepened, the words purring all the way down her spine.

"That's why I can't kiss you," he added in a more normal tone.

"Oh," she mumbled weakly. "Is that the only reason? Control?"

"The only reason."

Nerves, cold and squirming, flashed in her belly. If he doubted his self-restraint, she should too. But once Sabir returned, she would have to go back to keeping her distance from Lyre—and she couldn't. She couldn't stand this forced space between them.

Rising to her feet, she stared down at him with her heart in her throat. Was she crazy? Had she lost her mind?

He looked up at her, blinking in puzzlement.

Gulping down her doubts, she stepped behind the tree he was using as a backrest, hooked her hands over his elbows, and pulled them back. With a quick flash of green light, she cast a binding spell between his elbows, trapping him against the tree trunk.

"Hey!" he yelped, yanking the binding taut. "What are you doing?"

She circled back around and crouched in front of him. He snapped his elbows against the binding again, scowling at her.

"Damn it, Clio, I said I didn't trust my control if I kissed you, but I can bloody well handle anything short of that!"

Pretending her hands weren't trembling, she took her handkerchief and folded it into a strip, then reached for him. He leaned back with a snarl, trying to evade her, but she looped the strip over his eyes and tied it behind his head, blindfolding him.

"What the hell?" he growled, anger and a hint of viciousness coating his tone. "If you think this is funny, it's—"

He broke off when she pressed her palm against his chest. Kneeling in front of him, she sucked in a deep breath. She was crazy. It was the only explanation.

"Lyre," she whispered, barely able to summon any volume. "Now can I kiss you?"

His mouth opened, then closed. "What?"

"If you lose control, you can't hurt me. And you can't confuse my willpower with your eyes covered, right?"

"I—I guess—probably not? But still, Clio, this is—"

"Lyre. I need to kiss you. Right now."

He froze, not even breathing. She shifted forward, kneeling between his legs. The blindfold hid his eyes and what they might have revealed about his thoughts, but his shoulders were tense, his heels digging into the sand as he held himself rigid. He didn't like being immobilized, being vulnerable and powerless, but he wasn't fighting her. He trusted her.

Closing her eyes, she brought her mouth to his. Their lips melded together and she felt herself spiraling down into something dark and sweet and binding.

She pressed her mouth harder against his, wishing she could channel everything she felt through this connection between them. She didn't know *what* she felt, but she wanted him to feel it too—the way her chest had constricted with the fear of losing him, the need to be with him, to touch him, to kiss him. Need that had nothing to do with his magic and everything to do with *him*.

He leaned up, kissing her harder, and hit the end of the slack in his binding. She sank her fingers into his hair to hold him as she parted her lips. His tongue flirted hungrily with hers and heat shot through her.

She pressed closer to him, pushing him back into the tree. Their mouths moved together, erasing all thoughts from her head. With each touch of their lips, the connection between them fired stronger and hotter. She couldn't draw back. She couldn't stop, and her fatigue faded.

She'd only intended to kiss him, but she found her hand sliding down the side of his neck to his shirt collar. She followed it down, her fingers stroking his collarbones, until she found the top button of his shirt. With a twist, it came undone.

Keeping her mouth tight against his, she unbuttoned his shirt with growing urgency. When the last button came undone, she pushed the fabric aside and pressed both hands to his hot skin. He inhaled sharply.

She ran her fingers down his front, exploring the shape of him—the sculpted planes of his chest, the hollow between his collarbones, the shallow dip that ran down the center of his abs. Her hands curled around his powerful shoulders, muscles hardened by countless hours of archery. Tracing her fingers down his arms, she pushed his shirt off his shoulders until the sleeves caught on his elbows.

As his mouth moved against hers, she ran her hands over him again and again, memorizing every inch of skin she could reach. Shoulders, chest, abdomen. She slipped her thumbs under the waist of his pants, tracing the V-shaped dip of his hipbones. A soft growl rumbled from him and he caught her bottom lip in his teeth, a bite both gentle and dominating.

Breathless, she finally pulled back. He rose with her, trying to keep hold of her mouth, until he hit the end of the binding. Palms pressed to his chest, she blinked her asper into focus.

Golden light swirled around him, thick and intoxicating. But not *that* much. Not *that* bad. He still had control. Mostly.

And she needed more.

She leaned in again, bringing her mouth almost within his reach. He strained up with another growl, and she brushed her lips lightly across his mouth as she slid her hand down his arm to his elbow.

With a touch of magic, she snapped the binding spell.

He lunged off the tree, his arms closing around her as she fell backward. She landed on the folded robes and he came down on top of her, then his mouth was crushing hers.

She arched into him, unable to breathe as he kissed her deep and hard, his tongue stroking hers and sending liquid heat pulsing through her. She fumbled at the back of his head, pulled the blindfold off, and threw it aside.

He tore his mouth away from hers and pushed himself partway up. His eyes, black as night, slid across her face, drinking her in. She panted for air, a tiny thrill of fear running through her, but she didn't move as his gaze roved over her face then lazily slid down her body, taking in every detail.

His attention caught on her midriff and his hands curled over her hips. He lowered his head again—but not toward her face. He pushed her shirt up and his mouth pressed against her belly just above her jeans. She gasped.

He inched her shirt up, his mouth following, wet and hot. His fingers caressed her skin, sliding up her sides as his lips and tongue trailed up her middle. Her shirt bunched up under her breasts, then he pushed it up higher, over the swell of her chest to expose her bra.

Her hands found his hair and sank in, clutching his head as he dragged his teeth across the outside of her bra, teasing the sensitive skin underneath. His fingers slid over the fabric on one side while his mouth taunted her on the other side. All she could do was clutch him and remind herself to breathe as need spiraled deeper, the heat building in her center.

His thumb slipped under the cup of her bra and sharp pleasure shot through her. She arched into his hand with a moaning gasp.

With an answering growl, he pushed her bra up off her breasts, then his hand was cupping one and his mouth was on the other, his tongue teasing. She panted, tiny sounds escaping her as she squirmed under him, pleasure blazing through her and hot need gathering between her legs until she thought she might explode.

He shifted to support his weight with one elbow and his other hand slid down her stomach, over her jeans, then slipped between her legs. He pressed his fingers against her and she gasped wildly at the burst of pleasure.

Without warning, he rolled fully on top of her. She clamped her legs around his hips, pressing their bodies together. She could feel him, his need for her, and the barrier of clothing was unacceptable. He lowered his head, mouth brushing teasingly across hers. She grabbed his shoulders and pulled him down.

Or she intended to, but either she'd yanked too hard or his muscles were already on the verge of collapse, because his arms gave out and his entire weight came down on her. All the air whooshed out of her.

He swore and pushed off her. Rolling sideways, he flopped onto his back, breathing hard as he held stretched his arm across his chest.

She lurched up—and a wave of dizziness rolled over her. She steadied herself, wondering if she should blame Lyre's aphrodesia or the day spent in the blistering desert suns for her lightheadedness.

"Are you okay?" she asked Lyre breathlessly, pulling her shirt back down.

"Muscle cramp," he muttered as he gingerly rotated his arm and shoulder. "Damn it."

Desire still seared her, but her exhausted muscles were complaining loudly enough that she couldn't ignore them anymore. Wincing, she grabbed the nearest waterskin and passed it to him. "Drink. You need to rehydrate."

He sat up and drained the waterskin in a few gulps. Tossing it toward their pack, he refocused on her—and his black, hungry stare stole her breath. His hand found her cheek and slid into her hair, then he pulled her mouth back to his in a fierce, demanding kiss that made her head spin faster.

But the kiss was brief, and he withdrew, his fingers brushing across her jaw before he leaned back against the tree trunk.

He eyed her with irises that were lightening back to bronze. "Blindfolded *and* tied up. You're pretty kinky for a virgin."

"Lyre!" she gasped, mortified. She stood, intending to retreat out of sight, but he caught her arm and pulled her backward. She landed in his lap with a thump, too tired to control her fall.

He wrapped his arms around her, holding her prisoner, and she relaxed into his embrace. Sighing tiredly, she rested her cheek against his shoulder, head tucked under his chin. His shirt was still unbuttoned and she trailed her fingers down his chest.

Heat rolled through her, the fiery need to kiss him again. But after their hellish trek across the desert, she was too weary to move—and he had to be just as tired because she doubted anything less would have stopped him. Maybe it was a good thing their bodies weren't as willing as their minds.

She closed her eyes. Playing with fire didn't sound nearly as dangerous as toying with an incubus. What had she been thinking? Maybe the problem was she *hadn't* been thinking.

Or maybe the problem was she trusted him. She trusted he wouldn't hurt her, but he didn't trust himself, and if he was right and she was wrong, the next time she played with fire, they might both pay a terrible price.

SEVENTEEN

CONCENTRATION was proving to be an issue for Lyre lately. And by "lately," he meant the whole damn day. He'd resigned himself to the fact that, short of imminent death, the direction of his thoughts probably wasn't going to change for a while.

His gaze flicked to Clio, walking ahead of him, and his attention fixed on her swaying hips.

Who would have thought his innocent little nymph could be that naughty? In the grand scheme of kinks and fetishes, tying a guy up and blindfolding him was pretty vanilla, but for *Clio*? He sure as hell hadn't seen it coming. She just kept surprising him.

And now he couldn't stop thinking about anything else—her body, her mouth, her taste, her scent, the sounds she'd made as he touched and kissed her. And he couldn't stop thinking about all the things he wanted to do to her next.

Bloody hell. He needed a good long dunk in ice water.

If she had any idea how dangerous a line she was walking, maybe she wouldn't be tormenting him like this. At some point, when they had some privacy from Sabir, he needed to find a delicate way to explain why she should never do something like that again. His self-control was good—most of the time—but it wouldn't last long if she deliberately riled him up. He was lucky his exhausted body had quit on him before they found out how good his restraint really was.

Sighing, he forced his thoughts out of that arena. He had enough to worry about without pondering the dangers of taking Clio to bed. Luckily, he had many distractions—mainly, the fact that he was traveling through the *Overworld*. The idea was taking some getting used to, and despite their extra fun day yesterday, it still hadn't sunk in.

This morning, they had started early, with Sabir rushing them through breakfast while a heavy morning fog pooled in the gullies. Then it had been back onto the nonexistent trail through the rocky foothills. Lyre's legs had ached for the first hour as his muscles warmed up, but the early morning air had been cool and fresh. Without the desert's killer heat, it wasn't that bad.

The suns had burned off the mist by midmorning, revealing the summits rising on their left as they trekked parallel to the range. The mountains were a different shape than he was used to seeing—not the stabbing black peaks like those that surrounded Asphodel, but rolling mountains that sprawled lazily across the land, banded in orange, tan, and blue rock. Forests climbed some of the slopes in dense blankets of green and blue leaves.

Lots of blue in this world. Blue plants, blue rocks, blue hunks of crystal everywhere. It was kind of weird.

As the suns heated the earth, raising the temperature higher and higher, Sabir had led them farther north into the mountains. By the time the heat had grown unbearable again, they'd entered the cool shadows of a forest, where the rustle of leaves and the songs of wildlife had replaced the quiet of the foothills.

He hadn't seen any creatures, but he'd heard them—trills and chirps, buzzing and croaks, skittering claws on bark, and branches creaking as unseen beasts bounded through the canopy. Every few miles, a louder crash would erupt in the distance as something large trotted away, its feet thudding against the ground. Once, the thunder of large feathered wings had brought them to a halt, but they hadn't seen the source through the foliage.

They'd wound through the forested valleys for the entire afternoon. Game trails meandered drunkenly among huge, old-growth trees with gnarled trunks covered in soft, leafy vines. Sabir would follow the trails for a few hundred yards then push into the undergrowth again. Several times, he'd warned Clio and Lyre to avoid a certain plant—a tree with blue orbs hanging from its branches, a bush with orange-spotted leaves, a vine with tiny cobalt flowers.

Now, their guide was leading them up an uncomfortably steep ravine, and Lyre's legs were aching again. The suns hung low in the west, lighting the clouds in a spectacular canvas of red and orange. Shadows draped the ground.

Lyre's eyes narrowed as he watched Sabir climb over a boulder, then extend his hand to pull Clio up after him.

When their guide had returned last night, only minutes after Clio and Lyre had found themselves too exhausted to misbehave, Sabir hadn't seemed to suspect that anything was out of the ordinary. And that made Lyre suspicious. Lyre had been able to smell Clio's arousal, and his own scent had probably given him away. Unless Sabir had a stunted sense of smell, he *should* have guessed what he'd just missed.

So either Sabir had the senses of a human, which seemed unlikely, or he'd pretended not to notice—and done a hell of a good job considering his interest in Clio. A daemon interested in a female didn't just *pretend* not to notice another male making a move. That sort of polite bullshit was for humans. Daemons were a lot more direct—and more aggressive.

So if Sabir had been practicing his acting skills last night, he must have a reason to avoid confrontation. Problem was, Lyre couldn't guess what that reason was.

Ahead, the trees thinned and a rocky ridge jutted out from the forest. Lyre hastened his steps and caught up to Clio and Sabir as they clambered onto the rocks. Finally stopping, Sabir shaded his eyes with one hand as he looked toward the setting suns, then turned east.

"There it is," he said, pointing. "Irida."

Clio rose on her tiptoes as though the extra few inches would help her see better. "The Fallen Sisters! Lyre, come look!"

Lyre joined her and squinted at the horizon. Leaning closer, she pointed, aligning her arm with his line of sight as best she could, being ten inches shorter than him.

"The three slanted peaks, side by side, do you see?" she said eagerly, tracing them with her finger. "Those three mountains mark Irida's western border."

"Almost home," he murmured with a smile.

She beamed at him. "How much farther, Sabir?"

The daemon glanced at the sky, then scanned the surrounding terrain. The barren ridge zigzagged in an easterly direction before sinking out of sight beneath the forest canopy. Valleys, thick with trees, surrounded their location, and on their left, the mountains rose tall. On their right, beyond a steep ravine, the stark foothills sprawled. Barely visible on the southern horizon was a glimmer of sand.

"We'll reach the Iridian border late tomorrow," Sabir answered. "A mile farther, the ridge levels out. We'll camp there for the night."

"Right on the ridge?" Lyre frowned. "Won't we be exposed to the elements?"

Sabir shrugged and started forward. "There's a sheltered spot we can use. We can't go south because the ravine"—he gestured right—"is dangerously steep. And it'll soon be too dark to continue forward."

"What about this valley?" Lyre asked, tilting his head toward the forest on their left. "It doesn't look steep."

Sabir glanced at the valley. It sloped down from the ridge in a smooth, easy grade before leveling out. At the bottom, peeking through the trees, water glimmered amber and gold in the light of the setting suns.

"We don't want to go into that valley," Sabir said, quickening his pace. "We're in ryujin territory. There's a river down there."

"We're that close to ryujin waters?" Clio's voice was high with alarm. "I thought we were keeping to the edge of their territory."

Lyre twitched his shoulders. He didn't like the sound of these ryujin daemons.

"Would you rather tempt your fate with Ra patrols?" Sabir asked irritably. "The ryujin don't care if we come this way as long as we stay away from the water. I've walked this trail a hundred times and never had a problem."

He extended his stride, drawing ahead. Behind him, the suns dipped, the lower of the two vanishing below the horizon. Lyre glanced into the valley, then hurried to fall into step with Clio.

"Is Sabir underestimating the ryujin?" he asked in a low voice.

She bit her lower lip, and he had to look away before he started thinking about her mouth. This close, her scent filled his nose, distracting him.

"I'm not sure. Irida shares a border with Kyo Kawa, and my people are extremely wary of the ryujin." She grimaced. "They especially don't tolerate nymphs inside their borders."

"Why not?"

"There's a story that mothers like to tell their daughters." She pushed her ponytail off her shoulder. "A few centuries ago, the king of Irida was an ambitious man who wanted to expand our borders. Irida is hemmed in on one side by the uninhabitable Jewel Mountains, and on the other side it butts up against the Kyo Kawa and Ra borders. Expanding into griffin land wasn't an option, so that left Kyo Kawa."

She paused to climb over a boulder in their path, then continued. "Irida borders two other territories, but Kyo Kawa borders *five* kingdoms. The ryujin have spent thousands of years defending their land, but a couple hundred years ago, we nymphs had a cautiously cordial relationship with them. They permitted us to use certain trails through their territory, and a few individuals even engaged in trade.

"Well, this greedy nymph king figured the ryujin weren't that terrifying after all, and he wondered if he could take some of their territory for himself. But the thing is, ryujin cities are hidden. No one knows where they live. But then the king heard about a nobleman's daughter."

"A daughter?" Lyre repeated bemusedly.

"This girl claimed she had fallen in love with a ryujin and he'd taken her to his city. The greedy king forced the girl to reveal the location of the city, and then he paid a mercenary army to attack the ryujin and wipe them out so he could claim that part of their territory."

Clio's expression grew grimmer. "According to the story, the ryujin retaliated by slaughtering the invaders, forbidding all contact with other castes, and closing their borders for good."

Lyre winced. "What about the girl and her ryujin lover?"

"The girl died of grief and guilt. No one knows what happened to her lover." Clio shook her head. "My mother told me the story when I was younger—a much longer and more dramatic tale of love and tragedy. I'm sure she embellished the details, but that's the gist of it. I'm not certain how much is true, but they say that's why nymphs can never go into ryujin land."

"Hmm. I have to say, it's not a very patriotic story. I feel more sympathetic toward the ryujin."

"Yes, I always felt that way too. I asked my mother, and she said the story's message isn't about patriotism, or morality, or greedy kings and tragic wars."

"What's the moral of the story, then?"

"That people do stupid things when they're in love. The stupid ryujin showed the girl where he lived, and the stupid girl told her family about it to prove he loved her. That was my mother's interpretation, anyway."

Lyre snorted. "Aren't mothers supposed to encourage their daughters to find strapping young men to fall in love with and marry?"

"My mother taught me to not fall in love because I might turn into a complete dunce," she replied dryly. "But that lesson probably stems from her experience with—"

She abruptly broke off. He glanced at her, surprised to see her lips pressed together so tightly they'd paled. Seeing his questioning look, she flashed him a smile that he didn't buy at all.

"What lessons did your mother teach you?" she asked.

"None," he answered. "I never met my mother."

She stumbled and he caught her elbow. Straightening, she gave him an incredulous look that softened into sympathy. "I'm sorry. Did she pass away?"

He shrugged. "No idea."

Her lips quirked in a frown as she struggled with what to ask. "Don't you have a younger brother? Is he your half-brother, then?"

"Two younger brothers—Dulcet and Viol—but, again, I have no idea. I don't know who their mothers are." He arched an eyebrow at her befuddled look. "There are no succubi in Asphodel. Incubi and succubi don't get along, remember?"

"But then how do you … how did your father …"

He sighed, wishing he could go back in time and not introduce this topic. She didn't need to know the ugly truth about incubi and succubi's reproductive strategies. "Let's just say that being a single parent is the universal preference for incubi and succubi both."

Her frown deepened and he changed the topic. "Are there any other Overworld castes we need to worry about besides ryujin?"

She gave him a hard look, not fooled by his evasion. As the ridge broadened to a less precarious width, she linked her arm through his. The once-shallow valley beside the ridge had grown so steep that it resembled a cliff, and a mix of loose gravel and sparse shrubs clung to the precarious slope down to the wide river. The water was closer now, but the slope was far too steep to climb.

"Well," Clio mused, "ryujin are powerful, though no one is sure *how* powerful. Enough to protect their territory. But they keep to themselves, so when Overworlders talk about the dangerous daemons of our world, the ryujin don't normally come up."

"Who does come up?"

"Ra griffins." She ticked them off on her fingers. "The Valkyrs. And the jinns."

He'd heard of all three, but he didn't know much beyond the names. "That's it?"

"Around here, yes." Her eyes widened in emphasis. "Three is difficult enough. Griffins win by numbers alone. They have the largest territory and control a large portion of the continent either directly or through trade deals and other arrangements. The Valkyrs hold most of the western coast, and they're always clashing with the Ras over trade ports and territory lines." She smiled wryly. "The ryujin share their western border with the Valkyrs too. They really can't catch a break."

"Lucky them." He took a swig from his waterskin, lamenting that it was nearly empty. "What about the jinns? Is that a caste or a ruling family?"

"A caste. Jinns don't have a single ruling family but are broken into many smaller clans. They don't have a territory either. They're nomadic, traveling back and forth across the continents for their entire lives."

He considered that revelation. "Small, nomadic clans would make them much weaker than a unified nation like the griffins."

"Politically, yes, but no one messes with jinns. No one wants to tick them off."

"Oh?"

"You know how everyone in the Underworld gets that nervous look whenever draconians come up in conversation?"

"Yeah."

"Well, that's how Overworlders talk about jinns. They're really dangerous." She lowered her voice as though a jinn might be eavesdropping on her every word. "They're the assassins of our world. Their caste ability is terrifying."

Her eyes sparkled; she was having fun telling tales about the scary daemons of her world.

"What's their caste ability?" he asked, amused but a little wary of the answer.

"They call it 'shadow-step' and—"

"How does this look?" Sabir called, cutting through Clio's murmur.

Fifty feet ahead, a flat sheet of rock jutted from the ridge, forming a rough wall. Standing in the shelter it created, Sabir waited for them. Lyre grimaced. The rocky formation would block some of the chilly breeze, but it would still be a rough night.

As the last of the sunlight vanished below the mountainous horizon, they quickly set up camp and Lyre sat gratefully on his folded white wrap from their desert travels, using it as a cushion. Clio sat cross-legged on hers, fretfully glancing north where the river glinted under the light of the waxing planet, partially obscured by thick clouds.

Sabir ventured farther along the ridge and returned a few minutes later with an armload of tree branches. "What do you say to a fire and hot tea?"

Clio's face brightened. "That would be lovely."

Lyre said nothing, withholding his opinion that building a fire on an exposed ridge was a bad idea. The light would be visible for miles around. But it was that or freeze, he supposed.

Sabir made quick work of stacking the branches and lighting them with a spark of magic. As he pulled a metal pot from his pack and poured the contents of his waterskin into it, he asked Clio what kind of tea she liked. Their comparison of teas expanded into a detailed analysis of local botanical something-or-others and Lyre tuned them out. His day had been way too long for that kind of plant talk.

He was nodding off, the fire warm and the quiet pops of the burning wood familiar and soothing, when Sabir passed him a metal cup of steaming tea. He wrapped his hands around the warmth and inhaled the bittersweet smell.

Clio curled her hands around her own cup, still happily describing her favorite garden herbs with adorable animation. Lyre took a sip, not particularly impressed by the sweet berry flavor with a bitter undertone, and watched Sabir carefully scan the ravine on one side and the river valley on the other. Night had fallen, but the planet's silvery light leaking through the clouds held the darkness at bay.

As Sabir dropped dried vegetables in the leftover hot water, Lyre drank more tea. The warmth was pleasant and relaxing. His head nodded forward again and he let his eyes close, listening to Clio's voice rise and fall without really hearing it.

"What kind of tea is this?"

He started, jarred by Clio's razor-sharp tone. She held her full cup of tea beneath her nose, inhaling the steam. Her stare was fixed on Sabir, her back rigid and mouth pressed into a thin line.

Sabir blinked at her, his mouth quirking down. "It's greenberry leaf. Does it taste bad? I don't think it could have gone off already. I dried the leaves myself only a few weeks ago."

"It smells wrong," she said, hostility radiating off her. If she were a cat, her hackles would have been standing on end.

Lyre looked down at his near-empty cup. Well, fuck. "Did you poison it?"

Despite his calm tone, Clio jerked like he'd slapped her. Her face paled.

Sabir smiled as though Lyre had made a funny joke. "Of course not. Moldy greenberry won't hurt you. I'll just make something else."

"Did *he* drink any tea?" Lyre asked Clio.

Sabir held out his half-empty cup. Clio snatched it and lifted it to her nose. "*Yours* doesn't smell bitter. Why is mine bitter? Greenberry is sweet."

"Bad leaves?"

Lyre sighed. "What did you put in the tea?"

Sabir leaned back, propping himself up on one arm. "Hauling your pathetic ass this far only to poison you would be a complete waste of effort."

A fair point. Lyre fixed a cold, calm stare on the daemon. "But you did put *something* in the tea."

Sabir smirked.

"What did you do?" Clio demanded, clutching her cup as though it held the key to life or death. "Tell us!"

"Tell you what, exactly?" Sabir drawled, scanning the surrounding darkness. "I *could* explain all the reasons you two are the stupidest fools I've ever encountered, but ..." He pushed to his feet. "But it doesn't matter anymore."

Lyre shot up, ready to fire a rapid cast into Sabir's face—except when he called on his magic, nothing happened. A wave of sickening dizziness rolled over him when his power failed to manifest as commanded. He staggered sideways, the world spinning. In his wavering vision, Clio launched off the ground, her hands coming up defensively.

Sabir made a sharp waving motion, and Lyre expected the spell to strike him down. Instead, the daemon's blast hit the campfire, knocking over the pot, extinguishing the flames, and scattering the glowing coals across the ridge. The darkness deepened.

A spell struck Lyre in the back. He hit the ground on his knees, arms bound against his sides.

"Lyre!"

As Clio sprang toward him, the shadows behind her bubbled upward like a thick, inky soup. One moment, she was lunging toward him. The next, a daemon had materialized out of the darkness like a ghost. He grabbed her arm and hauled her back, then casually pressed the shining blade of a dagger against her throat.

"You're late," Sabir said irritably.

A shadow moved beside Lyre and a second unfamiliar daemon stopped beside him. He grabbed Lyre by the hair and forced his head back. Lyre bared his teeth, glaring at the new brown-skinned daemon as he tried again to summon his magic and was met with more whirling dizziness.

"Is this him?" his assailant inquired.

"Yes," Sabir answered as he stuffed his supplies back into his pack. "We should dose him with more Shade Rune before we get off the ridge."

"What about this one?" the other daemon asked, pulling on Clio's hair and forcing her onto her tiptoes. She whimpered and tried to shrink away from the dagger at her throat.

"The nymph slut? Who cares." Sabir's dark eyes flicked to Lyre. "It's the spell weaver I want."

Lyre snarled softly. That conniving bastard.

Sabir smiled with smug satisfaction, and without looking away from Lyre, he waved a hand carelessly at Clio.

"Kill her."

EIGHTEEN

"KILL HER."

Sabir's emotionless command fired a bolt of panic straight into Clio's heart. Her body tensed so much it hurt, but with a knife to her throat, she couldn't move.

Lyre lunged up but the daemon beside him shoved him back onto his knees. Sabir smirked at the incubus, then glanced at her captor.

"What are you waiting for?"

"You sure?" her captor asked. "Seems like a waste."

"She's worthless. Just kill her. Unless you want me to do it?"

Her captor grunted, his arm around her shoulders tightening in preparation to slit her throat.

"Wait!" she cried. "You heard about the bounty, didn't you? Are you planning to turn Lyre over to Hades?"

Sabir must have known Lyre was a spell weaver from the start; otherwise, he wouldn't have had time to arrange this ambush. Her gaze flashed to Lyre. Shade Rune—a drug that numbed a daemon to their magic, making it impossible to cast spells. That was the bitter substance she'd smelled in their tea.

"You know, Clio, I sort of liked you when we first met." Sabir pulled a long shining dagger from somewhere under his clothes. "If you'd only wanted me to take you to Irida—just you—I would have done it."

"If the bounty is what you're after," she pressed desperately, "then turn me and Lyre over to the king of Irida instead."

Sabir stepped toward her, a disparaging smile on his lips. "Why would I do that?"

"King Rouvin will pay you double the bounty."

He paused, flicking a glance at his companions before refocusing on her. "He might buy the spell weaver, but why would the Iridian king pay for *your* life?"

"Because I ... I'm his daughter."

Silence.

Sabir threw his head back in a harsh laugh. "Do you think I'm an idiot? The Nereid princess is, what, nine years old? Ten?"

"Petrina is eleven, actually," Clio said, struggling to keep her tone even. "She and Bastian are my half-siblings. I'm the king's daughter, but not the queen's."

"Oh, a bastard princess, then." He stepped closer and pressed the point of his dagger under her chin. "Why should I believe you, Clio?"

She held still, resisting the urge to lean away from the deadly point. "Because it's true. The whole reason I'm with a spell weaver is because my father and brother sent me to Asphodel to spy on Chrysalis. When Lyre came back with me, Hades put a bounty out for our capture."

Sabir's gaze flicked back and forth between her eyes as though reading the truth in each one. He slowly stepped back. "Interesting. But then why do you need a guide to your own homeland?"

"My escort was killed in Asphodel and I've never traveled the ley lines on my own."

Rocking back on his heels, Sabir nonchalantly tapped his dagger against his cheek. "Interesting."

"King Rouvin will pay double the bounty for my safe return—and Lyre's." She looked into Sabir's brown eyes and wondered why she'd never noticed their soulless emptiness before. "You don't want to deal with Hades, do you?"

Sabir smirked. "I never intended to deal with Hades for their pitiful bounty. A spell weaver like him is worth far more on the auction block."

"A-auction block?" she stammered.

Sabir sheathed his dagger. "And you, if you really are a Nereid, will be worth almost as much. Mimics are rare."

"B-but the king—"

"He'd probably love for his illegitimate child to disappear forever, and either way, he won't pay as much as I can make off the two of you." Sabir gestured at his companions. "Bind her and put her over there with the incubus. I want to dose them before we move on."

The daemon holding her lowered his dagger, grabbed her arms, and bound them behind her back with magic. Hauling her by the elbow, he shoved her onto her knees beside Lyre, then joined Sabir as he dug around in his pack for more Shade Rune.

She couldn't let Sabir drug her, but what could she do? She couldn't take on all three of them; she didn't even know what caste they were. Blinking her asper into focus, she looked at the second daemon. Like Sabir, he had a mysterious sparkly silver aura.

She flexed her arms and glanced anxiously at Lyre. His dark eyes turned to her, his expression taut. If he was upset to learn about her lineage, he wasn't showing it. They had more pressing matters to worry about. With a daemon standing right behind them, she couldn't even whisper to Lyre. Fixing an intense stare on him, she mouthed two words.

His brow furrowed in confusion.

"Distract them," she mouthed silently, exaggerating the shape of the words.

Understanding flashed across his face and he turned to Sabir and his pal, who was measuring water into a cup. Sabir held a small vial of dark powder.

"So, Sabir," Lyre began mockingly, "are all jinns vile slave traders, or just you?"

Clio, waiting for the others to focus on Lyre, started in surprise. A jinn? Sabir? Had Lyre figured out something she hadn't, or was he guessing?

"Are you an Overworld caste expert now?" Sabir asked with a snort. He shook powder into the cup of water.

"Not an expert," Lyre shot back. "And, just so you know, you're not making a great impression on behalf of your caste."

Sabir corked his vial. "Do you think knowing my caste will help you?"

"Who knows."

"You have no idea what we can do, do you?" Sabir weighed the cup of drugged water in his hand. "Why don't I demonstrate?"

Sabir's silver aura sparked violently. Before Clio's eyes, his body melted into dense, inky darkness. The black shape dispersed like smoke in the wind, disappearing entirely from her senses.

No, not smoke. Shadows. The jinn caste ability: shadow-step.

She frantically scanned the ridge but even his aura had vanished. Then light sparked in her peripheral vision and a shape bubbled out of the darkness behind Lyre. Sabir's body solidified as the shadows fell away.

Holy shit, Sabir *was* a jinn. Three jinns had captured them. Clamping down on her rising panic, she focused on the binding around her wrists.

Sabir grabbed Lyre by the hair and bent his head back, and the other jinn forced his mouth open. Lyre snarled, jerking away, but the daemons were too strong. Sabir poured the drugged water into his mouth, spilling it over his face.

"Swallow or drown, incubus," Sabir told him.

Clio contorted to see her wrists and bent her fingers painfully until she could touch a knot of glowing silver. A spark of her magic snapped the binding spell and she launched at Lyre and the jinns.

She crashed into Lyre, wrenching him out of the jinns' grasp. Their auras sparked and they melted into shadows. Lyre hit the ground on his side and spat out the tainted water. She reached for his binding, but silver sparks flashed beside her. Out of instinct more than conscious thought, she sprang away.

Sabir reformed from the shadows, grabbing for the empty space where she'd been.

She leaped away as the second jinn materialized from the darkness. Bolting ten paces down the ridge, she cast a light spell. Luminescence blazed across the rocky terrain, illuminating the ground around her.

The three jinns backed away from the light. Shadow-step. The ability to take a shadow form and flow through the darkness around them. While shadow-stepping, they were invulnerable to attack. It was the ultimate defense, and all they needed was a single shadow in which to hide.

Sabir smiled and silver light glowed over his fingers. "What's the plan now, Clio?"

She held her spell high above her head, ensuring no shadows touched hers. The cast forming in Sabir's hand was a blast that would take out her light—and then all three would be on her.

She couldn't take them all. She wasn't sure she could fight even one, not when they had an unassailable defense ability, and Lyre was drugged, his magic inaccessible. With only a second to decide, she looked across the ridge, then down the steep slope to the river glinting under the planet's light.

A faint blue glow shimmered in the water.

Sabir flung his cast. She dove out of the way as the magic javelin struck her light and shattered it. Darkness plunged back over the ridge and the three jinns melted into it.

She shot to her feet and froze, her heart hammering in her ears. She couldn't see them. Where were they? Where had they gone?

A flicker behind her. She jumped forward, barely clearing the jinn's reach. Whirling around, she raised her hands to cast but the moment after the jinn had missed her, he melted away again. She stumbled back a step. While the jinns were shadow-stepping, even her asper couldn't discern them. But when they went in and out of their shadow form, *that* she could see. And with that moment of warning, maybe she could survive—if she was fast enough.

Baring her teeth, she cast away her glamour.

Tingles rushed over her skin and renewed strength filled her limbs. Her clothes disappeared, replaced by simple white shorts and a chest wrap. She rose onto the balls of her feet, her bare toes digging into the gritty rock, then darted toward Lyre.

Sparks flickered in her path, and a jinn coalesced from the shadows, a cast glowing in his hands—but she was already flinging a raw burst of power at his chest. He disappeared again.

Sparks flashed behind her.

Sabir hooked an arm around her neck and pulled her off her feet. He jammed his hand against her side, magic burning against her skin as he started to cast. She rammed her elbow into his stomach and he grunted, his spell faltering. Her fingers danced in a swift cast and the spell ignited: crackling electricity that ran over her body. Sabir recoiled, then melted away.

Whirling on her toes, she sprang in a different direction. Sparks erupted again and she dove into a roll, evading the materializing jinn to buy herself time to finish two casts.

The jinn disappeared and she slid to a stop, waiting. One heartbeat. Two. Three.

Sparks kindled—two sets on either side of her—and she hurled both spells before the shadows had completely solidified. Her casts hit Sabir and the other jinn, and both crashed to the rocks with shocked yelps.

Green light blazed over her hands again. She had only a moment to strike with lethal force before—

A silvery flicker behind her and she threw herself forward. A gleaming blade whipped through the spot where she'd been. The third jinn held a long dagger in each hand. He wasn't trying to capture her anymore. He was trying to kill her.

Throwing an uncontrolled burst of power in his direction, she bolted for Lyre. The jinn disappeared—and Sabir and the other one had melted into nothing too. It was just her and Lyre on the ridge, trapped by the rock wall on one side and the dangerously steep slope on the other side. The jinns were invisible and invincible, and she'd be lucky to hit them a second time now that they were expecting it.

With no better options, she grabbed Lyre's arm and broke the binding on his wrists. Pulling him with her, she took two running steps and leaped off the ridge into the steep valley.

She and Lyre hit the slope feet first and slid on the scree. They careened downward as though riding a rocky slide. The water rushed up to meet them and she scrabbled desperately for purchase but there was no way to slow down.

They plunged into the cold shallows and hit the sandy bottom, jarring to a painful stop. Leaping to her feet in the waist-deep water, she clutched Lyre's arm as her gaze flashed across the river, sprawling fifty feet wide with its serene surface reflecting the planet's light.

"Uh," Lyre whispered breathlessly. "Isn't water bad?"

She didn't answer as her stare stopped forty yards upstream where blue light glimmered beneath the surface. The spot of light glided into motion.

With silver sparkles, a jinn appeared on the dark bank, smirking. "And what are you planning to do now, little nymph?"

She stood in the water, breathing hard. Her hands were underwater, obscured from view, and she curled her fingers, prepping two casts. The light reflecting off the river was enough to prevent the jinn from shadow-stepping any closer to her, but the safety the water offered was an illusion.

Upstream, the surface rippled as something passed beneath it, drawing closer.

She pulled her fist out of the water and flung her first cast into the air. The jinn started to melt away, but her spell erupted into a blinding flare that banished the shadows. He solidified with a garbled curse, and she unleashed her second cast.

A green band of power whipped out from her hand. It snapped around his waist and she yanked her end of the spell. With a crackling burst, he was flung into the air. He soared fifteen feet before crashing into the river with a splash—landing halfway between her and the underwater blue aura.

The jinn lurched to his feet and spat out a mouthful of water. "Damn nymph!"

Sparks flickered on the shore as the other two jinns arrived, but Clio ignored them. She grabbed Lyre's arm and yanked him forward. "Swim, Lyre! Across the river!"

His eyes widened but he obeyed, diving forward into a swift breaststroke. She plunged after him.

Behind them, Sabir's urgent shout rang out, his voice echoing off the water. "Get out of the river, you fool!"

The jinn in the water started to respond, then broke off. A moment of quiet.

The daemon screamed. Water exploded upward and Clio twisted to look back as a frothing wave enveloped the jinn. He vanished under the surface and bubbles erupted—red bubbles. A cloud of bloody water expanded from the spot, drifting downstream.

Fear clamped around her chest. She swam harder, glancing back with each stroke.

Sabir shouted furiously, then her light spell vanished in a burst as he shot it out of the sky. Darkness plunged over the valley again, broken only by the reflection on the water that the jinns couldn't cross.

But it wasn't the jinns that frightened her now.

The glowing aura under the water slid into motion—speeding toward her and Lyre. She swam as fast as she could, the water dragging at her limbs. She felt like she was barely moving. Lyre cut through the water ahead of her, swimming at an angle to the shore. It was too far. The blue aura was closing in, swift and deadly.

Then she saw it—the trunk of a gargantuan tree that had fallen into the river, its curved side protruding from the surface. That's where Lyre was heading: a natural bridge that extended almost halfway across the river.

They could reach it. They had to.

The blue aura swept in behind them. Lyre reached the colossal log and lunged out of the water. Right behind him, she grabbed the rough bark and hauled herself up. The moment she was on her feet, she whipped around with her hands raised.

The glowing light shot toward the log, then a splashing wave erupted. A huge creature burst from the water, jaws gaping wide.

She flung a wild blast of power into its face. Most of the magic rolled off its scales, but it jerked back and aborted its charge. It clung to the side of the log, long claws hooked into the bark a few feet from Clio and Lyre.

Its scales gleamed blue and green in the moonlight, its body long and sinuous with a dorsal fin running the full length of its back. Its reptilian head was small and elegant, with long appendages like a catfish's whiskers protruding from its snout and the top of its head. Three teardrop scales in the shape of a triangle glowed on its wide forehead.

It was a dragon. A silver dragon.

And it was about to kill them.

NINETEEN

LYRE GRABBED the back of Clio's top and hauled her out of the way as the dragon lunged at them. Its huge jaws snapped shut, missing her by inches. He shoved her in front of him, and she landed on her feet already running. He sprinted after her.

The dragon plunged back into the water, vanishing beneath the surface, but he didn't trust its retreat. Clio flew down the fallen tree trunk ahead of him, her feet barely touching the bark. Her hair streamed behind her, blond that shone and shimmered like moonlight on water, and faint green markings on her ivory skin trailed up and down her arms and legs.

If they survived the next five minutes, he would love to get a better look at her daemon form.

They raced down the tree and leaped into calf-deep water. Splashing through the shallows, they ran out onto the wide gravel bank. Beyond it, a forest of towering trees stood like a dark wall.

Breathing hard, Clio stumbled to a stop and turned. Lyre glanced back, his heart hammering and his head spinning from the damn drugged tea. On the far bank, Sabir and the other jinn stood well back from the river's edge. With the reflective surface of the water in their path, the jinns couldn't shadow-step across the river. One problem solved.

A faint splash.

In a wild spray, the silver dragon charged out of the river. Lyre backpedaled. Without magic, he was useless.

Clio sprang in front of him and flung a spell at the beast's face. It ducked its head. The magic hit its shimmering silver scales and sloughed right off.

Lyre tackled her around the middle, dragging her to the ground as the beast snapped its jaws shut where her head had been. The creature skidded to a stop, heavy finned tail whipping past and almost catching Lyre in the chest. It was right on top of them, deadly talons sinking into the gravel inches from their flesh.

Clio dove one way and Lyre rolled the other. As he lunged up, he shed his glamour. Strength flowed through him, washing away some of the dizziness. He still couldn't grasp or use his magic, but at least he wasn't as slow and weak.

The dragon whirled on Clio and snapped its huge jaws again. She danced back, grace and agility in every movement. As Lyre grabbed his bow off his shoulder and pulled an arrow, Clio sprang straight at the dragon's face. She grabbed its muzzle and used it to launch herself over its head. She landed on its shoulders, jumped off it, and dropped beside Lyre.

He barely managed not to gape. Since when was his clumsy, accident-prone nymph so nimble?

Flipping an arrow onto his bow, he raised it and fired. The bolt hit the dragon in the chest and shattered. Bloody hell. He needed his weaves but he couldn't use his magic to activate them.

The dragon lunged at him and Clio. She flung a binding at the beast that tangled its front legs. It stumbled, and Lyre used the extra moment to grab a dagger from the sheath on his thigh. He slashed at the beast's face.

The blade hit the scales of its cheek and skidded across them—right over the creature's eye.

Blood sprayed and the dragon lurched backward with a high-pitched whine. It stumbled again, front legs still bound. Lyre backed up, Clio beside him, and grabbed another arrow from his quiver—this one woven with his best armor-piercing weave. As he laid it on his bow, Clio touched the arrow and the weave activated.

He drew the string back and loosed the bolt.

It hit the dragon in the chest and sank in deep. Golden light flashed. The spell exploded in a spray of blood and the dragon screamed as it collapsed onto its belly. Lyre stumbled backward, catching his breath.

The light dimmed. He looked up as heavy clouds rolled across the planet's face. The light reflecting off the river disappeared and the water went dark.

He jerked around to face the opposite shore, but the two jinns had already disappeared. He scanned the black water, his stomach clenching. They were coming.

Realizing it too, Clio cupped her hands, preparing another extra-bright light spell. Lyre drew a new arrow and raised his bow, waiting for a sign of where they might appear.

Clio sprang backward. Sabir materialized out of her shadow, his dagger flashing. It caught her forearm, cutting up the underside and across her wrist. Her half-formed light spell burst apart and the concussion slammed into Lyre, throwing him backward. Clio crashed to the ground nearby.

Jolting half upright, Lyre fired his arrow. Sabir melted into nothing, then reappeared a step away with his hand extended toward Clio, magic flashing. With no time to grab another arrow, Lyre desperately called on his own magic but only sick dizziness answered.

A scream erupted, rising shrilly.

The other jinn had shadow-stepped onto the riverbank as well, but he hadn't joined the fight. He was alone on a stretch of gravel, on his knees and clutching his head. He didn't appear injured, but he shrieked as though his head were being crushed in a vise, his voice rising even higher until it cracked.

His agonized cry cut off but he didn't move, hands fisted in his hair and eyes squeezed shut. In the silence that followed, Lyre's entire body went cold. It took him a moment to realize why.

The slosh of water lapping at the bank had vanished. The river had gone utterly silent. Had he gone deaf? The clouds shifted and silvery light streamed down, illuminating the river once more—and Lyre knew he hadn't lost his hearing.

The water had gone as calm and still as glass. It reflected the sky like a perfect mirror, not a single ripple disturbing its surface.

And standing in the shallows of the unnaturally still river was a daemon.

The planet's light shimmered on the jewel-like scales that covered most of his body in a rainbow of blues, greens, and purples, and deep green hair fell to his waist. Not a splash or ripple of water broke the silence as the daemon paced unhurriedly to the shore. His tail, ending in broad double fins, lifted from the water, breaking his contact with the river, and the surface erupted in ripples as the current returned all at once.

Lyre didn't move. Couldn't move. What kind of power was this? What kind of daemon could control a river's current?

The daemon approached the immobilized jinn, still on his knees and clutching his head. Stopping in front of his victim, the daemon touched the jinn's forehead. Blue light flickered under his fingertips. The jinn arched in silent agony, then collapsed backward.

Dead. Dead before he hit the ground.

Sabir gasped, a sound of pain and disbelief. Clutching his dagger, the blade coated in Clio's blood, he melted into shadow.

The new daemon turned. His dark eyes slid across Lyre and Clio, and in the center of his forehead, three teardrop scales glowed, identical to the ones on the silver dragon.

"Ryujin," Clio whispered hoarsely.

The daemon raised his hand, the motion smooth and graceful. Blue light danced over his fingers, their clawed tips shining, and the scales on his forehead brightened ominously.

He whirled, swift and deadly, and thrust his glowing claws at nothing.

Except in the same moment that the ryujin struck, Sabir appeared in his path. Those gleaming claws hooked into the jinn's neck and, casual as that, the ryujin ripped his throat out.

Sabir staggered back a step, his dagger weaving drunkenly as though he couldn't understand what had happened. Lyre couldn't understand it either. How had the ryujin known where Sabir would appear?

The jinn crumpled to the ground and the ryujin pivoted again to face Lyre and Clio.

Still on his knees, Lyre grabbed an arrow from his quiver. As he slapped it into place, Clio reached to activate the spell, her injured arm pressed to her chest.

The ryujin swept both arms wide as though inviting the embrace of an invisible stranger.

Magic exploded out of him. The wave of fiery blue light hurtled across the riverbank. Clio lunged in front of Lyre and cast a green bubble shield over them. The blast, as powerful as anything Ash had unleashed on him, slammed into the shield, ripped it apart, and hit them, its force barely diminished.

The river and sky spun in his vision and he tumbled across the rocks, almost losing hold of his bow. Pain ricocheted through his limbs and his skull ached sickeningly. Scarcely able to move, he pushed onto his hands and knees and looked up. Clio was sprawled awkwardly a few feet away, unmoving, blood puddling under her injured arm.

Two dozen yards away, the ryujin glided toward them, finned tail swishing behind him and odd, narrow appendages flaring out from its base. Lyre reached for his quiver but lost his balance and half fell.

The ryujin was coming. He had to do something. He had to fight the daemon. Somehow, he had to find a way. Beside him, Clio was unconscious and bleeding. He straightened and grabbed an arrow. His vision blurred and doubled, but he got the arrow in place by feel alone. With unsteady hands, he raised the bow.

The ryujin stopped. Their eyes met, and Lyre clenched his jaw as he drew the string back, knowing the arrow was as good as useless without magic to aid it.

A quiet whimper.

The ryujin's head snapped toward the sound. The silver dragon Lyre had shot groaned again, its chest heaving for air.

Without so much as a glance at Lyre, the ryujin abandoned his course and sped to the dragon. Sinking to his knees, he pressed his hands to the beast's chest, a blue glow lighting under his palms.

Lyre hesitated, bow drawn and arrow ready. The ryujin didn't look up, his attention focused on the dragon. He was attempting to heal such a terrible wound? There was no way he could save the creature.

But if he intended to try, he would be busy for at least a few minutes.

Lyre stuffed the arrow back in his quiver, slung the bow over his shoulder, and heaved Clio's limp form into his arms. Lurching to his feet, he stumbled toward the dark wall of trees.

Just before plunging into the forest shadows, he glanced back. The ryujin met his stare with strange eyes, solid black with no sclera or pupils, colder than the depths of an ocean. Then the daemon returned his attention to the dying dragon.

Lyre fled into the trees, knowing that once the dragon died under his hands, the ryujin would come for them again—even hungrier for their blood.

HE SHOVED through the underbrush as fast as he could manage. Once he'd put a few hundred yards between him and the ryujin, he stopped, breathing hard, and laid Clio on the mossy ground. Blood smeared her arm and had splattered all over her pale skin.

He checked the wound, furious that he couldn't access his magic to stop the bleeding. With no better options, he stripped off his shirt and undershirt, then shredded the latter and tightly bound her arm. After redressing and strapping on his bow and quiver again, he picked her up, threw her over his shoulder, and marched on, hoping she wouldn't bleed out before he regained his magic. There was nothing else he could do.

He had no idea where he was going and he couldn't cast a light. All he could do was hope he was heading east. The undergrowth was thick and tangled, full of strange plants and unfamiliar trees. He tried not to touch anything; throughout the previous day, Sabir and Clio had warned him about poisonous plant life. A muted symphony of chirping, buzzing, and croaking from insects and amphibians filled the darkness.

The Overworld was beautiful, he couldn't deny that. But it seemed like the more beautiful something was, the deadlier it was as well.

Like those silver dragons. And the ryujin, with jeweled scales covering half his body. Beautiful but deadly. Clio hadn't been sure how powerful the ryujin really were, but having recently fought a draconian, Lyre was confident the ryujin rivaled the most powerful Underworld caste.

Clio eventually stirred awake. They exchanged a few terse words before continuing. The ryujin knew trespassers had entered their territory. There was no stopping, no turning back. He and Clio had to keep going.

The long night stretched on, the planet above waxing until its full round face glared down at the land. The foothills stretched endlessly, and with no guide and only a general direction to travel in, he and Clio struggled to find passable terrain.

Lyre's ability to use magic reawakened after a few hours, and he and Clio took their first real break so he could heal her arm. His healing skills were rudimentary at best and he knew he'd done a poor job, nothing like the perfect healing she'd performed on him. Her arm would scar, but otherwise, there would be no lasting damage.

They traveled onward. The foothills grew rockier and more impassable, forcing Lyre and Clio to detour back into ryujin territory. They trekked through a dark forest with tangled roots carpeting the ground and moss coating every surface, the sweet smell of rotting vegetation clogging their noses.

Their path carried them higher until they came out of the trees onto a ridge, not unlike the one where they'd fought the jinn. On one side was the valley they'd crossed, and on the other, the rocky terrain dropped in a sheer cliff. Across the gorge, a waterfall plunged into a narrow river where misty clouds shimmered faintly.

From the high vantage point, Lyre could see farther into the Kyo Kawa mountains than he'd yet been able to. He'd thought the Overworld was beautiful before—but he'd had no idea.

Miles of sweeping valley spread before them, and the dark forests were alight. Unidentifiable orbs shone softly, scattered through the trees like azure stars, and rising above the trees, thousands of lights in green, blue, pink, and purple danced and swirled.

"What …" he mumbled, awed but confused.

"Bell moths," Clio answered, her voice hoarse with fatigue. "And the larger lights are wellata pods—the fruit of a vine. Incandescent at night."

"It's beautiful."

She smiled tiredly, her pale skin radiant under the moonlight. He'd shifted back to his human glamour in case the ryujin could follow his unfamiliar Underworld magic, but she'd remained in her nymph form. Speaking of beautiful sights in this world …

"Irida is like that too. I think you'll—" She broke off, her lips pressed tightly together as she stared at the river below them. "I can see blue auras in the water. Either dragons or ryujin. They might be tracking us."

"Will they follow us into Irida?"

"I don't think so."

"Then we'll stay away from the water and keep going."

She closed her eyes, gathering her strength—her shoulders straightening, chin lifting, hands curling into fists. He did the same, summoning the stamina and endurance he would need to make it out of this territory. Fear would have to keep him going.

The ryujin frightened him—scared him on a deeper, more visceral level than Ash's manufactured terror ever could. The way the ryujin had mysteriously brought the jinn to his knees. The way the ryujin had calmly and callously murdered the daemon, and had just as calmly and easily ripped out Sabir's throat. The way the ryujin had turned an entire river to still, silent glass.

Pushing those thoughts out of his head, he focused on their journey through valleys and up ridges, back down into valleys, always avoiding rivers where ryujin might be lurking. The rocky ground evolved into soft turf so gradually that Lyre missed the moment of transition, and now he found himself walking through a magical Overworld forest.

Softly glowing azure pods hung from tree branches, long tendrils dangling from the bases like pale streamers. The radiant moss that covered every surface cast an enchanting but eerie turquoise hue over the woods. Insects flitted and darted, danced and swirled, their wings or bodies glowing or flashing, some as large as his outspread hand or even bigger. Their wings whirred quietly, filling the still air with a quiet hum, and delicate chirps that could have been birds or frogs echoed nearby.

The trees had reached monstrous proportions and their heavy roots coiled across the ground in waves and arches so large that he and Clio walked beneath them as often as they walked over them. Flowers bloomed from low plants and climbing vines, some aglow with bright markings or with thick bodies that held a luminous liquid. The equally vibrant insects fluttered among them in a feeding ecstasy.

Lyre walked a step behind Clio, staring all around. In the canopy high above, a pair of large green eyes blinked at him from a branch, then the small, furry creature hopped into the foliage and disappeared. Movement from the corner of his eye had him turning toward a fat tree root where a centipede-like insect, as long as his arm and almost as thick, scurried across the bark with countless legs that flickered with neon yellow light.

Clio stopped and Lyre almost walked into her back. His gaze flashed around in alarm.

"Look," she said breathlessly, pointing. "We made it."

In the distance, almost obscured by the foliage, a double line of green lights stretched into the trees. Lyre squinted, trying to figure out what the lights were.

Before he could ask, she rushed forward with renewed energy, weaving among tree roots and tall plant stalks with iridescent violet poofs on their tops. Lyre hurried after her, then slowed to a stop, letting her go on without him.

Ahead were two simple wooden posts topped with pieces of rough crystal that glowed electric green with a spell. The posts marked the beginning of a wooden boardwalk that wound into the trees, the simple planks flowing up and over patches of heavy underbrush or dipping under the looping roots covered in soft moss and vines. Every dozen paces, another pair of crystal lamps guided travelers along the trail.

From the head of the boardwalk, two paths forked—the first roads he'd seen since entering this realm. One headed west toward the ryujin mountains and one angled north. A post, its top holding another glowing crystal, had three markings carved into it, each indicating a trail.

Clio raced to the signpost and stopped to scan the unfamiliar markings. He watched her, marveling at this stunning creature in a forest more enchanting than any magic he'd ever seen or woven before. She moved without a hint of self-consciousness despite her minimal clothing, absolutely comfortable walking barefoot through the forest. The markings on her skin—spots and whorls in the faintest green— were almost invisible, but when the light caught them, they shimmered. With every tiny movement, she was art in motion.

Exhaling slowly, he started forward again. As he approached, she turned, her silver-sheen hair fluttering around her and her huge eyes shining with unshed tears.

"We made it!" Joy bubbled in her voice, overcoming her weariness. "We're in Irida!"

He smiled, enjoying her happiness. "You're home."

"Finally," she whispered, a single tear spilling down her cheek. Her gaze flitted across his face, then she slid her arms around his neck and tilted her face up, inviting him to lean down.

He responded without thinking, capturing her lips with his. Her arms tightened, and he caressed her waist, his thumbs running over her smooth skin and finding the strange, slightly rougher texture of the markings that patterned her skin. He slid one hand up her back and into the silk of her hair, deepening the kiss until she melted against him.

In that moment, it really sank in that he was kissing an *Overworlder*. He, an incubus, held a nymph in his arms. Cordial relations between residents of the two daemon realms were so rare that he and Clio fell into a tiny minority. Somehow, that realization took his breath away more than the beauty of the forest had.

She drew back, her homeland's lure too much for him to compete with. As she turned toward the boardwalk, she reached back and caught his hand, her fingers soft but her grip firm, holding him tight, keeping him close.

He stepped to her side, tracing the trail of lights as far into the distance as he could see. Irida. Finally. A painful knot of tension released from his spine. They were safe from the ryujin.

"If I remember correctly," Clio murmured, "we're about ten miles from the Iridian border with Kyo Kawa. It'll take another day of travel from here to reach the capital."

"Ten miles from the ryujin border already?" He glanced over his shoulder. "I don't remember crossing anything that looked like a border."

"I don't think anyone worries about exactly where the border is on this side. The ryujin don't come here, so ..." She shrugged.

"But isn't Irida under threat of invasion from Ra?"

"I'm sure there are soldiers along that part of the border."

He squinted thoughtfully. "I don't know the lay of the land here, but it sounds like the territories of Ra, Kyo Kawa, and Irida all come together at some point. Wouldn't that mean Ra could cut into ryujin territory to attack Irida from this side? Shouldn't your king be guarding this area as well?"

She frowned. "Maybe ... I don't know."

He glanced again at the empty forest behind them. Not a single soldier, scout, or guard. It was strange, but not their concern. He refocused on Clio. "Another day is more than I have in me. We need to rest—soon."

"Sleeping in the open in this forest isn't comfortable—the insects will drive us mad. We need shelter, but I'm not sure ..." Her eyes went out of focus. "Oh."

"Clio? What's wrong?"

"I just realized ... we aren't that far from ..."

"From where?"

She blinked slowly, her expression oddly slack as though too many emotions were crowding her at once. "Not that far from home."

His brow furrowed. "Home?"

Her eyes brightened again and she smiled, but her hand tightened on his like she needed a lifeline. "My old home, I mean. Where I lived with my mother. It's about eight miles northeast of here. We could rest there."

"Is it a town or a village?"

"There's a village two miles farther north, but the house is isolated. I don't think ... there's a chance someone else might live there now, but I doubt it."

"Sounds like our best bet," he agreed, suppressing his wariness over her reaction to the place. He took a step, his boot thudding hollowly on the first plank.

Clio stared down at the boardwalk as though afraid to step onto it. Her joy at being home was fading, and beneath her cheerful optimism, he sensed different emotions fueling her hesitancy.

What exactly had driven her from her homeland two years ago?

He hadn't yet asked her about her claim that she was the king's illegitimate daughter. He wanted to—he was dying to get answers—but they hadn't had the time or energy for that sort of discussion. She'd mentioned before that leaving Irida had been a favor to Bastian, the prince, but Lyre suspected there was more to it.

He was starting to suspect there was something ugly hidden in the unspoken details of her past, but he didn't know how to ask—or if he should ask at all.

Stepping back onto the dirt path, he wrapped his arm around her. She looked at him, her brow furrowed and eyes scrunched with emotions she was trying to hide.

With gentle pressure, he pulled her forward and together they stepped onto the boardwalk. She halted again, her body stiff under his arm, then she relaxed. When she started forward, he moved with her, his fingers curled over her side.

If she'd longed so desperately to return ... why did she seem so afraid?

TWENTY

SHE'D LOOKED forward to returning home for so long, but now that she was back, she didn't know what to feel.

Over the last two hours, the sky had lightened and the morning suns had breached the horizon. Golden beams streaked through the trees, illuminating trails and paths that had grown increasingly familiar. She'd never ventured as far west as the boardwalk, but here every tree, every rock, every signpost was familiar.

Her return wasn't anything like she'd imagined. Instead of arriving triumphantly in the capital with Kassia at her side and Bastian welcoming her with open arms, Kassia was dead, Bastian probably thought Clio was dead, and she had a fugitive Underworld spell weaver as her companion.

When she reached Bastian, would he be relieved to see her alive? Or would he be upset she had come to the capital, risking their family's safety with her presence? If Ra ever found out about her, they would use her against the king.

Exhaustion dragged at her limbs and every bone ached, but she didn't stop until she came to a familiar towering tree with huge roots that sprawled across the forest floor. Moss covered its ancient bark and vines hung from the broad boughs, their scarlet leaves forming thick curtains that swayed in the breeze.

The main trail continued past the tree, but a narrow path blanketed in leaf litter branched off under an arch in the tree roots.

"The village is at the end of the main trail," she told Lyre as he stopped beside her. "My old home is just up this path."

His gaze slid across her face. "Are you okay?"

"Yes … I think so. I haven't been here since … since shortly after my mother died."

He searched her eyes for a moment longer. "Together?"

He held out his hand. Dirt and dried blood smudged his skin but she didn't hesitate to grasp his fingers. Together. With her hand entwined in Lyre's, she walked beneath the arch and followed the trail between gargantuan trees.

After a hundred yards, the trees ended. Stretching before them was a small meadow with emerald grass, lush and tall, swaying in the breeze. In the center, a cabin stood, its walls covered in moss and vines so thick that the building appeared to have risen from the ground as naturally as the trees. Well beyond the house, three elegant *ceryn*, deer-like creatures with gold antlers, raised their heads to stare at the daemons, then bounded gracefully into the forest beyond the glade.

She and Lyre waded through the waist-high grass to a low wooden fence that kept wildlife from wandering right up to the cabin. She shoved the gate open, flattening the grass, and her steps slowed further as she approached the door, half hidden beneath vines. She reached for the latch, but her hand froze before she could touch it. For a long moment, she stood with her fingers hovering above the handle. Grief and loneliness flooded her chest, leaving no room for air.

She realized she was crushing Lyre's fingers in her grip and loosened her hold. "Let's go around to the back. There's a well. We can get a drink."

"Sure," he agreed. No impatience or exasperation touched his voice. No judgment. She could have kissed him just for that.

The grass in the backyard was even longer, hiding the squat well. Only its little peaked roof was visible, the same old bucket hanging from the center post. On one side of the yard, a more robust fence circled a large garden plot where plant stalks and leaves of all shapes and colors were tangled up in the grass.

"I don't believe it!" Releasing Lyre's hand, she ran to the fence and leaned over it. "There are vegetables!"

"Huh?" He joined her at the fence.

"I can't believe the weeds didn't choke out everything else." Brightening with excitement, she hopped over the fence and pushed the grass aside. "We can *eat* before we head for the capital. How about vegetable soup?"

He agreed enthusiastically and headed to the well while she sifted through the garden, getting an idea of what plants had survived and which were ripe for harvest. Crouching in a patch of low, broad-leaved plants, she dug into the soil and unearthed a cluster of fat gray bulbs.

Lyre returned from the well and stretched over the fence to pass her his waterskin—the only piece of gear they had left. It had been tied to his belt when they'd escaped, but the rest of their belongings were long gone.

Clio guzzled down the cool liquid, the tang of the well water painfully familiar, then handed the waterskin back. She gathered the bulbs and passed them to him. "Can you peel these?"

"Peel them? I guess …"

She frowned at his tone, then a laugh bubbled up in her throat. "You've never peeled a vegetable before, have you?"

"Um … that would be a no."

She swallowed a giggle. "Do you want me to show you how?"

He sank into the grass and leaned back against a fence post. "I think I can figure it out."

She returned to the garden and pretended not to notice when he shimmered out of glamour to access one of the short throwing knives strapped to his arm. If she acted like she hadn't seen, she could pretend her heart hadn't immediately started racing at that brief glimpse of his breathtaking true face. Luckily, once he had a knife, he slipped back into glamour and picked up a dull gray bulb.

"Oh hey," he murmured as he cut into the tough skin. "It's orange inside."

"It's a lot tastier than it looks when you first dig it up." She pulled out a clump of grass and a swarm of giant butterflies took flight from the stalks, their pink wings flashing.

"Hm." He continued peeling. "So you used to live here with your mother?"

"Yes." She crouched beside a large plant weighed down by green pods on the verge of over-ripeness. "My mother and I moved around a lot for my first two or three years, but I don't remember much of that. We eventually settled here, and this is where we lived until she died."

"How did she die?"

"Sickness." Clio's hands stuttered, but she forced herself to continue gathering pods. "She came down with a fever, but we didn't think it was serious. By the time we realized something was wrong … it was too late."

Lyre was quiet for a moment. "I'm sorry."

"It was six years ago … but I still have trouble talking about it." Finished harvesting pods, she carried them over to the fence and dropped them beside Lyre. "Can you cut the tops and bottoms off these when you're done with the rockroot?"

"Sure."

She ambled back among the plants, enjoying the warm soil under her feet and the morning sunlight streaking over the trees. Crouching, she stripped tiny round fruits off a bush, her thoughts wandering across the meadow where the ghosts of memories lingered. Behind her, the house was like a dark shadow drawing her attention.

"This place seems kind of isolated," Lyre commented, drawing her back to the present. "One woman and her child … why didn't you live in the village?"

"My mother …" Clio chewed on her lower lip. "Nymphs are very family oriented, but my mother and I had no other family, and because of that, we never fit in with the villagers. My mother tried—it's why we moved so much in the beginning—but she could never find a place that would welcome a single mother and child with no father or other family in the picture."

"So you were outcasts?" Lyre asked quietly.

"The villagers were nice. They were always polite, but … aloof. We were welcomed at the large gatherings and holiday feasts, but no one ever invited us to their homes or anything like that."

"It must have been lonely."

"Mother and I had each other. I was never lonely … at least, not until she died."

"What happened then?"

She stared at her hands. "The villagers helped me for a couple weeks. We held a parting ceremony for my mother, they gave me food, someone checked in on me every couple days, but … they eventually forgot about me."

"There was nowhere else you could go?"

"I felt just as alone in the village, and here I had privacy and no one judging me."

Quiet fell again, broken only by the raucous chirping of unseen birds. The startled butterflies had cautiously returned and were fluttering around the plants she had disturbed.

"How long did you live here alone?"

"Six months." She held up a red fruit and stared at it sightlessly. "Then one day, completely out of the blue, a man knocked on my door. I'd never met him before, but he introduced himself as my brother."

"Your brother?" A cautious note touched Lyre's voice.

"My half-brother. He said I didn't have to live in isolation any longer. He said he was bringing me home … to our father's home."

"Your father," Lyre murmured. "The king."

"The king," she agreed with a sigh. "Bastian had me pack my things that very afternoon, and he took me straight to the capital. I haven't been back here since that day."

She glanced at Lyre and found him watching her, his somber expression framed between the fence rails.

"If nymphs are so family oriented that you and your mother were ostracized by the community," he murmured, "why would the king welcome you into his family as a teenager?"

"He didn't." She carried the fruits over to the fence and poured them onto the ground beside the rockroots. "He didn't want me back. I'm a threat to his reputation. Bastian forced the king to accept me."

She picked up a rockroot and checked Lyre's peeling job. "Only the royal council knows I'm related to the Nereid family. My official position is as a lady-in-waiting for Petrina, the young princess." She glanced up. "Don't look so grim, Lyre. It's a hundred times better than living all by myself. I had everything I needed and more."

"And the king? How does he treat you?"

"I think he was warming up to me a bit, actually. Bastian arranged a family dinner once a month. Once the king realized I didn't want him to acknowledge me as his daughter and I wouldn't reveal the truth, he was friendlier."

"You don't want to be acknowledged? You don't want to be part of the family for real?"

"I …" She pushed to her feet and smiled brightly. "I'll pick a few more things for the soup."

She felt his eyes following her as she waded back into the garden and pulled up the Overworld equivalent of potatoes. It wasn't long before he posed a new question.

"How did you end up living on Earth?"

She pressed her lips together. She didn't want to explain anything more, but she owed him the truth. "The Ra threat. Bastian and the king were concerned I was too visible in the royal family's life. There were a few rumors—nothing serious, but questions about who I was and where I had come from."

"So they forced you to leave."

"Bastian asked me to, and I agreed."

"He made you nice and comfortable in his palace, then a few years later, he exiled you to Earth? Why couldn't he just move you out of the capital instead?"

She shifted uncomfortably at his disapproving tone. "Bastian wanted to send me somewhere out of the way. Somewhere safe. It was only temporary."

"A month is temporary, not two years," Lyre muttered under his breath, quietly enough that he probably hadn't intended her to hear.

She carried the potatoes over to him and added them to the pile. "Can you peel these too? I'll pick some herbs, then we can get started on the soup."

"This vegetable peeling thing is tiring." His tone was one of complaint but humor sparkled in his eyes. "Not sure I like this sort of work."

"Get used to it," she shot back cheerfully. "You have to do your own cooking now."

"Fair point."

"Besides," she added as she sifted through the grass and weeds, searching for surviving herbs, "*everything* is tiring right now because we're exhausted."

"Also a good point." He paused to yawn. "The sunlight is nice. Warmer than in the Underworld, I think."

She glanced up. He had leaned back against the fence post, his face tilted into the morning sunlight and his eyes closed. The golden beams lit his skin, gleaming on his pale hair and smoothing the haggard lines of weariness.

"This place is peaceful," he murmured without opening his eyes. "I like it. Feels … safe."

A butterfly bobbed out of the garden and danced above his head, fascinated by his hair. It dropped, wings fluttering against his face, and his eyes opened, buttery gold in the sunlight. He blew at the insect and it flew upward on the puff of air.

Clio's chest tightened. He was so gorgeous it hurt to look at him, like staring into the sun. He settled back against the post, his knife and a potato in his hands, but his eyes drifted closed again as though he couldn't help it.

Safe, he had said. She felt it too: an aura of protective tranquility. If her homeland was anything, it was safe. The nymph people were peaceable, lacking the aggression that many castes possessed. Their chimera allies, the other caste that shared this territory, were their aggressive protectors, standing as guardians in exchange for a heartfelt welcome in nymph land.

Irida was safe. It was quiet. It was a place where a damaged soul could heal.

Realizing the direction of her thoughts, she quickly focused on gathering herbs to season the soup. Lyre wasn't staying here. He couldn't. As much as he might like Irida's serene air, this was the

Overworld and he was an Underworlder. She'd never heard of an Underworlder *visiting* the Overworld before, let alone living here.

She bit her lip, unable to stop the forbidden thought now that it had reared its persistent head. What if he *could* stay here?

What if he could stay here *with her*?

Would he want to? Did he enjoy her company that much, or was their bond only as incidental allies? Did he care to tie his fate to hers permanently?

Was that what *she* wanted?

It was so easy to imagine more days just like this. Sunny afternoons. Working in the garden. Lazing in the grass. No dangers, no threats. Lyre's amber eyes glowing in the sun. His rumbling laugh that made her belly do somersaults. Here, he could weave the beautiful illusions he'd hidden from his family.

She glanced over her shoulder. Lyre's head had drooped, eyes closed and face slack, too weary to stay awake any longer. Gathering the herbs, she climbed over the fence and crouched beside him. He didn't stir, breathing slow and deep.

She hesitated, then lightly ran her fingers through his hair. He was so tired. So was she, but he had fought longer and harder than she had. He'd been exhausted in mind and soul before she'd even met him, and now he was exhausted in body and magic as well.

Her fingers trailed down the side of his face and across his lips as she remembered how she had kissed him. How he had kissed her. Was that how incubi kissed all women? Was it his charm and his aphrodesia that made her think he felt something for her—something stronger than just companionship or lust?

Her nerves twanged, and she pulled her hand back from his face. Shaking her head, she slipped the knife out of his loose grip and quickly peeled the last few potatoes. She threw the scraps into the garden, then filled the well bucket and rinsed all the vegetables. After dumping the water, she filled the bucket again, threw the vegetables in, and, holding the heavy bucket under one arm, turned to the cabin.

The dark windows stared at her, dusty and covered with vines.

Leaving Lyre to sleep, she crossed the yard to the back door and stood in front of it. Seconds passed. A minute. Steeling herself, she flipped the latch and turned the handle. The hinges creaked as she pushed the door open.

Dust roiled, sparkling in the sunlight. She stepped inside, her heart twisting at the familiar scent of wood and the unfamiliar odor of dust and dampness.

The main room looked exactly as she'd left it, minus the thick coating of dust. A kitchen counter on one side, a little island with pots and pans hanging above it. A large fireplace, the cooking grate still in place from the last meal she'd made six years ago. On the other side of the small room, hand-sewn pillows in bright colors muted by dust were piled on a wooden sofa.

She could almost hear her mother's bubbly laugh echoing through the room.

She carried the bucket to the counter and set it down. For a long minute more, she stood there, staring at every little thing. A wooden carving of a lycaon sat on the mantel above the fireplace. A wreath of dried flowers hung above the front door. A neat stack of worn books—her childhood textbooks—were piled on the floor beside the sofa.

Closing her eyes, she took a deep breath. Then she got to work. Start a fire, wipe the counter, clean a pot, fill it with water, set it in the fireplace. Chop the vegetables, mince the herbs, add them to the pot.

As the water steamed, she absently wiped down the counters and other dusty surfaces, lost in memories. She paused and squinted at her hand. Her arm was smudged with dirt. Her other arm was splattered from wrist to elbow with dried blood and an angry pink line traced the path of Sabir's dagger.

Throwing the cloth into the cleaning basin, she crossed to the bedroom door and opened it. Inside were two narrow beds with patched comforters in bright, sunny colors and a wooden dresser in the center. Flowerpots lined the windowsill, the plants in them dried to brown husks, their shriveled leaves scattered across the sill and floor.

Clio stared at the dead plants she'd left behind without a second thought. Plants she and her mother had nurtured for years, abandoned as worthless, as unnecessary and unneeded in her new life with her new family.

Tears spilled down her cheeks.

She choked back a sob as she went to the dresser and opened the top drawer. Empty. She'd taken her clothes with her when she left. Crouching, she opened the bottom drawer. It was stacked with neatly folded bundles wrapped in rough brown paper. She hadn't opened this drawer since the week after her mother's death.

She lifted out the first item and unwrapped it: a light flowing dress with an embroidered pattern of pink butterflies just like the ones in the garden. A hundred memories assaulted her at once: her mother in the dress, whirling around the kitchen as she cooked with abandon, ambling through meadow flowers swaying in the breeze, holding Clio's hand with their arms swinging as they walked to the village on market day.

She pressed her face into the soft fabric, her shoulders heaving. It smelled like stale paper and musty wood. It should have smelled like herbs and golden belle flowers. It should have smelled like her mother.

The floorboards behind her creaked. The air shifted with the movement of the door, then Lyre was kneeling behind her. His arms wrapped around her, enclosing her and the dress still clutched against her chest.

She wanted to stop crying, to apologize for losing her composure, but she couldn't. The grief rose through her in an unstoppable tide, and all she could do was weep the tears she'd refused to shed since the moment she'd last walked out of this house.

Lyre held her, saying nothing. Just held her, his silence full of understanding and compassion.

Eyes squeezed shut, she surrendered to the sorrow and to his embrace.

TWENTY~ONE

IF HER childhood home had been all peaceful tranquility, then Irida's capital was all frenetic energy.

Clio kept her pace slow to conceal her jumpy anxiety as she and Lyre walked the streets—though "streets" wasn't an apt description. Walkways, perhaps.

The small city rose before them, clinging to the steep mountainside. In the city's center, a waterfall poured off a high cliff and plunged into a narrow gorge that wound away into the forest. Ancient, colossal trees perched on the sloping earth, their twisting roots as thick as pillars. Plants, vines, and moss covered every surface, turning the entire city into a living tapestry of green.

Wooden houses with sharply peaked roofs were built in, on, and around the trees, their walls equally decorated with plant life. The higher up the mountainside she and Lyre climbed, the larger and more elaborate the homes became, and the interconnected halls and spires of the Nereid royal palace formed the topmost structure.

Everything was connected by walkways and bridges—some wide and lined with crystal-topped posts, others narrow and steep. They dipped and rose and curved and climbed around the city in a chaotic tangle that followed the shapes of the mountains and trees.

The late afternoon suns blazed, and under their warmth, the pathways bustled with daemons on their way to and from errands or heading home after a day's work. Nymphs with ivory skin and shimmering hair, dressed in minimal clothes similar to Clio's, passed them with long, curious glances directed at Lyre. Whispers followed them, and some nymphs circled back to trail in their wake, fascinated by the mysterious stranger.

Lyre hovered close behind her, and though she knew he was trying to keep calm, he radiated nervous tension. She couldn't blame him. She'd given him a dark green, knee-length cloak with a deep hood that he'd pulled low over his face, but he still stood out like a sunflower in a field of white lilies. He was taller and broader in the shoulders than the petite nymphs, his tanned skin strikingly dark compared to their ivory complexions, and his clothes were completely different.

And even with him hiding his face and suppressing his natural incubus allure as much as possible, masculine strength oozed from his every movement.

She smiled and nodded at everyone who was bold enough to make eye contact, and so far, no one had stopped them to make conversation. She strode purposefully, relieved she'd washed up and changed into some of her mother's old clothes before leaving the cabin. If she and Lyre had shown up covered in dirt and blood, they'd have drawn even more attention.

The winding boardwalk joined a busy intersection, and Clio ducked down a quieter, narrow side path between two houses. As the buzz of conversation quieted, she let out a long breath.

"I've never been stared at so much in my life," Lyre muttered. "And *everyone* stares at me."

"We'll reach the palace soon." She pointed upward. "Just got to get up there."

Wariness flickered across his face as he squinted at the elegant spires farther up the mountainside. "You live there?"

"I did. Not sure about now …" She sighed. "Bastian probably thinks I'm dead. I bet that's what Eryx told him."

"So, do you have a plan for—"

A low animal growl interrupted him. Lounging on the rooftop above them, two lycaons watched her and Lyre with critical dark blue eyes. The adult versions of the kit they'd seen at the poacher's stall in Brinford were larger than lions, with lean bodies, black and blue fur, and crests of yellow feathers. Their huge wolfish ears swiveled as they studied Lyre suspiciously.

"Good afternoon," she greeted politely as she blindly reached back and took Lyre's hand. With a respectful nod to the creatures, she quickly led him away. The lycaons didn't move, observing their retreat with perked ears and twitching tails.

"Uh," Lyre muttered. "Do those, um, talk?"

"No, they don't talk, but lycaons are very intelligent so my mother taught me to treat them like any daemon."

"I don't think they like me."

"They might be able to tell you're from the Underworld." She frowned worriedly. "Everyone here can tell you're not a nymph or a chimera, but they probably won't guess you're—"

She cut herself off as they stepped out of the narrow walkway onto an open boardwalk where, as though summoned by her mention of them, a trio of chimeras were walking by.

Their red hair swayed behind them in long braids, and tattoos covered most of their visible skin, which was a dull reddish hue like a human with a sunburn. Pointed, goat-like horns rose from their heads, and long tails reminiscent of a snake's body trailed after them.

They spotted Clio and Lyre, and their gleaming crimson eyes fixed on the foreigner with his face hidden.

"What's this?" one asked, stopping. "A visitor?"

Crap. She'd been hoping to avoid crossing paths with the fiery daemons. While nymphs were too polite to butt in without invitation, the same could not be said for chimeras.

"Yes," she replied neutrally. "We're heading to the palace."

"Oh, a *royal* visitor?" another cut in, grinning to reveal his pointed teeth. "Are they expecting you?"

"We're in a hurry," Clio evaded. "Please excuse us."

She started to walk past but they spread out, blocking her way.

"Who are you? Let's get an introduction," the third chimera said to Lyre, pushing her hair off her shoulders to reveal more dark tattoos. "We don't get many outsiders round here."

Lyre tilted his head up enough for the light to hit his lower face. He flashed a friendly smile. "Afraid we really are in a hurry, but I'll be here for a bit. Maybe later you can show me the best place to get a hot meal."

The female chimera blinked, probably caught off guard by his smooth, deep voice. Then she grinned and slapped him on the shoulder. "Good plan! A hot meal and drinks on me. We'll see you around."

Waving her companions to follow, she continued down the walkway. The male chimeras glanced back, suspicion glinting in their crimson eyes, but they didn't stop.

Clio and Lyre exchanged looks then hastened up the boardwalk, her feet padding quietly while his boots clomped with noticeably more volume. The path grew steeper, interspersed by ramps and stairs. They passed over and under broad tree roots, their rough surfaces covered in moss and dangling vines, and the waterfall's constant, low-pitched roar muffled all other sounds.

With each step closer to the palace, Clio's unease grew. She didn't know how Bastian and the king would react to her return, but it wasn't her safety that had her stomach in knots. It was Lyre's. How would the king and prince react to a spell weaver in their capital?

Perhaps they would welcome him as a potential ally. Perhaps they would be horrified and afraid of an Underworlder. Perhaps they would think him a spy and arrest him.

Sabir's sharp grin flashed in her memory. *It's the spell weaver I want.*

Spell weavers were highly valued for their skills, and Lyre was a Chrysalis master weaver. He was among the most elite weavers in the three realms, and that made him priceless. How many others would react to his real identity like Sabir? Any number of excessively wealthy and powerful daemon families would pay a king's ransom to have a master weaver at their beck and call.

If she brought Lyre into the palace, would the king of Irida see an enemy, an ally, or a tool to be enslaved for his kingdom's use?

Her hands clenched. Maybe she shouldn't have brought Lyre here. Maybe she should have left him at the cabin, safe and out of the way. A few days ago, she would never have considered the risk that her family might imprison Lyre—or sell him off—but after Sabir's betrayal, she no longer trusted her instincts.

They climbed the boardwalks in silence, passing increasingly elegant homes and expensive shops. The roaring waterfall grew louder until they were climbing wide stairs with the water tumbling downward just beyond the railing, its mist cooling her face. When they reached the top of the stairs, the railings ended in elegantly carved posts with fist-sized crystals set on the tops.

The mountain slope leveled into a plateau, and built upon it was the south wing of the palace—an interconnected web of buildings, their walls carved in the likeness of tree bark and twining vines, the stone itself covered in real vines and moss. Behind the front wing, spires rose high, climbing the rocky mountainside. Beyond them, the trees ended and the mountain peak rose, the striated rock layered with sparkling veins of crystal.

Beside the gates of the courtyard entrance, a dozen guards stood at attention—six lithe nymphs and six powerful chimeras. Astral perception paired with fighting ability and magical strength—a deadly combination.

She looked at the guards, then grabbed Lyre's hand and pulled him into motion—not toward the entrance but along the plateau.

"Where are we going?" he asked nervously.

"I think it would be better if I went in alone." She led him past the palace's vine-covered outer walls, as beautiful as they were functional. "To get a feel for the situation first."

On the other side, a stone archway revealed a lush garden. Cobblestone paths wound through explosions of vivid flowers and broad-leaved plants. Small trees with their branches weighed down by blossoms interspersed the shrubs, and scattered throughout were carved posts with crystals set on top. At night, the crystals glowed in a rainbow of soft colors and nocturnal insects danced for hours among the plants in a mesmerizing display.

She strode into the garden, pulling Lyre with her, and ducked down a narrow path that followed the back wall. In the farthest corner, well out of sight from the paths and benches, was a small storehouse. She opened the door, revealing shelves of fertilizer and a wall of gardening tools.

"You can wait in here," she said. "No one will disturb you."

"Are you sure?" he asked, his gaze darting across the garden.

"I used to come here whenever I needed a break from the bustle of the palace. It's quiet and the gardeners only work in the mornings, so no one will be back until sunrise. It's a public garden." She gestured toward the stone spires. "It connects to the palace and there are guards there, but they stay at their posts."

He pushed his hood back and light fell across his face, illuminating his grim expression. "Is it a good idea for you to go in alone?"

"Yes," she said firmly, her wavering hesitation solidifying into determination. She wouldn't reveal Lyre until she was sure it was safe. "If I don't come get you by nightfall, you should leave."

"Leave?" he repeated incredulously. "Clio, how the hell can I leave on my own? At best, I could backtrack out of the city, but I'll never find that desert ley line again."

"I—I know, but … if I can't come get you, it'll mean … I'll just have to find you later."

Jaw tightening, he backed into the shed. Shimmers rippled over him and his glamour fell away. The elegant dark blue and silver garb she had so admired when she first saw it was torn and stained with dried blood.

"Lyre," she said breathlessly, struggling to focus as her brain short-circuited. "What are you …"

From his pocket, he withdrew the pouch of spells Reed had passed on to him. He dug around it, palmed something, then tucked the pouch away again. His form shimmered, glamour sliding back over him.

He extended his hand. A pair of matching green gems sat on his palm.

"Linked trackers," he explained. "Activate one and it will trigger the other. We can follow them to find each other again."

She picked one up and examined the weave with her asper.

"If you don't meet me here by dark, I'll slip out of the city and activate the spell." He pocketed his gem, then placed his hand over hers, curling her fingers over the stone. "If you need my help, activate yours. I'll come find you."

Her throat constricted. "I'll be as quick as I can. Wait for me."

"I'll wait for you." He brushed his fingers across her cheek, then slid them around the back of her neck. She tilted her head up, lips already parting as he lowered his head. His mouth closed over hers, hot and urgent. Heat dove through her, but he was already pulling away. "Be safe."

With a shuddering breath, she stepped back. "Don't use any spells," she cautioned. "Nymphs can see it."

He nodded, his amber eyes gleaming in the shadows. She forced herself to close the door and shut him inside. Her heart raced with anxiety, her nerves screaming warnings at her. *Don't leave him.* The silent warning pounded through her. *Don't leave him.*

She pushed the pervasive dread away. What choice did she have? Taking him into the palace would be more dangerous, and they hadn't come all this way to turn back now. She had to leave him, if only for a short time. He would be safe. Only the gardeners knew about that shed, and they wouldn't be back until morning.

She exited the garden through the public archway and circled back around to the palace's front entrance. Raising her chin and pushing her shoulders back, she marched toward the waiting guards.

The first two pairs moved to intercept her. The nymphs wore pale green uniforms of soft fabric with leather belts holding simple short swords, while the chimeras were heavily armed and protected by leather armor. They carried long bladed pikes, the steel shining in the late afternoon sunlight.

She stopped and waited.

A nymph pursed his lips and squinted at her face. His suspicious expression cleared. "Lady Clio?"

She nodded, allowing a small smile. The chimeras glanced at each other, their stony expressions unchanged. The nymph guards were more familiar with the royal family and their attendants, so the chimeras probably didn't recognize her.

"Lady Clio!" the nymph exclaimed. "I didn't know you were returning. Is Her Highness expecting you?"

"I'm afraid my visit is unplanned," Clio said. "I'd like to meet with the king and Prince Bastian immediately. It's urgent."

"Urgent?" he repeated, his pale eyebrows drawing over his sharp blue eyes. He hesitated, then waved another nymph over. "Fetch an armed escort for Lady Clio and take her to the jade reception room. Have messengers alert His Majesty and His Highness that she's here."

The guard nodded and dashed away, his nymph agility carrying him out of sight in seconds. An armed escort wasn't for her protection. It was protection for the king and prince in case her "urgent" visit entailed any sort of danger, but she didn't mind. The guards wouldn't hurt her.

"Is Prince Bastian here, then?" she asked. "I wasn't sure if he might be out on business."

"I am not certain. If he is present, the messenger will alert him."

She nodded again, knowing better than to press. The guards were loyal to the Nereid family above all else; he would reveal nothing more.

The seconds stretched into minutes before her escort arrived—four chimeras and two nymphs. The chimeras' tails swished as they surveyed her from head to toe. The nymphs, too, examined her closely.

One pointed. "May I see the spell you're carrying?"

Keeping her expression neutral but inwardly cursing—she'd grown accustomed to being the only daemon around with asper—she withdrew Lyre's tracking spell and offered it to the soldier. He examined it, his eyes growing wide.

"This is a highly advanced weaving," he breathed. "Amazing. What's the range on this? It looks like it could—"

His comrade cleared his throat pointedly.

"Er, yes. Right. Lady Clio, I don't recognize the source magic. Who wove this? Is it griffin magic?"

The chimeras tensed, but Clio shook her head. "It is not."

"What is it?"

"I can't tell you, I'm sorry." She smiled amicably. "It's a tracking spell with a signal component, and as you can see, it can only be activated by touch. If you prefer, you may carry it for me."

He nodded, satisfied she couldn't use it to signal dangerous allies as long as he held it, and waved at her to come with him. He and the other nymph fell into step on either side of her, and the chimeras followed, watching her every move.

They swept through the beautiful entrance garden, shaded by two massive trees with broad boughs, and entered through the tall double doors. The main reception hall stretched before her—rows of carved pillars leading to a platform with a single empty chair. Vines of gold, decorated with emerald leaves and flowers of ruby and sapphire, wrapped its surface.

The guards didn't take her far, leading her left into the jade reception room—named for the design inlaid in the floor. A thousand tiny green tiles formed the Nereid family crest of a flower blossom with a jewel in its center, circled by a leafy vine. Wooden benches piled with soft cushions faced each other, and in one corner, water trickled down the wall to fill a pool in the floor. Tiny fish darted among aquatic plants.

An arched doorway on the far side opened into a garden courtyard, its carved pillars supporting a latticework ceiling draped with flowering vines. Another fountain gurgled somewhere out of sight.

Clio perched on the bench, her hands closing tightly around the wooden edge. The nymphs stood nearby while the chimeras split up, two at one entrance and two at the other.

Her heart raced faster with each minute she sat there. For so long she had dreamed of coming home, but everything was wrong. Suspicion, wariness, an armed escort. Lyre hiding in the public garden, waiting.

How would Bastian react when he learned she was here? What would he say when she revealed how Eryx had killed Kassia and left Clio to die? And, most importantly, what would he do when she explained why they had to destroy the clock spell?

She shifted restlessly. Her escorts were having trouble holding still as well, and as the wait dragged on, they glanced at the doors more and more frequently. She didn't understand why no one was coming. Were Bastian and the king in a meeting that couldn't be interrupted?

She was vibrating with tension by the time footsteps and murmuring voices echoed in the large reception hall. The chimeras at the door stepped aside, and with a burst of color and movement, a man crossed the threshold. Pale blue eyes, sharp with intelligence and surprise, flicked across her face.

She jumped to her feet, then went down onto her knees in a bow.

Rouvin, the king of Irida, stood before her, and she had no idea how her estranged father felt about her abrupt return to his palace—and his kingdom.

TWENTY~TWO

"RISE, CLIO, RISE," the king said.

Standing again, she straightened the short, fluttering skirt she wore and wished she'd chosen something more formal. The king, in comparison, looked like … well, like royalty. He was lean and limber like most nymphs, with age lines creasing his face and long silvery hair braided down his back. His garments were simple but very fine—a sleeveless tunic with silver embroidery and sapphires beading the collar and hem, fitted trousers of woven fabric in muted blue, and soft boots.

Behind him a dozen advisors and bodyguards crowded in, but he waved them away as he came into the room.

"Your Majesty," she greeted him.

"Your arrival is unexpected, my dear," he told her, throwing quick gestures at her escort. The daemons exited the room, with the nymph who still held her tracking spell lingering just outside the threshold.

She tensed at the ambivalent welcome. "I couldn't send advance word of my return, but …"

"Well, we're relieved to have you back. You've been missed."

"M-missed?" she stammered. Someone had missed her? Really? "I'm here because of something urgent. Is Bastian coming?"

"A messenger has fetched him." Rouvin folded his arms and surveyed her with austere blue eyes the color of a winter sky. "What is the issue?"

"I—I'd like to discuss it with Bastian here. I'm assuming he's kept you up to date on my … activities?"

"Generally he does, yes."

She bit her lip. Had Bastian told his father about the spell Eryx had stolen from Chrysalis? Maybe he'd wanted to get it working first.

"You look exhausted, Clio," Rouvin said before she could think of what to ask him next. "Sit down, child, and I'll have someone bring water while we wait for my laggard son."

As he snapped his fingers at an attendant waiting outside the room, she sank onto the bench again. Her hands were shaking and she twisted them together in her lap.

Her father stood beside her, as unreachable and impersonal as ever. She'd never been able to connect with him, never developed any camaraderie or even managed a comfortable conversation. In fact, she wasn't sure she'd ever had a conversation with him without Bastian present.

The king cleared his throat, a sound that suggested he felt the awkwardness as much as she did. "Petrina will be pleased to have you back."

"She will?" Clio mumbled.

"She was hurt that you didn't say goodbye before you left." A note of reprimand touched his voice. "You *do* plan to stay this time, don't you?"

Her head snapped up. "Stay?"

"Petrina felt your absence keenly. Not that she would admit it, of course; she takes after her mother that way."

Clio stared at him, struggling to read his regal features. "You want me to stay?"

"I never wanted you to leave."

Her hands clenched and tears spilled down her cheeks. "I—I don't know what to say. Thank you."

His brow furrowed as though he didn't understand her reaction, but he nodded, politely turning toward the fountain while she struggled with her emotions.

She quickly wiped her eyes. "I'm so glad to be back. I never wanted to leave."

The king glanced at her, his frown deepening. "Then why did you go?"

"I … I had to."

"So Bastian said," the king grunted. "I still think we could have found a less drastic solution where you would have been more comfortable."

A strange pressure closed over her chest like a cold clamp forming around her heart. The king hadn't wanted to send her to Earth? Had that been Bastian's idea?

"It was safer that way," she whispered.

"Safer?" Stern disapproval hardened his tone. "In what way has your safety been threatened within these walls?"

She shrank in her seat. "It hasn't yet, but the risk of—"

Bracing a hand on the back of the bench, he leaned closer and lowered his voice. "Though the only role I can fulfill in your life is that of your king, I have and will continue to be your guardian, as I am to every member of this household. Here, you are safer than in any Earth city."

Her mouth opened and closed, but no sound came out. Never before had the king spoken to her like that. Never had he even suggested he cared about her in the slightest.

"You—you are King Rouvin, aren't you?" she blurted.

His eyes widened and he straightened with a bemused expression. "I assure you I am, though with the look you are giving me, I wonder if I should check my reflection."

"I just—I mean—" Her cheeks heated. "I didn't think my leaving would bother you."

"How would you know my thoughts when you never gave me a chance to dissuade you?" He shook his head. "Fleeing in the dead of night without the slightest farewell wasn't helpful in that regard."

She tilted her head as though rattling the words in her skull might make their meaning clearer.

"Petrina was crushed," Rouvin added. "You may have some work ahead of you to win her trust again. She felt abandoned."

"I didn't run away," Clio protested, finding her voice. "I *had* to leave. To protect *you*."

"To protect me? Whatever from, child?"

"From … from …" Her brain fizzled, thoughts scattering. "I had to leave because of the Ra threat."

"The Ra threat?" The creases in his forehead deepened. "Tensions are higher than usual with the upcoming renewal of our trade agreement, but I would hardly describe it as a *threat*."

"Trade agreement?" she whispered.

"Irida and the Ras have a long-standing agreement that's renegotiated every decade. The politics are complicated and, yes, there are tensions and a certain amount of posturing involved in the negotiations, but I've successfully renewed the agreement every ten years since I took the throne."

"But what about … what about the threat of invasion? The possibility of war?"

"Invasion? *War?* Clio, unless you know something I do not, I assure you we are at no risk of war with *any* territory." He stepped closer and crouched to peer into her face. "You're white as a snow lily. What is going on?"

"Ra wants to invade Irida," she said blankly. "They've been pushing our borders for over a year. They've been commissioning special magic and preparing for war. You've been avoiding confrontation but you know that a conflict is coming."

"What are you talking about, Clio?"

The invisible bands around her chest tightened. "Their spies are looking for ways to undermine you. I had to leave the Overworld and go where they could never find me."

Rouvin stared at her, then gently grasped her hands. His skin felt fiery hot against her icy fingers.

"Take a deep breath, child. Inhale. Exhale. Good." He squeezed her hands. "Why didn't you tell Bastian about your fears?"

"Wh-what?"

"He tracked you down after you left, yes? He's been checking on you for two years now, but you never told him your real reason for leaving?"

Her brain wasn't working. Why didn't his words make sense? "My real ... reason?"

"He never mentioned your fear of spies. All I knew was you'd decided you needed time and space. I had assumed, or perhaps Bastian implied, that I ... bore some of the responsibility for driving you away."

She stared at her father, deafened by the sound of crashing stones in her head—the roar of her entire world falling apart around her.

"Bastian told you I ran away?" The words caught in her throat, and she had to choke them out. "He told you I wanted to leave Irida?"

Rouvin nodded cautiously.

"There is no threat from Ra? There are no spies? There isn't an impending war?"

"Not at all. Child, where did you get such an idea?"

She couldn't breathe at all. "Bastian."

"What?"

"Bastian told me about the increasing threat. He talked about it for over six months before he asked me to leave Irida for the family's safety."

"He *asked* you to leave?"

She barely heard him, her eyes wide. Rouvin's hands were her only anchor in the storm of realizations. "Everything I know about Ra came from him. No one else ever mentioned it, but he said it was confidential information, only discussed by the royal council. And he said—he said not to mention it to you because you were already stressed about it."

A hundred memories flashed through her mind. "On Earth, all Kassia and I knew was what he told us. Eryx never contradicted anything he said. Even though ... but why did he have me spy on Ra spell commissions?"

"Spy on Ra?" Rouvin squeezed her hands again. "Clio, breathe. Breathe, child. Come now."

She realized she was hyperventilating. "There *is* a Ra threat," she gasped. "There *has to be*. Otherwise—otherwise—"

"Otherwise my son has been lying to you for well over two years?" the king finished for her, his voice quiet. "And lying to *me*." He released her hands and rose. Turning, he strode from the room, his voice ringing out. "*Bastian!*"

Clio scrambled to her feet and raced after him. He was marching across the reception hall, his advisors clamoring around him.

"Find the prince!" Rouvin barked. "Immediately! I don't care what you interrupt. Drag him here naked if you must."

Clio hunched her shoulders, aware of the confused, critical stares snapping over her. "Your Majesty, what …"

"We will learn the reason for my son's deceptions shortly, Clio," he assured her, grim anger vibrating in his voice. "I am certain he has a *reason*."

She didn't understand the way he growled that last word. A reason. Could Bastian have a reason for his cruel deceptions? Was there an explanation that could make everything right again? He *must* have a reason, one so crucial and profound she and the king would forgive him—protecting her, protecting his father and his family, protecting his kingdom.

She and the king, surrounded by advisors, waited in the center of the grand hall. No one said a word; the king's anger held them all in silence.

A door slammed and running footsteps pattered across the hall. A nymph guard raced to the king and dropped to one knee.

"Your Majesty," the guard panted. "Prince Bastian's suites are empty. He was last seen an hour ago when a messenger informed him of Lady Clio's arrival."

"Where has he gone?" King Rouvin demanded. "He's here somewhere. Bring him to me."

"Your Majesty, he appears to …" The nymph cleared his throat. "He appears to have left the palace … covertly."

The pounding silence sucked all the air out of the hall.

"Find him." At those two quietly spoken words, every daemon in the hall leaped into action.

Clio shivered where she stood, arms wrapped around herself. Bastian had received a message that she was here—that she was alive after being taken prisoner in Chrysalis—and he had left the palace? *Why?*

"Huh?" The muttered exclamation came from behind her. "What the—"

Clio turned as the nymph guard dug in his pocket, his brow furrowed in confusion. He lifted something between two fingers: a green gem pulsing with soft golden light.

Lyre's tracking spell.

It was active? He had triggered the twin spell? But he wasn't supposed to use it until nightfall.

Sickening dread swept through her and she snatched the gem from the guard's hand. As soon as she touched the cool stone, sensation flooded her mind—a pulse calling her forward. The signal beat like a drum, coming from a point north-northeast of her.

A point much farther from the garden where she had left Lyre.

"How long?" she demanded, clutching the gem. "How long ago did it activate?"

"I—I don't know," the guard stammered, caught off guard by her urgent intensity. "I was paying attention to—"

He broke off and they both looked at the gem in her hand. With a stuttering flash, the light blinked out and the pulse in her head vanished.

The tracking spell had gone silent.

TWENTY~THREE

LYRE LOUNGED in the back of the storage shed, leaning against the wall with gardening tools stacked on either side of him. He rolled the green tracking spell between his finger and thumb as faint light from the gaps around the door glittered across its surface.

He hated waiting. He hated sitting here doing nothing. He hated feeling helpless and vulnerable, and he *really* hated feeling like a burden.

He'd felt like a needless burden since setting foot in the Overworld. They were here to get his KLOC back but he'd contributed nothing to their efforts. Now he was hiding in a damn shed while Clio ventured into the royal palace alone.

Of course, being the daughter of the king, she was *probably* safe. Then again, it was her brother's bodyguard who'd almost killed her, then left her to die in Asphodel. So he wasn't entirely sure.

But what could he do? Among a different caste, he could have disguised himself, but not here. Not surrounded by nymphs with astral perception. He didn't even dare leave the shed despite how vulnerable he felt in the cramped space where he couldn't see if anyone was coming.

He let his head fall back against the wall. Nymphs. Such an odd caste. Walking through this city had been an eye-opening experience. Males and females, all petite and beautiful, flitting around in skimpy clothes without a hint of self-consciousness. The boys were as pretty as the girls and difficult to tell apart at a glance.

The chimeras, however, were a whole different breed. Clio had explained the nymph/chimera arrangement so it hadn't come as a complete surprise, but seeing the tall, tattooed, red-haired daemons mixed among the ivory-skinned nymphs had still been a shock. And what the nymphs lacked in appropriate suspicion, the chimeras more than made up for in natural aggression.

All in all, he felt more comfortable among chimeras than nymphs. Chimeras, with their confident swagger and ready-to-fight attitudes, were reassuring in their familiarity. These gentle, cheerful nymphs were just … weird.

Clio being the exception. She was *his* gentle, cheerful nymph.

He tossed the tracking spell into the air and caught it again. How long would he have to wait? What if Clio didn't come back? Sneaking out of here in the dark would be a nightmare. He'd been hopelessly lost about two minutes into the city, and beyond that, he had even less of a clue. If Clio never came back for him … the prospect of being stranded in an enemy world with no escape was terrifying.

He tried to focus on something else—*anything* else.

Clio's childhood home had been nice. He'd liked the quiet meadow. The monstrously oversized trees commanded a presence of their own, like ancient, watchful guardians. He could have happily stayed there for a few days recovering his strength. Too bad they hadn't had the time.

With that, his thoughts slid right back into pointless, worry-filled circles. Assuming Clio's meeting with her brother went well, would he turn over the KLOC? Lyre doubted it. He fully expected he'd have to steal it back. *How* he would steal it was the big question.

Maybe he would have to tell them what the KLOC could *really* do— the real danger he hadn't revealed even to Clio. Maybe that would frighten them into returning it so he could destroy it. Assuming he *could* destroy it.

It was easier to worry about the KLOC. He didn't have the energy to think about what would come after. No matter how well things here went, when he was done, he would have to walk right back into the nightmare he'd left behind on Earth. Countless bounty hunters tracking his every move. A dark, dank city where he would have to find a way to survive. And, if he'd interpreted Reed's warning correctly, his father either planned to join the hunt or was already weaving his lethal webs in Brinford.

Whatever waited for him in the human world, he would face it alone. Clio would stay here, with her people and her family. Leaving her behind felt ... wrong, like a betrayal. They had escaped Asphodel together, and his subconscious had decided that meant they would stay together. But that had never been possible or even expected. She had her own life to return to, and he had a new life to build. Somehow. With Lyceus coming for him, Lyre doubted he'd get a chance to try.

Lost in bleak thoughts, he watched the floating dust motes dance in the line of sunlight leaking around the doorframe.

Then the line of sunlight darkened.

He stiffened. Something—someone—had moved in front of the door, blocking the light. Gripping the chain around his neck, ready to activate his shields, he didn't even breathe.

A rapping on the wood made him jump. Someone was knocking?

"I'm opening the door," a male voice warned, muffled by the wood. "Don't attack."

Lyre rose to his feet, back to the wall, as the door swung open. Light flooded the shed's interior, silhouetting the man standing in the threshold—a horned chimera with a bladed pike in his hand. The weapon carried by the palace guards.

The soldier backed away, leaving the doorway wide open.

"Lyre, isn't it?" a soft, refined voice called. "Please come out."

The breeze carried the scents of multiple daemons but Lyre didn't know how many. Staying in the dark shed seemed stupid, so he touched the gems around his neck, activating his defensive weaves, then pinched the tracking spell between his finger and thumb.

This spell was his lifeline. If he was captured, the tracking spell would lead Clio to him, and he couldn't risk them taking it.

Keeping the movement casual, he brought his hand to his face as though adjusting the hood of his cloak, and with the motion, he slipped the gemstone into his mouth. Empty-handed, he cautiously approached the doorway.

Five unfamiliar chimera soldiers waited for him in a loose half-circle around the shed. In their center was a nymph. His long blond hair was tied back and his features were too beautiful to call masculine. Unlike the half-naked nymphs in the city, he was dressed more conservatively in a gray-blue tunic and fitted pants, both expensive-looking garments. His ice-blue eyes watched Lyre carefully beneath elegant eyebrows, his cheekbones accented with the greenish markings all nymphs had.

Lyre wasn't sure if it was obvious to him because he was looking for it, but he didn't see how anyone could miss the family resemblance between this nymph and Clio.

Lyre crossed his arms and leaned one shoulder against the doorframe. At the same time, he used his tongue to tuck the gem into his cheek and hoped his aura hid the weaving's glow from the nymph's asper.

"Bastian, right?" he asked coolly.

"His *Highness*," a chimera corrected in a growl, "Prince Bastian Nereid, crown prince of Irida."

Bastian raised a placating hand to his guard. Lyre's eyebrows rose higher. Interesting how the prince had waited until *after* the chimera had finished spouting his titles before quieting him.

"And you would be Lyre Rysalis, master weaver and fifth son of Lyceus Rysalis, head of Chrysalis." Bastian smiled with cautious warmth. "You are the daemon I must thank for saving Clio's life."

Lyre returned the smile, keeping his expression smooth and pleasant. Well, well. With a mere two sentences, the prince had Lyre's instincts buzzing with warning. He had been playing deadly games of manipulation since he was a child, and with that experience, he could see subtle red flags all over Bastian.

"Have you talked to her, then?" Lyre asked, trying to get a feel for what Bastian knew—and what game he was playing.

"Not yet," he admitted. "I wanted to speak with you first."

Hmm, Lyre hadn't expected that honesty. "Why is that?"

Bastian folded his hands behind his back, his expression somber. His guards waited, their pikes held informally but their focus on Lyre.

"I learned of what befell Clio from my bodyguard Eryx upon his return," Bastian said, "so I know something of your role in her survival—and, I assume, her escape from the Underworld."

"Did Eryx tell you he killed Kassia, betrayed Clio, and left her to die?"

"He did." Bastian's expression hardened. "For his actions, Eryx has been incarcerated."

"So why are you here talking to me instead of Clio?"

Bastian didn't react to his accusatory tone. "I am here because my father is not a tolerant king. With the growing threats against our kingdom, he is especially paranoid. If he learns there is a Hades daemon in the city, I fear he may react rashly."

"But you're not prone to rashness, are you?" Lyre asked mockingly.

Bastian ignored that too. "I do not believe punishing you would be in the best interests of my family or my kingdom. You are a daemon of talent and skill—and of honor, or you would not have protected Clio at risk to your own life. I have come to speak with you, to ascertain your trustworthiness for myself, so I can convince my father to offer you asylum."

"Asylum?"

"A new home. A sanctuary where Hades cannot reach you."

Yep, he'd been right. This here was a walking, talking, scheming ball of slime in the shape of a nymph prince.

"And all you ask is my unswerving obedience, right?" Lyre unfolded one arm so he could flutter his fingers in Bastian's direction. "You'll shelter me in your territory, and in return, I have to weave whatever spells you request. If I fail to comply, well, who knows what will happen to me, isolated and under your power in a world I can't escape."

"That's a bleak outlook on a generous offer," Bastian said with a frown. "Providing a sanctuary for you would come with risks for us. Asking for your cooperation doesn't seem unreasonable, does it?"

"Well, that's the thing. I didn't come here seeking asylum. I came to get my spell back."

"Your spell?"

"Yeah, you know, the one your dear pal Eryx stole from me."

Bastian's frown deepened. "Eryx didn't turn over any spells when he returned. Are you sure he stole it?"

Lyre smiled, an expression that could almost be mistaken as friendly. "Do you really want to play this game with me, little prince?"

The chimeras stiffened but Bastian merely raised his eyebrows.

Pushing away from the doorframe, Lyre stepped out of the shed. "This territory is something else, you know. Nymphs are unlike any caste I've encountered in the Underworld. They're almost like children—so trusting and naïve." A sharp edge crept into his smile. "It must be so easy for a guy like you."

"I'm afraid I don't understand."

"Still pretending, huh?" Lyre ran his hand through his hair, pushing his hood off. As it fell back, the chimera guards went rigid and their wide eyes darted over his face as they got a good look at him. Bastian's expression didn't change.

Lyre took another step closer. He wished he could use aphrodesia but the prince would see it with his asper. "I'll tell you something, Bastian. You might be a smooth bastard compared to all these carefree nymphs, but to me, you're a clumsy amateur."

Bastian's mouth thinned. Aha. A reaction, finally.

"In my world," he continued, "lies and deception are the air we breathe. You don't have the skills to play this game at my level."

The prince studied him, his expression indecipherable. For all Lyre's condescension, Bastian wasn't *that* much of an amateur. But the taunting was all part of the game.

"I see," the prince replied. "I presume you wish me to be as straightforward as possible?"

"Yeah, that's right. We don't have all day to stand here verbally sparring, do we?"

"We do not," Bastian agreed, and this time, when he smiled, it was as sharp and mocking as Lyre's smile had been. "Then I will be honest,

Lyre. I want you to work for me. You will be protected, safe, and comfortable. In exchange, you will weave at my command."

"You propose it as though I've never had an offer like that before."

"I expect you will find life significantly more pleasant here than under your family's employment, but should you refuse, I'll arrest you as a Hades spy."

Lyre *tsked* softly. "Another amateur move, Bastian. Don't make threats you have no intention of carrying out."

"I assure you, it is not a bluff."

"Oh, but it is. You won't arrest me and throw me in a dungeon. Too much risk you'll lose control of the situation before you can get what you want."

"And what do you think I want?" Bastian asked coolly.

"We both know perfectly well." Lyre dropped his voice to a malevolent purr. "The clock spell. You're standing here with your guards, trying to persuade me to come quietly, because you can't unlock the clock spell without my help."

Bastian's eyes flashed—chagrinned surprise followed by anger.

"You won't throw me in a dungeon. You don't want the king or anyone else at the palace to know I'm here. That's why you came to find me before talking to Clio." He canted his head. "Let me guess. Your spies informed you about a stranger with a gold aura and lots of fancy spells heading toward the palace, and you guessed where Clio would ditch me—in her favorite private spot in the garden."

Bastian raised his hand. The five chimeras snapped their pikes down, the blades pointing at Lyre's chest.

He arched an eyebrow. "Didn't we just agree that you don't plan to kill me?"

Stepping backward, Bastian nodded pleasantly. "We did, and your shields will prevent those pikes from piercing your flesh."

Lyre's jaw tensed. A diversion. Bastian wanted Lyre to focus his defenses on the threats in front of him, but the attack would come from somewhere else.

An instant—that was all he had to decide. Fighting back would be pointless. The moment he tried to cast, Bastian would see it. With no spells in hand and his enemies so close, six against one were impossible odds. And if he attacked the crown prince of Irida, whether he won or lost, he'd end up dead.

So in the instant he had to act, he caught the tracking gem on his tongue and triggered it. The spell pulsed in his head as its twin activated, and with no better way to keep the weaving hidden and close, he swallowed it.

Bastian's gaze flicked up, focusing on something above Lyre. A signal.

A rope dropped over Lyre's head. The noose snapped tight around his neck and yanked, half strangling him even with his shield. He grabbed the rope but the nearest chimeras caught his arms and forced them away from his body. The noose pulled up until he was lifted onto his toes.

"Begin a cast and I'll have them beat you unconscious." Bastian stopped in front of Lyre and touched two fingers to his chest. Hot magic washed over him, followed by a cold wave as the nymph dissolved his protective wards. "Would you prefer to walk under your own power or be carried?"

Lyre wheezed, the rope crushing his throat. He rolled his eyes up and caught a glimpse of the chimera crouched on the roof of the shed — a familiar chimera.

"Fancy meeting me again, eh?" Eryx barked a laugh. "I can't believe you got out of there alive, but it worked out well for us, didn't it?" He hauled on the rope, lifting Lyre off his feet by the neck. "Not so much for you, though."

"Bind him," Bastian ordered. "Gag him as well."

As the chimeras pulled his arms behind his back, Lyre sneered at the prince as best he could while hanging from a rope, but he couldn't come up with a witty insult. Helpless and captured *again*. What a fun pattern this was becoming.

The tracking spell pulsed in his head. With the weaving's light lost in his aura and muted by his body, the prince hadn't noticed it—yet.

Bastian wrapped his hand around Lyre's spell chain. A touch of his magic snapped the links and he pulled the chain off to examine the weavings. "We can have a long and profitable relationship, or we can have a short and violent one. The decision is yours, but either way, I will get what I want from you."

As he turned away with the spell chain, he glanced back, pale eyes gleaming like arctic ice.

"I'll tell you something, Lyre," he murmured—the same phrase Lyre had derisively used. Bastian's smile returned, crueler than a blade. "You may know how the game works, but you'd lost before we even began to play."

TWENTY~FOUR

CLUTCHING the silent tracking spell, Clio waited for the signal to return. If it didn't reactivate, how would she find Lyre?

Throughout the reception hall, voices buzzed and advisors, messengers, and guards rushed around. Rouvin was barking orders, so focused on locating his missing son that he'd barely glanced her way when the tracking spell went off.

Why had it gone off? Why was Lyre so far from the garden storeroom? Her shaking hand tightened on the stone. If the palace guards had captured him, they would have brought him inside, not taken him away.

Why had the signal stopped?

"Lady Clio."

She looked up. The nymph guard who'd been holding the tracking spell watched her warily.

"What is that spell?" he asked. "Why did it activate?"

She glanced at her tightly closed fist, the gem hidden in her grip.

"Were you signaling someone?" His voice hardened with suspicion. "Do you have someone waiting at the ley line?"

Her head snapped up. "Ley line?"

"I felt the signal," he said, his tone suggesting he thought she was playing dumb. "The only thing in that direction besides wilderness is the North Road and the White Rock ley line."

A ley line. There was a *ley line* north of here. She stared at the guard, her mouth hanging open. If Lyre had gone through a ley line, that would explain why the tracking spell had cut off. It couldn't signal his location if he wasn't in the same realm as her.

"Your Majesty." A guard knelt before the king. "We've expanded the search into the city. Prince Bastian appears to have left the grounds."

Rouvin folded his arms. "You found no indications of where he's gone? Are we certain he left under his own power?"

"His guards are also missing," the chimera replied. "I assume they're with him. We found no indications of where he might have gone, but there are signs of a disturbance in the east garden."

Clio's lungs seized.

"What kind of disturbance?" Rouvin asked.

"The storage room door was open and there were footprints in the dirt and signs of a struggle. We don't know if it's related."

"Find out," the king commanded, and the daemon saluted.

Clio stared blankly at the chaotic bustling. A disturbance in the garden where she'd left Lyre. Signs of a struggle. Lyre activating his tracking spell and heading toward a ley line he shouldn't know existed.

Bastian missing. His guards with him. Gone from the palace grounds. *Signs of a struggle.*

It was too much of a coincidence.

What were the chances that Bastian knew she hadn't arrived alone? Hundreds of nymphs in town had seen Lyre's golden aura and the strange spells he carried. She'd thought she'd have time to talk to the king and Bastian before rumors of a mysterious visitor reached the palace.

She looked at the king, tall and commanding amidst his people, then turned around. With purposeful steps, she walked away. In the bustle of soldiers and messengers, Rouvin didn't glance in her direction. Everyone was focused on their tasks, too busy with their orders and searching for the crown prince to worry about the princess's long-lost lady-in-waiting. Everyone except—

"Where are you going?"

The persistent nymph guard trotted after her.

"I need to check on something," she answered through clenched teeth.

"On what?"

She marched faster. As she headed out of the reception hall and into a long corridor, he swung in front of her, forcing her to a stop. "You don't have permission to—"

She flicked her fingers. Her binding spell was so fast he only had time to gasp before it immobilized him.

"I'm sorry," she said. "I'm leaving. Tell the king ... tell him I'll be back as soon as I can."

Stepping around the frozen guard, she broke into a run. Her nymph swiftness carried her through the familiar halls in a flash and she burst out of a side door. She'd lived at the palace for over three years and knew how to avoid the guards. In only a few minutes, she had hopped the outer wall and was pounding down a path.

She'd never traveled on the North Road before, and if not for the signpost, she would have run right by it. She'd expected an actual road, but it was scarcely more than a worn track through the grass that branched off from a city avenue. She launched down the trail, hoping the ley line wouldn't be difficult to find.

She wished she was leaving with her father's blessing and the assistance of the palace guard, but she couldn't risk it. She had to do this alone.

Sabir had shown her how other daemons, even Overworlders, could react to a rare master weaver. If she told Rouvin about Lyre, he might decide the incubus was a tool, a bartering chip, a spy, or a criminal. Rouvin hadn't known about Bastian's lies, which meant he didn't know Bastian had sent her into the Underworld.

She ran on, long grass whipping at her arms, the trail nearly invisible. The enormous guardian trees petered out, replaced by smaller ones with needle-like leaves that were more suited to the rocky terrain and cool mountain weather. The road wound among crystal-veined outcrops and colossal boulders from ancient rockfalls, and soon the grass disappeared until she was jogging across a trail of fine gravel.

Even as her feet pounded the ground, she knew this was a fool's mission. Ley line travel was untraceable. Bastian could have taken Lyre *anywhere*.

But if he had left the palace, it was because he didn't want anyone to know about Lyre. They weren't in Irida—she would have sensed the tracking spell if it was that close—and going to another Overworld territory would risk the attention of another caste or ruling family. Which meant he'd probably gone to Earth.

Brinford was the only human city she'd been to, and the only daemon-friendly one she was familiar with, so that's where she'd start. As long as Lyre kept his tracking spell active, she could find him.

What she'd do once she reached him … that she wasn't sure about.

She needn't have worried about missing the ley line. It was easy to find—protected by a troop of nymph and chimera soldiers, positioned in an open valley, with the ley line running through a gully at the end.

She stopped on the trail and scanned the valley, but there was no way to sneak up on the line. Leaving the road, she trotted down the slope. The soldiers watched her come, and a pair of nymphs broke off from the wooden shelters where the rest were positioned.

"Lady Clio?" The nymph frowned at her. "I hadn't heard you were back. This ley line is restricted. What are you doing here?"

"I'm following Prince Bastian's instructions. I need to go through the line."

His frown deepened. "He didn't mention you."

So Bastian *had* gone through this line. She lifted her chin. "Why else would I be here? I need to catch up with him. It's urgent."

The nymph exchanged a look with his comrade, then shrugged. "Go ahead, then, but make sure to return with His Highness."

With a nervous nod of thanks, she approached the ley line. At a fast jog, it had taken her almost an hour to reach this spot. Bastian and his men must have captured Lyre almost as soon as she'd left him and traveled to the ley line. She was so far behind.

Her stomach twisted. She had to get to Lyre. She was the only one who knew what had happened to him. No one else could save him.

No one else would even try.

The realization came on a wave of quiet grief. She was the only person who cared about him, who would fight to save his life. Besides her, there was just Reed, and he had already done all he could.

She was the only one. Lyre had no one else.

The burn in her lungs and the ache in her legs faded. Determination lit through her, and her hands clenched into fists. She would not fail him. She would be there for him.

She stepped into the ley line.

THE MOMENT she stepped out of the line, she felt it: the pulse of the tracking spell. A beacon in her mind summoned her onward, calling her to follow.

She stumbled away from the ribbon of blue and green light and gathered her bearings. Though it was early dusk in the Overworld, on Earth, it was already dark. The stars glimmered in a clear sky and the three-quarter moon illuminated the scrubby forest that surrounded the ley line.

The tracking spell beat in her head, telling her which way to go.

She shoved through the underbrush, ignoring the thorns scraping across her exposed skin. Ahead, an old highway peeked through the foliage; she'd last traveled that road with Sabir on their way to the line a few days ago.

As she broke into a steady jog, timing her pace with the pulse of the tracking spell, her mind raced ahead. Bastian had brought Lyre to Brinford. She hadn't wanted to hope it would be this simple, but it made sense. Brinford was the human city Bastian was most familiar with. He'd been visiting it at least once a month for two years.

Bastian had lied. The sick realization had hovered in her mind since her talk with the king, underscoring every thought. Bastian had lied about *everything*. Why? Why had he tricked her into leaving Irida? Why had he convinced her their homeland was in danger and sent her to investigate Ra spell commissions? Why had he asked her to steal warfare spellcraft from Chrysalis?

Why?

No matter how she twisted and wrangled the questions, she found no answers. She didn't know where the truth ended and his lies began. With each question that spun through her head, the numb shield of disbelief cracked. Beneath it, pain waited — and beneath the pain, fury simmered, its heat growing swiftly.

Her legs burned and her throat ached from thirst, but she didn't slow. She had to catch up. She had to find Lyre and stop Bastian from … from whatever he intended to do.

In the distance, a smattering of white and yellow lights glittered among the blanket of darkness: Brinford. The tracking spell called her onward. It was so pervasive she almost missed the second, softer beat of another spell — the beacon that marked a Consulate.

She hesitated, slowing to a walk. The last time she and Lyre had been there, they'd stolen the Consulate's car. Had the Consulate recovered their vehicle?

Making a snap decision, she rushed down the long drive. The elegant manor came into view, its front lights glowing welcomingly. Ignoring the front drive, she cut through the trees to the hidden garage and narrow back driveway. A bolt of magic snapped the lock on the door and she flung it open to reveal the pitch black interior.

She cast a light spell and the green glow washed over the dull paint of a gray sedan parked in the center of the garage. Old, rusting, and far more beaten than the car she and Lyre had stolen, but it was a car nonetheless.

She pulled the vehicle's door open and a musty smell wafted out. Dropping into the driver's seat, she pawed at the various nooks and crannies where the keys might be hiding. Last time, Lyre had hot-wired the car — an unexpected skill she'd meant to ask him about — but she had no idea how to do the same. She needed the key.

She searched the car, finding nothing, then scoured the garage. Swearing under her breath, she considered how long it would take her to find the keys. Every wasted minute felt like a risk, but the time she lost here could be made up by driving into the city. At any moment, the tracking spell could disappear and she might never find Lyre again.

She shimmered into her human glamour so as not to draw too much attention, then raced through the trees to the back of the property. Cracking the back door open, she entered the gourmet kitchen where she'd cooked pancakes. It was empty and lit only by the lights under the cabinets. She hurriedly poured a glass of water and drank, her thoughts consumed with the question of where the Consuls would keep the keys to their vehicles. Not anywhere a daemon could stumble upon them.

After downing two glasses of water, she tiptoed across the kitchen and into the corridor, listening for any signs of life. The building was quiet except for the rumble of voices and the tinny crackle of a radio emanating from the basement.

Stopping in front of a door, she pressed her ear to it. No sound on the other side. A crude lock spell glowed across the wood and she dissolved it before trying the handle. It jiggled but wouldn't turn, physically locked.

Adding a magical boost, she shoved down on the handle. The lock snapped with a loud crack and she froze. No change in the rumbling conversation downstairs.

Pushing the door open, she rushed into an office dominated by a large mahogany desk. Despite the opulence of the woodworking, the room was cold and businesslike, the desktop empty, and the floor-to-ceiling bookshelves filled with bland leather spines.

She jumped over the desk and grabbed the first drawer. Locked. She used magic to break it open and rifled through the contents, finding nothing resembling keys. She broke open the next drawer and dug through it, dumping folders of paper on the floor in her haste.

"Damn it," she hissed as she broke into the third and final drawer. Boxes of envelopes, paperclips, and other office supplies. She flung them onto the floor and sifted through the pile. Nothing.

"What the hell are you—"

Clio shot to her feet. The young apprentice girl stood in the threshold, one hand on the door. Her furious glower morphed into surprise.

"Clio?"

"Piper?"

"What are you doing?" Piper demanded. "This is the Head Consul's office! You'll be blacklisted for this."

"I don't care. This is urgent."

"What's urgent?" Piper pointed accusingly. "You and that incubus stole my father's car when you left, didn't you? When did you come back?"

"Just now." Clio clenched her jaw. "Piper, I need another car."

"*What?* You already stole our good one! How can you even—"

"I *need* it!" Her voice went higher as the frantic need to move, to keep going, to reach Lyre before she lost him pounded through her head. "I don't have a choice."

Piper blinked, her anger subsiding. She lowered her hand from the door but didn't move from the threshold, blocking Clio's path. "What's going on? What's so urgent?"

"My friend—the incubus—he's been captured."

"Captured?" Piper's green eyes widened. "By who?"

"I can't tell you, but his life is in danger. I have to reach him before—before it's too late."

Piper looked from Clio to the mess on the floor and back again. "He's in that much danger?"

Clio nodded. "I have to get to him as fast as possible."

"Where is he?"

"In the city. I've already lost too much time running from the ley line—"

"*Running?* You ran the whole way?" Piper's gaze snapped over Clio from head to toe as though reassessing her. The girl shifted her weight, a furrow forming in her forehead. "Damn it. I'll get grounded for a month for this."

"For what?" Clio asked blankly.

"For helping you." The girl's hesitation vanished behind an excited grin. "Let's rescue your incubus friend!"

Clio blinked. "*Let's* rescue …?"

Piper marched across the room to the bookshelf, rose onto her tiptoes, and grabbed a thick volume from the top shelf. It jingled as she flipped the cover open. The interior was hollowed out, and inside it sat several sets of keys.

Piper lifted out a key chain, shut the book, and replaced it on the shelf. "Let's go!"

"But—but Piper, I can't take you with me." Clio rushed after her toward the door. "It's too dangerous for—"

"You're *not* stealing our only other car," Piper said, waving the keys over her shoulder as she strode into the hall. "I'm going with you."

Clio bit her lip, then raised her hand at Piper's back. The binding spell hit with a flash and Piper pitched forward, landing with a loud thud. The keys skittered across the floor.

"Hey!" Piper yelled. "What are you doing?"

"I can't let you come." Clio stepped over the girl and grabbed the keys. "I'm sorry. It's too dangerous."

"I can help!"

"No, you can't. You don't understand."

"Wait!" Piper squirmed, furiously trying to free herself. "Do you even know how to drive?"

Clio hesitated, biting her lip. "It doesn't look that difficult."

Piper's eyes bulged. "You'll wreck our car! Let me do it."

"You know how to drive?"

"My uncle taught me."

Clio bounced from foot to foot, anxious to keep moving. How much time would she lose figuring out how to operate the car? She hadn't paid all that much attention when Lyre had driven them into the city before.

Whirling back around, she crouched in front of Piper. "You can drive me, but once we get there, you'll drop me off, turn around, and come right back here. Agreed?"

Piper grimaced. "Agreed."

Clio touched the girl's arm and the binding spell dissolved.

Piper popped back up and bounded ahead of Clio, leading the way to the kitchen. "I'm going to kick your butt later for putting a binding spell on me."

"You can try," Clio muttered. Piper might have better hand-to-hand combat skills, but Clio could out-spell the girl in her sleep. Based on the girl's strange aura, she didn't have enough magic to cast anything, let alone defend herself.

In the garage, Piper wrestled the overhead door open, then jumped into the driver's seat, grinning the whole time. For the girl, this was a grand adventure—a daring rescue mission to save a handsome incubus.

As Clio climbed into the passenger seat, sending up a cloud of musty dust from the upholstery, she wished she could feel that kind of innocent excitement. But this journey wasn't an adventure for her or for Lyre. She wasn't sure what it was, but as Piper revved the engine and the car peeled out of the garage, Clio couldn't shake her growing dread.

She loved her brother. She was sure he cared about her too, and no matter what happened, she shouldn't be afraid of him. But deep in her heart, icy fear pulsed in time with the tracking spell.

Cherished sibling or not, she couldn't trust Bastian, not with Lyre's life … or her own.

This wasn't an adventure. This wasn't a rescue mission. It was a life-or-death confrontation with a daemon who had the power to destroy everything that mattered to her.

TWENTY~FIVE

LYRE'S BACK hit a hard surface. Hands grabbed his shoulders and forced him down until he was sitting, then the blindfold was pulled off his head.

Daemons circled him. The chimera guards had shifted into glamour, their uniforms replaced by unremarkable dark clothes. They didn't hold weapons, but all it would take was a quick shift out of glamour to rearm themselves.

The nymph prince stood directly across from Lyre, arms folded as he surveyed his prisoner. He, too, had donned his glamour. His stylish black coat and slacks gave him the look of a young, wealthy businessman about to sit down at a fancy restaurant with some clients.

Lyre glanced past them, trying to get a handle on where he was. A human city, obviously, which he'd known by the stench of garbage and damp pavement. They were in an abandoned park, surrounded by dead or dying trees with a few yellow leaves clinging to their branches. Rotting wood benches lined the cracked pavement, and across from him was an old fountain, no water flowing from it. A war memorial, as broken and dirty as the rest of the park, acted as his backrest, the once polished surface carved with hundreds of names, now illegible and forgotten.

Surrounding the park, the shadows of old buildings with elegant architecture were visible through the trees. Behind them, skyscrapers rose—including a distant pale tower that looked white even in the darkness. It was familiar and unmistakable: the Ra embassy.

So they were back in Brinford, where all the assassins and bounty hunters were waiting for him. Lovely.

With a clatter of wood on stone, a chimera guard dragged over a simple wooden chair and set it down behind Bastian. The prince sat and crossed his legs at the knee, getting comfortable.

Steepling his fingers, he studied Lyre. "Shall we begin?"

"One thing first." Lyre shifted uncomfortably with his arms bound behind his back from wrists to elbows. "What's with the chair?"

"I beg your pardon?"

"That *chair*." Lyre pointed at it with his chin. "Where'd it come from? Why do you have a chair in the middle of an abandoned park? Do you perform interrogations here so often that you keep a stash of furniture handy?"

"I prefer to be prepared for all occasions," Bastian replied coolly. "From this point onward, I will ask questions and you will answer."

"And if I don't answer?"

"Then my guards will persuade you to be more cooperative."

Standing just behind Bastian's left shoulder, Eryx flashed an eager grin at Lyre.

When Bastian first captured him, Lyre had assumed the prince would hide him somewhere in or near the nymph city, giving Clio plenty of time to arrange a rescue. He hadn't expected the prince to whisk him right out of Iridian territory. On Earth, there would be no rescue.

He sighed. It was going to be a very long night.

"Start asking, then," he said dully.

Bastian folded his hands into a more relaxed position. "We will begin with the clock spell."

"Kinetic Lodestone Obversion Construct."

"What?"

"That's what it's called. KLOC for short."

Bastian's eyes narrowed.

"Kinetic means moving parts," Lyre explained, oozing as much condescension as he could while sitting on the ground with his arms bound behind his back. "I designed it to clear remnant weaves from lodestones, hence the next part of the name. Obversion means—"

"What does the spell do?"

"It obverts magic. That's why I called it the Obversion Constr—"

"The spell *consumes* magic. That is not the same as obversion."

"Obversion is a more accurate word." Lyre arched an eyebrow. "It means to turn something into its opposite, which is what the KLOC does. When it contacts other magic, it converts that energy into more of itself."

"Meaning what?"

"Meaning it turns regular weaves into … shadow weaves."

"Shadow weaves," Bastian repeated.

Lyre nodded. He wasn't keen on sharing anything about the KLOC, but he would reveal enough tidbits to make Bastian think he was being open about the spell. The information wasn't any more dangerous than what Bastian would have learned from Eryx or deduced from his own examination of the clock.

"What is a shadow weave?"

"Well, you looked at the KLOC, right?"

"Of course. You mean the dark tint to the weaves. How did you create it?"

Lyre rolled his shoulders, the muscles aching from too long in the binding. "I'm not sure."

The prince scrutinized him, debating how much he wanted to push. So far, Lyre was cooperating and Bastian probably wouldn't apply significant pressure over one evasive answer.

"How does the spell work?" he asked.

Lyre relaxed against the wall. No torture yet. Hooray. "Once triggered, the initial outflux of the shadow weave will obvert any magic it contacts, at which point the converted magic will undergo an outflux as well, expanding by a factor relative to the input energy. If it contacts more magic, it will obvert and outflux again, continuing the chain reaction until it ceases to encounter any more fuel and exhausts its reach."

Eryx blinked stupidly and looked at Bastian.

The prince drummed his fingers on his knee. "So, in essence, this spell doesn't consume magic so much as transforms it into more of the shadow weave, perpetuating its existence … and its reach."

Hmm. A deceitful, conniving, *and* intelligent prince. He understood the nature of the spell better than Lyre had expected.

"How fast is the chain reaction?" Bastian asked.

"Up to a radius of a hundred feet, its near instantaneous. It may slow as it expands, but I haven't tested it on a larger scale."

"What kind of magic can it obvert?"

"All kinds." Lyre hesitated, but Eryx had already overheard the next part. "From embedded weavings to a daemon's power reserves."

"What happens to a daemon when their power is consumed?"

"Beyond having their magic completely wiped out? Physical weakness, severe fatigue, loss of glamour." He shrugged. "It isn't fun."

Bastian considered his next question. "Where does water come into play?"

"The fluid resistance slows the shadow weave's expansion, reducing its reach."

"So you used the KLOC in a bathtub to limit it."

Lyre nodded, tension threading through his muscles. Bastian had asked all the easy questions, and he would soon run out of queries that Lyre was willing to answer.

"How would I safely use the KLOC?"

"Put it in water. The more water, the better."

"How would I safely use it *for a purpose*?" the prince clarified impatiently.

"If you want to clear lodestones, put them in the water with the KLOC."

Bastian observed him for a long minute. "How do you activate it?"

A sharp breath slipped from Lyre. There it was. The question he couldn't answer.

When he said nothing, Bastian straightened. "Lyre, I recommend you continue to cooperate. I will have the answer regardless."

Again, he held his silence. What could he say? There was no plausible lie for how to activate the KLOC that Bastian wouldn't see through.

The prince leaned forward, bracing his elbows on his knees. "This has been nearly pleasant so far, Lyre. Consider my earlier proposal. Working for me would not be taxing or demeaning. I would treat you well. You would have reasonable freedoms."

"I don't consider basic autonomy a 'reasonable freedom.'"

"It would be a better life than what you've come from. Would you rather die here in this reeking hole of a human city?"

Lyre met the prince's ice-blue eyes. "Actually, I would."

Bastian sat back. "You will answer no more questions, will you? Why did you answer any of them?"

Lyre twitched his shoulders in a shrug. "Did I tell you anything you hadn't already guessed?"

Bastian's lips thinned. "I see. Well, we will begin with the question of how to activate the KLOC. Once you answer it, we will move on to the next."

He waved at Eryx.

Grin returning, Eryx walked up to Lyre, grabbed him by the arm, and hauled him up. The other guards closed in, and together they pulled Lyre past Bastian to the fountain. Two tiers in the center stood about eight feet tall and the main basin was a large square with high walls. Murky water from the recent rainfall filled the basin, reflecting the city lights.

Lyre's stomach dropped sickeningly, then someone behind him pulled the blindfold back over his eyes. He tensed, unable to stop himself from resisting as they dragged him over the sidewalk, then pushed him down. His stomach hit the basin's lip, crushing his diaphragm and ramming the air out of his lungs.

A hand grabbed his hair, and before he could catch his breath, they shoved his head into the cold water.

CLIO CLUTCHED the interior door handle and wondered if she should have driven the car herself. If she died in a wreck, who would save Lyre?

Piper grinned fiercely, clutching the steering wheel as the car tore through the streets and dodged garbage. There were so few running vehicles left in the city that other traffic wasn't a concern, but Clio still feared for her life.

"Is the signal still straight ahead?" Piper asked, slamming on the brakes to whip around a dumpster sticking out into the street.

"Yes," Clio gasped breathlessly, gripping the chest strap of her seatbelt. "You should slow down. We should approach cautiously."

Piper let off on the gas pedal, her young face alight. "Not much farther, right?"

"Not much." The pulse in Clio's head was growing stronger and stronger, coming from a point dead ahead. "We're almost there."

Slowing the car, Piper adjusted her grip on the steering wheel. "How are you going to save the incubus guy?"

"I don't know yet."

"Can you do it all by yourself?"

Seeing exactly where the girl's line of questioning was headed, Clio nodded firmly. "I'll figure it out."

"Wouldn't it be better to have backup?"

She shot Piper a stern look. "The daemons who have my friend are expert magic users. You can't help."

Hurt flickered through Piper's eyes and her face fell.

"I'm sure you can fight," Clio added quickly. "But you'd need a lot of magic to stand any chance against these daemons."

Piper flexed her jaw. "How did you know I don't have magic?"

"I ... I can tell."

"I'm a haemon," she muttered tersely. "I should have magic."

Clio didn't know what to say. The girl might be a haemon, but her aura was far from normal.

The road ended at a T-intersection, and directly ahead was a thicket of trees with a paved walkway that disappeared into the darkness.

Piper stopped the car and squinted at the park. "Should I go around?"

"No." The tracking signal pounded in her skull. "This is close enough."

Piper reached for the key in the ignition. "I can—"

Clio grabbed the girl's hand, stopping her from shutting off the engine. "You will turn around and drive home. You don't want to lose your apprenticeship, do you?"

Alarm flashed in her gaze as though she'd never considered the possibility.

Clio unbuckled and pushed the door open. "Straight back to the Consulate, okay?"

"Okay." Piper leaned sideways to watch Clio climb out. "Be careful, Clio."

"I will." With a reassuring smile, she swung the door shut and stepped onto the sidewalk.

Piper steered the car in a tight U-turn, then the engine revved as she took off back down the road. Clio waited to make sure the girl didn't stop and turn around again, then she faced the night-swathed park.

Her heart hammered painfully in her chest. Touching her throat, she cast a cloaking spell over herself, then started forward at a brisk walk. The path zigzagged through the trees, silent and empty. The tracking spell called her onward, hammering so loudly in her head that she almost wanted to deactivate it. But not yet.

She reached the edge of the trees as something splashed loudly, followed by hacking, wet coughs. Ahead, a memorial wall blocked her view. Barely breathing, she crept to the edge and peeked around it.

The first thing she saw was Bastian's back. He sat in a wooden chair that was completely out of place in the decaying park, facing a crumbling water fountain. Six daemons with red hair and tattoos stood at the edge of the fountain, and she didn't need her asper to know they were his chimera bodyguards.

Slumped at their feet beside the fountain was Lyre, a blindfold over his eyes and water dripping off his chin as he coughed violently. Convulsions wrenched his body as though he'd inhaled an entire bucket of water.

"How much longer, Lyre?" Bastian asked, his calm voice painfully familiar. "Next round, I'll double the time."

Lyre continued to cough up water.

When he quieted, Bastian rubbed his chin. "You are exceptionally stubborn. Tell me how to activate the KLOC or we will continue."

Lyre sucked in an unsteady breath as though to speak, but instead he spat on the ground in Bastian's direction. A clear answer.

Bastian waved his hand and leaned back in the chair, looking bored. The chimeras grabbed Lyre by the arms, spun him around, and shoved his face into the fountain.

Lightheadedness swept through Clio. Lyre writhed, his arms bound behind his back and his feet scraping helplessly at the ground. A guard snickered cruelly and rammed his knee into Lyre's back, pinning him to the basin's edge.

Bastian sighed. "This is tedious. I didn't expect him to hold out so long."

Clio didn't even realize she was moving until she'd burst out from behind the memorial. She hadn't decided to act, but her body was in motion and the only thing in her head was a raging fury so hot that it was like a poison flooding her body.

Focused on Lyre, the men didn't notice her until she was almost on top of them. The prince lurched up from his chair and three chimeras whipped to face her, but she had already reached Bastian, her arm pulling back.

She struck him across the face with all her strength.

He staggered, and then a blast of magic from a guard hit her in the chest, throwing her backward. She landed hard and two daemons sprang at her, their glamours vanishing and swords jumping into their hands.

"Stop."

The chimeras halted at Bastian's command, the points of their weapons aimed at her chest. She pushed up onto her elbows, too angry to feel fear. At the fountain, the other three guards hauled Lyre out of the water and dumped him on the ground. He retched and coughed, shaking violently.

How long had they'd been drowning him in that water over and over? Tedious, Bastian had called it. Callously torturing another daemon was *tedious*?

She turned her enraged focus back to Bastian—and the daemon standing beside him. Eryx grinned delightedly. Her fury cracked at the sight of him, grief and helpless anguish rising through her, but she choked it back.

"Clio," Bastian murmured. The side of his face was reddening but he didn't acknowledge that she'd hit him. He flicked a glance at Eryx. "Check if she came alone."

Eryx sped away into the trees.

"How did you find us?" Bastian asked her.

"If I don't answer, will you drown me in the fountain as well?"

His mouth thinned. "I would like to know."

She stuck her hand in her pocket, pulled out the tracking spell, and threw the gem at him. He watched it clatter on the crumbling pavement, then peered at Lyre with his brow furrowed.

She glanced at Lyre as well, squinting with her asper as she wondered how he'd hidden his spell for so long. All she could see was his aura.

Bastian made a soft sound of surprise. "He *swallowed* it?"

Lyre lifted his head, his lips pulling back from his teeth in a humorless grin. "Surprise, asshole."

Irritation flickered across Bastian's face. He turned to Clio again. "I'm pleased to see you alive and unharmed."

"Are you?" Ignoring the chimeras and their weapons, she got to her feet. "Are you equally pleased that Eryx murdered Kassia in a cowardly surprise attack, or that he left me to die in Asphodel?"

"His methods may not be what I would choose, but Eryx is a loyal servant."

"Loyalty is important, isn't it?" she sneered. "You like everyone to be loyal to you, no matter how many lies you have to tell them to win them over."

"So you have spoken to the king." Bastian sank back into his chair, calm and composed as though they were discussing their holiday plans. "What did you learn?"

"That you've lied about everything!"

"'Everything' is an exaggeration."

"You lied to me about the threat of a Ra invasion! You tricked me into leaving Irida! You sent me to get military spells from Chrysalis when there isn't even a war!"

He smiled faintly. "But there will be a war, Clio."

She balled her hands into fists, trembling with fury. "You're a filthy liar. Why should I believe anything you say?"

"I rearranged the truth, nothing more. Would you like to discuss this, or would you rather rage and shout?"

Anger spiraled through her at his patronizing tone. She sucked in air, fighting for control. Breathing deeply, she unclenched her hands. "You owe me an explanation, Bastian. For everything."

He appraised her as though analyzing an interesting specimen in a laboratory. "You told me many times over the last two years that you wanted to help protect our homeland. That is what you've been doing, Clio."

"But there is no threat—"

"There is very much a threat, one that my father and his predecessors have ignored." He tapped a finger on his knee as though to emphasize a point. "Centuries ago, Ra forced a trade agreement on Irida. They made us purchase our own sovereignty, and we continue to pay for it centuries later."

She glanced from her brother to Lyre, who was on his knees beside the fountain with three guards surrounding him. "I don't understand."

"My father is too fearful of conflict to resist, but I am not. Before the trade agreement is next renewed, I will end Ra's dominion over us." He rose to his feet and slid his hand into his pocket. "Ra sees us as weak, but I will prove otherwise. You have helped me prepare for that day, and I am almost ready to forge a new fate for our kingdom."

He withdrew his hand to reveal Lyre's spelled clock, its gears glittering with jewels. "You did very well in Chrysalis. Far better than I had hoped."

"You left me there to die," she choked.

"Eryx's choice." Bastian ran his thumb along the clock's edge. "No single life is more important than our goal. This is about saving Irida."

"Saving Irida from a *trade agreement*?" She struggled to gather her strength, searching for the hot fury that had died beneath his cold logic.

"I would have gone to Chrysalis even if you hadn't lied about a Ra invasion. Why did you send me to Earth?"

"To protect you. It was my mistake ... I shouldn't have exposed you to danger by bringing you into the palace in the first place. It wasn't safe for you, Clio."

Her hands clenched as she searched his face. His sincerity sounded perfectly earnest ...

"No, Clio." Lyre's hoarse voice startled her. His shoulders were hunched, his head hanging, the blindfold dripping water. "He brought you into the palace to show you the thing you wanted most—a family—then he took it away. He did it to make you dependent on him. He held your dearest desire hostage against you."

Clio stared at Lyre, then turned back to Bastian. His expression seemed blank but his eyes had narrowed and his mouth had tightened. Anger. Displeasure.

Pain ricocheted through her chest as her heart broke piece by piece.

"Was that your plan?" she whispered, her voice shaking. "From the very beginning? You wanted to use me all along ... your secret mimic."

"You did well, Clio. You learned the skills you needed quickly, and you were ready to enter Chrysalis sooner than I had anticipated." Bastian hefted the clock like it was a well-earned prize.

She pushed her anguish aside. "You can't use that spell. It's too dangerous. You can't control how far it will spread or how much magic it will eat."

"Does that matter? If unleashed in the correct place, its uncontrolled spread will work in my favor."

"But—"

"I will purge Ra's shadow from over our kingdom, Clio. I will bring Irida back to its former strength and glory. The question is ..." He fixed his cool stare on her. "Where do you stand?"

"What?"

"You have proven yourself resourceful and resilient. Your loyalty has ... strayed somewhat, but it is nothing I am unwilling to forgive. You've proven your commitment to protecting Irida." He walked toward her, stopping a few feet away, and he smiled—the gentle smile of welcome that had won her over so easily when they'd first met. "Will you join me in the battle to free our people from Ra's shadow?"

Her throat constricted until it ached.

"I have used you," he admitted softly, "and I regret that I have hurt you, but this is for Irida. Help me protect our people, Clio. Fight for them at my side, not as a tool but as a valued ally."

The pain in her shattered heart turned to icy flames. "Free Lyre first."

Bastian's brow furrowed. "What?"

"Let Lyre go. Prove you're better than Ra and Hades and the other power-hungry warlords who do nothing but hurt and oppress whoever they think they can control."

Images flashed through her mind—Lyre in chains in Asphodel's basement; Reed with his eyes shadowed by helplessness; Ash covered in blood and bruises as he walked unresisting into a prison cell.

She raised an unsteady hand and pointed at Lyre. "Prove it, Bastian. If you won't free him, then you're no better than Hades and you have no right to call yourself a prince of Irida."

"Clio ..." Bastian sighed. "He is far too useful, and too dangerous, to let go."

She lowered her arm, the last of her hope crumbling like bitter ash. "I defended you to Kassia," she whispered brokenly, "but she was right all along."

Bastian's face hardened with annoyance. Then a different voice spoke right behind her, its familiar arrogance triggering a cascade of loathing.

"I told you she was too stupid to understand."

She gasped as a man's arm clamped around her torso, then the cold edge of a blade pressed against her throat.

"Two for two," Eryx whispered in her ear.

Bastian dropped back into his chair. "Take the blindfold off the incubus."

A chimera ripped the cloth strip off Lyre's head. His eyes, black with fury, jumped straight to Clio and he snarled at the sight of Eryx with a knife at her throat.

Bastian snapped his fingers, drawing Lyre's attention.

"Now, Lyre, let us try something different. My patience has worn thin, and I would like to proceed without further delay." He tilted the KLOC, the gems glittering in the moonlight. "Tell me how to activate the spell or Eryx will slit Clio's throat. You have to the count of ten."

TWENTY-SIX

"TEN," Bastian began, his voice cool and emotionless.

Lyre clenched his teeth so hard that pain shot up his jaw. Bloody hell.

"Nine."

Things just kept getting worse. His gaze darted from the prince to Clio, her eyes wide and Eryx's dagger at her throat.

"Eight."

He wished he could go back in time and destroy the tracking spell. He wished he'd never given it to her.

"Seven."

He'd thought she would bring help—palace guards or something. He'd never imagined she would come alone, bursting in without a plan.

"Six."

Damn that prince. He'd twisted Clio in his emotional games for so long she probably hadn't considered the possibility he would turn on her like this.

"Five."

To someone else, maybe her actions would seem willfully stupid, but he understood. Even after everything Lyceus had done to him, part of him still wanted to please his father. It had taken years of outright abuse to crush the ever-kindling hope that the person he most wanted to love and protect him wasn't actually that bad.

"Four."

Clio was learning the hardest lesson of all. Her brother would never love her. He had never cared about her.

"Three."

She had refused to submit to him. She was standing on her own two feet—and therefore, she was useless to him.

"Two."

And now he would kill her.

"One."

The blade gleamed in Eryx's hand. Lyre tore his gaze away from Clio and focused on Bastian.

"Fine. I'll tell you."

Clio gasped in horror. "No, Lyre, you can't—"

Eryx clamped his hand over her mouth and pressed the knife into her throat. A trickle of blood ran down her neck.

"An excellent decision, Lyre," Bastian complimented.

He bared his teeth. "Get that knife off Clio."

"No, I think the knife will remain where it is in case you're inclined to be difficult again."

Lyre growled silently. "Unbind me."

"Why would I do that?"

"If you want the key to the KLOC, then unbind me."

Bastian's eyes narrowed, then he nodded at a guard. "One suspicious move and Eryx will cut her throat."

Clio made a furious sound through Eryx's hand. A chimera snapped the magical bindings on Lyre's arms and pain shot through his shoulders as the strain on his muscles released. He sucked in an unsteady breath and climbed to his feet.

"Well?" Bastian asked softly.

"I'm going to drop glamour—briefly. Don't overreact." When Bastian nodded his permission, Lyre let his glamour fall. Tingles rushed over his skin, and as power washed over him, he let a touch of aphrodesia spill out of his aura. He grabbed the chain around his neck—protected in his daemon shape—and snapped the silver skeleton key off.

He pulled his glamour back into place. He could sense the faint presences of the chimeras standing around him—too close for their own good and unaware he'd begun to ensnare them.

He glanced once at the key he had carried since the day he'd realized how dangerous the KLOC was, then tossed it to Bastian.

The prince caught it, his gaze flicking over the ruby in the bit. "What is this?"

"The key for the clock."

Bastian's jaw flexed as he realized Lyre's reference to a key hadn't been figurative. "Explain."

"Insert the key in the back of the clock and turn it counterclockwise to wind one minute." Lyre let more aphrodesia leak out while the nymph's attention was on the KLOC. "When you remove the key, the second hand will count down. In sixty seconds, the spell will activate."

Bastian flipped the clock over to check the back. "That seems needlessly complicated."

"Tell you what. When *you* design never-before-conceived magic, you can craft the trigger however you like."

Ignoring that, the prince continued his examination. "I see. This explains why I had such difficulty understanding the weaving or discerning a trigger method. Fascinating."

Lyre was about to slip more aphrodesia into his captors when Bastian inserted the key into the clock's back.

"What are you doing?"

Bastian glanced up at Lyre's sharp tone. "Testing it. You don't expect me to take your word, do you?"

"You can't use it *here*."

"Why not?"

"Don't you understand how easy it is to lose control of the spell? If it touches our magic, it could spread for—I don't even know how far, but—"

"There's water in the fountain," Bastian interrupted dismissively. "I chose this location for more than one reason."

"It's too risky," Lyre insisted. "Even I don't know its exact range, in or out of water. If you misjudge—"

"Why would it concern you if everyone here has their magic devoured? It will hardly make your situation worse."

Lyre snapped his mouth shut. Shit.

"You look nervous, Lyre," Bastian observed silkily. "Why does your spell frighten you? Have you omitted information I should know?"

Lyre let out a rough exhalation. He didn't want to reveal how catastrophic the KLOC could be, but he couldn't allow Bastian to use it carelessly. Lyre using it on himself in Asphodel had been insanely dangerous as it was.

"The shadow weave infects any magic it touches," he growled unhappily. "*Any* magic."

"So you've said. Your point?"

Lyre ground his teeth. "Ley lines are magic."

Bastian stilled. "Are you suggesting this spell could obvert a *ley line*?"

"I don't know, but are you willing to take the chance? Ley lines are a planet's arteries. If the shadow weave touches even one ley line, it might spread to them all. It could wipe them out."

Bastian glanced at the clock. His expression should have been terrified, but instead it was thoughtful.

"We can jump from one world's ley lines to another's," Lyre snarled, urgent demand in his voice. "What if the shadow weave can reach through the Void? You could wipe out the magic in all three realms at once. Every ley line, every daemon, every magical creature. All magic gone in one sweep."

The chimeras standing around him shifted nervously, but Bastian was still considering the clock like it was a damn lottery ticket.

"You're holding a doomsday spell, you fool!" Lyre yelled. "You can't use it! You can't ever risk it touching a ley line!"

Bastian tilted his head thoughtfully. "If it's so potentially devastating, why didn't you destroy it?"

"It absorbs any magic that touches it. I don't know *how* to destroy it."

The prince balanced the clock on his palm. "There are no ley lines anywhere near here."

"Are you fucking serious?" Lyre jerked his head toward the skyscrapers beyond the park. "The Ra embassy isn't that far. How much magic is in there? Enough for the shadow weave to cover the whole city? All it would take is a few daemons in the wrong place for the shadow weave to make the jump to the nearest ley line."

"That is extremely unlikely." Bastian inserted the key in the clock again. "We take great risks every day, and this one is slimmer than most."

Lyre lunged forward but the guards grabbed him. One of them bent his arms behind his back, trapping him in place.

"Um, Prince Bastian?" Eryx pulled the knife a few inches from Clio's throat. "Not that I want to agree with the incubus mongrel, but maybe you should test that spell under more controlled circumstances."

"Why do you say that?"

"That bastard hasn't lost his cool over anything else." Eryx squinted at Lyre. "But *now* he's scared. If he's freaking out over this, I don't think we want to fool around."

Lyre held his breath, waiting to see how Bastian would react to words of caution from his right-hand man.

The prince pursed his lips, then sighed. "I abandoned caution when I left Irida without leave. I can't afford further delay. Now that we have begun, to pause would be to invite defeat."

A sickening feeling sucked at Lyre's innards, and he looked at Clio. Eryx's hand still covered her mouth, his dagger hovering a scant two inches from her throat. Her eyebrows scrunched together, and her stormy eyes moved from Bastian to Lyre.

They stared at each other for a moment that lasted an eternity, unspoken words passing between them. Bastian would risk everything in unleashing the shadow weave—and Lyre would risk everything to stop him.

Even though his next move would likely mean Clio's death.

He tore his stare away from her and let his focus sink inward. As Bastian turned his attention to the clock, Lyre ripped his arms out of the chimera's grip. Then he dropped his glamour and slammed the full force of his aphrodesia into the daemons surrounding him.

CLIO STARED into Lyre's black eyes. She knew. She knew he was about to act—and that her survival was in her own hands.

Eryx had shifted the blade away from her neck when he'd cautioned Bastian against using the clock. She couldn't believe Bastian had disregarded Eryx's warning. Eryx embodied reckless arrogance, so if *he* felt caution was needed, how could Bastian ignore that?

But the prince was ignoring it, and she focused on getting through the next thirty seconds alive. She twisted her palm toward Eryx's torso behind her.

In a surge of movement, Lyre lunged free from his captors and dropped his glamour. His aphrodesia hit her like a punch to the chest but she stayed focused and unleashed her cast. The simple spell slammed into Eryx's lower belly, flinging him backward. She ducked away from his dagger but it sliced across her cheek.

Eryx shot up as fast as he'd fallen. She whirled on him, hands raised. His dagger shone red with her blood as he flicked a glance away from her.

She dared to look away at the same time. Lyre was out of glamour, his fists bristling with throwing knives. Two chimeras stood unmoving, caught in his aphrodesia, and the other three were backing away as they also dropped glamour.

Lyre flicked a blade in the air, caught it, and whipped it into the face of an enthralled chimera. The daemon pitched over backward, the knife protruding from his eye socket.

"Take him down but don't kill him," Eryx barked at his men. His crimson eyes, darkening to black, swung back to her. "I'll deal with the girl."

She widened her stance and slid sideways, bringing Bastian into her peripheral vision. But he hadn't moved. Holding the KLOC, he stood in front of his stupid chair and watched Lyre fight.

Just her and Eryx, then.

"I kind of wish things had turned out differently," the chimera said, his lips pulling into a cruel grin. "I would have liked to strangle you to death. I imagined it so many times while we were in Asphodel."

"Strangling sounds like your style," she agreed, curling her spread fingers like claws. "It suits a coward."

Shimmers washed over him as he dropped glamour. Goat-like horns sprouted from his head and a long tail snapped out behind him. Weapons were strapped to his body, and his grin widened to show pointed canines as he drew a second long dagger.

She should have been afraid. She should have been quaking with terror, but rage and anguish pumped through her veins. He had killed Kassia, and she had no room for fear. Only hate.

She dropped her glamour as Eryx sprang at her. Lunging backward, she flung out simultaneous blasts. He rammed right through them, a shield glowing across his chest, protecting his vitals while leaving his weapons unrestricted.

Spinning away, she began two more spells. He came in fast and she ducked. His dagger whipped across the space where her throat had been, and he skidded on the pavement, tail lashing for balance.

Fast. He was too fast. Nymphs were quick and agile, but that wouldn't give her much of an advantage over him.

She flung a pointed green dart. It hit his shield and shattered it, and she threw her second spell right behind it. He lurched away and the bladed disk glanced off his shoulder, shredding his leather armor.

"That was a mean spell, Clio." He flipped his dagger over and hurled it at her.

She cast a hasty shield and deflected the weapon. Eryx charged in, his second knife flashing toward her chest. She dove for the ground and tucked into a roll, barely clearing his weapon. The blade hit the pavement in a burst of sparks.

Still rolling, she snapped a gem off the decorative belt around her waist and started to weave.

Pulling another dagger so he again wielded two, Eryx lunged for her as she shot to her feet. She cast the powerful bubble shield she'd learned at Chrysalis.

With a snap of his tail, Eryx darted around her, dug his feet into the ground, and launched at her from behind. He slammed into her, the physical hit bowling her over even with the shield spell. She crashed down and rolled again, losing her shield.

Pain seared across her upper arm as his dagger grazed her flesh. Hand clenching, she flung the gemstone at his face.

The brand-new weave erupted into crackling electricity that rushed over his body. He fell to his knees, paralyzed by the binding, and she lurched back to her feet, breathing hard. He was immobilized. Raising her hand, she started to cast again.

Green light flashed.

A blazing orb struck Eryx in the back. Green light washed over him and her binding spell dissolved. He lunged to his feet, and a dozen paces behind him, Bastian turned back to watch Lyre's struggle with the other chimeras.

Eryx charged her, his daggers whirling in his hands, and magic shimmered over them. He channeled fast, simple spells down the blades—too smart to try to out-magic a mimic.

He attacked hard and fast, giving her no time to cast anything but shields. As he circled on dexterous feet and she frantically defended, fatigue pierced her intense focus. After her desperate journey from Irida's capital to Brinford, she was tiring too quickly. Her leg muscles cramped as she retreated from Eryx's flurry of attacks.

As she spun around to keep Eryx in front of her, gold light flickered in her peripheral vision. Lyre's aura.

Clenching her jaw, she slapped one hand to her chest and cast a shield with the other. Heat washed over her as she focused on the color, the taste, the feel of Lyre's aura—almost as familiar to her now as a nymph's aura.

Power rose through her. Fixing her eyes on Eryx's, she unleashed her new aphrodesia.

TWENTY~SEVEN

STANDING on the fountain's edge, Lyre kicked a chimera in the face as he slashed at another with a throwing knife. He hadn't had a chance to activate his defensive weaves. Fending off all four was the best he could do.

He hopped backward, knives in one hand, and tossed a light-flare spell upward. The four chimeras flinched back, blinded. Unleashing another wave of aphrodesia into the nearest guard, he snarled, "*Freeze.*"

The daemon froze. Lyre sprang off the basin edge, shoved the chimera's head up, and sank a knife into his jugular.

A crushing blow hit him in the back. He and the dying chimera crashed to the ground. He tried to roll but he was cornered against the fountain as the three furious chimeras lunged for him.

An invisible wave of sultry heat whooshed over him like an intangible wind. Burning desire seared his body and he *needed* to touch the source of that magnetic power.

Aphrodesia. But *he* was the only incubus here.

His distraction might have cost him his life if his opponents hadn't been equally sidetracked. They turned away from him, fixating instead on—on Clio? Lyre jerked halfway up, his gaze snapping toward her. Scalding desire hit him again. The aphrodesia—it was coming from her. *How?*

Mimic. Apparently, her power wasn't limited to copying spells and weaves.

She'd caught Eryx in her imitation aphrodesia, the daemon struck dumb and helpless, and the other chimeras were enthralled as well. Being female, her power was far more effective on male daemons than his was.

He was half caught too, but he'd been swayed by aphrodesia enough times that he could still think—and act.

Lurching to his feet, he grabbed the chain around his neck and activated a physical defense weave. Then he grabbed a chimera by the hair, pulled his head back, and cut his throat before they could react. No sense in wasting magic on a death spell when a blade worked just fine.

Shocked back to their senses, his two surviving opponents whipped around to face him, their black eyes glittering with rage.

If he hadn't gotten a shield up, he wouldn't have lasted long. With only two, they weren't getting in each other's way—and defending against them became *more* difficult.

Splitting up, they circled around him, striking from both sides at once. He flung out two trip spells, but he caught only one and the chimera recovered fast. Lyre retreated and they followed, staying close, giving him no space. He jumped back to evade a glowing blade and almost tripped on that damn chair. Its owner had moved away, steering clear of the fight, and Lyre didn't have the luxury of worrying about Bastian.

Ducking a blow, Lyre sprang at the other chimera. A punch of aphrodesia startled the daemon, then Lyre grabbed the back of the chair and swung it. It smashed over the guard, who crumpled to the ground. Whirling on the other, Lyre struck with a fast binding spell. The chimera shielded, but Lyre's spell snapped right over the barrier, pinning the daemon's arms to his sides.

Lyre jumped back three steps, opening a space to pull his bow off his shoulder. An arrow was in his hand an instant later, and he activated the spell as he slapped it onto the bow for a point-blank shot that would go right through the chimera's skull.

A flash of movement out of the corner of his eye. He glanced away for an instant—and saw Clio fall in a shower of green sparks. Eryx lunged for her, his dagger arcing for her chest.

Lyre had three seconds to save her life, but the angle was wrong. He couldn't shoot Eryx without hitting Clio.

Spitting a curse, he lifted his bow and loosed the arrow.

SHE'D MISCALCULATED and now she would die.

Green sparks burst all around her. Bastian's spell, cast from outside her line of vision, had struck her just when she'd found an opening in Eryx's defense. A heady dose of aphrodesia hadn't been enough to incapacitate the chimera warrior, but it had slowed him down. She'd been about to deal the final blow.

Then Bastian had struck her with a spell.

She fell backward, and Eryx was already closing in. Bastian's cast sizzled over her, preventing her from retaliating. She had no weapons, no defense, no magic. She hit the pavement and Eryx's dagger swung down. She flung her hands up in a futile block.

Out of nowhere, a glowing arrow flashed toward her—and struck her upraised hand.

A shriek erupted from her as the arrow lodged in the middle of her palm. Eryx's blade stuttered, the chimera as surprised as her. Lyre had shot her. He'd *shot her*. He could hit the same spot on a moving target three times in a row, but he'd hit *her*?

The spell on the arrowhead blazed, and through her shock, understanding bloomed.

She clenched her hand around the arrow shaft, her vision going white from the pain. But she didn't need to see. As Eryx descended on her, she thrust her hand up. The spelled point of the arrow hit him in the chest and sank right through his protective shield, right through his leather armor, right through his flesh.

He staggered backward, tearing the arrow out of his chest and wrenching her hand. She choked on a scream and yanked the bolt out of her palm. Her vision fizzled to white then to black, but she clung to consciousness. Dragging her head up, she found Eryx again. He clutched his chest, blood gushing over his fingers.

She staggered to her feet and flung a rough blast into his face. He crumpled to the ground and didn't rise, grasping at the mortal wound as though he could hold on to life with his bare hands.

Stumbling with pain and exhaustion, she whipped around, taking in everything in one glance.

Golden light flared again as Lyre flung a spell at one chimera, knocking the daemon to the ground. In a blink, he'd flipped an arrow onto his bow, pulled it back, and fired. It struck the second chimera in the chest. A flutter of golden light, then the arrow exploded, opening a crater in the daemon's torso as he fell.

Bastian stood in the center of the open space, holding a small object as green light danced over his fingers. Lyre snatched another arrow, pivoted on one foot, and brought the bow up—his black stare fixed on the prince.

Clio's heart stopped. It just stopped. Bastian was her brother. He had betrayed her and tried to kill her, but he was still her brother. And Lyre was about to kill him.

Lyre's arm drew back as though in slow motion and the arrowhead lit with a shield-piercing weave. His hand opened—and the last surviving guard tackled him in the legs.

The arrow whipped past Bastian's head. Blood splattered and he jerked sideways as crimson spilled down the side of his face and stained his hair. He raised the object in his hand—a gemstone.

Clio's gemstone.

The stone into which she'd woven one of Lyre's powerful binding spells while fighting Eryx. Bastian had picked it up—and he'd repaired the weave.

Lyre slammed his bow into the chimera's face and twisted free, but Bastian's arm was already in motion. With one hand, he cast a glittering orb at Lyre, then tossed the glowing gem after it. The orb burst against Lyre, dissolving his defensive shield, and the gem clattered to the ground at his feet.

With a flash, the weaving activated. Electric power surged over him and the chimera, and they both collapsed to their knees, immobilized by the binding.

Clio stood frozen, as paralyzed as Lyre was.

Bastian hissed angrily. "*Five* of my best guards," he complained as he slid his hand into his pocket. "Such a waste, incubus, and for no gain at all."

He withdrew the KLOC and its key from his pocket. Smiling at Lyre helpless in the spell, he pushed the key into the back of the clock.

Her heart seized a second time. Bastian was going to test the KLOC by unleashing it on Lyre and his own guard. He wasn't even going to test it in water. How could he be so careless? How could he be so *selfish*?

Her heart launched back into a frantic beat and she unclenched her bleeding hand. Magic sparked across her fingers.

Bastian glanced toward her as she flung the binding spell at him. He batted her cast out of the air like it was nothing more than a crumpled paper ball.

"Really, Clio?" he asked, his voice soft and dangerous in a way she'd never heard before. "You wish to fight me?"

"You can't use the clock spell," she said hoarsely.

"I can do whatever I please. You cannot stop me."

Who was this daemon? He wasn't the prince she'd thought she knew. "You're putting the realms at risk."

He shrugged and tucked the KLOC back into his pocket, the motion almost hiding the way green light sparked up his arm.

She cast the master-weaver shield and his spell exploded against it. Dissolving the barrier, she began two more casts. Across from her, Bastian began to cast as well. She hurled back-to-back attacks.

He cast the same shield she'd used. That fast, he had mimicked it.

Her spells exploded harmlessly against it. Jaw clenched, she began to cast again. Light flickered over her fingers as the same glow danced over Bastian's hands. As much of her attention was on his spellwork as on her own as she tried to anticipate his casts before he finished them.

But he could anticipate hers too.

She threw spell after spell and he countered them all. Magic exploded in the space between them, the concussion blowing her hair back from her face. She cast again, using the rarest spells she knew to catch him off guard.

But he had organized most of her education. He knew almost everything she did—and more.

A wave of magic nullified her last cast, and then the spell in his other hand shot toward her. It hit the ground at her feet and burst. The blast hurled her backward and she landed hard, pain flaring through her joints. Gasping, she rolled over and staggered to her feet.

Green light glimmered over his hands. She flung a shield in front of her, but his first cast obliterated it and the second one exploded against her chest. She skidded across the rough pavement.

Her head spinning, she pushed up on shaking arms. She'd barely staggered to her feet when his next spell hit her. She tumbled across the ground, coming to a stop on her belly.

Footsteps crunched as Bastian walked toward her. She raised her head, struggling to make her arms and legs move. Only a few feet away, Lyre was still immobilized. She had fallen at the edge of the binding spell that held him prisoner, a constant stream of electric magic crackling over the ground.

Bastian's footsteps stopped beside her. "Kindly stay there for a minute, Clio, hmm? Just one minute."

Metal clicked above her. Panting and dizzy from pain, she lifted her head. Bastian stood at her side, blood drenching his face, as he grasped the key sticking out of the clock. The gears ground loudly in the otherwise quiet park as he wound it.

Tremors ran through her body as she wiggled her arm forward. Her bloody fingers touched the glowing green edge of the binding circle.

The gears clicked. The clock was wound.

Digging her fingernails into the pavement, she cut through the circle with her magic and the binding spell evaporated—just as Bastian pulled the key out of the clock and the countdown began.

TWENTY~EIGHT

THE BINDING SPELL dissolved. For a single heartbeat, Lyre's abused muscles refused to respond. Then he surged to his feet and lunged at Bastian.

The prince backpedaled, magic flaring in his hand, and Lyre bared his teeth. A mimic against a master weaver.

Snapping his bow out, he hooked it over Bastian's head and yanked him forward—right into his fist. The nymph's head snapped back, and Lyre grinned fiercely. He might be a master weaver, but he knew better than to rely exclusively on magic.

Fifty seconds.

Hauling on the bow, Lyre grabbed for the clock. Bastian clutched it and ducked out of the bow. Lyre dropped the weapon to free his hands, light spiraling over his fingers and up his arms. Limbs wrapped in magic, he launched at the nymph.

Shimmers rushed over Bastian as he dropped glamour. Retreating with startling agility, the nymph cast. Lyre flicked his fingers and his spell pierced the nymph's, shattering it before it finished forming.

Forty seconds.

Snarling, Lyre pressed close, magic blazing over his hands in a continuous cast as he blended one spell into another until Bastian was frantically shielding—too slow to keep up, mimic or not. Lyre couldn't weave powerful spells at this speed, but against a nymph, he didn't need power.

Bastian cast a bubble shield, and Lyre almost laughed aloud as he jammed his fist into it. Ripples rushed over the barrier and it burst apart. He'd invented that spell; of course he knew how to defeat it.

His other hand lashed out, and the swift blast of power knocked Bastian clean off his feet. He landed on his back, still clutching the clock.

Thirty seconds.

Bastian's eyes flicked from the clock to Lyre. He rolled out of reach, then jumped to his feet. As Lyre sprang at him, he cocked his arm back and flung the clock away. It spun through the air and clattered to the ground somewhere behind Lyre.

A smug grin flashed across Bastian's face. Then he turned and ran.

Twenty seconds.

Lyre swore and whipped around. Clio was leaning against the fountain with blood streaking her arm and face, and a few feet away, the last chimera was trussed up in her binding spell. Lyre scoured the uneven pavement, bodies and blood everywhere.

Where was it? *Where was it?*

Fifteen seconds.

He shot toward Clio. If he couldn't find the clock, then they had to get clear of it. He skidded to a stop and pulled her to her feet.

"It's there," she gasped, pointing.

He whipped around. Twenty feet away in the shadow of an unmoving body was the glimmer of something reflective. Indecision chained him. Get away from the spell or grab it and try to get it into the water?

Ten seconds.

Green light erupted from back in the trees. A glowing line raced across the ground toward him and Clio. Lyre flung out a fast counter. His spell hit the prince's attack and light exploded everywhere.

Six seconds.

Get away. They should get away. Without them, there was no magical fuel for the KLOC to consume. He clamped an arm around Clio, intending to sprint away from the spell.

Five.

Clio gasped and he looked back. The body beside the clock had moved—*not* a dead body. Eryx lifted his head and his hand stretched toward the clock.

Four.

He was alive! And now the clock would trigger on top of him, and his magic would fuel its expansion. It would catch Lyre and Clio, and uninhibited by water, it would burst outward—reaching the bound chimera and Bastian—and from there it would expand even farther.

Three.

His eyes met Eryx's black stare. Blood ran from the chimera's mouth. In that instant, a wordless understanding passed between them.

Two.

Grunting from the effort, Eryx threw the clock. It sailed twenty feet and Lyre snatched it out of the air. No time to get away.

One.

With the clock in one hand and his arm clamped around Clio, he turned and threw them both into the fountain's black water.

Zero.

BREATHING was almost too much effort.

Pain dug into his chin where it rested on the basin's edge, his head leaning against his arm, the rest of his body still in the water. The clock, its gems quiet and dull until it was once again triggered, hung from his hand.

Beside him, Clio was slumped halfway out of the fountain. He must have pulled her out of the water, but he didn't remember doing it. All he remembered was plunging into the cold liquid and desperately pulling glamour back over his form to protect his spelled arrows and lodestones just before the shadow weave ripped through his body.

His glamour was gone again, but he'd saved his spells. And since the earth wasn't collapsing around him, he assumed the shadow weave hadn't traveled far. Had it converted his entire arsenal of weaves, that might have been a different story.

Twenty feet away, Eryx lay on the pavement, his hand reaching for the fountain. His dead eyes stared blankly. Throwing the clock to Lyre had been his final act.

Lyre's senses prickled and he laboriously lifted his head.

Bastian stopped a step away, smiling pleasantly. "It seems it works as promised. A successful test run, I would say."

He reached down, and there was nothing Lyre could do to stop the prince from plucking the clock out of his hand. His magic was gone and his body was too exhausted to move. This time, he didn't have Clio standing by with fully charged lodestones to replenish his strength, and it was all he could do to stay conscious.

Bastian examined the KLOC for damage, then held it up to the moonlight, watching the gems sparkle. With a groan and a clank of weapons, the last surviving chimera guard pushed to his feet and stumbled to his master's side with blood splattered over his face.

"Excellent," Bastian murmured, returning his attention to Lyre. "What to do with you now, master weaver? You've proven yourself both highly skilled and excessively troublesome."

Lyre said nothing, unwilling to expend any effort on a reply.

"Should I kill you?" Bastian tapped a finger against the KLOC. "You invented a spell that can consume any magic *and* infinitely expand its own power. Killing you would be a waste of a brilliant mind."

He slipped the KLOC into his pocket. "Perhaps you'd like to help me rework this spell into something more … containable. I'd be delighted to eradicate the magic of an entire daemon army but if it's powerful enough to wipe out the ley lines, I'd rather avoid that."

"There's no way to control it," Lyre snarled hoarsely. "It should be destroyed."

"Hmm. A shame."

Lyre couldn't summon the strength to move. His body had given out.

"Well, I suppose in that case, I will—"

Bastian leaped sideways like a startled cat. A dark blur flashed by, then a sickening crunch. The chimera guard, standing a step behind where Bastian had been, toppled over with a knife hilt in his chest. The prince scrambled backward.

Red light flared. In a swirl of black fabric, a hooded reaper appeared with a curved scythe in his hand.

Another blaze of red and a second reaper materialized on Bastian's other side. The prince's eyes darkened as he skittered away, his gaze darting between the two Hades daemons cloaked in black with deep hoods pulled over their heads.

"Did you think you could throw around that much magic without drawing attention?" a reaper mocked in sibilant tones. He flicked his blade menacingly. "Surrender and we'll spare your life."

Bastian took another step back.

"Run and we'll kill you," the other daemon threatened. "No one can escape a reaper."

Bastian stopped retreating, his gaze fixed on the reaper. Sudden concentration tightened his features.

Red light flashed over the nymph, then he vanished.

"What?" a reaper spat. "He's gone!"

"Did he *teleport*? What caste is he?" the other snarled. He swore angrily. "We'll catch up to him as soon as we've secured the weaver."

The breath hissed out of Lyre's lungs and he wished he had the power to stop his heart. He'd very much like to die now, but without the strength to lift his arm, he couldn't even take his own life.

He should have realized their battle wouldn't go unnoticed. The city was packed with bounty hunters, and the only reason no one had shown up sooner was that the park was otherwise deserted. But now that the reapers had arrived, there would be no escape. They would capture Lyre, take him back to Asphodel, and hand him over to Lyceus.

The closer daemon stepped in front of Lyre and knelt. His bony fingers grasped a fistful of Lyre's hair and pulled his head up. Red eyes shone faintly within the darkness of the reaper's hood.

"Ready to go home, weaver? Your father is waiting." White teeth flashed as the daemon smiled. "But he'll have to wait until Samael is finished with you. The warlord will want to hear *all* about this spell that can eradicate an entire army's magic."

Horror crushed Lyre's lungs. They'd *heard*? Damn Bastian and his gloating. Hades's warlord couldn't know about the KLOC. His *father* couldn't know about it. Bastian's reckless ambition was nothing compared to that of Samael and Lyceus, and with the shadow weave, they would destroy the realms.

The reaper pulled Lyre's head farther back until pain shot through his neck.

"You can't resist at all, can you? Is this what the spell does?" He laughed softly. "Most intriguing."

He let go of Lyre's hair. His chin hit the basin's edge and the taste of blood filled his mouth. Swirls of light and dark swam across his vision but he clung desperately to awareness. Sickening, defeated lethargy sucked at his mind. It was over. This was the beginning of the end.

The reaper rose to his full height and looked across the park. "What's taking him so long?"

"Hey!" the second daemon shouted to the empty park. "Hurry up before that other one gets too far!"

A chill whispered through the air, a hint of terror carried on the breeze.

From the darkness behind the memorial, the shadows coiled and shifted. A figure melted out of the night, unhurriedly walking toward the fountain, his steps silent on the cracked pavement. Shuddering cold swept through Lyre, pulling him back from the brink.

Ash.

The draconian stopped a few long paces away from the reapers, his dark eyes lingering on Lyre. A multitude of weapons were strapped over his armored clothing and his wrap once again covered his lower face. He rested one hand on the hilt of the short sword belted to his thigh.

"Finally," a reaper snapped. "Secure the weaver and the nymph girl."

Lyre stared at Ash, a cocktail of emotions twisting through him. Ignoring the Hades daemons, Ash held his stare as though prying into Lyre's mind with nothing but his eyes.

Lyre's vision blurred. He struggled to hold on to Ash's face but his sight fractured and darkened. As the world spun and he felt himself falling, Ash turned his attention to the reapers. His deep, rumbling voice shuddered through Lyre's bones as he finally answered.

"My orders are to kill."

Lyre's breath escaped in a shuddering exhale, and as he lost consciousness, he didn't know whether he felt terror ... or relief.

TWENTY~NINE

AS LYRE'S EYES glazed over and his face went slack, Ash focused on the reapers. "My orders are to kill."

"I'm changing the orders," the reaper growled. "You heard what that other daemon said—the spell he spoke of."

Ash glanced again at the unconscious incubus, slumped over the fountain. A sickly scent of weakness clung to him. The nymph hung off the basin beside him, unmoving, her shining hair dragging in a pool of blood.

So *this* was the mysterious spell the girl had stolen from Lyre's workroom. The one she'd used to save his life and that his family had discovered, causing them to turn on him. And this was what it did—it devoured a daemon's magic and left them utterly helpless.

"A weapon with that kind of power?" the reaper continued. "We are *not* killing this weaver. Not anymore."

Ash had heard that Lyceus had argued to bring Lyre back alive but Samael had issued the execution order anyway. Samael must not know about the spell—yet.

Ash's stare slid from Lyre to the two reapers.

"Secure him," the reaper ordered. "We're going after the other daemon."

Ash scanned the dark trees, his senses stretching to their limits as he searched for signs of nearby life. His hand tightened on the hilt of his sword, the leather grip creaking.

"Draconian," the reaper barked. "Don't make me—"

Ash pulled his sword from its sheath. Moonlight gleamed across the steel as he snapped it through the air in a lightning-quick strike.

Blood sprayed from beneath the reaper's hood.

The blade continued in a smooth arc and the second daemon had no time to react before the point plunged into his chest. Ash drove it in up to the cross guard, twisted the hilt, then pulled it out. He flicked the sword to clear off the worst of the blood before sliding it back into its sheath.

Both reapers hit the ground, unused weapons clattering out of their limp hands.

Disobedience. Treachery. Treason. Ash rolled the words over his tongue as though tasting their essence, then discarded them as easily as he'd discarded the reapers' lives.

Stooping, he picked up the bow lying near his feet and slid his fingers over the supple grip. A fine weapon, well used and well cared for. He hooked it over the baldric on his back, then turned to Lyre and his nymph accomplice. Grabbing the nymph by her top, he lifted her off the basin and slung her limp body over his shoulder. Then he grasped the strap of Lyre's quiver and hauled the unconscious incubus out of the fountain. Water sloshed from the basin, merging with the puddles of blood.

Carrying the nymph, he dragged Lyre across the park to the edge of the trees. There he stopped and faced the fountain again, dead reapers and sprawled bodies scattered around it. Drawing in a slow breath, he raised his arm, hand clenched into a fist.

Power built within him and burned along his nerves as it flowed through his arm and gathered in his fist. The air around him sizzled.

He snapped his fingers open and black fire exploded from his hand. The dark inferno ripped across the pavement in a crackling tidal wave, consuming everything in its path. Red and orange flames erupted as his dragon fire ignited everything flammable and melted the rest.

He lowered his arm and watched the crackling heat spread, cleansing the battle and the bodies from the earth. The evidence of death would disappear, and with it any sign that something far more terrible had been unleashed.

A spell that can infinitely expand its own power.

Eradicate the magic of an entire daemon army.

Powerful enough to wipe out the ley lines.

Some magic was too dangerous to be unleashed. Some magic was too catastrophic to exist. A power that should have been impossible to create had come into existence.

And it could *never* fall into Hades's clutches.

As the black flames faded and natural fire spread hungrily to the carpet of dead leaves beneath the trees, Ash grabbed Lyre and heaved him up. With the incubus over one shoulder and the nymph over the other, he turned away from the burning park and strode into the night.

TO BE CONCLUDED
IN SPELL WEAVER: BOOK 3

THE BLOOD CURSE

ABOUT THE AUTHOR

Annette Marie is the author of YA urban fantasy series *Steel & Stone*, which includes the 2015 Goodreads Choice Award nominee *Yield the Night*, and romantic fantasy trilogy *Red Winter*.

Her first love is fantasy, but fast-paced adventures, bold heroines, and tantalizing forbidden romances are her guilty pleasures. She proudly admits she has a thing for dragons, and her editor has politely inquired as to whether she intends to include them in every book.

Annette lives in the frozen winter wasteland of Alberta, Canada (okay, it's not quite that bad) and shares her life with her husband and their furry minion of darkness—sorry, cat—Caesar. When not writing, she can be found elbow-deep in one art project or another while blissfully ignoring all adult responsibilities.

Find out more at www.annettemare.ca

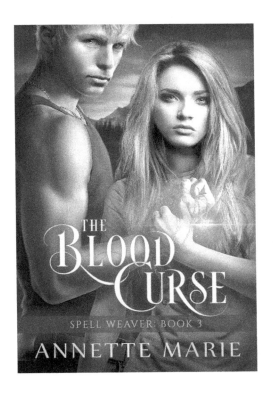

THE BLOOD CURSE
SPELL WEAVER: BOOK 3

When Clio conned her way into the Underworld, she thought she was helping protect her homeland. Instead, she exposed Lyre's most calamitous spell, and now Bastian plans to wield it against the powerful Ra family. Clio and Lyre have to stop him before he can unleash it, but Bastian isn't their only adversary.

Chrysalis wants the shadow weave—and they want Lyre dead. And this time, they aren't trusting mercenaries to get the job done. Lyre's father is coming for him, and no magic can defeat the most lethal weaver in the three realms.

From the scorching deserts of Ra to the darkest corner of the Underworld, Clio and Lyre must chase the shadow weave as both the hunters and the hunted. To make it out alive, they'll need magic more devious than they alone possess, and if they fail, the realms will pay the price.

www.annettemarie.ca

 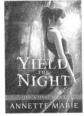   

THE STEEL & STONE SERIES

Five years after the Spell Weaver trilogy, the story continues ...

The first rule for an apprentice Consul is *don't trust daemons*. But when Piper is framed for the theft of the Sahar Stone, she ends up with two troublesome daemons as her only allies: Lyre, a hotter-than-hell incubus who isn't as harmless as he seems, and Ash, a draconian mercenary with a seriously bad reputation. Trusting them might be her biggest mistake yet.

www.annettemarie.ca

THE RED WINTER TRILOGY

A destiny written by the gods. A fate forged in lies.

In this exotic, enchanting fantasy, Emi Kimura's life as a mortal will soon end, and her new existence as the host of a goddess will begin. But when she discovers that her long-awaited fate is not what she was led to believe, she makes a dangerous bargain with a *yokai*—a spirit of the earth and an enemy of the goddess she will soon host—to find the truth. As her final days as a mortal approach, she must choose whether to bow to duty … or fight for her life.

"Red Winter completely immerses readers in a beautiful world mined from the richly fertile and varied landscape of Japanese myths and mythos." – Flylef Reviews

"Vivid, beautiful characters that ripped my heart out at times … and a fantasy world that has enough realistic touches to be relatable." – Red Hot Books

"It was a thrill to go on these adventures with all these amazing characters and fantastical creatures and learn more about the world." – Linsey Reads

www.annettemarie.ca